INFILTRATION

infiltration

Frank Wallis

The Book Guild Ltd
Sussex, England

This novel is a work of fiction. Names, characters, places and incidents are the product of the author's imagination and are entirely fictitious. Any resemblances to actual events, locales or persons living or dead is entirely coincidental.

The Book Guild Ltd
25 High Street
Lewes, Sussex

First published 1995

Set in Meridien
Typesetting by Raven Typesetters, Chester, Cheshire

Printed in Great Britain by
Antony Rowe Ltd.
Chippenham, Wiltshire

A catalogue record for this book is
available from the British Library

ISBN 1 85776 003 4

1

The stewardess shook him. 'Mr Clarke, Mr Clarke we're about to begin our final descent into Heathrow. Would you please fasten your seat-belt and put your seat back in the upright position. The captain has also switched on the "No Smoking" signs. We shall be landing in about twenty minutes.'

Fred Clarke woke up. Another rotten flight – ten hours in an aluminium tube flying at seven miles high and at a speed of six hundred miles an hour. It didn't matter if you went first class or in the tail section, you always felt the same – bloody lousy; the human body wasn't meant to withstand such treatment. It would be cheaper if they gave you a whiff of gas on take-off and brought you round again on landing. Everybody would feel much better and they wouldn't need to keep feeding you with stuff you didn't want – that would make you feel better for a start! Fred was in another of his down moods. He ached as if he had just got over a cold or something and he felt lethargic. In fact, he could quite happily stay on the plane when everyone else had left and just sleep. He couldn't be bothered about anything and the thought of driving around the London orbital motorway depressed him even more.

Mind you, he had nobody else to blame but himself, because as always he had overdone the socialising bit. By day the Japanese are one of the most hard-working people on God's earth, but what a different story when night falls! They don't have many vices but one they go in for in a big way is getting stoned out of their skulls, and it's even more of an excuse when an honourable foreigner is present.

Fred reflected on the past week. Three nights on the trot he'd eaten raw fish, drunk more beer than he would in a month or even longer, and sung every well-known Sinatra number through the Karaoke machine. He knew he had no one else to blame for his condition and it would take him days to recover – it always did. No wonder the Japanese had the highest suicide rate in the world if they kept up this pace throughout the year. One thing he could never quite understand though. They went out for a good time and started off by really letting their hair down, but the more the night went on so the more maudlin they became. They would drink more but it didn't seem to make any improvement. Perhaps it was catching!

Gill knew what state her husband was in from the sound of his voice over the phone. She didn't mind his European trips; at least he always came back almost as cheerful as he went. But she hated the Japanese ones when he would mope about the house all weekend. As usual she would keep out of his way and let him get on with it.

Fred eventually surfaced from his bed a day later, shuffled to the bathroom, showered and then looked at himself in the full-length mirror. It was not a pretty sight. He was way overweight – he looked pregnant! His neatly cut brown hair was losing its battle against the grey but he consoled himself with the fact that he still had a full head of hair at nearly fifty-five years of age. His eyes were still bloodshot and he felt he could tear off the lining on his tongue. He looked away in disgust.

When you wear a suit, shirt and tie all week the last thing you want to be at the weekend is smart, so Fred found his old comfortable 'about the house' slacks at the bottom of the wardrobe and his favourite sweater; both made him feel immediately more at ease with himself. He joined Gill in the living-room.

'I'm glad you've only got another six months to work, otherwise I reckon these trips would be the death of you,' she said, by way of greeting. 'You know you can't keep up with all these heavy drinkers any more, not with your gout.'

Fred looked at her. It was funny, he thought, it was never put down to jet lag, overeating or even hard work

– it was always the gout that was responsible. But she was right: only six more lovely months to go to early retirement in December. The thought in itself made his aches seem less. When you're young and fresh and just starting out you have a master blueprint on how you're going to steer your life and career through the years. Then Sod's Law comes into play and cocks the whole thing up. In his early years he had drifted from job to job and finally ended up in the drawing office of a large engineering outfit. Then he'd applied for and got the job as a sales representative selling the company's range of pumps. He'd been given a company car, but that had turned sour over the years. The job was all right but the driving had become a joke. It had got more and more difficult to get to appointments on time, there were roadworks everywhere with twice as many cars about now; in fact, life on the roads had become a sheer lottery – he'd lost count of the number of serious accidents he'd seen. It had all started to get too much for him. Then one Saturday morning he'd sat down with Gill and discussed their future. They were both fifty at the time and he couldn't bear the thought of working to sixty or, worse still, sixty-five. They'd worked out the plan together. If they both continued to work until they were fifty-five then they could opt out of the rat race. For a start, the mortgage would be paid off, money would be due from their endowment policy and he could also start to draw out his private pension. Then they could move to a smaller property north of Ipswich, and spend a more relaxed time together. If necessary, they could even do some sort of part-time work just to keep the funds topped up. The thought of stacking supermarket shelves three hours a day appealed to Fred; no driving, no responsibility, with the brain in neutral all day.

Gill broke his chain of thought. 'Don't forget we're going sailing next weekend, will you?'

Fred acknowledged her question then returned to his thoughts. The ink was hardly dry on his masterplan when disaster had struck. It was Christmas 1991 and he remembered quite clearly telling Gill about it in the hallway while she was decorating the tree. After ten years they had made him redundant. The recession had claimed him. He knew from his sales figures things were pretty bleak, but probably like thousands of others, he was not prepared for the axe when it came. Oh yes, he'd got some redundancy money but it was peanuts in the grand scale of things. It had all come too early, he still needed another four years' money for their master-plan even to start to function. He'd trudged round dozens of companies over the next four months and seen possible hope turn to abject despair. At each interview it was either 'you're too old' or 'we'll let you know'. He couldn't even stack the supermarket shelves, all those vacancies were given to youngsters on cheap government training schemes. Nobody wanted a fifty-year-old. He remembered cursing because he no longer had a car – how the wheel of fate had turned!

Then one day there was a possibility. He'd seen the job advertised in the *Daily Anglian Times.* It was commission only, selling made-to-measure quality furniture. He was taken on for a trial period but had to provide his own car. That hurt, a great slice of their savings went. The company was based in Essex, near Dunmow, and had been founded in the year dot by the great, great something or other of the present owner. In all they employed seventeen craftsmen, who were all good with the chisel and the French polish. The furniture was excellent but far too expensive for the average punter in the middle of a recession – and what a recession! All the politicians of the time were knocking each other over to appear on television to tell the nation that better times were just round the corner. It was a sick joke. There were so many companies going to the wall that there wouldn't be any left to start up again once these promised times came. He had never trusted politicians, they were the sort of people who lined their own pockets first and foremost before giving a toot about anyone else.

The first few months of his new job had proved disastrous. He couldn't even sell the stuff at prices that left him with no commission, and his savings were dwindling by the day. Gill managed to increase her hours at the office where she worked part-time but things were looking very grim indeed. Then he remembered how he'd struck lucky one day while sitting in a roadside café enjoying a well-deserved cup of coffee. His feet ached. He had spent most of the day peddling his wares around a housing estate without so much as a 'maybe'. All doors were closed in his face before he even got a chance to speak.

He'd got chatting with the café waitress, who'd explained that a motel was to be built next to the car park, which was why two men were measuring it up. In for a penny, as they say – he had nothing to lose. He went out and talked to them, asked them when it would be built, who was supplying the interior fittings and gave them each a card. Three weeks later his company was invited to tender for built-in wardrobes and other furniture for thirty-two bedrooms. He remembered well the row he'd had with his chairman. The idiot didn't want to lower his company's standards to meet the contractors' low price requirements, but Fred had pointed out in no uncertain terms that it was better to do this and remain in business than be out on the street – what price his company's reputation then? Reluctantly his boss had backed down and agreed. They now had enough work for everyone for seven weeks – things were looking up at last. In its own small way the company went from strength to strength. Two more motels were planned before the end of the year and word got back that they would get the orders for these as well. Then the fun really started.

One day one of the young, poorly paid apprentices brought in the piece which he'd made for his City and Guilds examination. It was modelled on a pre-war radio. The reproduction was an incredible piece of work from an eighteen-year-old lad, all nostalgia with knobs and a large clock tuning dial. Everybody was very impressed with it – even the chairman, which made a refreshing change. And then some bright spark suggested that the company should make things like this as they would sell well. Fred was given the job of getting it costed out, and in three months the first range of five radios was ready – all hand finished. A local printer came along and took photographs, and in a matter of weeks a three-page glossy colour brochure was produced.

Fred laughed out aloud. Gill turned to see if he was all right. She knew from the look on his face that he was reminiscing about his career, as he always did when he was too tired to do anything else. She let him get on with his thoughts. At least he didn't look as miserable or ill as he had earlier.

One of the radios disappeared some days later and everyone suspected everyone else until the chairman admitted taking it home – the quality had been officially approved! Then came the big push to sell them; stands at all the spring fairs and the Ideal Home Exhibition, and adverts in the Sunday supplements. The orders came in thick and fast initially and then settled down to a trickle, but it was steady business and jobs were reasonably secure. He was even put on a salary and could call himself sales manager – heady days indeed!

It had been his suggestion that they try their luck abroad, again by exhibiting at all the relevant trade fairs across Europe. Enter Mr Kyokuto, the man had come onto their stand at Frankfurt and was interested in selling the radios in Japan. It was the wrong way round! Here was this executive from the biggest exporter of electronic equipment in the world wanting to buy old-fashioned sets made in England and sell them in Japan. He'd even visited the plant in Essex where, after lots of handshakes and low bows, he'd got his wish and was now the exclusive agent for the whole of the Far East. That was two years ago. He'd done well – in fact, most of the production headed east these days.

This last trip had been Fred's fifth, and as his chairman kept reminding him, the visits were necessary to continue to 'cement relationships' – although he never volunteered to go himself. Fred always felt bad after one of these trips. No wonder, Kyokuto's two sons drank like fish. One moment they would have full glasses in their hands, you blinked or turned away for a second and they were empty, although you never actually seemed to see them drink the stuff.

In due course, Fred reckoned, Kyokuto would find somebody cheaper to make the sets and would abandon his English connection; in fact, he would probably end up exporting them here. Still, only another six months and then he wouldn't give a damn, they could do what they liked. He hadn't told his boss about his plans yet but no doubt the old company would struggle along without him for several more generations.

Gill brought him back to reality. 'So you didn't want your cup of tea then?'

'Sorry. Forgot all about it, I was just mulling over things.'

'I know. You've been going over your biography again, haven't you? You always do when you're in one of your funny moods.'

'Funny moods?'

'Yes, funny moods. You're like it when you come back from your overseas trips. You just sit and think, and you've no energy. Look at you now – all tired and withdrawn. In fact, at this very moment you'd agree with anything I said just for a bit of peace and quiet. It's a good job I know you well enough after twenty-eight years of marriage. If I was a calculating, scheming woman I would have a wardrobe full of new clothes and a brand-new car in the drive by now.'

Fred protested, 'I'm not like it after every trip, though. The, Japanese ones are always the worst, I know that myself.'

'Yes,' Gill agreed, 'it's not them all. But I just can't understand you sometimes. You come home from Japan feeling all depressed and yet you always say the business went well. But that time in Germany last year when you said it was a waste of time, not even worth going for, you came home full of it, remember? You wanted to take me out dancing – I think you were still drunk. You were ready for anything, you even argued with the carpet-fitter that there was a crease in the middle of the piece he'd just laid. He said it would drop out it had happened on the roll, but you would e of it, you gave the poor man a whole lot of verbal abuse and even told him he was useless at his job. He couldn't get out of the house quick enough, poor man. But you won't listen, will you? I think you're a masochist at heart. The doctor told you to cut down on alcohol and watch your diet otherwise you'd keep getting these attacks of gout. I go to a lot of trouble making sure you don't eat the wrong things at home and yet when you're away you probably stuff God knows what down your throat. You can't expect too much sympathy from me, can you?'

Fred knew she was right, of course, and that there was no point in even replying. After all these years the toss of that mane of auburn hair meant the matter was decided, and anyway he just couldn't be bothered to argue the point further. The attacks of gout when they came were bloody painful. They got him across the shoulders and in every joint in his arms and legs. It was as if he had to pay a penance for his recent excesses. It normally took a full two days before the aches and the general pains disappeared again. He would definitely make this his last visit to Japan. Things would be better when he retired, Gill would make sure of that.

He and Gill were not sailors. In fact, he couldn't remember the last time he'd even been on a ferry, but it was too late now, they'd agreed to go sailing. Like most things that had happened in his life, it had come about purely by coincidence. They had met Mick and Betty many years ago in the local pub, and become good friends, but they had always declined suggestions to make up a holiday foursome. Perhaps he and Gill were anti-social, but they preferred their own company and didn't want to be tied into what seemed to be some mini-package. The boat thing had started about a year ago. Their friends had come into the pub looking remarkably healthy, having spent the previous weekend on a yacht, and tales of their experience totally dominated the whole lunch – both were still very much on a high. Mick was self-employed and had been carrying out work at the East Anglian Brewery. The second brewer turned out to be an avid sailor who'd mortgaged his house to buy a yacht, and chartered the boat out. Mick had been sold on the idea and had booked a weekend for himself and Betty on the spot. They described it as some of the best days they'd ever spent and pestered the Clarkes into joining them the next year.

Now the weeks had flown by and they were about to embark on a new experience in their lives. They both had reservations about the whole thing, which hadn't been helped by the fact that Mick had booked a bank holiday weekend, so they would be at sea for nearly twice as long as originally planned.

They all drove down to the south coast the following Friday night. Port Solent Marina was impressive. It was stuffed full with all sorts of craft and some of the prices on boats for sale were beyond belief.

'How the rich live.' Mick commented. 'Impressed so far?'

'Very much so, Mick, but you need to be approaching millionaire status to do this sort of thing. You said your brewer friend was hocked up to his eyeballs, so how can he afford to moor his boat here?'

'Luck. He has a distant cousin who lives here but doesn't own a boat at the moment so he allows Alex to moor here for next to nothing. He started out doing his charters on the River Orwell near Ipswich. However, more were cancelled than took place because of the conditions in the North Sea. The Solent is far more gentle and there's much more to see and do.'

'Just as well,' replied Gill, who was looking very apprehensively at all the masts swaying to and fro.

Alex Hayward was everything you would imagine a brewer and a sailor to be. He had a full beard, lots of curly hair and a portly but strong frame. His most outstanding feature, however, was his laugh – it could be heard across the whole marina. Fred took to him straight away. He introduced them to his yacht, a 36-foot Westerly. Mick was right, it was impressive; teak and mahogany everywhere and there were two good-sized double berths, each with its own toilet and shower. It had every modern convenience except for a television but they would soon forget such a thing had been invented. Gill was comforted by the number of safety instruments, the satellite navigation system and the ship-to-shore radio, whilst Fred was happy to learn that it had a bloody great big Volvo engine so that they didn't have to rely on the sails.

They spent the first couple of hours going through the safety procedures and being shown a few useful knots, and then finished the evening off sitting in the cockpit drinking wine. Already layers of stress were beginning to peel away.

The smell of fresh bread wafting through their cabin door got them out of their bunk the following morning. It took them about two hours to motor down the river to the sea and, encouraged by the skipper, everyone was soon playing an active part. The weather was kind: blue skies and a force four breeze, just right for a smooth crossing to the Isle of Wight, so Alex informed everybody. Fred soon got the hang of the steering-wheel and had never imagined that a boat under full sail could be such an exhilarating experience; Alex almost had to prise his hands from the wheel when he needed to take over.

The skipper had another hidden talent; meal-times were a treat to behold. His wife prepared the food beforehand and then froze it. All the containers were labelled with a full set of instructions and as they were required they were heated up in the small oven. There would not have been many people, even in expensive restaurants, who ate as well as the five of them did that long weekend. Every course was a delight, as was sitting in the open cockpit with a drink in hand, watching the sun go down.

Sunday night saw them moored at one of the marinas at Cowes and they all went off to explore the narrow streets of the sailing town.

Gill took her husband aside. 'Fred, please, slow down a bit, will you? You're dashing about on that boat as if you were in your twenties. I know you're enjoying yourself, so am I, but I don't want you to end up with a heart attack, and I'm sorry to nag again, but you're drinking an awful lot of beer and wine. You know you'll suffer for it next week.'

'I know, but I feel great, honestly, and you didn't think I was old last night, did you?'

The reference brought the smile back to his wife's face. They continued their stroll hand-in-hand; it was a long time since they'd done that.

The final tying-up back at Port Solent brought mixed feelings; nobody wanted it to end. Mick suggested a mutiny so that Alex would have to sail off to the south seas, but the skipper said it wasn't necessary, he would go voluntarily. His laugh echoed around the quayside as they said their goodbyes, all promising to do it again the following year. Fred knew he would bore everyone to death with his stories for weeks to come. Before they turned in for the night Gill asked him how he was feeling.

'Great! Last week I was a physical wreck and now I feel fit and well, and yet I've probably drunk more and eaten more good food this weekend. The body's crazy, the way it reacts to things, isn't it?'

'Perhaps your problems are stress-related. I must admit you looked really relaxed over the last few days even if you had forgotten your age!'

Fred smiled. 'We'll soon see, not long to go now.'

September soon came round and Fred handed in his notice – three months as stipulated on his sales manager's contract. His boss flew off the handle, convinced he was either going to a competitor or that Mr Kyokuto had poached him. He couldn't understand that Fred just wanted to retire early. Fred thought about saying it was for health reasons, but why should he make excuses? He'd waited a long time for this moment and he didn't want it ruined by some bloody Spanish inquisition. The chairman wouldn't give up his tirade, though. He felt Fred had let the side down.

'Can't understand your reasons, Clarke. I'm sixty-eight and still work. What are you going to do with yourself, eh? Sit around the house all day? It's not healthy. I find your whole attitude ungrateful. You came to me almost begging for a job five years ago and now you want to leave just as we're becoming successful. No, can't understand you at all.'

Fred let it go. Silly old sod, didn't know the meaning of the word work. He'd inherited the family home, set in twenty-six acres, and only came into his office in the mornings, and then only needed the slightest excuse to disappear off with one of his cronies for a long lunch. Fred had seen the expensive cars this lot arrived in. If this was work, then he would certainly stay. The bloody cheek of the man. The chairman owed *him* a debt of gratitude, not the other way round. Who'd got the first order that had started the ball rolling? He had. And what about the youngster who'd made all the money for the company with his radio? He'd let him go as soon as his youth employment scheme had expired – some loyalty indeed!

The remaining three months dragged by, during which he made two European trips and survived both well. Fred's main task was to appoint a successor. He advertised in the local press and was astounded by the response: 437 letters. Some of the CVs made pathetic reading: people with more qualifications than Einstein, others with none but swearing they either had the experience or could do the job. It took him a week to read them all; he felt it was only fair to do so. And then he broke with convention. There was no short list drawn up or first interviews, he just liked what he read from one hopeful who had been unemployed for more than a year. He invited him to visit, approved of what he saw from the start, and gave him the job. He got him to fill in a new application form eliminating the word 'unemployed' – the chairman would not approve. In his ivory tower he felt the unemployed chose not to work and were, therefore, just layabouts; Fred reckoned too much inbreeding had made him a complete berk! The new man was ecstatic. No doubt so were his wife and four daughters when he broke the news to them.

The final send-off was quite a do. It was only a week

before Christmas so everybody was in high spirits anyway. The lads in the factory presented him with a miniature version of one of the radio sets. Fred was touched. There was also a very nice letter from Kyokuto which invited him to stay at his home anytime he was visiting Japan. Somehow Fred thought he would give this one a miss! The only absentee from the party was the chairman. He sent a note saying that although he couldn't attend in person, due to a previously arranged appointment, he wished Fred every happiness in his retirement – well, at least it was better than nothing. The chairman's secretary told Fred the other pressing engagement was to catch a plane to Florida to start his Christmas break.

Fred caught a bus home and sat with a huge grin on his face. His fellow passengers would think he was just another drunken office worker celebrating the festive season, not someone now out of it all and by choice.

Gill was standing with the door open, smiling. She had watched him walk up the garden path, grinning from ear-to-ear.

'Well, how's it feel to be just another statistic?'

'Great! It's like a giant millstone's been taken off my shoulders. I'm free!'

Gill laughed. 'It sounds as if you just been released from prison.'

'No, it's better than that. If I had been, I'd still have worries, wouldn't I? I'd still have to find a job and pay off the mortgage and touch my forelock every time the boss walked in. Now I'm stress-free. I've got a blank sheet of paper to start my, our, lives on again.'

'But you'll still send your poor old wife out to work!'

Gill's reflexes were excellent. She avoided the cushion by inches.

'Only until we decide what we're going to do and I see what pension I get. If that's all right with you, breadwinner!'

They both laughed and had a cuddle. Things were looking good. Gill was pleased. Fred could settle down healthwise, the things that were responsible for his mood swings were now behind him. It was also quite exciting for her; they could choose a totally different way of life if they wanted to. There were not many other families who had this option.

It was one of the best Christmases anyone could remember. They were joined by their daughter, son-in-law and grandson. Everyone remarked on how laid back Fred was. He felt like a different person as well.

The 'board meeting' took place during the first week of January and there was only one item on the agenda – 'the future masterplan for Mr and Mrs Fred Clarke'. It was agreed early on in the meeting that they would sell the house as it was far too big for just the two of them. But where to move to? They discussed the possibilities for well over an hour. East Anglia was still one of the quietest and most rural places left in England and they both agreed North Suffolk was particularly appealing. They liked Scotland too, but not the winter weather. Fred asked the leading question.

'All right, given a free choice, where would you move to?'

'Right now somewhere warm. I went out to the garage earlier on to get our dinner out of the freezer and it must be minus five out there. The wind cut right through me.'

Fred was surprised. 'Are you serious? You would consider moving abroad?'

'Why not? If we're going to change our lifestyle, why not do it completely. Mind you, we'd have to live on your pension. Could we afford that?'

'I don't know at the moment, I'm still waiting for the breakdown of what I'll get. But where would you move to? Australia? The South of France, like that lot in the book? Where?'

'I need to think about it first,' Gill told him.

'Well, we'll have plenty of time. I doubt if we'll sell the house for many months to come, the way the market is so depressed at the moment.'

The whole thing had taken on a new dimension. Fred had never even thought about retiring to some foreign country, and now it had been suggested by his wife there was certainly a lot to mull over. Whatever happened, the new year was certainly going to be totally different to all those previous ones lost in time.

It took two days before someone came out from Crossfields estate agency. The young man spent a couple of hours jotting down all the details and measuring floor areas. The Clarkes were out of touch, houses were sold by the square metre now and theirs would be advertised as a four-bedroomed detached house occupying some 220 metres of floor area; it didn't have that homely ring about it any more, but it conformed to the latest European Community legislation, they were told. A photograph of the front was taken and then the man became deadly serious. He told them of his company's sliding scale of charges for selling properties. If they agreed to all of this he would prepare a leaflet and bring it back in two to three days' time for their final approval. He would also bring along all the paperwork for them to sign. The house went on the market for £95,000, which Fred thought low and Gill considered fair. After all, they had paid only about a tenth of that price themselves.

Fred sat for days working out his worldly wealth, and no matter which angle he approached it from it always came to the same bottom line. With the hoped-for house price, the cashed-in endowment policy and their savings they had the grand sum of £117,042. His pension amounted to £893 a month and at present Gill bought home £312 a month. He worked out their outgoings, fuel, council tax, water rates, electricity, car tax for Gill's car, the lot. His best estimate was that they would have £450 a month to live on or £762 if Gill carried on working. Of course, if they bought a cheaper house somewhere they would be able to get some more cash from the interest on the capital left over. He showed Gill his neatly set out lists with the various options headed and underlined. She sat studying them and he was convinced she didn't understand his calculations, she had looked at them for too long. She finally spoke.

'If we moved abroad to somewhere warm, we wouldn't need fuel bills or a lot of these outgoings. I doubt if we'd have to pay council tax for a start. In fact,

I'm just working to pay off all this lot.' She pointed to all the unwanted items. 'I don't understand the ins and outs of it all but if we stayed in the UK, wouldn't your pension be taxed? Abroad it's tax free, isn't it? If you're out of the country for most of the year or something.'

Fred listened. What his wife said made a lot of sense. Why not spend their hard-earned money on themselves, instead of giving it back to the Government?

'Thank you, madam chancellor, for your sound advice. I'll make some enquiries tomorrow.'

'That's all right,' Gill said graciously, 'all part of the service. My fee will be forwarded in due course.' She was in good form. The excitement of the unknown suited her.

The house went on the market almost a week later, and things moved ahead quickly from then on. In two months they were lodging with their daughter on the outskirts of Cambridge whilst their best pieces of furniture were stored in her garage. The house had sold for the asking price within the first week to the manager of a supermarket opening up in the area. Gill did all the negotiating, and Fred was impressed. They decided to leave some items of large furniture as well as the carpets and curtains.

Gill was sitting up in bed one night reading whilst Fred was looking at his building society pass book for the umpteenth time. The sight of all those noughts seemed to mesmerise him. She only said one word.

'Cyprus.'

'What about Cyprus?'

Gill explained. 'Let's move to Cyprus. It's warm, they speak English and we've both enjoyed our three holidays there. We've always said what a lovely place the island is and that we wouldn't mind staying longer.'

'Cyprus, eh? I must agree I like the place. The people are so friendly and it's always amazed me how safe the streets are to walk about at night.'

'Precisely. Have you seen the paper today? This country's getting as bad as America.' She threw the paper across the single beds. 'Have a look. Nearly every news page has some depressing article on violence, riots, rapes or muggings. I tell you this place is beginning to fall apart at the seams.'

RIOTS IN MANCHESTER the headline screamed out from the front page. Fred read the article. Black gangs had fought running battles with the police in Moss Side. Several policemen were critically ill in hospital, over one hundred arrests had been made, firemen had been stoned trying to put out fires in shops that had been deliberately torched and looting was widespread. The police had also been condemned for their heavy-handed approach by the reporter, who had accused them of over-reacting and being almost as bad as their adversaries.

Fred put the paper down. This was not some isolated incident, he reflected. Gill was right, Britain was falling apart at the seams. The television news always reported something similar in their daily bulletins. All sorts of crimes were at an all-time high; youngsters roamed the streets in gangs; women were advised not to go out on their own at night; Birmingham now outstripped New York for the dubious prize of more murders per day, and then there was talk of arming all the police, not that a lot of them weren't anyway. Prison sentences were ludicrous. You could be sentenced to a longer term in gaol for not paying your television licence than for killing somebody with a car. As always, the politicians made calming noises and pointed out that these events were only 'isolated incidents', and even the Prime Minister made numerous broadcasts soothing the nation and promising tougher action and penalties. But nobody believed him. It was all so much hot air. He'd changed his mind so many times before, why not again? As captain of the ship, he steered it round in ever-decreasing circles and all the while lots of people with fancy social occupations argued that the breakdown was due to high unemployment or that children had been smacked when little or anything else that sounded fashionable. Whatever the cause, the politicians failed to recognise and act on it. How long before there was a total collapse of society, and then where would the politicians be? All in different positions, no doubt, and all washing their hands and claiming it was their predecessor's fault. If they all moved around enough then none of them ever had to accept any blame for anything and they could then concentrate on making even more money from all their executive directorships. Fred stopped his train of thought, it was making him bitter and annoyed.

'Okay. Let's opt out. Let's go to Cyprus'. He was ready to turn in but Gill was not finished, she'd just had a brainwave.

'Supposing, just supposing, we found that after a while Cyprus was not what we really wanted. If we'd bought somewhere we'd be stuck with it and would have to go through all the selling rigmarole again. I know we could probably rent it out but it wouldn't bring in enough cash for us to do much else with, would it? How about us renting out somewhere first, for say a year, and then see how we feel? The interest we're going to get from the money in that book you sleep with would pay for something and the capital would still be there at the end of our chosen time.'

'Brilliant, just brilliant now I know why I married you!'

Package tours were abundant during March and they had no trouble arranging a three-week holiday for the price of two, with a small car included. Paphos was to be their temporary home for the next twenty days. It had also been their favourite holiday spot. Tucked away in the south-west corner of the island, it had escaped the massive building chaos that had overwhelmed Limassol and there were still places out towards Coral Bay and beyond where you could find tranquillity.

Their spirits dropped gradually over the first few days, and every night they would return to their hotel feeling slightly more depressed. It had now been three years since their last visit and the price of properties had rocketed. Two things had happened: a lot of people with the same plans as themselves had created a sellers' market and the British pound had plummeted against its Cypriot counterpart. A small two-bedroomed apartment was just about within their budget, but their dream villa with private swimming pool might as well be on the moon. Over dinner, with beer in hand, Fred toasted the Chancellor of the Exchequer for ballsing up the UK economy. They were down but not out; Gill saw to that. They switched their entire thoughts to just looking at rented accommodation.

Having lived together for nearly thirty years, they both knew they had found it the moment they saw it. The white villa was high up on a hill overlooking the Tomb of Kings and had great panoramic views over both the valley and the sea. The leaflet said 3,600 Cyprus pounds per annum fully furnished and that it was empty and ready for immediate occupation. At £6,000 sterling it was more than they had planned for, but then they had to adapt to the current market. They reckoned that their interest would just about cover it. The local agent mentioned it was owned by an elderly Scottish couple who had gone back to the UK so that the husband could be treated by a specialist. He was quite adamant that it was to be rented out for eighteen months and not twelve. Fred offered a compromise. They would make the owners an offer of £7,500 sterling for the full eighteen months, paid in advance. The agent huffed and puffed a bit. He clearly hadn't expected the likes of Fred, someone who watched his pennies, and was used to dealing with a more affluent clientele, people to whom the odd few thousand pounds made no difference. He said he would have to consult with the owners.

To pass the time, Fred and Gill looked at other properties, but it was always the same – the nicest ones were above their ceiling and by a considerable amount. They hung around the hotel for days in case there was any message. Ten days later Fred's name was called out over the hotel tannoy system. The agent was standing in the reception area and smiled as Fred approached.

'Mr Clarke, I am happy for you, the villa can be yours for the next one and a half years. You are pleased?'

Fred was ecstatic! He thanked the man and said they would come into his office first thing in the morning to deal with the paperwork. Like someone who's just found out he's passed all his exams, he rushed back to tell Gill. They now had their place in the sun. It was only temporary, but eighteen months was a long time. The British pound could kick its Cypriot colleague into touch during this period – anything could happen. Although the rent came from their capital, Fred reckoned the remainder would gain just about the same in interest over the eighteen months. They moved across on 15th April, bringing with them only three suitcases full of clothes.

The villa was a two-bedroomed semi-detached bungalow. Patio doors from both the master bedroom and the living-room led out onto separate tiled verandahs, and the kitchen-cum-dining-room was Gill's dream – it had every conceivable modern appliance. The living-room occupied the prime aspect and enjoyed the best of the evening sunshine. There was a reasonably sized garden which was almost cut in half by a very blue swimming-pool, and most of all they were not overlooked by the neighbouring villa, which was occupied by a typical Greek Cypriot family. Initially Fred was concerned that the four young children would be noisy and ruin the peace, but how wrong he was. The kids were the epitome of good behaviour and manners. Fred and Gill had to admit that they were too used to basing things on their past English experiences and that from now on it was time to learn certain things from scratch again. Within days they were all friends and were giving their barbecue a new lease of life as the temperature began to climb into the thirties. They were both happy and totally convinced they had made one of the better decisions of their lives; the old adage would have to be changed – life may just begin at fifty-five!

The neighbours treated the Clarkes like their own family; the wife would never think of driving into town without asking Gill if she wanted a lift. Gill had taken up her offer a couple of times when she needed to see an optician for some prescription sunglasses. They were still not ready for collection on her third visit, and the reputation that Cyprus was the best place to buy spectacles was beginning to slip.

'Any joy?' Fred called out from the pool area when she got back.

'No, but I've got a job!'

'But you can't work here, you haven't got a work visa. You'll get arrested. What job?'

'Calm down and I'll tell you. The optician is on his own at the moment. His wife is having their first child and normally she does all his paperwork. George may be a good optician but he hasn't a clue about records, he's in a mess and it shows – he didn't even send my prescription off to the Nicosia factory until last week. Anyway, I offered to sort his paperwork out for him – it's all in English. I felt sorry for the poor man so I offered to do it for nothing until his wife comes back. He was so pleased he made me a proposition.' Gill's face was a picture as she tossed back the mane of hair.

Fred grinned. 'Did he now!'

'No, not that sort, although he is very good-looking!' Gill could tease as well. 'He can't pay me – I didn't expect it as I volunteered. Anyway, he has a brother who runs a car-hire company and he has an old high-mileage Suburu 800cc car I can use to get into town with. George says we can use it for pleasure as well.'

'You've certainly had a good day. Not only a job, but a company car to go with it.'

This would suit Gill down to the ground, Fred thought, a few hours' work every day, catching up with the news from home from all the British clients. She was always happiest when she was doing something rather than just sitting. He looked at her, she was full of it. He just couldn't resist saying, 'Calm down and stop rushing around like some twenty-year-old or you'll end up having a heart attack!' He ended up in the pool.

Life took on new pleasures and meanings in the weeks to come. They were invited to the christening of George's baby and attended a Greek wedding as guests of their neighbours. They used their little runabout and discovered some excellent village taverns where the food was good and the wines refreshingly cheap. Gill worked mornings while Fred caught up on books he'd always wanted to read. He even started to lose some of his excess weight, eating fresh salads rather than meat and two veg. For the first time in his life he became interested in the garden and spent several hours every morning tending it. In due course it reflected his efforts.

It was just another typical morning. Gill returned home at her usual time and, same as ever, the first thing she did was take her dress off, hang it over the chair and jump into the pool. 'That's better. Can I get you anything when I go indoors?'

'A lager please,' Fred requested.

The first one hardly touched the sides – he had worked hard in the heat. The next time Gill was up on her feet he asked for another. He finished off his bit of weeding, sat down on the lounger and began to sip at this one. After only a few minutes he didn't feel right – something was going wrong, his mood was changing, he began to feel lethargic and depressed. He went indoors convinced he'd been in the sun too long and had drunk the first beer too quickly. The sight in the kitchen struck him like a body blow. There on the draining-board were two empty cans of Japanese lager; he knew the brand name only too well.

'Where the bloody hell did you get those cans from?' he called out to Gill, who came running in thinking he'd had an accident.

'I shopped at a different place yesterday and they didn't have your usual local make so I got a four-pack of these instead. Anyway, it's all much of a muchness. What's all the fuss about?'

It was their first argument on Cyprus, not that it could really be called that – Fred couldn't be bothered to argue. All his energy seemed to have gone. It had been months since he'd felt so rough; the only thing he wanted to do was go to bed. It was a good two days before he felt right again. Gill was her usual philosophical self about it and said that it was probably as a result of doing too much in the garden in the hot sun. The next time she was in town she was going to buy him a hat.

The only things Fred did properly for the rest of the week were to empty two cans of lager down the toilet and sit and twirl his hair round and round with his fingers. It was something he always did when he mulled things over.

2

Temperature is relevant. An Eskimo would no doubt have thought twenty degrees Celsius warm but Fred and Gill found the Cambridgeshire weather cold. They were on their first visit back home. Cyprus has its own rules and regulations, which allow foreigners a maximum stay of three months; then the visa has to be renewed. There are ways and means of extending it, but as yet they hadn't got round to sorting it out. They needed to come back anyway. Fred wanted to sort his pension money out so that it was paid directly into the bank's Paphos branch. He had also arranged to visit his solicitor in Ipswich, otherwise they had no pressing engagements until their return flight the following Wednesday.

'Jenny and I are going to Norwich on Monday,' Gill told him. 'Do you want to come with us? We'll probably stay overnight and be back Tuesday afternoon.'

This would mean a visit to her sister's, so he declined. He didn't like Gill's sister one little bit and he knew the feeling was mutual. The term 'toffee-nosed' summed her up nicely. Two sisters, and he could have ended up marrying the wrong one and spent a life time of purgatory. Fred didn't feel sorry for anyone but her husband came very close to it.

'No thanks, I think I'll take Alex Hayward up on his offer and see if he'll show me around the brewery.'

Gill stopped what she was doing and glared at him. 'Don't start.'

'What do you mean?'

'You know perfectly well what I mean. You've got some bee in your bonnet about your beer being poisoned. If you've mentioned it once over the last month you've mentioned it a dozen times. You want to see if it's true, don't you? Well, don't forget you're supposed to be retired, you know, relaxed, not involved in anything any more – and don't forget I've got to live with you and your moods. Please just forget about it.'

She was right, of course. Fred did tend to become obsessive about things. She had read him perfectly; he could only lie.

'It's nothing like that at all, just thought I'd see how the stuff's made. After all, I've drunk enough of it over the years.'

'You're a nuisance, we wanted to take the car.'

'Don't worry, I'll catch the bus. I've also done enough driving in my time – I've retired from that as well!'

Alex could not make the following Monday, he had too many meetings, but he said he would be delighted to give Fred the grand tour on Tuesday.

The bus journey took about one and a half hours and to pass the time Fred bought a newspaper. The news was depressing, he only glanced at each page; human beings didn't deserve to run the planet. He discarded the paper and finished the journey looking out of the window at the rolling countryside.

The brewery was not difficult to find; it occupied a very prominent position right in the heart of the city. The building was old, built out of red bricks, and on one wall a large sign spelt out its purpose in life: 'The East Anglian Brewery Company Limited, Established 1792'. Steam poured out of several metal chimney-stacks. The site was much bigger than he had expected, and the reception area was like an art gallery – dozens of oil paintings adorned the walls and generations of family members gazed down at him. The lady at the desk said it was still a private company in the hands of the descendants of the founder. He was admiring some old photograph taken at the turn of the century of the entire workforce assembled outside the same building, everyone wearing hats and ties, when his thoughts of better times were shattered by an unmistakable voice.

'Fred, nice to see you again, how are you? It's a bit early for a beer but let's have a coffee and you can tell me what you've been up to.' There was hardly any pause for breath.

Alex looked well, the sort of health you acquire from a lot of outdoor activity. Fred asked about the yacht. Since April he had chartered it out nearly every weekend – he was a very happy man.

'So what do you know about the brewing of beer then?' Alex asked.

'Absolutely nothing,' Fred admitted. 'Never even tried to brew it at home. I've drunk it and that's about all. That's why I took you up on your kind offer and I really appreciate your inviting me here to learn something about how it's produced.'

Alex went to a cupboard in his office and handed Fred a white coat. 'Let's go and have a look round, shall we?' With that he bounded towards the door. His enthusiasm was still as great as it had been on the boat. 'Ask as many questions as you like as we go round.'

They walked to the brewhouse, and Fred remarked on the very pleasant smell.

'Malt,' Alex replied. 'Our main brewing material. It's derived from barley. We go to great lengths to make sure that we only get the best crops each year. The process isn't carried out here, by the way, it's done by our maltsters in the depths of East Anglia. They take the barley and soak it in water first, which allows the grain to germinate and converts the insoluble starches into sugars. Once this is achieved the process is halted by drying the product in kilns and the end result is malt. This not only gives the final beer its body and strength but is also responsible for a lot of the colour and its flavour.'

They stopped next to some very noisy pieces of equipment.

'This is where we start once we've bought in the malt. It's crushed through these mills into a coarse powder. We have our own words in breweries, Fred, and this crushed malt is now called grist.' Alex pointed to a very large vessel and even from where he stood Fred could feel the heat coming off it. 'The mash tun,' Alex continued. 'Here the grist is boiled with water. Remember the sugars in the malt, yes? Well, they are now extracted and dissolved into the water to produce a sweet cloudy brown liquid. Two more words for you Fred, the liquid is called wort, and water in a brewery is always called liquor.' Alex wrote them down for Fred. 'The wort is taken off the spent malt grains and these go off to keep the cows happy. The wort continues on its journey and ends up in those copper boiling vessels over there. Yes, I know they're made of stainless steel now, but originally they were copper and so the name has stuck ever since. Hops are now added and the whole lot is heated up until they have imparted their bitterness into the liquid. This normally takes about two hours, after which the hopped wort is run off and cooled. The spent hops are sold off for use in fertilisers so nothing's wasted. Now we're ready to start making an alcoholic drink. Follow me please. I'm afraid the next part of the process happens in a different part of the brewery and it's quite a long walk.'

With that Alex was off again. They walked down numerous corridors where pipes of all sizes ran along the walls, crossed a busy yard and entered a fairly new building. Throughout their entire journey Alex never stopped his running commentary. 'The Egyptians were the first to produce beers; technically an ale is a drink without hops; everything here is measured in hectolitres these days, but I still think in terms of barrels. There are thirty-six gallons to a barrel.'

'Where do you get your water, sorry, liquor from now?'

'The brewery was originally founded on this site because there was pure water available in underground wells. It's no good now, too full of nitrates which have found their way in from all the fertilisers used around here. We use town mains water these days; of course we have to treat it first, but by the time we've finished with it it's so pure we even have to add some hardness back to it! Right, here we are – the fermentation block.' Alex held open a heavy insulated door and ushered Fred inside. The temperature was much lower than outside. 'The hopped wort is pumped across here to these large conical vessels.'

Fred felt like someone straight out of *Gulliver's Travels*. He stood underneath row upon row of massive stainless steel vessels shaped like rockets, disappearing through holes in the floor above.

'This is where the yeast is added. It acts like a catalyst and starts to convert the sugars into alcohol. This fermentation process can take anything up to two weeks to complete.'

'So you have to buy a lot of yeast as well?'

'No, just the reverse, in fact. The process creates more yeast, another by-product that's sold off for use in health foods and the like.'

'And why does it have to be so cold in here?'

'A very good question, and an important one as well.' Alex looked suitably impressed with Fred's few questions so far. 'I don't want to bore you with all the technical details, but basically temperature is crucial at this stage otherwise the yeast gets up to lots of little tricks and makes the wrong sort of alcohols, which can give the beers certain "off" flavours. One more room to see, follow me. This is the conditioning block.'

Alex opened the door and a blast of icy air hit Fred in the face. 'After the yeast has been removed the green beer is matured in here. The final beer ends up very slightly cloudy and has to be filtered to remove the last pieces of solid material and then it's ready for drinking, and that's about it. Come along and I'll show you our canning line.'

This was obviously where the majority of the workforce were employed. Two circular machines were whirling around like they were possessed.

'Each one is capable of filling over 300 cans a minute. Not bad, eh?'

Like soldiers on the move, the thousands of cans marched forward on a conveyor belt towards a large oblong box which was the focal point of the room.

'That's called a tunnel pasteuriser,' Alex explained. 'It kills off any bacteria in the beer so that it's sterile and therefore has a good long shelf life. We do a similar exercise with keg beer. However, cask-conditioned ale – real ale – is not filtered before going into the cask, so it has to be consumed relatively quickly. Have you any more questions?'

'Yes, you've only mentioned beer, what about lagers?'

'Sorry about that, I call everything beer whether it's a bitter or a lager. By and large lagers are produced along similar lines just using different types of malt and hops, and, of course, most importantly a different strain of yeast. But yes all lagers are produced in a very similar fashion to what you've just seen.'

'And chilled and filtered?'

'Yes, very good, spot on!'

'Have I got this right then? After the beer has been made it is cloudy and needs to be filtered to make it nice and bright?'

'We'll make a brewer out of you yet.' Again Alex laughed loudly.

The sample room was in an old cellar. Sepia photographs lined the walls and in between hung old cooper's tools. Alex explained that the art of making wooden barrels was now almost extinct but that at the turn of the century it had accounted for well over half the workforce. In one corner of the room was a row of fifteen or so beer pumps, not behind a bar but attached to the wall. Some were labelled with the company's trade names, others just numbered. Fred was taken to the opposite corner and offered a seat.

Alex returned with a glass of beer. 'An exceptional pale ale we are particularly proud of, see what you think of it. About this time every day we have a taste panel. While it's in progress I would ask you not to talk, but please help yourself to as much beer as you want.'

Over the next five minutes eight people, including Alex, took over the table and chairs in the middle of the cellar. What followed next looked like a time-honoured ritual. Fred sat quietly; he was both amused and engrossed in what he was witnessing. In turn a cellarman gave everybody a glass of beer from one of the numbered pumps. Like hamsters, noses sniffed the brown or amber liquid whilst glasses were swirled vigorously, then the beer was used as if it were a mouthwash and spat unceremoniously into a bucket. Occasionally someone got up and went to the relevant pump for a further sample and repeated the whole exercise. Away from the table, the testers filled in columns on sheets of paper. Between each sampling crackers and cheese were consumed from a huge plate which adorned the centre of the table. At the end of the dozen or so tastings Alex asked each member of the jury for their various verdicts.

'Number three too fruity; number seven had a slight trace of diacetyl; numbers one, four, five and nine all identical – excellent, clean full-bodied.'

Someone obviously caused slight consternation with one of their comments. There was a rush to the pump to re-sample this particular beer. The solitary opinion was finally judged to be wrong. The panel was wound up, several members lit up cigarettes, beers were poured for consumption this time and Alex introduced Fred to several of his colleagues. The peace of the last half-hour was broken. 'What do you think of the pale ale?' Alex asked.

'Excellent.' In fact it was sliding down Fred's throat very nicely and he ended up having four glasses of the stuff. They returned to Alex's office, where he went to his cupboard and produced a small plastic carrier bag which had the company logo on it.

'Something to remember your visit by. You can think of us when you're lying in the sun, and remember, serve it chilled.' They said their goodbyes.

A slightly tipsy Fred found his way back to the bus station. He was in a good mood, having just consumed the right amount of alcohol to make him feel at peace with the world. He laughed at some of the thoughts going round his head. Perhaps he could get a part-time job on the taste panel, start at nine and to hell with the crackers! He peered into the bag Alex had given him. There were four cans of the same pale ale he'd been drinking. He would enjoy them.

He'd only been back indoors a few minutes when the phone rang. It was Gill. She would be back much later than planned, they were still shopping in Norwich and her sister had invited them back for dinner. She didn't want him to worry where they'd got to and hopefully they would back between nine and ten. She mentioned that there were some bits in the fridge he could use for his dinner. Fred caught a glimpse of himself in the mirror. The back of his hair was standing up in little twists, but he couldn't even remember doing it.

He couldn't be bothered cooking for just himself so he made an enormous cheese and pickle sandwich and settled down to watch some early evening television. British television was a novelty to him again after all the months away. A comedy film started. It was all bar-room humour, full of *double entendres*, and he found himself laughing out loud at some of the sketches. During the first adverts the lure of the beer cans grew too much for him and in the next hour two met their end. The more he watched the screen the poorer the film seemed to become. Some of the humour was becoming pathetic. He switched it off and missed the finale. How could grown men and women behave so stupidly? Had they sold all their pride for money? He felt like throwing an empty can at the set but sat there fuming instead about how programme planners insulted your intelligence.

Gill arrived back on the dot of nine, and had obviously had a good couple of days; in each arm were two bags from well-known department stores.

Fred couldn't remember formulating the question in his mind but it was said nevertheless. 'And I suppose you've been spending all our bloody money again?'

Gill stood still and stared at him. He hadn't even said hello first. Jenny made a discreet exit with her son – they were tired and going to bed. Gill announced that she was going up as well.

'You've obviously sampled the beer you saw being made. I'll talk to you when you're more sober and in a better mood.' With that she left, slamming the door after her.

Fred continued to sit. What was the matter with him, for Christ's sake? He knew what he'd said was totally uncalled for, he'd known Gill was going shopping, she'd even told him what she'd hoped to get and how much it was likely to cost, and anyway it was not in her nature to overspend. Years on the poverty line when they were first married had seen to that; he'd always had to persuade her to go into shops when she saw something she liked. He didn't even know if the bags were hers, Jenny could have bought all the things. No, he was totally out of order and had snapped at her for no apparent reason; in fact, he was still itching for a row right now.

He looked at his watch. It was still early, there was no way he was going to bed just yet and anyway he felt wide awake, indeed he felt very good. Gill had probably misunderstood him. He tried to convince himself he'd meant it in a light-hearted way and he certainly wasn't drunk, no way! He'd had four glasses at the brewery and felt great, and anyway those would have worn off by now, and he'd only had two cans tonight. No, Gill had taken it the wrong way, she was probably tired after all that walking around the shops.

He helped himself to another beer and switched on the television once again and flicked through all the channels with the remote control. He stopped at one programme; four panellists and a chairman were sitting around a table discussing something. He recognised it as some political forum where members of the audience ask leading questions and hope the panellists will squirm in their seats whilst making up answers. It looked more like an argument than a debate; the chairman was having problems controlling the panel, who were going hammer and tong at each other. He turned the sound up and listened for several minutes. One voice rose above the rest. 'If we are to secure employment for all our members then it is high time the government took action to stop the influx of cheap labour from abroad.'

'Thats right. Send the black bastards back!' Fred had said it out aloud. He looked around the empty room in embarrassment. What was he saying? He'd never be been a racial bigot in his life. What was happening to him? He turned the television set off and lay back on the settee.

He awoke the following morning cold and cramped and looked round the strange room to get his bearings. Three empty beer cans lay on the coffee table. He swore at them.

The flight back to Cyprus wasn't until late in the afternoon and during the morning the women kept well out of his way. The drive to the airport was tense; Gill and Jenny kept up a conversation in the front of the car. Occasionally they would turn to see the child in the back seat, but each time Fred only received a piercing glance. He had a beauty of a headache but kept the news to himself to avoid any 'told you sos'. His trouser belt felt tight against his distended stomach from too much liquid yesterday.

It was now normal procedure to check in for all international flights at least three hours before take-off. Security had really been tightened up. In the last two years four aeroplanes throughout the world had crashed following bomb explosions. One of the planes had been forced to crash onto a factory in the Far East. It transpired that some maniac who had been sacked from his job smuggled a handgun on board and forced the crew to fly over the industrial estate where he used to work, then shot them all and aimed the plane, kamikaze fashion, onto his old firm. It didn't seem to bother him that not only did he kill his old boss but four hundred of his old workmates as well – not to mention the other five hundred people in the plane and the adjacent buildings.

Farewells were said to Jenny and young Simon, then the long wait began. Fred apologised to his wife and conceded that he'd had too much to drink and promised to behave himself in the future. In fact, he almost made the vow to give up drinking beer altogether. One nice thing about Gill was that she didn't bear grudges – well, not for too long. She accepted his excuses and soon the matter was forgotten.

Gill hated flying but it was the waiting that really got to her. She went off to buy some magazines to pass the time until their flight was called, and returned with a newspaper for Fred. The front page of the tabloid carried a picture showing people trying to climb over the railings of Buckingham Palace. Banners proclaimed; 'MONARCHY OUT', 'PARASITES', and similar slogans. The authorities had arrested forty people, and three policemen had been injured, one seriously. Fred's head still hurt, he didn't want to know any more.

'Do you fancy a coffee or something to eat?' he asked.

'No thanks, we all had a good breakfast this morning and I'm not going to pay their exorbitant prices.' If she was going to rub it in about money she didn't.

'Think I'll stretch the old legs and have a sandwich.'

The coffee was stewed and bitter so he left it but the ham roll was fresh and made him feel a bit more human. He watched other people eating and then walked and browsed round the shops but the niggling feeling would not go away. Why had he been all right at the brewery but so aggressive later on? What had gone wrong? Was it really just an accumulation of alcohol over the day? Why had he not started to feel angry at the brewery? The beer was the same, the effect so different. He couldn't shake off the feeling that something inside him had been altered. He walked past a row of telephones, but they were all exposed so everybody else could eavesdrop on your call. In all he walked past them four times before he made his mind up and grabbed the first receiver and got the number from Directory Enquiries. He had no pen so he desperately tried to remember the digits for the few seconds it took him to punch them in. He kept looking around and felt guilty standing there, convinced that Gill was watching him, that somehow she knew what he intended to do. He heard Alex introduce himself down the phone.

'Hello, Alex. Fred Clarke here. We're at the airport, just wanted to thank you for all your time yesterday, the visit was a real eye-opener. I shall remember it for a long time to come. Also thank you for the cans of beer. They will be much appreciated in due course. Looks like the same stuff as I had in the sample room. Is it?'

'Yes, it's exactly the same, same batch, same recipe, everything. Of course, the ale in the cans has been chilled and filtered, whereas the stuff you drank in the sample room was cask conditioned. You remember me telling you about the much shorter shelf life of the cask variety? Well, it wouldn't be any good giving you that to take back, would it? You'd have thought our beer tasted horrible when you drank it in a few days' time.' The laugh made the earpiece tremble.

'So the only difference is really this filtration thing?'

'Correct.'

'And what does it consist of?' Fred persisted.

'Oh Fred, now you've asked! It's a very complicated state of affairs. Far too involved to discuss over the phone. Look, I'm in a meeting at the moment, I'll transfer you over to my secretary. Give her your address and I'll dig out some literature and send it on to you, how's that?'

Fred hung on. His mind had gone blank, so he ended up giving the girl on the other end the Cambridge address because he couldn't remember the spelling of all the Cypriot words. When he got back Gill remarked on his long absence.

'Oh, I've just been browsing around the tax-free shopping area. You were right about the price of coffee, by the way. It's cheaper to buy a bottle of perfume!'

The flight took over four hours. The captain announced that they would be flying by a longer route over Romania and Turkey as air space over what had been Yugoslavia was still prohibited.

Fred pretended to sleep for most of the journey but he kept repeating over and over to himself Alex's remark about 'the beers being exactly the same except that the stuff in the cans had been filtered'. He couldn't get to grips with all of this. If you filtered something then you took something out not put something in. Alex had said it himself, the brewery filtered slightly cloudy beer to remove the solids so that it looked bright and sparkling when it was served. The only sensible conclusion to his behaviour was Gill's – he had just had too much to drink throughout the day. He fell asleep on this thought.

Gill had the last laugh on the whole episode. Two days after they got back his gout struck; it took the rest of the week before the aches and pains finally receded.

3

During August Jenny and the family came to stay with them for a fortnight's holiday. It took them a few days to adjust to temperatures in the high thirties to start with as it sapped their energy. The English summer was doing its usual thing, wet and windy with temperatures only in the mid-teens. Fred and his son-in-law, Brian, had always got on well together, the trouble was they never saw enough of each other. Brian had trained as a civil engineer and went wherever the work was. For the past year and a bit he had been on contract to the company converting the Edinburgh to Newcastle road to motorway status. He worked long hours and only got back home every four weeks. At least he managed it, some of his workmates never bothered. Jenny had accepted it all very philosophically many years back, 'needs must when the mortgage is hungry', was her favourite saying on the subject.

Fred and Gill babysat whilst Brian and Jenny explored the island in their own rented car. They liked the place and could see the attraction that had drawn her parents to it. They all had some great evenings round the pool together and one night even the neighbours joined in the fun – it looked like a battlefield the following morning! It was not strictly true that 'they' babysat. In the mornings it was Fred's turn as Gill went off to work as usual to stop George drowning under all his paperwork. She always returned to find them fast asleep on the same poolside chair, both exhausted, with water everywhere, and she had great trouble keeping a straight face when the little boy insisted on spilling the beans on what he and Grandad had been up to.

It was almost a week before Jenny gave her father the brown foolscap envelope.

'Sorry Dad, I threw this in the case first and I've just found it. It came a week or so ago so thought it better to bring it, probably quicker to – I hope it's not too important.'

It was addressed to him. The postmark was Colchester and it was franked East Anglian Brewery. Fred opened it cautiously, aware the others were close by, and pulled the contents out a few inches. It was a booklet entitled something or other Filteraids, he couldn't make out the name in the split-second before he rammed it back inside its cover.

'Anything interesting?' Gill asked.

'Just some boring information regarding my pension. I'll read it later,' he lied. Fortunately, Gill didn't pursue the fact that it had been sent to Jenny's address whilst all other business letters came direct to the villa.

They were all sitting on the verandah one night, each with their own thoughts, watching a fantastic sunset when Jenny disturbed the peace.

'Dad, what are your plans for next year?'

'You mean staying in Cyprus?'

'Yes.'

'You just want to come here for holidays. I know you!' he answered, and everybody smiled.

'It would be nice, but seriously, what are your intentions? Mum says you're in charge.'

Fred nodded to Gill in thanks. 'To be honest, I don't know yet. You've seen some of the island and what it has to offer, and you've also seen that it's full of Brits. With so much aggro back home they're flocking over here to buy property. Of course, only those at the top of the heap have the wherewithal to do it, and as a result property prices are going up all the time. We certainly couldn't afford to buy this place at today's prices.'

Brian joined in the conversation. 'So where does that leave you both?'

'At the moment we just about get by on my pension and, touch wood, we haven't broken into any of our capital as yet. In other words, we're standing still, which is not a bad thing, I suppose.'

'What could you buy with your money then?'

'Probably an apartment tucked away somewhere without a sea view and with a communal swimming-pool; certainly nowhere on the same scale as this villa. God knows what the prices will be next year. I suppose if it were possible we could continue to rent this place for ever and a day, but then I imagine after a few years the rent would be so high we'd be eating into our capital to pay for it, and in due course we'd have nothing left – you two would get a knock on your front door one night from a couple of down-and-outs! Anyway, it's not what Gill and I want to do. As you can imagine, you feel a lot more secure when you've still got cash in the bank. There's a further alternative, of course – we could always look to a different country where prices are cheaper.'

Gill didn't like this last comment at all and added her bit. 'And go through all the whether we like it thing again first, oh no!' The subject was dropped. The sunset was far more interesting than boring money talk.

Their family returned home and life returned to a normal routine again. Gill went off to work whilst Fred busied himself with removing leaves from the pool, reading and generally keeping the garden in trim. In the afternoons they would have a siesta and when the mood took them go for long walks in the cooler evenings. Life was as good as it gets.

One morning Fred was looking for a small electrical screwdriver which he felt sure was in one of the kitchen drawers somewhere, and instead he found the brown envelope. Curiosity got the better of him. He pulled out the booklet and something fell onto the floor. He bent down to pick it up. It was a small clear plastic self-sealing envelope which had a very fine pale yellow powder in it. It looked and felt like custard powder. A printed label spelled out its contents: 'Purflo Filteraid Grade P5'. Underneath someone had written in pen, 'as used on East Anglian Brewery's filters for the clarification of keg beers and lagers (not cask ales, stouts or barley wines)'. Attached to the brochure was a brief hand-written note.

Dear Fred, Hope you are well and as promised please find enclosed a booklet outlining filtration. As you will see, it is a very detailed subject in its own right. I hope you are not thinking of going into competition!! Kind regards. Alex Hayward

Fred could imagine Alex laughing as he wrote the last sentence. He checked, the writing matched that on the label. Jenny would have had a fit if she'd known she was carrying some unknown powder through customs, and Alex or his secretary obviously thought it would never leave England.

The booklet was titled PURFLO FILTRATION BULLETIN NO. 3, and the front cover had a panoramic view of a white desert-like landscape. In the foreground of the photograph was a sprawling factory with several large silos in the middle of it. The first two pages gave an explanation of how solids could be separated from liquids. Fred stood in the kitchen and read it once. It was no good, he was going to have to read it several times before he would grasped the fundamentals. He went outside and sat by the pool and reread it. Very slowly it began to make some sense. He read the most interesting paragraphs quietly out aloud to himself.

Filtration is carried out by forcing a dirty liquid under pressure through a cloth or screen mesh – the septum – and in theory, the liquid should pass through the openings of the mesh and the unwanted solids remain on the septum. This does indeed happen where the impurities are hard and retain their shape. However, in most food products the solids to be removed are not rigid in structure. They tend to be jelly-like and capable of changing shape, and so under pressure they are formed into flatter structures which will join up and cover the passage ways in the mesh. This slimy, impervious layer will no longer allow the liquid to flow.

What is needed is a hard product which can be added to the dirty liquid to keep these soft particles both in place and apart, so that flow can still take place through this new addition – the filteraid.

> Therefore, this product has to be very open and porous. The ideal material must be chemically inert; it must not impart any flavours or tastes to the liquid; it must be insoluble over a wide range of both acid and alkali conditions; it must be rigid in structure and capable of forming very porous filter beds and, of course, it must be available in a number of reproducible different grades to cope with the wide range of liquids industry produces.

Fred summed up his interpretation of things in his own way. So you add something to the dirty beer which stops the squashy lumps forming a solid wall and then this something, the filteraid, which has lots of holes in it, not only holds the solids in place but allows the beer to pass through itself. Yes, he could visualise this in his mind. So something is added in order to take something out. It was not what he'd imagined at all.

The next section stood out in bold print, THE PURFLO RANGE OF FILTERAIDS.

> To achieve all of the above is a difficult request. However, the inorganic mineral Favusite meets the challenge and much more. The material is a complex silica compound which has a honeycombed structure with the actual solid substance only occupying about ten per cent of the volume, leaving the remaining ninety per cent as holes which are capable of trapping very fine solids as well as permitting the flow of liquid through the structure.

On the next page there was a picture of Favusite taken with a powerful microscope. The quality was excellent and it showed a three-dimensional shape with holes going all the way through it. To Fred it looked like a cross between a sea sponge and, yes, a honeycomb.

There was a page on how it was mined and processed into a complete range of grades, and time after time Purflo was referred to as the company's trademark for its Favusite products. The funny-looking stuff had many other uses – the list of applications ran over into two pages. As it was light so it made good insulation board;

as it was absorbent it was good for soaking up oil spillages and so on. There followed a section on its chemical and physical properties. Fred could have sat all day reading this bit and still wouldn't have been any the wiser so he quickly turned the pages. Then there was a chart outlining all the grades available and their possible applications. Three subheadings were included: *Fine*, *Medium* and *Coarse*. Under fine was Purflo P5, the sample currently resting on his lap; 'for the clarification of beers' was its only recommended use. The coarsest grade was P35, and this was for 'removing solids from liquid sugar obtained from sugar beet'.

Fred had a break and walked round the pool and then returned to the booklet with renewed interest – he hadn't done anything like this for years, it was like swotting for an exam.

The next section he found interesting and read the lot. It described how the material was used in practice: a ten per cent slurry was first prepared, using either clean water or product – the choice was the end-user's. Just before the dirty product reached the filter this slurry was injected, using a dosing pump to control the amount, which could vary, depending on the level of solids to be removed, and was called 'the bodyfeed'.

The last few pages described the operation of the various types of filters found in industry and cutaway cross-sections were shown. Fred was no qualified engineer but he had been around hardware such as pumps long enough to know that they all seemed much of a muchness. There were stainless-steel pressure vessels with row upon row of mesh septum supports to strain out the dirt mixed in with the filteraid. Some had vertical meshes, others horizontal, but they all operated on the same principal. The clean liquid flowed through the mesh and into a sealed chamber and was then directed out through a central pipe. Meanwhile, the cake built up on the septum and started to fill in the space between the chambers. Once these areas were full the filter was stopped and the dirty filteraid backflushed away through a large valve in the bottom of the vessel. The clean filter was ready for action once again.

Enough was enough. Alex had been right. It was too difficult to explain over a phone line and was a specialist subject in its own right. He threw the booklet down onto the grass, the back cover face upwards. He leant over to read it and saw it gave some company details – Union Mining and Minerals Inc., head office in Sacramento. A sticker had been applied to the page, *Distributed in the UK by Midland Trading Limited, Dukes Street, Nottingham*, and underneath were their telephone and fax details.

Fred leaned back on the lounger, hands behind his head. What had he learnt in the last hour and a half? A lot, but basically that some beers were clarified with Favusite filteraids, the keg type, whilst others such as cask beers were not. It had taken him all that time to reach the same conclusion that Alex had spelt out in one sentence on his note. Now, he knew a bit more and had quite enjoyed the exercise. He looked at his watch and jumped up quickly. He had to get the envelope back into the bottom of the drawer before Gill returned.

The day resumed its more normal activities. However, later on in the afternoon Fred asked Gill where the dictionary was. With a 'how's this for service' smile she extracted it from her handbag.

'I've been taking it with me,' she explained. 'Some of the words George uses are new to me. Anything I can help with?' She was curious to know why he wanted it. She knew he didn't do crosswords, he'd always hated them and thought them a complete waste of time.

'No, not really. Thanks anyway.' He looked up the word that had puzzled him all day: '*Inorganic* – having no definite organised physical structure, or mineral origin, not organic. Not arising by natural growth'. He flicked through the pages; '*Organic* – of animals and plants, of chemical compounds containing carbon in its molecule; not inorganic'. Why was it the dictionary always gave you the opposite, it seemed like some sort of cop-out to him; '*hot* – opposite of cold'! It was too late to make excuses up now, Gill was peering over his shoulder. 'All right, then mastermind, what's the difference between organic and inorganic then?' he challenged her.

'Easy! Organic means things that grow, like vegetables and us. Inorganic are things like minerals, salts and nitrate fertilisers; there's leaflets everywhere back home in the supermarket – it's the in thing to buy organic foods which haven't been sprayed or contaminated with inorganic chemicals. My consultancy fee will be forwarded in due course, sir!'

The dictionary was too heavy to throw, Gill was easier to push into the pool. She looked very enticing dripping wet.

Fred had recently taken on the shopping. Gill gave him a lift in, then he walked back to the villa with the groceries. He was always surprised at the size of the supermarket and the fact that it had two aisles devoted purely to alcoholic drinks. For a start, he had not expected there to be so many different types or brands of beer. He had walked up and down on several occasions and counted them: two types of stout, twenty-three imported lagers and two local varieties. One of the twenty-three was the Japanese 'poison' he swore he would never, ever touch again. There were no brands from Alex's brewery. The manager had watched this strange counting ritual being carried out and decided he either had a very fussy customer or the Englishman was having trouble with his selection. One day he decided to intervene.

'Can I help you, sir?' he asked politely.

'No thanks, I was just admiring your extensive range. Why do you stock so many different brands?'

'For you English. To remind you of home! We have a good selection, yes? You will try some? They are all newly sent here.'

Fred was sorely tempted to buy a can or two. It had been weeks since he'd had a beer and the thought of a cold lager on a hot day made him lick his lips but no, he would resist the temptation and stick with the local wine. It didn't upset him, and his relationship with Gill was stronger than it had ever been. Why spoil it?

They did have one little argument, although it took the

form of a strongly worded discussion rather than anything else. The first six months had come round very quickly and he'd forgotten to do anything about their visas. Panic ensued! Fred dashed into town and visited all the travel agents but with no success, none of them had flights available to England in three days' time. He couldn't even start to blame Gill, he'd said from the start that he would always sort this side out. She saved the day, nevertheless – she'd picked up the brochure on her way home one day.

'Why don't we go somewhere else instead?' She showed him the information. A four-day cruise to Haifa in Israel on the *Princess Cypria II*, it was even cheaper than the UK air fares and it would be a new experience for both of them. Fred thought it was an excellent idea – it also got him off the hook! Gill was delighted. Perhaps she still remembered Fred's behaviour on their last visit home – he certainly did, but then he had the guilty conscience.

The trip turned out to be a memorable one – especially on the boat, Gill was feeling particularly romantic at the time. They were not prepared for what they saw on landing in Israel though, large groups of uniformed young people of both sexes patrolled the streets. The look on their faces was almost one of hatred and aimed at the world in general. 'Don't try anything with us' – their message came across loud and clear. If somebody had blown the starting whistle they would have knocked each other down to get to the action first. Fred had read somewhere that the average Israeli felt betrayed by their own government, who'd given back some of their occupied land to the Palestinians a few years back. He didn't really understand it all, wasn't it their land in the first place? He was glad he had opted out and didn't have to worry about such things.

As soon as they returned they applied for their long-term resident's visas. George helped them with the form-filling side of things and went with them to the municipal building. They were now totally in charge of their own lives, at least for the next year. Perhaps there was method in George's assistance or perhaps he was genuinely just being helpful, but two weeks later Gill announced that she'd volunteered to work longer hours. At present all George's customer records were kept on cards in numerous boxes. However, he now felt it was about time to move into the computer age. This was right up Gill's street, she'd done this sort of thing many times before in her various office jobs. Not only would she transpose all his records over for him, but as she was now a genuine resident, he said he would also pay her a wage; not a fortune by any means, but the extra cash would certainly come in very handy to pay for heating bills now that the cooler winter months were approaching.

Gill reckoned that it would be chaos for the first weeks until she got the system up and running and that she might have to work not only longer hours but also most days. Fred didn't mind, she always seemed happier and more loving towards him the more she had to occupy herself with.

Fred changed his shopping routine. He now went into town with his neighbour's wife. They both went their own separate ways but met up again once they'd finished their respective chores. He now had door-to-door service, so the weight of shopping he used to carry back was no longer a problem.

He really didn't know why he'd done it, but there they were on the kitchen table. Two cans of Irish stout. He'd checked Alex's note over several times: 'Stout is not filtered.' Neither was the pale ale in the sample room, and he'd been all right drinking that. Two cans: they weren't going to do him any harm; anyway, he needed a change, he was fed up with drinking nothing but wine all the time. He wanted a long, cool drink – a typical North European drink. He'd talked himself round and was convinced he'd done the right thing. He did wonder how they kept it from going off in the cans if it wasn't filtered, but decided some other technique like pasteurisation must be used – anyway, it wasn't his problem. He would drink them tomorrow when Gill was out. He searched round for somewhere to hide them and felt guilty, a grown man smuggling two cans of beer into his own home. But he would prove he was all right drinking beer first and then tell her. No, that would only prove he was doing something behind her back; he decided he would cross this hurdle when he came to it – in other words, he didn't have a clue what he would do.

He wasn't relaxed at all, it was all too clinical. He sat by the pool and looked at his watch, emptied one can into a glass and drank it as he normally would. It was warm but he hadn't dared to leave the cans in the fridge, and it was also very good with a rich malty taste to it. The second can was consumed in the same hour. What now? Wait; it was ridiculous. What was he waiting for, hairs to appear on the backs of his hands? He didn't know what to do. He felt more than slightly embarrassed and even looked round to see if anyone was watching him. Another hour passed and he still didn't feel any different, no worse than if he'd had his usual wine spritzer at this time. He pottered about in the garden, read and went for a short walk. Gill returned home at four. They talked about her day; he was attentive, made her tea, dried her hair after her swim, all normal events. Not one raised voice. He was quite pleased with his little experiment and just hoped he'd buried the cans far enough down in the rubbish sack.

Visits to the supermarket became bi-weekly events over the next month. At first it was just for cans of stout, then it developed into 'Fred's research programme'. One day he bought four completely different brands. One thing he always did, though – he always left the Japanese variety on the shelf. Gill would know he was up to something if he tried that one. The supermarket manager asked him if he was throwing a party – after all, this Englishman never bought so much normally. Fred felt both sneaky and vulnerable. Suppose the man told his wife? What was he going to say and why was he doing it, for God's sake? He knew why. Gill had summed it up previously: it was in his make-up that once he got something fixed in his mind he had to worry it to death. The 'something' would start out as a germ of a thought and slowly take him over completely.

Perhaps he was unique, perhaps everybody did it. No, that wasn't right. Gill, for instance, let things go for ever like sand through her fingers. Perhaps advancing years were speeding up his phobia level.

He returned home clutching his latest bag of 'experiments' and walked round and round the property looking for a secure hidey-hole. There was a small outside cupboard attached to the house, something to do with the swimming-pool. Gill never went near it during the day.

Every lunch-time he tried one make of beer and then summed up his reaction to it. His findings were not dramatic; along with the stout, two of the lager brands – one locally produced and one imported – had no effect. He was convinced, however, that the other two lagers, both imports, made him feel slightly more aggressive. He couldn't explain it properly but he became restless and things started to annoy him, like one particular fly that kept buzzing round his head. He was tempted to drink more of these two to see if he could identify the effect more positively but decided the consequences weren't worth it. There was one possible indicator, though – after drinking the stout and the two 'harmless' lagers, he had no problem dozing off for an hour or so but found it impossible with the last two; his mind was too active and his hair a mass of twists. He was certainly not going to be able to write a thesis on the difference experienced when drinking filtered and unfiltered beers – there were too many unanswered questions everywhere. The two brands of 'harmless' lagers must have been filtered, he reasoned, and yet they produced no more effect than the stout. These three qualities achieved what you would expect from drinking a five per cent alcoholic drink and that was all; was the 'aggressive effect', as he called it, from the other two just a figment of his imagination?

He realised he was becoming too obsessed with the whole thing. It was only a matter of time before Gill found out or he blurted something out by mistake. He should have told her in the first place – what was wrong with buying the odd can of beer? She probably wouldn't have minded anyway. He decided there and then to finish with it before he worried himself into an early grave.

But as the days passed the thoughts wouldn't leave him and he read the same page of his novel over and over again until it was dog-eared. It was even worse on their walks, he would remain silent for ages. Gill would ask him what he was thinking about, and he would lie and tell her that the view in front of them didn't really need words to describe it. He tried hard to forget it but some little voice inside his head kept reminding him. Then a wicked idea struck him. Perhaps the little voice whispered it to him? Somewhere he had a sample of filteraid. He could prove to himself once and for all if it was responsible for his mood change.

He found it hidden in one of the kitchen drawers, 'Purflo Grade P5'. He took a glass tumbler, added some bottled water, and stirred in two teaspoonfuls of the off-white powder. It took about five minutes for the water to clear. He could feel himself sweating, he was so nervous. He closed his eyes and took a full mouthful and at first was reluctant to swallow it, then it was too late, it was in his stomach. He sat on one of the kitchen stools and waited. Nothing. All afternoon he expected some violent change to take hold of him at any moment, but nothing did, it had no effect on him whatsoever. Then it suddenly dawned on him and he cursed his own stupidity. *They filter beer with this stuff not bloody water!*

He decided to repeat the exercise, using stout. It was not filtered and it didn't affect him, therefore, he argued to himself, any change in his behaviour would be totally down to Purflo. First he would have to return to the shop to buy some more. He tossed and turned all that night and was up early. He even goaded Gill to get a move on otherwise she would be late for work, and made various excuses about having to go into town early to buy something for the garden. At the store he couldn't bring himself to buy just a pack of stout so he added some totally unwanted items to the basket. He caught a taxi back – money didn't matter where science was involved!

Without a minute to waste he rummaged around the cupboards, found the coffee filter papers and the funnel device, poured the stout into a jug and mixed in some spoonfuls of the powder. He decided that there was more stout in the jug than water in his previous test, so he added two more scoops. He poured the lot into the funnel. A fine stream appeared and started to fill up the empty jug. He was all tense. He had to calm down and behave normally – it was no good being on some sort of anticipated 'high', it might ruin his test. He left the dripping stout to its own devices and went outside. He pottered about, picking dead heads from some of the plants and watching next door's children playing a ball game on their lawn. He talked with them for several minutes about what they were doing at school.

The stout was completely flat but still tasted okay. He drank it down slowly and started to tidy up the mess in the kitchen. He could feel the effect of the alcohol. Satisfied Gill would never know he had used the kitchen as a laboratory, he grabbed his book and went and sat by the pool and waited. The breeze kept blowing the page over. It infuriated him so he threw the book down angrily and it landed in the water. He tried to retrieve it but couldn't reach it so he went off to fetch the leaf-catcher. It was at the back of the outside cupboard, hemmed in by other tools. He swore out loud and threw all the other implements onto the lawn. It took him what seemed like ages to get the book back. He threw all the tools back into the cupboard and slammed the door. The bloody noise from the kids next door was getting on his nerves. He went across to the dividing hedge and shouted at them to be quiet, and they all ran indoors. He felt really bad-tempered and aggressive but could do nothing to get to grips with it. Coffee – that would help. He drank three strong cups of the stuff over the next hour and even shouted at the kettle to hurry up and boil. The black liquid made not the slightest bit of difference; he daren't let Gill see him like this so he left her a note.

Dear Gill, have come down with some stomach bug and have decided to try and sleep it off.

He went and lay down on the bed but the last thing he could do was sleep. Instead he felt wide awake. His mind was working overtime, he wanted some form of action, anything. Gill looked in on Fred several times during the evening to find he was lying diagonally across the bed. She needed her sleep as well, so she used the spare room for the first time.

Fred woke up mid-morning and looked at the clock. Gill would have been at work for a couple of hours now. He felt fine and remembered quite vividly what had happened. The first thing he did was go round and visit the neighbours and make it up with the kids. He apologised and said he had not been feeling very well; the mother understood. He felt like some Jekyll and Hyde character and sat and mulled over his experience for days. Now he was convinced that something in filtered beer affected him; it was not the beer itself that was at fault, the filteraid was the culprit. But over the weeks he must have drunk several brands that had been filtered. Why didn't they affect him? He didn't understand it and the more he thought about it the less sense it made. He reread the Purflo booklet to see if it would shed any more clues, but all he really did was flick through it – a lot he still didn't understand. He stopped at the page outlining possible applications. One of the grades, P27, was recommended for swimming-pools.

Enthusiasm started to flow back. The cupboard, the one they never bothered with, the one where he'd kept his beer samples and thrown all the tools back in – it was, he concluded, some sort of filter room for their swimming pool. He rushed across to it and for the second time in twenty-four hours threw all the bits and pieces out. Apart from the tools there were some plastic bottles – he could smell chlorine coming off them – and in one corner a pump sat merrily humming away. Next to it was what looked like a large propane gas cylinder with a small electrical panel screwed onto the wall directly above. The agent had explained that as long as the panel showed a green light then everything was working properly, but if it ever went red they were to contact somebody. Who? Fred didn't have a clue, he had always poked his nose round the door at night when the green glow showed up better and so far there had been no need to call anyone out. He inspected the cylinder more closely; there was a label on the side: *Serviced by Makris Pools, Agiponoras Street, Paphos; in case of emergency, telephone 06-34-8671 (24 hours).*

It was too late once the bell on the reception desk had been pressed. Fred didn't really know why he'd gone or what he was going to say, his stupid obsession with bloody filteraids was just carrying him along. The street was only next door to the one where Gill worked – what if she saw him going in? Would he just get away with telling her there was something wrong with their pool? He convinced himself he would.

A very large gentleman came through from the back of the premises. Fred didn't let him even get to say hello.

'I'm Mr Clarke and I live in the villa on the Lemba Road, you service the swimming pool—' Fred was stopped from going on any further.

'I'm sorry, you have a problem? My humble apologies. I will see somebody goes there straight away, I am Mr Makris.' He stretched out a very hairy arm.

'Well no, it's not exactly a problem, the pool is working very well, I would like to ask you a question please. It's out of curiosity, I suppose.'

'I will try to help, ask your curious question please.'

Fred hesitated. He had only been retired a short while but had already lost the salesman's knack of always being ready with the next question. The words stumbled rather than flowed as intended. 'The metal container, the thing in the cupboard outside – is it a filter? Does it use filteraid?'

'Come with me, I show you.' He led Fred through an office. Paperwork lay everywhere. Gill would never be out of work in Cyprus, Fred thought. The far door opened onto a warehouse and workshop where three men were sitting on packing-cases and drinking coffee.

They drained their cups and hurried back to their previous activities as soon as they saw the big man.

'Here, this looks like the one in your room, yes?'

Fred nodded. With deft turns of a spanner Makris undid a large nut and bolt and removed a retaining strap. He lifted the lid off and placed it on the bench, then he reached inside and carefully lifted out the innards and placed them alongside the lid. A central hollow tube supported twenty evenly spaced circular plates about fifteen inches in diameter. The tops were covered in mesh gauze, the bottoms were made of solid metal.

'This wire mesh is welded at the edges and so is watertight.' Mr Makris made a great point of showing Fred this. 'The plate is hollow, water goes through the mesh and down into the hollow plate and then out through the central pipe. There are holes drilled into this pipe especially for this purpose.'

The demonstration continued. Fred was shown how, when it was all plumbed in, dirty water could enter via a pipe in the side of the vessel, flow through the mesh and then come out as clean water through the central pipe, which connected to another pipe in the lid. It was all very interesting but he had to ask his question while the going was good.

'And the filter powder?'

'Ah, yes. The filter powder, like this the dirty water would stay the same, not good for business, eh?' He laughed. Fred knew somebody else with a similar laugh. Mr Makris explained that all the top meshes were covered with a thick layer of filteraid which would take out all the dirt and keep the pool like new. Fred did not understand properly.

'So no powder is added to the water?'

The laugh this time reverberated back off the walls of the building. 'So you want to sit by the pool all day with a bag of powder and a shovel? You joke with me, Mr Clarke?'

Fred knew he shouldn't have said it. 'Don't they add it like that when they filter beer?'

The eyes glared back at him. 'So maybe you are a spy

for one of my competitors? You know more about filtration perhaps than you admit?'

Fred tried to extricate himself from the hole he had just dug. 'I have absolutely no experience at all, I can assure you, but some years ago now I went round a brewery and saw it done like that.' There was at least some element of truth in his story.

The big man's stare disappeared and he started to smile again. 'You are right about beer, it has many solids to be removed and so needs lots of powder, but the filter only runs for a short time. The pool water on the other hand is very small in solids, it will not make the filter cake dirty as quickly and therefore will not become blocked up for many months, maybe even a year, so the filter can be filled up with a new powder before the lid is put on.' He went through the motions of shovelling in imaginary powder and then put the lid back in place. 'You understand now, eh?'

'Yes, thank you. Do you use Purflo filter powders, Mr Makris?' Fred asked, his confidence restored.

'Excuse me. I did not hear the name.'

Fred repeated the name more slowly. Makris shrugged his large shoulders and indicated for Fred to follow him to a corner of the warehouse. In amongst pallets of tiles, bags of cement, tins of paint and all the other items necessary to make up a swimming pool business were three shrink-wrapped pallets of white bags.

'This is our filter powder.' He dug into one of the bags and emptied the contents of his huge fist into Fred's cupped hands. The product was brilliant white, not yellow, it was also much coarser than his sample and reminded him this time of granulated sugar.

'Now you know all about swimming-pool filtration, Mr Clarke. Any more and you will be an expert and want to set up in business, eh?' He slapped Fred across the back and the powder went flying. 'You are satisfied? You will recommend my company to all your English friends when they come to live on our beautiful Island of Aphrodite?'

Fred knew there would not be another opportunity.

'Yes, I have learnt a lot, thank you. I have something further to ask you, Mr Makris, a favour. I must come clean . . .'

The last sentence was totally unintentional. The giant started to laugh. 'You English people have such a sense of humour! Come clean, like a filter!' He roared with laughter again and went off to tell the men the joke. He laughed, they laughed, he returned wiping his red eyes with a handkerchief. 'So this favour?'

Fred surprised himself. The bullshit rolled quite easily off his tongue. 'We have a small drinking-water filter back at the villa. It uses filteraid, that's why I really came to see you, to see if you could sell me a small amount.' He was about to get the sample out of his pocket when the giant held up his hands again.

'You can throw it away, Mr Clarke. The drinking-water is from the gods themselves; it comes straight off the Troodos mountains, it is pure, it is good for you, it is the best in the world.'

'Yes, I appreciate that, and it is very good water, but I have a little problem.' Fred patted his stomach. 'I have to have water with few inorganic minerals in it.'

'This filter, how big is it?'

Fred gave the dimensions with his hands.

'You will bring it here, we will make it work.'

'Oh, that's not necessary really, what I'm looking for is some more of this.' Fred held out the small sample of Purflo P5. He had transferred it to a white envelope from the original packet – he hadn't wanted anyone to see where it had come from in case it gave the game away. There was only a small amount left, it wouldn't have filled an eggcup.

Makris ripped a corner off and rubbed some of the powder between his fingers. 'It is very fine, yes, very fine powder not like ours. Please wait here.'

Fred consoled himself with the fact that what he'd said was not a complete lie. There was a little water-filter gadget which they'd used back in Suffolk – the water there was awful due to the enormous amounts of fertilisers running off the land into the underground reservoirs. Gill had got fed up with the taste and had bought the small plastic device for only a few pounds. You poured your dirty water in at the top, it trickled through a filter cartridge and there you were, pure water in the bottom receptacle. It was last seen on Jenny's windowsill in Cambridge. God knows what was in the cartridge, though, Fred thought.

Makris had obviously got through to whoever he wanted on the telephone. He spoke for five minutes, there was a lot of shrugging of the huge shoulders and plenty of arm waving, then he slammed the receiver back and started talking while he was still yards away.

'Our agent in Nicosia knows of this product. It is popular in mainland Europe but it is a competitor. He is happy there is none here in Cyprus, so he has all the business! I am to send him this sample, he will have it analysed and send me a sample of his company's same product. This is good eh? You come back in two weeks and I will give it to you, yes?'

Fred could hardly contain his satisfaction at the outcome, and thanked Makris warmly.

'It is no problem,' Makris assured him. 'We must look after your belly so you can swim in my pool and make it dirty so I can sell more filter powder.' He was still laughing when he showed him the door.

Fred found the nearest store, bought a good quality whisky and returned to the pool company and presented Makris with it. He had the top off in seconds and insisted Fred join him. Fred patted his stomach and declined. Makris boomed out some foreign words and the three men came running into the office. He poured each of them a generous measure into their dirty cups which they raised in some sort of toast. The whisky would be short-lived.

Fred stood outside, realised he was near Gill's place of work and quickly started to walk back to the villa. He felt good, in fact he had not felt so on top of the world for weeks. It had all turned out much better than he had anticipated. To be honest, he had not expected anything from his visit at all and now he had so much. It was clear in his mind, and so simple – the local beer had no effect on him because it wasn't filtered through Purflo.

There were other types of filteraid in use and he was going to get a sample of one of them. He could then test it out in the stout and compare the effect against this Purflo stuff and prove his case once and for all. His persistence and perseverance – but not obsession – was beginning to pay off. He smiled all the way home. He would have made a good detective, he felt.

Gill's birthday, her fifty-fifth, fell on the following Tuesday. There was the choice of two Saturdays to take her out to dinner. Fred wanted to celebrate two things early so he chose the first date and booked up a table by the window at one of the harbour restaurants. He started with a small local beer and was surprised when Gill made no comment. They had a bottle of local wine with their meal, and while Gill went to the powder-room he ordered some genuine French champagne. She was worried about the cost, but he said it was worth it, she was worth it, plus she deserved it for working. They strolled along the harbour wall and took a taxi home. Both of them were in the right mood and they made it a night to remember. Fred was delighted, and as a bonus he had no adverse effects from the drink. Deep down he somehow knew he wouldn't, he was now convinced what the problem had been over all the past years.

The euphoria didn't last. By Wednesday of the following week he had started to mope around the villa and couldn't settle. He knew he had at least another week to wait but his patience was beginning to wear thin, very thin indeed, and he began to mumble to himself about the laid-back attitude of the Mediterraneans. Why couldn't they do things quickly? He had one vital test left to carry out and they were treating it as a non-priority. At one stage he decided to visit Makris a week early, just in case, then he changed his mind again. The last thing he needed to do was upset the big fellow, then he would end up with nothing. No, somehow he had to summon up the will-power to just sit it out for the full two weeks. With only three days of his ordeal to go disaster struck. He'd heard voices in the drive and just assumed Gill was talking to neighbours. He was sitting in the kitchen eating a sandwich when she burst in, her face like thunder, her eyes looking daggers.

'Would you mind telling me what in hell's name is going on?'

'What do you mean?'

'You know bloody well what I mean,' she retorted. Fred could not remember the last time he'd heard her swear. 'I've just been talking to a young man on a motor cycle who said he was from our swimming-pool cleaning company. He gave me a parcel and said it was for my husband as requested for his drinking-water filter. We haven't got a drinking-water filter! I asked him what was in the package and he looked at me as if I were an idiot and should have known. He said it was filteraid, of course. I felt like a proper idiot. Why order something for which we have absolutely no use? I want some explanations. I've had enough of your moods, one minute blowing hot, the next cold – and don't tell me you're not drinking, some days your breath stinks of beer. I'm warning you, Fred Clarke, any more and I'm off, I promise you. I'll go back and stay with Jenny while you go completely round the bend.'

She threw the small parcel into Fred's midriff, wishing it had landed lower down. He gasped and she stormed off into the garden. Without turning she shouted back, 'Some explanations and soon!'

Fred ripped the package open, there was a copy of a letter.

> My dear Mr Makris, We have tested the sample of Purflo Grade P5 which you forwarded. Our nearest equivalent is our A200. Please inform your client that our product will not only perform much better, but unlike the P5, does not contain any organic material and is therefore much purer.'

There was a further two paragraphs of personal chit chat – something about Andrea's wedding in January – which had been scored through once with a thick black line. the signature could have been made by a spider. Right at the bottom of the page was one more sentence: *'Enclosed 1 kilo sample of A200.'* Fred examined the plastic package. The powder was white and felt like salt.

He tried to postpone the inquisition for as long as possible so he could rehearse what he was going to say to Gill. She gave him the good grace to remain silent whilst he explained what he thought – no, now knew – that something connected with Purflo filteraid altered his personality, and that whatever it was, was transferred into the beer at the breweries.

Gill occasionally shook her head in obvious disbelief. 'You mean to tell me you think somebody is deliberately trying to turn beer-drinkers into aggressive people? You are going off your bloody trolley. This is 1995 and the real world, not some science-fiction planet. I warned you to drop it – you'll end up being taken away to the funny farm. And there's me thinking you're up here relaxing and stress-free and all the time you're drinking beer to see what it will do to you! Dear God! Well, I've said it before: no more and I mean it. Okay?'

Fred knew from the tone of her voice that she meant it. She didn't see red that often but he could still recognise the signs when she did. She hadn't finished either. She picked up the sample of A200, went out into the garden and scattered it over the flower-beds. They hardly saw each other for the rest of the week; the spare bedroom was occupied once again.

But Fred couldn't drop it, not just like that, not his pet project. He slouched in his chair for two days and wrote a summary of all the events and his findings: the depressed moods associated with the Japanese lager, although he couldn't offer a satisfactory explanation unless they used a totally different filteraid in Japan; the angry, aggressive moods now proved with Purflo; the difference between unfiltered beers; his various experiments. He put it all down and rewrote it four times before he was satisfied it was all in the right chronological order. He had to admit to himself that some of it sounded far-fetched and that he didn't have much, if any, evidence to support his outlandish theories.

At dinner he broke the now usual silence. 'Gill, will you do me one last favour and then I promise you I'll drop the whole subject for ever and try and return to normal?'

He explained that he felt he would like to send his report to someone; just getting it down on paper had made him feel better anyway.

Gill's reply took him somewhat by surprise. She was willing to drop the matter if he was. 'Yes, I'll type your wretched letter for you if it makes you feel any better and on the firm understanding that you forget the whole thing.'

It was agreed. The problem was where to send the letter. Gill's suggestion wasn't constructive. The letter hung around the villa for days and in the end, just to get rid of it he sent it to the only important address he knew – Number Ten Downing Street. The weeks passed and the experience faded with each one. Fred had made his promise and started to keep it; he avoided all makes of beer and lost the urge to meddle with them.

Christmas brought mixed news. Fred was thinking back to his retirement and couldn't believe how quickly the year had flown by, when the agent visited. One of the owners, the husband, had died some weeks ago of cancer and his widow wanted to sell the villa. Were they interested? But the asking price was beyond their resources. It was catch twenty-two. If they didn't have to pay the rent then the interest added to their capital would give the right amount in about four years' time, but obviously there was no way the widow was going to hang around in limbo for all that time. They considered asking George for a loan in lieu of Gill's wages, but they would be in their eighties before the capital was paid back, assuming he had cash to lend them in the first place, and Gill was still alive to work! Fred wrote asking if the Scottish lady would continue to rent the villa to them. A solicitor replied saying that although the owner sympathised with their dilemma she needed the cash to buy her own place. The letter went on to say that at the moment she was lodging at her sister's.

They had three options open to them: spend the rest of their lives renting villas, buy a very much inferior apartment in Cyprus or return to Suffolk and look at cheaper rural properties. Gill liked the first idea; she liked the island and its way of life. Fred on the other hand was less optimistic. He pointed out that rents would rise, probably quite sharply, whilst knowing their luck, interest rates on their savings would fall. They would then have to use more and more of their capital, which could cause a situation where, by the time they were in their mid-sixties, health still permitting, all their savings would have been consumed, leaving them no roof over their heads and just a pension to survive on. They would indeed be knocking on Jenny's door! Still, they had another nine months to sort something out, so they would do what most people do in a similar situation – continue to enjoy themselves now and panic at the last moment.

The late February days were beginning to warm up again, making it possible to sit outside most of the time. Fred heard the car doors slam but thought no more about it until two men walked down the drive. They looked like those irritating people Fred had no time for – Jehovah's Witnesses. He mumbled to himself about nowhere being free from pests. One of the men was blond, well over six foot tall and dressed in very casual clothes; Fred reckoned he was in his early forties and summed him up as being typically American. The other fellow was a good deal older and a good foot shorter and bald, apart from a smattering of hair above his ears; he was also overweight and dressed in a brown suit. He looked as if he was out to sell something, and to Fred's mind looked British through and through.

'Can I help you?' Fred was ready should Bibles or some other literature suddenly appear in their hands.

'Mr Clarke? Mr Fred Clarke?' It was the little man who was doing the asking. 'Hi, my name is Arnold Henderson. This is my colleague Paul Somerbee.'

The tall man said 'Good morning.'

Fred had been right about the nationalities but had got them the wrong way round. He wasn't going to waste his time so he asked them outright if they were from some religious organisation, and knew straight away from their broad smiles that he was not about to be saved from eternal damnation.

Henderson handed over a business card. 'No, we're both from the World Health Organisation. May we come in please? There's something we'd like to discuss with you.'

Fred was reluctant to invite them into the house so he offered them chairs on the verandah; en route he read the card. Inspector Henderson was based in Zurich.

'Inspector Somerbee and I would like to ask you some questions regarding your letter.'

Fred had honestly forgotten all about it by now and replied, 'Letter? What letter?'

'The one you sent to London. You know, the one outlining your work on beer.'

It all came flooding back. It had been nearly three months since he'd sent it. He wondered how many desks it had landed on before it finally settled on the one in Zurich. 'Yes, I remember now, what do you want to know? It was all in it, everything I'd done, there's no more to tell really.'

'Understood, Mr Clarke, but it's always nice to hear things first hand. If you would be so good as to run through it for us we'll tell you our side of the affair.'

Fred related the story, and after about five minutes was once again engrossed in the contents. It was like a good therapy, at last he was getting rid of any remaining pieces from his mind. Neither of the inspectors spoke throughout his entire monologue; they nodded or shook their heads in all the right places but remained a good listening audience. Fred looked at his watch. Gill wouldn't be home for at least two hours yet, but Sod's Law would probably intervene and she would walk through the garden at any minute. She would certainly have grave doubts about what was going on and might even think he'd arranged their visit – and be on the first plane back to the UK. He tried to hide his nervousness.

'Well, that seems to confirm what we have established, doesn't it, Paul?'

'Exactly,' replied Somerbee.

'Now, let us tell you what we know and what has happened Mr Clarke. It's the least we can do after all your efforts and concern.' Henderson continued. 'We also have been aware of some sort of problem for the last year now and have managed to trace it to a contaminated batch of cereal used by the brewing industry. Some French farming consortium inadvertently sprayed their crop with entirely the wrong chemical – a fungicide instead of a pesticide. We are not entirely sure which one at the moment as our chemists are still investigating. Anyway, all the remaining stocks have been destroyed and the co-operative fined very heavily indeed. Some of the stuff, unfortunately, got through and was used by several large breweries throughout Europe. The chemical goes all the way through into the final beer. It's not poisonous or anything like that and only a few people noticed any side-effects anyway – mainly migraine and asthma sufferers and of course those with sensitivity to changes in their metabolism, such as people with gout. But nevertheless it shouldn't have been there in the first place, so no excuses.'

Fred was curious and at the same time genuinely interested in finding out as much as possible. 'What sort of cereal was it?'

'Maize. Anyway, Mr Clarke, the whole episode is over and done with and we understand that most of the beer has either been consumed by now, or what was still in stock in the various outlets has been destroyed. As far as our organisation is concerned, the matter is history. One of the reasons for coming to see you was to thank you for your concern and vigilance. There are too many rogues in the world trying to dump substandard goods on an unsuspecting public. We need and rely on people like yourself to keep watchful eyes on things. Once again, thank you. Oh, by the way, did you send a copy of your letter to anyone else?'

'No, I kept the carbon copy and eventually sent it back with some other personal correspondence to our family solicitor in Suffolk. We have nowhere in the villa to keep confidential paperwork. Why?'

'Good, if you had we would have let them know the matter's resolved,' Henderson answered. 'We don't want them chasing around on an issue when we already have the answer, do we?' They both stood up to leave and once again thanks were proffered. Throughout the entire visit Inspector Somerbee had only uttered four words.

Gill arrived home much later than normal and was in a very good mood. As a thank-you for all her efforts in getting the computer system up and running George had insisted on a treat. His wife had taken her round some clothes shops and bought her nearly £300 worth of summer clothes. She was going to have a shower and then Fred could have a floor show. She was like an excited teenager all over again; there was never going to be a better opportunity to tell her.

'I had visitors today,' he began. 'Two inspectors from the World Health Organisation in Zurich came to thank me for pointing out the problem in the beer. Seems there was some contaminated raw material. It's all cleared up now.'

Gill stopped dead in her tracks, one arm out of her sweater. When her face emerged it showed both horror and disbelief, but before she could pounce Fred showed her the visiting-card. 'Good, well now the matter is well and truly closed,' she said, and went off to the bathroom.

Fred felt vindicated. It had all been worth it, after all, and in some small way he might just have prevented a major catastrophe. He was glad he'd written his letter.

The following day Fred prowled around the pool. The more he remembered and dwelled on yesterday's meeting the more disturbed he became. The same questions kept coming up. Wouldn't the breweries check the quality of the cereal? After all, it was their main ingredient. And wouldn't they have found the presence of something alien and refused to accept it? Also, Alex at the East Anglian Brewery had said that they only used malted barley and had never made any reference to maize. And why no mention of the different effects he'd referred to in his letter between cask and keg beers from the same brewery? They would be on the same raw material even if it was maize. And not the slightest mention of filteraids, which had been his number one culprit. He had written more on this than anything else in the letter – in fact, he'd gone to great lengths to point out the differences between Purflo and the Greek stuff and had mentioned the presence of organic material more than once. And what about his comments on the different depressing effect experienced with the famous Japanese beer? He came to the conclusion that they obviously hadn't read his letter. And how did they know he had gout? Had he really got it all wrong and was his imagination up to its old tricks again? What had he really done, in effect? Just drunk some contaminated beers with pesticide in and then others that had used a different crop? He couldn't make any sense out of it, but it really didn't matter any more, enough was enough. He said out loud, 'No more.' It had nearly wrecked his marriage, and his sanity was probably not far behind either. He couldn't do any more anyway, not just one non-technical man, and he had also made a promise to Gill and he would honour that promise. No, he would erase everything to do with the bloody filtration of beer from his mind – he would even go one step further and would never, ever drink any more beer. He would also stop playing with his hair!

4

'Well, Inspector, what did you make of our Fred Clarke then?' Henderson asked his colleague.

'I thought he was genuine,' Somerbee replied. 'Certainly not a crank. He honestly believes somebody is adding something to his beer, which is then responsible for his mood swings. He's done quite a good job with his detective work, for an amateur.'

'You going to put him on your payroll then?' quipped Henderson. 'If you ask me, I'd say the guy's bored out of his skull and just looking for things to stick his nose into, but who knows?'

Both men were sitting in the bar of the Beach Hotel, less than two miles from Fred Clarke's villa. They had decided to spend the night in Paphos. It was rumoured there was a good nightclub.

Peering through the Bushmills in his glass, Somerbee remarked: 'Don't you ever get confused with all the different visiting-cards? It's a wonder you can remember your own name.'

If Fred Clarke had been slightly concerned about some of the irregularities of Henderson and Somerbee's visit, he would have had a heart attack if he had known the truth.

Paul Somerbee was Andy Lockwood; Arnold Henderson was Derek Madden, and neither worked for the World Health Organisation, neither had a clue about poisoned beer or any knowledge of contaminated maize.

Andy Lockwood was thirty-nine years old. Born in London, he had joined the army as soon as he turned seventeen. Through hard work and study he worked his way into the junior officer ranks and saw action in the Falkands conflict in 1982. Somebody had obviously been monitoring his career and spotted his potential, because in the late eighties he was invited into his colonel's office to meet some high-powered civil servant down from London. He didn't like what he saw one little bit, he was one of those grey-suited patronising types who always used the royal 'we' in conversation. He said he was recruiting 'men of a special calibre' to look after Britain's security and safety and said that the work would mainly be abroad, assessing any situation which might ultimately rock or upset the nation's status quo. Andy didn't volunteer as such, but it was stated in no uncertain terms that it was in his best career interests to accept. So for the last seven years he'd worked, as he'd always done, for the British Government, but he hadn't a clue for which department. The rules were quite simple: after one job was finished he would telephone the London number he'd had to memorise and be told either to take a break or to contact someone else, always abroad and in person, as soon as possible. He would then travel to the foreign destination, be briefed by the local go-between, and get on with whatever the instructions required. In due course, sometimes days or even weeks later, he would report back to his local contact and then he or she would give him a date when he should contact his London number.

He soon found he enjoyed the job. It offered him the chance to travel abroad, was not too difficult to do and so far had not been particularly dangerous. Not meeting his superiors he considered a bonus! He had to be careful, of course, how he carried out his surveillance and how he obtained certain information, but perhaps he'd been lucky to date, and as far as he knew he'd never aroused any foreign government's suspicions. In fact at times he felt quite guilty 'holidaying' in some exotic location, all at the taxpayers' expense. He also found he enjoyed working on his own, and although he'd grown up as part of an army team, he had always felt better when assigned individual duties. Basically he was an introvert and would never be classed as the life-and-soul-of-the-party type; perhaps that's why he'd never married. (He had been engaged for about four years back in the early eighties but had broken it off when she'd started nagging on about a wedding ring and babies.) One day, just out of curiosity, he might get around to tracing the phone number and the one address he'd also been given. The latter was a post office box number, again in London, and any non-classified stuff he obtained could come via this channel, he was told. So far the only time he'd used it was for his expenses claims. There were never any queries on this front and all monies he asked for were quickly paid by the British Government into his bank account. One day he would also check to see what this now totalled as he'd hardly touched his salary for years now.

Andy had received his brief instructions the week before. Some faceless local shoved the envelope into his hand in the small foyer of the Hong Kong hotel where he was staying.

> Fly to Cyprus, accommodation arranged at the Air Force Base at Nicosia. Meet Station Commander Fenton on Monday 24th February. Seek out and familiarise yourself with your opposite number, Mr Derek Madden.

Andy had got there on the twentieth and left a message that he would be in the mess bar between noon and two in the afternoon and again after nine in the evening. Derek had come up and introduced himself the following day. Perhaps opposites attract, but they had got on well from the start. They exchanged only very general information but Andy learnt several interesting points about his new friend.

Derek Madden was ten years older, for a start, born in Brooklyn fifty years ago. He was divorced, but even with his short, overweight frame and lack of hair, still liked to think of himself as a ladies' man. He worked for the CIA and was seconded to the Institute of Terrorism; Andy had to do his best to hide a smile when he found this out. After all, it was only the Americans who could have dreamt up such a department! Derek had worked for the Agency since leaving university. Family connections had introduced him to the right people, and for most of his life he'd held numerous desk jobs. He was quite open with Andy, a total stranger, and said himself that he was not a high-flyer. However, after fifteen years of this pen-pushing he had got totally pissed off with it all and volunteered for a one-off foreign assignment. Whether they had no one else available wasn't relevant now; they picked him, and he not only surprised his bosses but also himself by doing a good job. He never went back on the inside again.

They knew the rules, the pair of them, and during all the conversations they held there was never any reference to previous assignments. Derek didn't know Andy had flown in from Hong Kong, where he'd spent three weeks assessing what the Chinese were up to. Most of the Colony's population were dead against handing over the place in under two years' time and some were becoming quite militant. To counter this the Chinese paid certain gangs very well indeed to stir up as much trouble against the British 'illegal imperialist regime' as possible. Andy had gone in as a tourist and worked in conjunction with the undercover Police Department R12; probably right now his report would be forming the basis of some committee meeting back in London.

By contrast, Derek had made the shorter journey. He had been in Germany and, being of the same faith, working closely with a guy from Mossad on a fact-finding mission regarding the sudden increase in membership of the Nationalistic Front and the National Offensive, both banned Nazi organisations, and also to find out who was responsible for selling them some of the latest ex-Soviet small arms. Like Andy's, his report would now be on his boss's desk, together with a list of all the new members' names.

Their interview with the Station Commander was over and done with in a matter of minutes. He was very friendly and not only welcomed them to his base but offered them any assistance they might require. He was also extremely bogged down, judging by the amount of paperwork piled on his desk and, they got the impression, slightly annoyed at having to act as a postman.

Derek took the plain brown envelope from him. They found a quiet corner in the Mess room and in turn read the two letters in silence. One was from a Mr Fred Clarke, the second, which bore no address or signature, said they were to interview this gentleman with reference to the contents and assess its validity; included were six or seven paragraphs of suggested answers they could give to any questions that might be raised. One further sentence was heavily underlined. It stressed that Mr Clarke had to be assured that any problem, if there ever was one in the first place, had now been resolved. The final paragraph was not only underlined but stated in bolder type: **Meeting arranged 10.00 a.m. Monday 1st March; the Marriott Hotel, Lexington Avenue, Manhattan, Suite 1012. Repeat 10.00 a.m. prompt.** They both turned the page over but that was it.

Derek spoke first, 'I don't know about you, my new-found English accomplice, but this is a new line of investigation for me. Sounds more like a job for the local cops, if you ask me.'

Andy had to acknowledge that it was a long way off his normal path as well.

They agreed they would visit this Mr Clarke in Paphos on the Wednesday. It said in the letter that he was retired, so he shouldn't be too far from his pad, and even if he was out for the day then they would find a bar and try later on. They also mutually agreed that there was no need to warn him of their visit in advance, they would just turn up, take him off guard and assess his unprepared answers. Derek would do the talking, Andy the assessing bit. They would also arrange to hire a civilian four-wheel drive vehicle.

'We don't want to give him the wrong idea and frighten the life out of him by turning up in some military vehicle, do we?' Derek had said, running his hands over his non-existent hair.

They spent Tuesday in Limassol. Derek described it as a sight-seeing day. He spotted the two likely females in a bar, both were in their late thirties and looked like sisters, and this was the first time Andy saw his partner use his card trick. Derek marched straight up to them and offered to buy them drinks, adding right away that he was vice-president of an American oil company *en route* to inspect his company's operations in the Middle East. Most of this crap fell on deaf ears as they turned out to be a couple of German housewives having a short holiday break, but they were impressed, however, when he gave each of them a business card and they worked out between them what the words meant. *Hank McEvoy, Vice-President, Standard Southern Oil, Inc., Texas.* They giggled a lot to each other, but after several drinks the two couples left the bar and headed off in the general direction of the women's hotel.

Andy was impressed with Derek's technique. It was not bad, not bad at all for a bald, short, overweight, middle-aged man.

'I never go anywhere without at least half a dozen different calling-cards,' Derek explained on the drive to Paphos. 'They always come in handy, I can tell you. I can never resist those printing machines at airports and always get a couple more run off before a flight. I reckon I must have over a hundred on file now – perhaps there's a special name for this hobby of mine?'

Andy was not prepared for the cold, and their first stop in New York was to a store, where he bought himself a waterproof jacket and scarf, whilst Derek couldn't resist an overcoat he'd spotted amongst the sale racks. By the time they walked up to the Marriott Hotel they were both well protected from the chilly wind. At precisely 10 a.m. they rang the bell to Suite 1012. The door was opened immediately by a leftover from the Neanderthal age. He was the same height as Andy, but much younger; his neck and head were the same size and he had the minimum crew cut possible without being bald. He asked for identification, then, satisfied, he brought himself to utter some words. 'Follow me.' He was obviously not employed for his personality. He led them into a large lounge where four hard-backed chairs had been placed in a straight row facing a magnificent period writing-desk. Two of the chairs were occupied, and both Andy and Derek nodded greetings to the occupants, but before any introductions could be made the hired help opened a door to an adjoining room. It was difficult not to laugh at the sight of the man who came through it. He was dressed from head to foot in denim: shirt, jacket, jeans, the lot. On his feet he wore training-shoes. All very trendy on somebody in their teens or early twenties, but not on a fat man in his late fifties, no more than five foot tall and shaped like a 'D'. His hair was plastered down with gel, which made his fat face look even more oval. There was worse to come. He had one really outstanding feature, and Andy could see out of the corner of his eye that Derek was staring at it. The little fat man had an enormous nose, more of a beak really. He walked across the room and stood in front of the desk, weighing up his audience.

'Good morning. I am General Oliver Hutton.' There was a pause. If this was supposed to bring a round of gasps or applause there was none. 'The introductions can be dealt with later. Needless to say, you are all under oath, including you, Lockwood.'

He was about to continue in his funny squeaky voice when the door opened and a female voice shouted out, 'Albert is taking me shopping, Oliver. See you at our table at noon.'

Andy caught a glimpse of a very thin old woman with a severe face. It was obvious Hutton did not like being called 'Oliver' in front of his subordinates; his face had taken on a very red colour. He composed himself again before resuming his speech.

'Our leaders and the heads of several foreign governments have become increasingly concerned about the growing amount of violence and the escalating number of conflicts taking place throughout the world. As far as I am concerned, most of them are beneficial to this country. I don't really care if all the Chinese and Koreans annihilate each other or if the niggers are running amok over those fascist bastards in South Africa. I doubt if some of our allies give a shit either. No offence intended of course, Doc.'

The black man referred to as 'Doc' stood up and very calmly and precisely said, 'None taken from this fourth generation all-American nigger.' He sat down again and stared at a picture hanging behind Hutton's head. The General's face started to bulge and took on some strange colours, including a bright purple hue. He looked as if he was going to say something but then decided to forget it.

'As I was saying,' he continued, 'concern is growing even more now it has spread to our own backyard with the recent riots in the Midwest. You all read the newspapers and watch the news bulletins on television so you know what I'm talking about. It has been mooted that there may be a definite pattern to the events taking place and that somehow they are being orchestrated. Our leaders have decided this possibility is worth investigating. They have come up with several hunches and want them all checked out, no matter how crackpot they may appear on the surface.' He added the last sentence with a very sarcastic tone to his voice.

'One far-fetched notion, proposed by the English' – again he paused, and stared at Andy as if he alone was to be held responsible – 'is that somebody, or some organisation, may be tampering with the world's beer production.' Hutton made no attempt to hide his utter disbelief at the idea. 'You, gentlemen, are to be given the privilege of investigating this absurdity. I want you to begin as soon as possible because the sooner you put an end to this nonsense the sooner you can get back to doing something useful and more beneficial for the United States.' At this point the denim shirt puffed out so taut that gaps opened up between the buttons to reveal a white vest. 'I am also in charge of many other projects investigating much more likely solutions and shall be extremely busy. You can appoint a team leader who will compile all the information and keep me informed – I don't want you all bothering me! As I don't expect this project to run for very long before you disprove it, then I will need a final summing-up report. Got it? Questions?'

Derek stuck his hand up. There was silence and a look of thunder came over Hutton's face. 'Yes, what is it?' he stormed.

'If you think all this beer theory is a load of crap, then firstly, why pursue it at all, and secondly, why choose people like us who are not really trained in this line of work? Why not people from the Food and Drink Administration?'

A well-rehearsed reply was fired back. 'To the first part of your question, it is out of my hands. To the second part, can you imagine the outcry if word got out that we were even considering the possibility that something had been added to beer? We would have more riots and problems than we have now. I would have thought that even you would see that, but obviously not! We want the investigation to be as covert as possible so no one is ever aware it took place.'

Derek sat down again, reprimanded like some schoolboy who had just been told off for bad homework. The General made to leave.

Andy stood up. 'General, why should I be involved? I note that the original thoughts came from Britain but you give the impression the investigation will be in the States, a place I have no working knowledge of.'

Derek nodded; he obviously thought it was a reasonable question to ask. The General didn't.

'I did not say anything at all about the investigation being confined to anywhere, did I? That's up to your project team leader to decide. You are part of the team because your English government insisted someone was present on all the projects they'd had an input in, if not they would exclude Americans from theirs. Pure blackmail, if you ask me. Personally, I'd have been happier without a foreigner present.'

Andy wasn't hurt by the remark, he was too long in the tooth to be affected by some puffed-up little midget like Hutton. What puzzled him more was why Americans always insisted on calling it England and not Britain.

There were no further questions. Hutton reeled off a string of numbers. 'This is the telephone number where you can leave messages for me. Once you have established a base, let me know so that my chauffeur can collect any reports, etc. Oh! and one other thing – expenses. Keep them down. I shall not approve any exorbitant claims, so keep your hotel and car rentals to the middle ranges and remember, you are under my command for this exercise, not on some James Bond extravaganza! Let yourselves out, gentlemen.'

They all shuffled into the corridor and waited for the elevator. Nobody spoke. The only noise was the Doc expelling a great sigh.

Derek broke the ice first. 'Thrown out onto the streets by General Odd-Job. Just wait until Miss Moneypenny hears about this!' The other three laughed or smiled; at least it was a start. 'Listen,' Derek went on, encouraged, 'I know a bar on the next block. I'm sure we could all do with a drink whilst we discuss our next move. All agreed, team?' They all nodded and began to wrap themselves up against New York's weather.

'Do you know where I can get some poisoned beer for Hutton?' It was the Doc's voice.

They all sat down in the back of the bar and ordered their respective drinks. Derek ordered whiskey, the rest stuck to warming coffee. He polished it off in one go, asked them to order another when they could catch the waiter's eye, and went off in search of a telephone. He returned some five minutes later. 'Gentlemen, we have temporary shelter, about a thirty-minute taxi-ride away. Take your time, there's no panic.'

The apartment was on the eleventh floor. It was fashionably furnished and the view overlooking the river was impressive. 'It's my ex-wife's *pied-à-terre,*' Derek announced to everyone. 'She still allows me to use it when I'm in town. It's handy for the odd shower and change of shirt, and even the odd bit of sex – yes, we are still good friends! Oh, one house rule, by the way. We have to leave the flat as we found it.'

Derek disappeared and came back with a bottle of whiskey. 'Don't worry, it's my bottle, kept here in case of emergencies.' He poured everyone a generous measure but the Doc refused, so Derek drank the fourth glass as well and proposed a toast. 'To our team. I suppose we had better make some introductions. Let me start.'

Derek gave them a brief history of himself and who he worked for. He kept it fairly light-hearted, and by the time he had finished his guests were not only warm but more at ease. He then introduced Andy Lockwood to the assembled few. First he said he was very, very welcome and to disregard Hutton's comments. The other two reciprocated these sentiments.

Andy gave a good account of himself and hoped that they could understand his British accent. They all said they could. Derek poured some more drink for himself and turned to face the youngest member of the team, who looked quite nervous at what he clearly considered an ordeal. Slowly and encouraged by Derek this obviously shy young man began to settle into his stride.

'My name is Ben Hansen, I'm twenty-nine years old and work for the Internal Revenue Service in a Special Projects Department linked to the Treasury. I'm supposed to be considered something of a computer expert and I've been involved in unearthing several major frauds involving the illegal transfer of billions of dollars between companies.' He stopped – that was going to be it. Andy did not know if Derek was thinking along the same lines but what was a very smart young man in his blue suit, power tie and gold-rimmed glasses doing sitting with a couple of reprobates like them? What was he going to contribute to this beer project? He had to ask.

Ben Hansen hesitated and then actually blushed. 'Well, there is something else.' Again there was a pause, almost as if he was too embarrassed to continue. It came out in a rush eventually. 'I'm a computer hack, that's what I'm really good at, I have been ever since I was twelve.'

'You mean you break into other people's computer programs to obtain illegal information?' Andy asked.

'Yes, that's correct.'

'And you get paid for it at the same time?' Derek threw in.

'Yes.'

'Excellent, Ben. Welcome to the club of spies,' Derek told him.

The Doc coughed. Derek turned to him. 'Sorry, if you're not one we'll make you an honorary member. How's that?' The Doc smiled through two rows of impeccable white teeth.

Derek turned back to Ben. 'So what have the powers that be told you about this little operation then?'

'Nothing really. I was asked to attend today's meeting by my boss and told to assist, should my expertise be required, in tracking down any large sums of foreign money being fed into any organisation, I suppose to fund this beer allegation thing.'

'So you know none of the background?'

'No.'

'Don't worry, as soon as we've heard from the Doc here, I'll fill you in.'

On cue the Doc stood up. He was dressed in a creased white lightweight suit and wore a red bow-tie. He looked the oldest on the team; his white hair was set off by the contrast with the colour of his skin. 'Pleased to meet you all. My name is Larry Fletcher. I run one of the government laboratories for the Federal Drugs Unit based in Los Angeles. As you can see, it is warmer there at the moment!' He ran a hand over his summer suit. 'I'm also a guest lecturer at the university. My experience, as you may now have guessed, is helping to identify various types of drugs and where they were made. We have been quite successful in helping to break up several drug operations. You can tell by the way the base chemicals are put together where drugs such as crack and breeze were made, and sometimes even who was responsible. We broke up one syndicate by checking the records of a chemical company who had legitimately sold on a particular raw material. It has a lot in common with forensic work: synthetic products are all slightly different, a bit like fingerprints. I suppose I'm included in the gang of four to help identify any substances that might be found in the beer but I must admit I know nothing about the make-up of it at this stage – I never drink the stuff. For the record, I am fifty-seven years old, married, have two grown-up daughters and live on the outskirts on Santa Monica, and yes, I know I look a lot younger than my age!' If Ben Hansen had been brief with his curriculum vitae, Larry Fletcher had gone into lecture mode. However, everyone took an instant liking to the Doc; he was easy to listen to – if he'd been a medical doctor he would have been described as having a good bedside manner.

In unison both Andy and Derek asked the same question: 'You've met the General before, then?'

'Yes, unfortunately, once. About ten years ago now, I suppose. Similar type of operation in a way, looking for a drug coming into the country disguised as something else. He's an arrogant bastard, strutting about like he does. I wasn't looking forward to this meeting one little bit, I can tell you. You know, he has never seen action in his life, he's a total armchair soldier, yet he thinks he is single-handedly saving the American nation from the bad guys. All this talk about expenses, he lives off the taxpayer to the full – best hotels, best restaurants. I wouldn't be at all surprised if his wife's shopping's on an army credit card! There's very few people I dislike, but he certainly tops the list.'

'What about his nigger business then?' Derek asked.

'Somebody on our last little exercise found out that he originally came over from Germany with his family in 1937. His real name is very Teutonic, so I'm led to believe. He likes to forget about all of this and for everyone to consider him one of the original all-American heroes.'

'He's certainly no oil-painting, is our General. That nose! More like Captain Hook!' Andy remarked. Everyone laughed, and whether he liked it or not, the little fat general had a new nickname.

They all encouraged Ben to open up some more. It worked. He gradually started to relax and accept that he was amongst friends, not everyone was like Captain Hook. They learnt that he lived near San Francisco and worked in the city itself, that he wasn't married but lived with someone and kept fit by jogging with his partner in the hour before work. His whole life seemed to revolve around computers, however.

The Doc had one request to make. He didn't particularly like being called 'Doctor' and asked everyone to start calling him Larry. He hated the formality of the title, plus it also reminded him of someone else with a handle! His request was unanimously accepted.

Derek called the meeting to order to discuss their future plans but before he could start Andy interrupted him. He proposed Derek be elected team leader, and this was agreed by the other two. They sat and pooled what information they had. Larry's was sketchy, to say the least, whilst Ben's was non-existent. Andy dug out the letter from Fred Clarke and passed it around, and Derek explained some of the finer points they had gleaned from their meeting in Cyprus. Larry asked the first question.

'Presumably somebody on your side of the water must have found some sort of evidence to support this man's claim?'

'I would assume so,' Andy answered, 'otherwise it's a lot of trouble to go to if it's just on the whim of some civil servants back home.'

They all agreed that there must be some evidence somewhere, otherwise it was pretty absurd, as the General had suggested, to have four men about to investigate the possible contamination of beer based on the findings of one untrained retired man many thousands of miles away.

Derek disappeared to the toilet to lose some of his whiskey and was gone for a good five minutes. 'By the way,' he said on his return, 'the General's number rings through to the State Department. Just thought you would like to know!' He took centre stage once again. 'Right, let's run through this plan to see if we all agree. First, we need to establish if there *is* a problem. To do this we're going to have to get numerous samples of this filteraid stuff, both here and in Europe. Larry can then test them to see if they do contain any drugs. That's okay, isn't it, Larry?'

'Yes, fine. I'll need about 100-gram samples – enough, say, to fill this tumbler.' He held up Andy's empty whiskey glass.

'Andy, will you go back to Europe and look after that

side of things? I'll sniff around here.' Derek was now in full flow, dishing out the instructions. 'Larry, is it worth checking out various different makes of beer to see what they contain? Good. I'll leave that for you to organise. Ben, while we're grabbing handfuls of powder for Larry, can you delve into your computer and find out the details of the companies who manufacture Favusite or any other type of filteraid?'

'No problem,' replied Ben. 'May I ask a question?'

'Of course.'

'What happens if Larry finds something in the beer samples, but nothing in these filteraid materials?'

'Then stage two comes into play, my friend – we panic! Seriously though, we'll cross that bridge when we come to it. We'll need somewhere to meet in future and also a telephone number so we can keep in touch. Any ideas, anyone?'

Larry volunteered his office straight away. 'It makes sense, I'm the one who'll be static all the time and in LA, and we won't be too far from Ben either.'

Derek liked this offer. 'Excellent suggestion. Thanks. On the West Coast we'll also be the furthest point away from Captain Hook as well. Good thinking Doc! Sorry – Larry.'

Everyone wrote down Larry's telephone and fax numbers and his office address. He also gave them his university telephone number just in case. They set a time limit of two weeks for their next meeting. The date was fixed but not the time, so that it became flexible for those travelling, plus it also steered clear of horrible words like 'prompt'.

Larry had a further request. 'Don't hang onto your samples until there are dozens of them. Please send them off as soon as you get hold of them, it'll take me a couple of hours to analyse each one and I don't want Derek shouting at me in a few weeks' time when I haven't got any results! And please send them in plastic bags so that they don't get contaminated en route. Thanks.'

The meeting broke up. Three of them went their own separate ways, each with his own task and thoughts on how best to deal with it. Derek stayed behind to tidy up the room. He glanced at his watch. There was time for a bath before Ruth got home from work. Perhaps he would ask her if he could stay the night. She usually said yes, and it might turn out to be a lucky one – especially if he took her out for a nice meal first.

5

Andy had to wait six hours for a flight. He looked at his watch; with London time five hours ahead he would arrive at Heathrow about mid-morning. Flying into the day was not that bad, jet lag didn't catch up with you as quickly if at all. Not that Andy suffered much in that direction. Anyway, he always worked on two principles: one, no alcohol in flight and, two, no matter what time your body clock said, you stayed awake until it was dark and time for bed in the foreign land. Once in London he would hire a car and buy a large bunch of flowers for his favourite lady. He decided he'd better ring her first to warn her he was coming – she hated surprises, and no doubt, would spend the day tidying up even though the flat was always spotless. It was strange, really, that after all these years he still called her 'Mum'. He'd had his own property in London several years ago but, being away so much, had hardly ever used it, so he decided to rent it out. What a disaster! Perhaps it was just that particular family who were not house-proud, but it had cost him thousands of pounds to put the damage right; he would never forget the state of the carpets! Every room had needed to be redecorated and it still annoyed him.

'Animals!' He'd said it out loud and the man in the next seat turned and stared at him.

He'd left it empty the next year, but squatters had broken in and he'd had to go through the whole messy business of eviction orders to get them removed – no easy task when you're abroad most of the time. That was it, he'd had enough of it all, so he'd sold his 'little castle'; mind you, he'd had the last laugh though. It was boom time late 1990 and he'd got a very good price. During a month's leave he'd had a good look round Eastbourne and bought his mum a two-bedroomed flat with sea views, central heating, the lot. She was over the moon; her old downstairs flat on the outskirts of London was damp and dark. She'd soon made lots of friends her own age and been introduced to the world of antiques; now she had a stall in the old town hall twice a week. He always stayed with her when he returned from his overseas jaunts, and like any other mother, she always wanted to know where he'd been and what he'd been up to. Most of the time he told her lies, but they were enough to satisfy her curiosity. She was convinced her only child worked as some sort of security consultant advising large foreign companies on the best ways of keeping their respective properties safe and sound.

Andy was one of the first into the library the following morning, no worse for all the travelling and the late night from answering all his mother's questions. He had to be shown where the business directories were kept but found what he wanted. He was both surprised and yet, at the same time, disappointed. As a teenager in London he remembered breweries being everywhere; they had been landmarks for centuries, and now there were only three listed in the book. He scanned the rest of the page. There were only twenty-three companies listed nationally and they were well and truly scattered around the country. It was going to be pot luck which ones would provide the most useful information.

He looked across the almost deserted room and watched an ancient pensioner struggling with a newspaper. Andy was still having trouble getting to grips with this job. On several occasions in the past he'd risked life and limb, had even been ready to use a gun if pushed into a corner, and now here he was about to visit a British brewery to get samples of filteraid! It didn't quite seem to add up. He rubbed the early signs of stubble on his chin and formulated his plan. He might as well start off in the south of England. Why travel hundreds of miles on what might turn out to be a wild-goose chase? He started to write down several names and then the thought struck him: why bother with visits to the breweries themselves? He would either have to break in and steal a sample or go through the lengthy procedure of arranging an appointment and then bluffing his way through an interview with some brewer – why not just go straight to the company supplying the wretched stuff in the first place! He went back to the reference book but couldn't find the company or the trade name Purflo. Then another brainwave struck him and he laughed – next time he wanted inspiration he would have to remember to visit a library. He left and made one phone call. He picked a brewery at random from his list and called them and asked them where, as a fellow brewer, he could buy Purflo filteraid from. The receptionist put him through to their purchasing department and he explained his predicament – he wanted to filter beer and needed some filteraid, Purflo had been recommended but he hadn't a clue where to get it from. The man on the other end of the phone couldn't have been more helpful; Purflo was sold through an agent in the UK call Midland Trading Limited, based in Nottingham. He even supplied a telephone number. Andy would never know it, but Fred Clarke could have supplied this information from the back of his brochure. The next call was to Nottingham. Another helpful man on the other end of the line said he would be delighted to receive him, but added that it was more usual for them to visit the potential client on his own site, to see the set-up first hand. Andy quickly interrupted and said he had other business to attend to in their area and 'was killing two birds with one stone' so to speak, and an appointment was made for three o'clock the following afternoon.

Andy presented his card to the girl on reception. It spelled out *'Henry Taylor, Managing Director, Taylor and Company Limited, The Brewery, Exeter, Devon. DV9 3GJ.* All fabrication – he had taken a leaf out of Derek's book, stopped at a service station on the motorway and printed the cards off on one of the machines in the foyer. The minimum quantity was twenty cards for only three pounds – not bad value for a scam; perhaps he would start a collection as well! He told the girl he had an appointment with a Mr Parker to talk about Purflo filteraids and spoke in a voice which indicated he was used to getting his own way. He was offered a seat and some fresh coffee and biscuits, and was just about to start to scan through a brewing journal when a voice called out his name.

'Mr Taylor, I'm Michael Parker. Sorry to have kept you waiting, I was on the telephone to one of our principals. How may I help you?'

'I own and run a small brewery down in Devon. We are expanding rapidly and I've been told, or advised, that I need to filter my beer.'

The tall, very pale young man asked, 'So you don't treat it at all at the moment then?'

'No,' Andy was starting to struggle and inwardly cursed himself. He had gone headlong into this project without any preparation at all. It was sheer complacency on his part because he wasn't treating the whole thing seriously. It was a good job his life didn't depend on his answers this time. He pretended to blow his nose whilst his mind raced for suitable answers.

Mr Parker saved the situation for him. 'So you must produce only cask beers at the moment. Are you going into keg beers then, perhaps a lager?'

Andy nodded. 'Yes, that's right, we're going to start manufacturing a lager.' He hoped the relief didn't show on his face.

'Have you bought a filter yet?'

'Not exactly, my engineer is looking at some this week.' Again Andy hoped this inquisitive young man would not ask any questions about filter machines. He had been on this planet for thirty-nine years so far and had never felt a need or desire to get involved with such equipment!

Mr Parker invited Andy into a small office. Pictures of filters lined the walls and brochures relating to Purflo were neatly stacked in the centre of the small and only table. During the next hour he was subjected to the history, technology and usage of filteraids. Most of it he found boring but he made every effort to assimilate as much information as he could and made a point of remembering that it was only the finest of the Purflo grades that were used for beer filtration. Mr Parker finished off his talk by saying that the exact grade chosen would depend upon the flow rate required and the final clarity necessary to meet his specifications.

'How many grades are there then?' Andy asked trying to ignore the cramp in his legs.

'We supply six different grades to the breweries; as I said, it all depends on what is required from the filtered product.'

'And what grade would you recommend for my lager, Mr Parker?'

'Probably not the very finest.' He drew Andy's attention to a chart in the brochure. 'Not P1 or P3, probably more like the P5, P7 or P9 grades.'

'Excellent. Would it be possible to have some samples? I'll get our technical people to carry out some small-scale trials in order to see what the differences are.'

'Certainly.' Parker went out of the office and returned several minutes later saying that some small sample packets would be available for him to take away. The salesman in Parker now wanted to get down to the commercial aspects of the meeting: had Andy any idea how much he would require per annum? How was he going to buy it, by the pallet, by the tonne, perhaps five tonnes at a time? He pointed out that the larger the delivery the less the price. He was about to talk about transportation costs when Andy cut him off short. He couldn't be bothered with all of this and told Parker he had no idea at the moment, but that hopefully if the lager sold well, then it would be beneficial to both parties. Whatever the outcome, he would always place his business with Midland Trading as a thank-you for setting him on the right track to start with. This last comment satisfied Mr Parker. Now it was time for Andy to fish around a bit.

'Do you manufacture these Purflo filteraids in the UK then?'

'Oh no. We are only distributors. They are all processed in America and we receive the finished grades already bagged and palletised.'

'So how do you know the quality of each grade is always up to scratch? Do you sample incoming shipments?'

'Well no,' It was the first time the younger man showed any signs of hesitancy. 'We don't have the facilities here, we rely on our American principal's quality-control set-up. Each shipment and each grade is coded and comes with a certificate of conformity, though.' Parker noticed the puzzled look on his future client's face and so continued, 'It guarantees that the grade meets all the very high standards laid down for it.'

'And what are the main standards then?'

'Well, permeability to ensure that the throughput is always the same from batch to batch, colour, lack of odour and generally that the grade is pure and free from organic matter.'

'Just one more question please, Mr Parker, then I must leave you to get on with your own work. If you do have a problem with one of your grades do you have to send it back to the States for analysis?'

'No, it takes too long and keeps the customer waiting – not that a problem happens very often, you understand.'

Andy nodded sympathetically.

Parker continued, 'No, we send it to Union Mining and Minerals' offices in Brussels. They have their own set-up in Belgium; laboratories, warehouses, sales offices. They handle the rest of Europe directly themselves.'

The samples arrived and Parker looked quite relieved. This visitor was asking too many leading questions for someone who didn't even buy from him. He carried the box out to the car.

Andy thanked him and shook his hand repeatedly. 'It's really nice to know there are people like you about who are absolutely dedicated to your subject – your explanations were superb, you obviously know your stuff inside out. I came here knowing next to nothing and am leaving with my head crammed full of useful facts. Thank you. With such good products and sound technical service no wonder you are number one in the business. I doubt if you have any competition anyway.'

The flattery worked. Parker smiled. 'Thank you, Mr Taylor. It's very nice of you to say so. Yes, we are the biggest supplier to the brewing industry, but like everyone else we do have our competitors.'

Andy waited, but any further information was going to have to be prised out of Parker. 'Who are they then?'

'Only one, really, a French company called Liseux.' He spat the name out; it was almost as if he'd blasphemed.

Andy drove back south, satisfied with precisely one hour and twenty-five minutes' work. He had one-kilo samples of five different Purflo grades, two brochures and a lot of knowledge about filteraids in general. He also knew that nobody interfered with the product between the American plant where it was first made and the final customer who used it. There were still far too many loopholes in his information, but in his usual methodical way he would find answers to these as well. He only hoped the exercise was not just some crackpot idea dreamt up by a grey suit in Whitehall. No, it wouldn't be a single person, it would have to be a committee at the very least!

Andy caused Mrs Lockwood a lot of consternation when he suggested that they go away for a few days' holiday together. They could take her car across the Channel and spend a few days in Paris, take in a show or two and splash out on some good food at well-known restaurants and then drive back via Belgium, stopping over in Brussels and Bruges. They could be back by Sunday. There was no rush though, they could take it as it came.

First of all she argued that she had a fair on Saturday and then that it was really too short notice. The real reason, Andy knew, was that the thought of foreign travel frightened her. At seventy-one years of age she'd only been abroad once, and had hated it. Andy's father had been dead now for nearly twelve years and she'd never really wanted even to discuss holidays since. Years ago he'd actually bought her a three-week cruise on the QE2 and then gone away on business, but she didn't go, said she had flu at the time, and he was not sure to this day if it was just an excuse or not.

It was hard work, but he won this time – she eventually agreed.

In March, Paris was quiet and it was fairly easy to do the tourist bit – the Eiffel Tower, the Louvre, plus visits to several of the main shopping areas. His mother's inbuilt fear dissipated. She started to enjoy herself and returned to her more normal relaxed happy self. Everything about the city lived up to expectations, and on the second night when they returned to their hotel at ten o'clock, they agreed they were tired out and needed some sleep.

Andy gave it about an hour before he changed into jeans and a navy-blue teeshirt. Nobody saw him slip through the reception area. Once on the Paris inner ring road, he soon found the turn-off to Chartres. The drive took him nearly two hours and twice he had to reverse to look at signposts. It would have been difficult enough finding the small village in daylight, but on a pitch-black night amongst rolling countryside he was struggling, and it eventually took him twice as long as he had planned.

It was easy to spot his objective once there, though – it was bathed in light and resembled a quarry of some sort. A row of cabin offices stood in darkness with the name LISEUX plus some smaller letters painted on the wall. He parked just off the main road and took stock of the situation. From the noise, the majority of activity was going on behind the offices. He could hear machinery on the go but could not see any people. At the far side of the hole in the ground was a large black shed, which he assumed was the warehouse – his target. He reached across the seat and grabbed a small torch, knife and some small plastic bags, but had to search for the marker pen, which had rolled onto the floor. He smiled to himself. His 'tools' were hardly those a regular burglar would have chosen! He got out and checked that the car would not be spotted. Satisfied, he made his way around the back of the store.

All the doors were open, and he had the place to himself. Pallet upon pallet of bags were laid out along the entire length of the building. He worked his way down, only stopping when he came upon a different code number. A small stab of the bag with the knife and enough powder flowed to fill up his small plastic bag. As he leant against one single pallet to add the reference number to the self-seal envelope, something prodded him in the small of his back. He turned round cautiously; it was a foot. Then he heard heavy breathing. One of the workers had been at the anisette – he stank of it. Andy shone the torch on his face and decided he would be out cold for hours – his workmates would probably end up carrying him home when the shift changed.

There were only four grades to collect and within forty minutes Andy was speeding back to Paris. The new receptionist probably thought he'd just been out for an early morning jog. He had a shower, changed clothes, and was already at the breakfast table when his mother came down at the prearranged time.

In Brussels, Andy found them a hotel just off the Grand Place. They did the tourist bit, had an early dinner and again his mother retired early, tired after the drive. He walked to Union's offices on Frederick Avenue and couldn't believe his luck, the main door to all the various offices was open. Cleaners were busy mopping the foyer, so he walked straight in and exchanged a few everyday greetings with the two women. From his confident manner they would assume he worked in one of the companies and had either forgotten something or was going to burn the midnight oil.

The suite of offices he wanted was off a central corridor and there were four or five possible doors he could enter by. It was going to be sheer guesswork. He tried them all; they were all locked. He selected the easiest type of lock, took some wire from his shirt pocket, and within thirty seconds was inside what looked to be the general office. All the other offices had interconnecting and unlocked doors onto this room – he had struck lucky!

After an hour he had found nothing to contradict Parker's information; Purflo came into Europe via Rotterdam and was already bagged and palletised. It was stored in warehouses in Aalst, here in Belgium, ready and awaiting orders. He found invoices from as far apart as Germany, Finland and Spain. One of the rooms looked to be a small support laboratory, there were several containers of dirty beer in a large fridge and some white plastic drums labelled *Standard Liquor (Sugar Beet)*. It was obviously where they matched the correct grade of filteraid for the job requested by a particular client. There were several miniature dustbins full of Purflo grades. It was too good an opportunity to miss so he collected six grades in six manilla envelopes.

The best office was reserved for the manager and expensively furnished with a small bar in one corner. The name-plate on the desk suggested the man was of French origins. Andy carefully went through the desk drawers. Most were unlocked; the bottom ones on either side weren't, but it didn't take long to open them. His adrenaline started to pump faster, as it always did when he was about to delve into the unknown. It was not what he was looking for; the Frenchman had a penchant for very obscene pornographic literature – the drawers were crammed full of the stuff. He returned to the foyer, where the cleaners were taking a smoke-break. He held up the envelopes, yes, they would think he had forgotten to do something important – like post them. It never ceased to amaze him – and he'd seen it and taken advantage of it many times before – how companies relied on the cleaners to be responsible for security whilst on site. It never worked.

He was glad to get back to his room well before midnight. Although he desperately needed some sleep, there was still one more job to do. Carefully, he transferred the contents from the paper envelopes into the plastic ones and made sure they were all properly labelled.

There was no urgency from now on. Next morning Andy drove to Bruges. His mother fell in love with the place and they stayed another day. He deliberately drove slowly back to the French port of Calais so that they missed their planned ferry and had to rebook on a later one. He wanted time to visit one of the hypermarkets. He had to admit that he was impressed with the size of the place, whilst his mother was struck with the ridiculously cheap prices, compared to her local shop. He grabbed some packs of beers; she bought cheese, butter and numerous sticks of bread.

Andy unloaded the car once they'd got back to Eastbourne. His mother would have been horrified if she had known that, tucked in between her shopping, were plastic envelopes full of white powder. A son and his mother on a short holiday into Europe, all very normal and a very nice cover. Keep it discreet, they had said, so discreet it had been. But to Andy's way of thinking it was still all a bit over the top, the whole exercise, the whole idea.

He did something unusual the following day; for the second time in twenty-four hours he went shopping, this time to an English supermarket. He bought seventeen different brands of beer. He had to buy four-packs of them all and got some funny looks at the long checkout queue – he was either an alcoholic or going to throw one hell of a good party. On the way out he helped himself to a large sturdy empty cardboard box, found a quiet spot in the car park and began to pack his container. When he had finished it held sixteen samples of filteraid and at least one can of beer from twenty-three different breweries scattered all over the UK, Ireland, France, Belgium, Germany and Italy.

'This should give Larry something to get his teeth into and decide whether they're drugged or just downright enjoyable!' he mumbled to himself. The he dumped the unwanted cans into an aluminium-recycling skip, walked to a newsagent's, bought some strong sealing-tape and used the telephone outside. The voice on the London number asked him to wait, they would action his request in a few moments. He hung on for minutes before getting a reply and then was told to take his box to an RAF station in Norfolk, where they would ensure it was forwarded to Dr Larry Fletcher as soon as possible.

He arrived back in the flat in the early evening and was just about to take a shower when his mother called out. At first he thought she had been taken ill, and rushed into the living-room. She stood motionless, pointing towards the television screen, which was showing scenes of violent fighting on the streets of some city. As the camera panned back there were the unmistakable sights of the Grand Place in Brussels with the Rathous in the background. The newsreader was saying that a peaceful march by Flemish demonstrators had been barracked and heckled by a large crowd of Walloons. Then stones were thrown and the situation got totally out of hand. The police separating the two rival factions were now embroiled in the battle themselves. The voice-over stated that the cause was historical and deep-seated – the Flemish were demonstrating against French becoming the number one language.

Andy's mother stared at the screen in horror. 'Andy we were there only three days ago. It's all so reminiscent of the thirties.'

It would be a long, long time before she would consider setting foot outside Britain again, Andy realised – not that it was any better here. It was all just a lottery, you could be in the wrong place at the wrong time and witness similar scenes almost anywhere. He felt frustrated. Here he was, a trained operative, running around supermarkets whilst the world was falling apart.

He got dressed and went out to find the nearest telephone box – he couldn't say what he wanted to on his mother's phone. He rang his London number and was told to call back in ten minutes. They were obviously going to have to search round the right gentlemen's clubs to find their – his – boss. He walked up and down the street rehearsing his speech, rang back exactly on time and put his prepared case forward.

The well-spoken male voice was sympathetic, almost

patronising, but shot him down in flames. 'You have your instructions, so would you mind getting on with them, please? Sometimes none of us like what we are doing, we may totally disagree with the logic behind it, but things have to be done all the same, as I'm sure you understand. Good night.' The line went dead.

Andy remembered his first sergeant-major, whose motto in life had been quite simple: 'Orders is orders, never begin to query 'em, just carry 'em out and make sure you do 'em right. Got it, laddie?'

Yes, Andy had got it, all right. He made his mind up. He would see it through to the best of his ability, he wouldn't necessarily agree with it, but he would give it his best shot.

He lay in bed and reread the copy of Fred Clarke's letter. There was one further job to carry out. Clarke had mentioned a Greek supplier whose material was okay and didn't affect him, he couldn't rely on the word of some retired guy; no, he would have to get samples back to Larry - After all, if the job's worth doing, and all that. He checked with the local travel agent first thing in the morning. Thursday to Athens, back to Frankfurt, and then a non-stop flight to Los Angeles, getting him there late Saturday night. He made the bookings and spent one last day taking things easy.

The receptionist at the Herodian Hotel in Athens found out what he wanted: the Greek Lacunite plant was near a place called Fagrinkon. He checked his map, it was four hundred miles away on what could be bone-shaking roads - and all for some handfuls of dirt out of the ground! He hired a car and, with gritted teeth and fists clenched tight around the steering-wheel, set off on his latest trek. When he had gone about a hundred and fifty miles he was already dehydrated; the heat and dust were unbearable. If he opened the car window a fine cloud threatened to choke him, with it shut it was like an oven. His shirt and shorts were damp and sticking to the seat. At the next sighting of a taverna he would pull in and buy their entire stock of cold drinks! The thought made him lick his lips but it was another fifteen miles before he spotted his oasis. There were half a dozen lorries parked up, their drivers all sheltering inside the café; it was only mad dogs and Englishmen who carried on when the sun was at its zenith! He bought his drinks, nodded to the semi-dozing drivers and left; just another tourist on his way through. He stretched against the side of the car and drank two bottles of the mineral water and looked around. He did a double-take – two lorries up was a flat-bed truck loaded with pallets of material in bags, and he could see quite clearly printed on the side the word LACUNITE. He approached and counted four different grades – A50, A100, A150 and A200. The majority of the load was A150. Within minutes he had samples of each. There was no time for labels, so he just hoped he could remember the chronological order he'd stolen them in. A bonus indeed! He turned round and drove the car back to Athens wondering what the purchaser would think when he found knife slashes across four of the bags. Perhaps it was par for the course in this part of the world. He fixed his mind on a long cold shower and the air-conditioning blasting out back in his hotel room.

Andy scrounged a large envelope from reception and addressed it to Larry. Later that night, suitably refreshed, he drove the short distance to the American Embassy. The third assistant to the ambassador first checked out who he said he was and then promised to send the package on. He just hoped he had labelled the plastic envelopes correctly.

He had another bout of the blues on the plane to the States. He still didn't like what he was doing and felt like a soccer player who had just been relegated to a minor league. Perhaps those in power were trying to hint that he wasn't considered very good at his job, after all. Perhaps a memo had been circulated – 'give Lockwood the bum jobs because that's all he's good for.'

On the other side of the Atlantic Derek Madden was not being at all philosophical about his job. He was being paid to do this and his life was not in danger as he was unlikely to be shot at in a brewery. There was no foreign language to contend with and he would not have to keep visiting the toilet with a case of the squirts after eating some totally unrecognisable foreign food. No, if his superiors wanted him to do this assignment then he would do it gladly; in fact, he would enjoy it and treat it like a holiday.

There was one thing he had never done but had always fancied and that was to drive across America, coast to coast. Now he had the opportunity and two weeks to do it in. He sat back in the chair in his ex's flat and studied the map. He'd marked on most of the major breweries, and without too much dog-legging he would be able to visit six, maybe seven, on his intended route. For good measure he would phone Larry every two days to keep up to date with any developments. And to hell with the expense and that bastard Hutton, if he was going to do all that driving then he would do it in a quality car not some cheap imported compact.

Derek wasn't laughing two days later, he was drowning his sorrows with some very large whiskeys. He was really annoyed with himself – two breweries crossed off the list already and nothing to show for it. He'd thought it was going to be a pushover and it had totally caught him out.

The first brewery was two hundred miles south-west of New York. He had driven round it the night before and got the lie of the land. It was a massive complex and, unbeknown to him, the largest single site in the world. It was capable of producing over twenty-five million barrels of beer a year – almost enough to quench the thirst of all the beer drinkers in England. His plan had been very simple. He would join one of the guided public tours held every two hours, slip away from the party, find the filter area, do his thing and rejoin the group further on with his pockets bulging with samples. What he was not prepared for was the security. The tour was organised along glass-sided gantries which looked down on the various stages of brewing carried out below. There was no way into the bowels of the plant – even the odd doors which led off were all locked and, unlike Andy, Derek couldn't pick a lock to save his life. At the end of each corridor were security cameras, so even if he could slip away there was every chance his movements would have been monitored anyway. At one stage of the tour he heard the guide state, 'And this is where the beer is filtered in order to remove the slight cloudiness it has; it is then sparkling bright, ready to drink and exactly as you would serve it.' Derek cursed his luck, or lack of it, and looked down on the filters through the glass. There were ten of the bloody things, but he couldn't get any closer; he felt as if he was walking down one of those perspex tunnels at Sea World where you could reach out but couldn't actually touch the fish. At the end of the tour the party were invited into a hospitality suite, where everyone was given a free drink and a presentation pack of four bottles of the most popular brand produced. He could have bought them at any liquor store instead of wasting a day!

Brewery two was set deep in the heartlands of mid-America and although only a fraction of the size was still a considerable producer. Again Derek joined the official visitors' tour, but this time he managed to slip away unnoticed. He found a white dust coat hanging on the back of an office door and slipped it on. The few people he passed even nodded and said good morning. It was the classic disguise. After thirty minutes he still couldn't find a room full of pallets of filter powder, so he reluctantly stopped a man in a blue boiler suit and explained that he was on an induction course and had got lost; could the man point him in the direction of the filter powder bag store? The man told him that there were no bags, all filteraids were purchased in bulk. He even took Derek the hundred yards to show him the silos and explained that it was blown straight from the delivery tanker into these large metal containers. There were two such vessels, one smaller than the other. Both were labelled Purflo; P5 on one, P15 on the smaller one. His new-found friend said one was used to precoat the filter, the other grade added as a bodyfeed. This meant absolutely nothing to Derek. Neither silo had sample point access, they were totally sealed, there was nothing he could do. So near and yet. . .

He thanked his friend, tried to conceal his frustration

and just caught up with the official party as they disappeared into the sample suite, where once again he got his complimentary goodies. No doubt the cleaners would wonder why a perfectly good white coat had been thrown into a waste-paper bin.

He had now failed twice, and this was not Derek's style. From now on he would move up a gear. He dug out the box of fictitious name-cards from his suitcase and found appropriate ones.

Within the next seven days Derek acquired twenty-seven samples of filter powder. His new *modus operandi* was always the same: he would march up to the security gate and present his card, which not only looked impressive but said that its owner worked for the Government as some sort of environmental specialist. He would then demand to see the warehouse manager. He enjoyed it when the guards asked him if he had an appointment. He would let rip that the whole purpose of his visit was to drop in unannounced to ensure that the store was complying with all the numerous health regulations required in a food-processing plant.

After the first of his new-style visits he knew what to look for, and the other six were almost routine. He always asked to be left alone to walk around the place in order to make his official assessment. It was then quite straightforward to help himself to samples; he learnt as he went along. It was too slow spoon-feeding the powder into small bags, it was much easier to fill up a plastic coffee cup and slap the lid on. On several occasions the store manager would insist on hovering not too far away, watching his every move. He would get rid of him by getting him to measure the distance between rodent traps on the far side of the building and then swap places with the man if he wanted to be on that side of the building himself. Only one company refused him entry, so he made a scene and threatened to shut them down. They soon allowed him on site.

He was a stickler for detail. Each night he would sit in his motel room transferring the powder from cup to bag and then attach a detailed label with the trade name, company name, where it came from and the date. He posted them off in ten-sample lots to Larry. Most were Purflo samples, some of the others were new to him. He liked Klearites from a company in Oregon because of the very simple method of grading: extra fine, fine, medium and coarse. You knew where you were with those classifications.

He lay back on the bed after one of his better visits and reflected that a lot of things in life ended with *ite*. If he had a product it would naturally be called Maddenite – no, it didn't sound commercial enough. The earlier shaky start was now far behind him and he was pleased with his recent successes. The way things were going he would be in California on Thursday. He decided he would drop any remaining samples off to Larry and then visit both a brewery and an old flame in San Diego. So far there had not been any news from either Andy or Ben but he assumed they were doing okay.

Andy arrived in Los Angeles early Sunday morning and phoned Larry at home. The others had agreed to meet the following afternoon at four, Larry told him.

He hired a car and found a suitable hotel on the San Diego road. The weather was hot and dozens of joggers and roller skaters were using the beach road. The temptation was too much – he was soon amongst them. It seemed like weeks since he had had any proper exercise.

The two-storey white building in the Palos Verdes district of South Los Angeles was just a stone's throw from the Pacific Coast highway and it only took him about fifteen minutes to reach it from his hotel. Not a bad place to work, he decided. The sign stood out, red letters on a white background, STATE OF CALIFORNIA, DEPARTMENT OF SOCIAL AND HEALTH SERVICES. A small driveway led up to a security building. The entire site was surrounded by high chain-mesh fencing but inside the gardens were well-manicured with lots of large tropical-looking red flowers already in bloom. The guard had him down on his 'expected' list, so he lifted the barrier and pointed the way to the visitors' car park. In all

Andy passed about fifty to sixty cars, which gave him some idea of the workforce. He also noticed security cameras, including night infra-red devices, fixed onto every corner of the building.

Larry was already waiting for him, his hand outstretched. 'Welcome to California, Andy. Please come over here, I'm afraid you've got to sign in with this security man first.'

Andy did as he was told, showed some identification and was presented with a visitor's pass.

'We have to be careful, of course, you know, with security. There's a lot of drugs and things kept in this place. So far nobody's attempted to try and break in, but you never know. We'll go straight to my office, I've got some coffee on the go.'

Larry was the sort of person anybody would have found easy to get on with, Andy felt. What you saw was what you got. He was neither complicated nor devious – a refreshing change.

They walked through double doors to the right of the reception area, and Larry explained the set-up as they went along the corridor. 'All the laboratories are on this first floor, six of them, including mine. The wing opposite is used for stores and technical support, whilst the second floor is mainly taken up with administration, a restaurant and a library.'

Andy was confused. 'The building only has two storeys, so how come it has a second floor?'

Larry laughed. 'We Americans like to do things differently to everybody else! We call the ground floor the first floor, that's why.'

They stopped to look into one of the laboratories through the glass panels along the corridor. The white benches were packed with all the latest hi-tech equipment. It was a far cry from the brown wood, bunsen burners and rotten egg smells Andy remembered from his school-days.

'Here we are.' Larry directed Andy into his office. It was spacious and well lit by daylight, but above all it was air-conditioned, it was also very tidy and showed an organised mind. The far wall was covered in shelves, each piled high with books and scientific journals. On one wall various framed certificates hung in pride of place, whilst the clear glass window opposite looked out onto a large well-equipped laboratory where two technicians were busy poring over some very complex pieces of apparatus.

Andy had been the first to arrive, and as they drank coffee Larry asked him about his family and England – he'd never been there but one day would like to visit. The phone rang; the other two had arrived, half an hour late. Larry made some joke about the man from England being early while the two local boys were late, and went off to collect them. Andy felt underdressed for the occasion. His choice had been dictated by the weather and he was only wearing a shirt and slacks, whilst the Doc had a suit on – and his familiar red bow-tie. Ben was the first through the doorway and Andy was relieved to see that he was also casually dressed – but not Derek, who still had on the same heavy suit and tie he'd been wearing in Washington. Larry poured some more coffee whilst all the hellos and handshakes were taken care of and then beckoned them to join him round a small table by the window. When they were all seated, he started.

'Well, it's nice to see you all again. I hope you all had pleasant journeys to Los Angeles. I have received a huge box from you, Andy, together with a large envelope from Greece. I've also received three envelopes from you, Derek, including the one you dropped off yourself. Are there any more to come?'

Both sample men shook their heads so Larry continued. 'Good. Oh, by the way, the three technicians working for me are all fully vetted and have signed all the right and relevant bits of government paper. However, they are not being told the exact nature of the project. So far, we have examined over thirty-five samples of various filteraids, some are still to be looked at. Quite a few of them are the same, nevertheless we are treating them all in their own right. As you know, these products come out of the ground and are inorganic. Our first test was to examine them all for traces of organic matter, which is something that the manufacturers claim should be absent. To date, we have found none in the Klearite range supplied by you, Derek, nor in half the Purflo samples, and none in any of the French Liseux range; this type is a different mineral to all the others. However, we have found about 0.3 per cent by weight of organic matter in the other Purflo products.'

'Which half, Larry?' Derek asked.

'The finer grades, namely P1, P3, P5, P7, P11 and P13. From the list, it sounds as if there should be a P9 but we have no sample of this one yet. The organic matter is a type of protein but at present we have not been able to identify exactly what sort.'

'You mean protein as in make you grow big and strong protein?' Derek asked, rubbing the large area where hair used to grow.

'Yes, exactly the same stuff that's found in all types of food and which is vital for a healthy existence.'

Derek added, 'So it's not a drug that's present, then?'

'Absolutely not. Well, not in the sense that we here talk about drugs, that's for sure. It's certainly not even remotely related to any of the so-called hard drugs and it definitely won't give any of the effects described by the man in Cyprus.'

'How do you know that for certain Larry?' Andy asked.

'Gentlemen, if you follow me there's something I'd like to show you.'

Larry stood up and was about to open the office door when Ben asked his first question.

'But all the same, it's not supposed to be there, is it?'

'No,' Larry replied. 'All the literature I've seen on these products says they should be completely free from organic matter.'

'So what are they doing selling something which contains this material?'

'I really don't know, Ben. After all, it's only a very small amount and may just be down to bad quality-control procedures. The literature also states that the mineral is heated up to very high temperatures to burn off all the organic products, so perhaps it's not hot enough and not doing the job properly?'

'And will this organic matter be protein, Larry?' Derek asked.

'That's a very good question and the missing piece at the moment, but no, I wouldn't have thought so, it's more likely to be carbohydrate from decayed vegetable material.'

Larry led off, the others followed in single file behind him. They walked the entire length of the laboratory and stopped next to an insulated door covered in various symbols which meant nothing to the laymen present. Before revealing what was behind it Larry added, 'What you are about to see is normal in institutions like this, so I hope none of you will be upset by its contents.' Then he swung open the heavy door and ushered them inside.

The temperature was a lot warmer and the lighting in the windowless room was subdued. On one side ran a white workbench scattered with various pieces of equipment. However, it was the other side that took everyone's immediate attention. Spaced evenly in racks were row upon row of clear plastic boxes lined with sawdust and containing groups of white mice. Stainless-steel mesh lids were clamped over the boxes to contain the rodents and each container had been carefully labelled. Once Larry's guests had adjusted to their new surroundings he continued his talk.

'Over the last week we have fed various groups of our friends here with large intakes of all the Purflo products we know contain protein material, others with some of the organic-free grades, and a third group nothing but their normal diet – to act as a control. Our conclusions have all been the same. In not one single case have we found the slightest behavioural difference between any of the groups. As you can see, the mice are all perfectly happy in each other's company and are just getting on with their own lives.'

He invited them to inspect the individual cages in more detail. He was right, the entire colony of mice looked exactly the same. Some were asleep, others were cleaning themselves, whilst some of them were negotiating their water bottles or feed tubes; it was all very peaceful.

'We started with a fairly small addition to their normal food supply but over the days have increased it enormously. The amount they are consuming now would be our equivalent of eating a small bucketful of the stuff a day! If anything was going to happen we feel it would have shown itself by now. It's certainly not the same in here when we administer drugs to them. Pandemonium breaks out, I can assure you.'

They all returned to Larry's office and drank some more coffee in silence.

Derek broke into everyone's thoughts first. 'Any clues how this organic matter will affect the beer? Will it make it taste different for a start?'

'It will make absolutely no difference. Beers are full of protein anyway. Let me show you. Again it's probably easier than trying to explain it.'

They all traipsed back into the main laboratory and assembled in front of a large piece of equipment.

'This is called a high-performance liquid chromatography unit,' Larry told them. 'It analyses the different molecular structures between chemicals and displays them like this.' He held up a sheet of continuous stationery which resembled some sort of graph paper. A red pen had drawn out dozens of jagged peaks on it. He turned, had a few words with one of his assistants and then continued, 'He's just about to run through one of your English beers, Andy.'

They all watched as the operator fiddled with some buttons, then paper started to appear out of the far end of the machine while the pen darted up and down like something possessed. They hardly dared breathe in case they upset the moving pen's concentration. It suddenly stopped. There was silence.

'That's it, that sample's completed.' Larry tore off the three-foot length of paper and turned it round so everyone could see it properly. It looked like some horrific mountain range with very severely pointed summits and valleys. He took out a black pen and began to draw circles round several of the sharp points. 'These are the alcohol peaks; the big one here is ethanol, the main one in beer; the smaller ones are secondary alcohols. You obviously don't want too many of these present, otherwise you'll develop hangovers and headaches the next day.' Larry continued his circling spree, at the same time stating what such and such a peak represented. Further along the chart was a group of peaks and he circled them all. 'This is the protein range.'

'Do all the beers you've looked at have the same pattern of peaks?' Ben asked.

'No, similar but not exactly the same. It will all depend on how the beer is brewed and the choice of raw materials used. The main point is that the protein in the Purflo grades does not show itself as a separate peak, it is completely masked by all the other dozens of proteins naturally present in the drink. That's why we can't identify what it is at the moment – we can't get at it!'

Again a demonstration was called for. Larry pulled open a large drawer in the cupboard underneath the machine and took out a sheaf of charts and a clear plastic sheet. He held this up so they could all see it. There was a scale and one medium-sized peak drawn on it in bold black ink. To Andy it resembled a shark's fin sticking out of the water. Larry placed the sheet on each of the graphs in turn and in all cases the black peak was overshadowed and swallowed up by the much larger red ones.

'So you see our Purflo protein peak is always masked by the more dominant ones found in the beers themselves. There is one further very important thing. Whatever the protein is in this Purflo, it is barely soluble in water, so there can't and won't be much, if any at all, transferred to the beer during filtration.'

Derek took over the chair. 'Thanks, Larry, you've certainly been very busy. As I see it at the moment it's all very interesting but not a major problem, am I right?'

Larry nodded and fiddled with his bow-tie – there was little else he could say.

'Well, Ben old son, let's hear what you've been up to then.'

Ben removed several pieces of paper from a small case and handed one each to his three companions. 'I don't know if I've done the right thing putting all the information down on paper – you know, with this being a classified project and all that.'

'That's fine, Ben. After all, we're hardly a threat to national security, are we?' Derek replied.

They all studied Ben's report. It was excellent, precise, to the point and exactly what he'd been asked to do. He had listed all the countries producing beer during the last year. The grand total was 870 million hectolitres, with the United States topping the list with 249, followed by Germany with 127, Russia with 70, Japan with 53 and so on right down to Uganda with only 0.1 million hectolitres. In all 74 countries of the world produced beer of one sort or another. On the reverse side of the page there was a chart and further tables showing a top ten by area. Now Europe collectively took over pole position, with the US, Japan, China, Mexico, Canada, Australia and South Africa following in ever-decreasing volumes.

Ben interrupted everyone's concentration.'The figures for Russia also include the Ukraine and Belorussia.'

'You're a stickler for detail, Ben old son,' Derek added, trying not to sound too sarcastic. At this stage of the operation who really cared about the Ukraine!

'Well, I suppose you have to be when you're dealing with figures all day. The bottom line must always add up correctly. I have some more information I'd like to give you.' This second page was entitled *World production of mineral filteraids*, and Ben suggested he talk everyone through it.

'As you can see, there are two types of minerals used as filteraid, namely Favusite and Volcanite. The first is found in areas where there have been earthquake faults, with the main deposits lying in the western area of the United States and Mexico, whilst much smaller amounts are found in Europe and the Far East. Volcanite, on the other hand, is found wherever there have been volcanic eruptions and is, so I understand, related to lava; the main commercial deposits are in

Turkey, Greece, Iceland, Japan and the Philippines. As you can see from the table, a total of 950,00 metric tonnes of filteraid is mined and processed annually. Union Mining and Minerals are top of the league, with approximately 400,000 tonnes of Favusite; Oregon Mining comes next with 120,000, again Favusite; then Liseux, with about 100,000 tonnes of Volcanite – in fact, most of the remaining tonnage is volcanite. There are about a further fourteen other companies scattered throughout the world but I only have figures for two of them; one's in Greece, the other Turkey. Both report an annual metric tonnage approaching 35,000.' Ben finished off on a low note, 'I don't suppose any of this matters now from what Larry has said, but thanks for hearing me out anyway.'

'It's our pleasure, Ben. Don't for one minute think it was a waste of time. You've done extremely well ferreting out all this information. I daren't even begin to think how you came across some of it!'

Ben completely missed the hint of flippancy in Derek's voice. 'It was very easy really, all the information is available from the Food and Agriculture Organisation of the United Nations in Rome,' he replied dryly.

Derek changed the subject completely. 'I'm fascinated, what's the little box of tricks in your case for, Ben?'

Nearly half an hour later Derek wished he'd kept his mouth shut. Ben explained that it was his laptop computer, that he always carried it with him and that it would even plug into his mainframe unit at work. He was a changed person now that he was talking about his pet subject, his shyness had completely disappeared. It was obvious from their eye contact that neither Derek nor Andy understood any of his explanations, only the technical man, Larry, seemed to understand the language.

It was now just after seven o'clock. Larry went off to tell the technicians to call it a day and returned with some more charts. 'They have just finished work on your Greek samples, Andy. They couldn't find the slightest trace of organic matter in any of them.' He turned to Derek. 'What's the plan now? What do you want to do next?'

'I suppose we'll need to write Captain Hook a report. I'm quite happy to do it now and get it out of the way, and I'm sure you've got more important things to do with your time and people than testing beer samples all day. Would it be all right to use your office for a couple of hours or are you strapped for time?'

'Please help yourself, Derek. The building's open twenty-four hours a day and I'm not in any hurry to get away.'

It was agreed that Larry would send out for some food, and Derek, with Ben's help, would compose a report consisting of Larry's findings, together with some of Ben's figures. Ben offered to type the lot onto his machine to save time but Derek said he preferred to write it out in longhand. The truth was he was very suspicious of Ben's little gadget; for all he knew, the information, which might take them an hour or so to feed in, could be lost for ever if the battery failed. No, in Derek's mind there was nothing like having stuff recorded once and for all on paper.

The food arrived and it didn't take the four of them long to empty the various boxes. Larry offered more coffee but they all declined, they were almost swimming in the stuff.

'Well, there are plenty of beers in the cupboard. If you fancy one, please help yourselves. I'm, afraid it's not cold, though, but at least it won't do you any harm!'

They all laughed. Derek opened the door and took out a box of six bottles. One was missing; it had been through the analyser.

Andy was now a spare part in the next phase of the operation, a point not overlooked by his host. For the sake of completeness he still needed to finish off some tests on the last batch of samples Andy had sent in, so he invited the Englishman to join him in the laboratory and was pleasantly surprised at how quickly his guest picked up on his instructions. In no time at all he allowed him to conduct a few tests on his own. The time flew by, with everybody totally engrossed in their own respective tasks.

Then the peace and tranquillity in the laboratory was suddenly shattered.

'Well, do the fucking thing yourself then!'

Both Larry and Andy exchanged glances and rushed towards the office. Only Ben was visible through the glass. He was standing up, shouting and gesticulating furiously.

Larry made it to the doorway first. 'What's going on? What's the matter?'

Ben's face was full of anger. 'It's that bastard Derek, he insists on writing everything down himself. I've told him time after time there's no need to. We already have the charts and now he wants to copy them out. But will he listen? At this rate we'll be here the whole goddam night. I give up on him, that's for sure!'

This was a different Ben to the one they'd seen earlier. He was full of rage, even his normally placid eyes had a look of hate about them. Throughout all of this tirade Derek remained seated. He looked up at the others and shrugged his shoulders.

Larry reacted quickly. 'Right, that's enough for tonight. We've all had long days recently and some sleep is called for. We can finish off tomorrow. I'll organise some taxis to take you back to your hotels and I suggest we meet up here again at, say, noon.'

Andy looked at the clock. It was only a few minutes after ten.

6

Larry phoned Security – taxis would be there in five minutes. They all walked slowly to reception and waited, and on cue the cabs arrived. A security guard unlocked the main door and let them out. Andy said his goodnights and started to walk towards the car park, but Larry grabbed his arm and beckoned him back inside.

'If you're not too exhausted, can I have a few words with you please?' Lights were still burning on most of the first floor, and as if to read Andy's mind Larry said, 'It's quite normal for people to work long hours here. Some of the projects we take on demand it. After all, if some tests require monitoring every hour or so you can hardly go home for a normal eight hours' sleep, can you? I stay overnight from time to time but not as much as I used to. That's the beauty of being old and senior, you can delegate to your younger staff. I think you know what I mean, Andy. I was watching you earlier tonight – you were absolutely enthralled in what you were doing. Time was irrelevant.'

'Only in case I pressed the wrong button and broke something.' The reply was more of an excuse really. Yes, Larry was right about him, once he got absorbed in his work time did become unimportant.

They reached the office. It was a tip. Andy started to throw some of the beer bottles into the waste bin.

'Stop!' Larry shouted at him, and then apologised for using such a stern voice. He pointed to a chair and asked him to sit down. He was going to have a coffee, would Andy like one as well? He remembered this time, no sugar.

'What did you make of that little outburst then?' Larry asked.

'Not a lot really, just two very tired men who had rubbed each other up the wrong way. Just a conflict of personalities.'

'You didn't find it strange that Derek was so subdued? From what I've seen of him so far, he's a bit of an extrovert, yet he just sat there and took an earful from Ben as if he were a naughty schoolboy receiving a telling-off from the headmaster.'

'I admit I was impressed with Ben,' Andy added. 'I didn't think he had it in him. He's certainly gone up in my estimation. Before, I thought he was a bit of a wimp. Now I know he'll only be pushed so far. Anyway, what's going on in that head of yours? You obviously think something else happened.'

'Do me a favour will you, Andy. Derek was sitting where you are, right? Ben over here. Can you find all the beer bottles or cans Derek had, and I'll collect Ben's.'

It was an easy task. All Ben's were in the waste-paper bin, the rest scattered on one side of the table were Derek's. Larry asked him to total up the volume of each brand. Again it was a simple task: Derek had drunk seven bottles, each containing 330 mls; five were the same brand, the other two were different makes; all the beers were American-brewed. By comparison, Ben had only had three cans; they were all different but each can contained 500 mls, one was American the other two of European origin.

'Well, what do you think then, Andy?'

The reply was to the point; 'That they were both on their way to being well and truly pissed. No wonder tempers started to fray.'

'You've seen Derek drink – he can hold his liquor. At his ex-wife's flat he drank, what, four very large whiskeys and what happened? He became more outgoing and brash. I still remember some of his jokes. Derek's a happy drinker, I suspect, not one to get all depressed.'

Andy suggested, 'Perhaps he was just tired. You can't be on top form all the time. At the moment I feel shattered and slightly irritable myself. It's been a long day, as you said.'

'It's just a hunch, but perhaps their personalities did change tonight because they were drinking beer filtered through Purflo. All the qualities – well, the American ones they drank – use it, according to Derek's information, and the effects are similar to those reported by the man in Cyprus.'

Andy couldn't believe his ears. Here was a highly qualified and technical expert bending the circumstances to fit the facts. Surely this was not very scientific, and why so much credence being placed on some idiot in Cyprus. The fellow could be a troublemaker or just a crank. All this effort and technical know-how for what?

Larry guessed what was crossing Andy's mind. 'Yes, I know I've already said there's nothing in Purflo that can cause such effects in beer, but the change in the two of them tonight was strange. Believe me, I don't want to find anything in beer. Perhaps I've been watching the mice for too many years now and reading too much into things. Anyway enough, time to go home.'

Larry walked Andy to his car, and the Englishman sat and watched the back of the crumpled suit going back into the building. Was the Doc going home or would he spend the night pacing up and down pondering his new theory?

The weather was magnificent, not a cloud to be seen. The sprinklers had been busy during the morning and the grounds of the Institute smelled fresh and scented. Andy had slept long and well. Another day and he would be able to move onto some other project his people had selected for him.

Larry met him at the entrance. He had shaved but still wore the same shirt – most of the creases were hidden by his long white coat. No, Larry had not been home. The office was back to its usual pristine condition and smelled of furniture polish. There was not a sign of any beer cans or bottles, and the only item on the table was a file containing Derek's extensive but as yet unfinished report. Both Derek and Ben were in the main room, talking to one of the technicians, and seemed to be on speaking terms.

Larry called the meeting to order. It took the form of a question-and-answer session to start with.

'How are you both feeling today?' Larry began.

Ben replied first. 'Fine, apart from a slight headache. I certainly slept well. Didn't wake up until ten this morning.'

'And you, Derek?'

'As normal, I suppose.'

'Do either of your remember what happened last night?'

'I remember getting slightly annoyed with Derek. He was really dragging things out. I suppose I'm used to my little computer doing everything for me.' He tapped the case which was his constant companion. 'Our methods differ, and I lost my temper. I've apologised to Derek.'

Derek duly nodded to acknowledge this had been done.

'Do you normally get annoyed like this?' Larry asked.

Ben paused. He was beginning to get a bit embarrassed, but eventually answered, 'No, not really. I don't know what you all think of me but I've never been very pushy. I suppose it's the way I'm made. No, normally I'm a very placid, quiet sort of person.'

'But last night Derek annoyed you so much that you became irritable. Something snapped and you lost your temper, right?'

'Yes.'

Derek made to interrupt but Larry waved his hand and continued, 'Left to your own devices, what would you have done if Andy and I hadn't intervened last night?'

Again a pause. 'I don't really know. At one stage I remember feeling I wanted to hit Derek and walk out.'

'And you remember all this clearly?'

'Yes, why?'

'In a minute please, Ben.' He turned to Derek. 'And what do you remember?'

'Drinking some beers, doing a lot of writing and clean

sheets on a lovely big bed.'

'Do you remember Ben's outburst and that you just sat there and stared back at him, that you just accepted his tirade of abuse?'

Derek shook his head. 'Not really. I must admit I wasn't thinking too much about anything at that stage. I just wanted to curl up and sleep. That goddam drive across the country must have taken more out of me than I thought.' Derek stood up and reached across the table to take Ben's hand. 'Sorry if I caused any offence, didn't mean to. Too much beer.'

Ben also apologised for the second time. 'Yes, too much beer,' he added.

'Yes, I think it was the beer as well,' Larry stated. It was the way he phrased it plus the tone in his voice. One by one the penny dropped and the implication of his statement sank in. The meeting went silent as coffee was ordered.

'Now it's my turn to offer a possible explanation,' Larry resumed. 'I have no proof, of course, and you might think what I'm about to say is a bit out of line, but please hear me out. I think you both drank beers that changed your personalities. Derek drank one type, and instead of it increasing his usual outgoing nature, he went the other way. He became withdrawn, quiet and lethargic. Ben, on the other hand, changed from a normal quiet polite person into an aggressive character. Yes, it might just have been the alcohol but I would like you to consider an alternative, that there is something else in the beer that sets these changes off. I've checked the beer Derek drank – it is all filtered through Purflo P5. One of the brands Ben drank is also passed through Purflo, either P3 or P5. And this is where my explanations fall down. Why the changes should be different, I just don't know. Derek, may I ask you some more questions?'

'Sure, fire away.'

'What happens to you normally, even when you're tired, when you drink a lot? Please forgive me for asking such a personal question.'

'No problem, Larry. Normally? Well I become very

verbal and randy! Mind you, I must admit I don't drink more than four pints of beer these days in a session, otherwise I'm up all night peeing. Usually I stick to whiskey – the effect's the same though.'

'Well, both Andy and I saw you last night. You were certainly not very verbal and the last thing I think you had on your mind was sex!'

Derek turned to Andy. 'What happened to you, then? You were drinking as well.'

'I only had one can in the end. Larry got me all involved with his flight decks out there. Perhaps once a night isn't enough!'

Derek burst out laughing at Andy's *double entendre*. 'Anyway, Larry,' he said with a smile still on his face, 'you're leading up to something. What is it?'

'I'd like to repeat the exercise.' Larry stood up and quickly left the room saying he had to pass on some information to one of his men. The real reason was to give them a chance to discuss his proposition. They must think him mad even to suggest it, he thought. He watched them – a full-scale debate was going on inside his office. Then Derek went out and asked him to come back in.

'To be honest, Larry, we all think the idea's crazy. However, for two reasons we're all prepared to go through the exercise again. One, because it will stop you worrying about it, and two, we can put an end to it once and for all. It's not as if you're asking us to inject ourselves with herioin, is it? Drinking a few beers is no hardship. How do you want to play it then?'

'First of all, thank you, everyone. If you all agree, we can try the experiment again tonight in my office, but under strict rules this time. If I do see any sign I'm not happy with then we stop. Okay?' It all sounded very melodramatic.

Andy and Derek volunteered to be the star turns that evening. In the meantime, Derek and Ben agreed they would finish off the original report and that charts would be included. Andy would visit a local shopping centre and buy stocks of various beers – Larry wrote him out a list. He himself would be busy in his laboratory. The afternoon dragged by. They all went out for a very early dinner. The guinea-pigs were not allowed to consume any alcohol.

Just after seven, the test started. They were on their own. Larry had sent all his staff home. Apart from the beers, Andy had also brought back a small parcel. Derek's curiosity was killing him. He burst out laughing when he saw what it contained and had trouble getting the words out.

'My God, the world's falling to pieces and going down the pan fast and the ace team of rescuers are going to sit tonight drinking beer and playing Monopoly. Heaven help you all, folks!'

Andy explained that it was pointless just sitting watching each other for every little twitch or unusual tic. They had to have some focal point to pass the time. Even Derek admitted it was a good idea. The game started. Larry served them beer in glasses this time so that there were no preconceived ideas as to what it was or where it came from. There was no pressure to drink fast or heavily. When they requested more, he gave it to them. Andy was fascinated by the board. He hadn't played the game for years, but still remembered some of the street names and railway stations on the British version; the American streets and utilities added a novelty value. It ran neck and neck for the first hour. After a while he forgot all about Larry and Ben watching, even the point of the exercise. Then he saw an opening. He had three cards of the same colour – a set. He began to buy houses and then hotels. Derek always seemed to land on them, much to his annoyance to start with, but then he became resigned to the fact and just accepted it as fate. By nine thirty Andy was taking squares in lieu of payment. Another fifteen minutes and Andy was incredibly rich, at least on paper – he owned the lot. Larry refused to make any comments that night.

They all reconvened in the office at ten the following morning. Both Andy and Derek looked at Larry expecting him to tell them his findings. Instead, he handed the meeting over to Ben, who seemed at a bit of a loss where to begin and started to read his notes out aloud.

'During most of the first hour, very little happened. Both players seemed absorbed in the game. Andy then started to buy more property. On several occasions he punched the air with his fist after each victory. He was very excited. Twice he tormented Derek that he would soon finish him off and that he didn't stand a chance. He wouldn't allow Derek any credit, always demanding he pay his debts off straight away. Once he had won, he let out some sort of war cry and told his opponent they should have been playing for real money. Derek, on the other hand, began to accept defeat gracefully to start with, but then started to sulk in the later stages. At one point he said it was a stupid game and he didn't know why he was playing it. Twice he admitted defeat and said Andy was the winner, but Andy insisted they play to the bitter end.' He finished reading his observations and turned to Larry for support.

'Gentlemen, those are not my words, they are Ben's. However, I agree with every one of them. Both of you did change temperaments as the game progressed. Andy, you were drinking the same beer Ben drank last night, and you, Derek, had exactly the same stuff as before. I'm now convinced one type creates a high, the other a low feeling. Why? I don't know. But I do know that there may well be some truth in the Cyprus man's results. Can I ask you, Andy, how did you feel last night? By the way, you drank five glasses of your chosen beer.'

Andy remembered enjoying the game and the fact that he'd won. He couldn't remember punching the air, it wasn't his style. Nor could he remember goading Derek about losing. Larry told Derek he'd drunk six glasses and again asked him for his comments. All Derek remembered was his total lack of interest in the game and how he was glad when it was over so he could turn his brain off!

'So far, Ben and possibly Andy have seen the changes in the other's personalities. If you've no objections I would like to continue the trial once more so Derek can see it.'

'Listen, Larry, there's no need to convince me,' Derek

protested. 'I believe your findings, but if you want to run a couple more trials then I'm sure we'll all take part in any capacity. But how about you, you're convinced something's happening, why not take part yourself so one of us can witness how you alter?'

Larry shook his head. 'If it's all right with you, I'd prefer to monitor the results.' There was a pause. The Doc's face took on a pained expression. 'I have a confession to make. Many years back I had a bereavement in the family. I was pretty cut up about it and took to the bottle. It's a long story, but to keep to the point, I'm a reformed alcoholic. I've been on the wagon now for nearly eight years. I would normally –'

Derek cut him off in mid sentence. 'You continue to monitor the results of as many trials as you wish, Doc. You have three willing "white mice" over here, doesn't he?'

Both Ben and Andy nodded. Larry nodded his appreciation back. They all now understood his predicament. Perhaps it was Captain Hook's idea of a sick joke to give a project involving alcohol to a reformed addict. Andy wondered what the temptation must be like; after all, Larry spent long nights on his own next to a cupboard of booze.

The meeting needed to lighten up. Once again Derek came to the rescue. He offered to take them out for lunch – as long as Andy paid with the fortune he'd won last night! It was now Wednesday. The breathing-space did them all good.

That evening, Larry planned to ask Andy and Derek to play the board game again, but unbeknown to either he would give them both what her termed the 'high' beer. They were both strong personalities and he wanted to see what they would do and how they would react if taken together to a more extreme point. He would take no chances though, he'd already informed Security that they were to come running immediately he contacted them. He was sure Ben wouldn't mind being a spectator once again. He wasn't; on the contrary, he looked quite relieved when told.

The game started at seven o'clock. Again, little

happened in the first hour. However, Derek had learned from his earlier defeat and wasn't so susceptible to Andy's tactics this time. Ben began to look bored very early on, so Larry did his usual sociable bit and offered to show him some of the instrumentation in the laboratory. As a computer buff he would understand it better than Andy.

'Instead of doing all these trials, couldn't we just feed some of your mice with different beers and see how they react?' Ben asked politely.

'As you know, we tried that out in the first few days of this project but we couldn't detect any noticeable changes or effects.'

'Would you mind if I had a go? I've never done anything like this before. I find the whole exercise very interesting.'

Larry didn't really want this totally unqualified young man fiddling about with things. But it would give Ben something to pass the time, and allow Larry to concentrate on the two in his office. He took Ben to the end room and pointed out two cages he could use. One should be used as control, the other he could use to feed the mice beer, he explained, and left him to it.

The telephone rang just after eight. Larry was annoyed. He'd told Security not to put any calls through as he didn't want the concentration broken. But he'd been summoned by his boss upstairs and had no alternative but to go. He looked at the players. They were okay; in fact, they were laughing and joking, both determined to land on the one unsold square first. They would be all right for at least the next half an hour. He topped their drinks up, found Ben and explained his predicament. He would be no more than fifteen minutes at the very outside. He wrote down an extension number Ben was to ring immediately he even suspected anything was changing. True to his word, Larry was back inside the time he said he would be. Ben went off to see how his new-found friends were doing.

The state of play was as Larry had left it. Again he refilled their glasses, and as before used a different jug for each of them. By ten o'clock the game was well advanced. Competition was fierce. It was difficult to tell who was winning and who was losing. Tensions were running high and both men were drinking more whilst waiting their turn. Both were equally aggressive verbally, each claiming imminent victory. Derek was throwing the dice with a particularly bellicose shake. Larry was convinced he was trying to knock Andy's houses onto the floor. But he was ready. He wouldn't let the situation become too explosive.

Ben came flying in through the door. He was very white-faced and looked as if he would burst out crying at any minute. His rapid entrance into the room startled the two players and they stopped their game. They all looked at Ben, waiting for him to say something, but he couldn't get the words out – he just kept pointing to the far end of the laboratory. They all walked quickly to the animal room. One cage was not a pretty sight. Three mice lay dead, surrounded by their own blood, huge chunks missing from their heads. Another was wandering about with an eye hanging out. The other two were in some form of stand-off. Occasionally they would snap at each other. Larry quickly put on a glove. He transferred the two healthiest ones to individual cages and destroyed the badly maimed one. In the other cage, the control, everything was peaceful. Most of the mice were asleep, completely unaware what their neighbours had been up to.

'I think you'd better tell me what you've been up to, young man,' Larry requested. 'But first let's get out of here and go back to the office. We could all do with some coffee.'

'And we can finish our game,' Derek added. 'After all, I was winning before we were so rudely interrupted.'

'No you bloody weren't, I was,' Andy retorted.

Larry stopped them in their tracks. 'No, no more. The game's over. It was a draw, all right?' As soon as he reached the office he did two things. He scooped up the board, thereby destroying the order of play, and emptied the remaining beer in the jugs down the nearest sink. 'Right, Ben, what happened?'

'You know you said you'd tried feeding the mice beer and nothing happened? Well I thought I'd try mixing some powder in with it first. I'd worked out that breweries must add about four grams of powder to every litre of beer, so I found some powder and did just that.'

It was obvious for all to see that Ben was distressed. Larry coaxed him on with his story. The voice started to tremble. 'Before I could give it to them, you asked me to stand in for you as an observer whilst you were called away. When I got back to the beaker the powder had settled so I went and filled the drinking vessels in one cage with the clear beer. That's all I did, honestly.'

'So this was a good two hours ago?' Larry asked.

'Yes, easily.'

'When was the last time you saw the mice and were they okay then?'

'Probably about half past nine. They looked fine then, so I started to do some work on my laptop. I'm sorry – those poor mice.'

It took an arm around Ben's shoulder to console him. 'Please calm down and don't worry. These things happen.' Larry had another problem to contend with. The other two were still arguing about the game on the other side and he had to separate them. He gave Andy the job of finding the Purflo brochure and asked him to dig out what amounts they recommended for beer filtration. He sent Derek off into the lab to find the sample of filter powder Ben had used.

'Between 100 to 200 grams per hectolitre,' Andy shouted out.

Derek returned with the plastic envelope. 'One of mine – Purflo P5.' It was obvious to Larry what Ben had done. He had assumed that all filteraid production was used to filter beer and overdosed his beer sample with up to four times the recommended level. He had completely overlooked the fact that half the grades at least – the coarser ones – didn't get anywhere near the stuff. At this stage they didn't even know exactly how much of the world's beer production was even filtered using fine Purflo grades. He looked around at his colleagues and decided it was pointless discussing this with them now, in their present moods. But one thing was certain: Ben, the total novice, had found the key to the problem. (Larry would never know it, but weeks before Fred Clarke had come up with the same experiment in his kitchen, but had decided it sounded too amateurish to include in the final letter he'd sent.)

It wasn't planned, but they all got down for breakfast very early the following morning. Each had his own reason for not sleeping the previous night. Andy still had a bit of a headache but otherwise felt reasonable and was dressed as casually as ever, whilst Derek as always still had his suit on. His sleep had been disturbed on more than one occasion as he'd had to get up for a pee – as he'd said, beer ran straight through him. Both of them were surprised at Ben's appearance – he was back into a shirt and tie again. He hardly spoke. It was as if he was expecting to be hauled up before the boss and torn off a strip for meddling. It was only half past eight by the time they got to the laboratory, an hour earlier than agreed, but they realised Larry would have been there since first light, if not all night. They knew the routine off by heart now. Stop at Security. Open boot of car for inspection, park, walk to reception and sign in. Higher up the page were their names from the previous night. Larry had written against address, *Drug Enforcement Agency, Washington* – it filled the lines up if nothing else. There was a second book, for employees to sign themselves in and out. Andy glanced across the last page. Larry's signature was missing from the last column – he had been here all night.

Larry arrived just as they were pinning their visitor's badges on. Yes, it was the same shirt and bow-tie again, mostly hidden by a brand-new white dust-coat. Tired or not, his greeting was as warm as ever. He announced that coffee was on the go in his office.

When they were all seated he began. 'After you'd gone last night I found the beaker Ben used. It still had the filteraid in the bottom. I dried some of it off and checked for organics. Nothing, absolutely nothing. It's all been transferred into the beer.'

'It's early Larry, refresh my memory. I thought you

said before that it wasn't soluble in water?' Derek stroked his bald patch. It was unintentional, but gave the others the impression that his brain really did hurt.

'No, it isn't soluble in water. But there are lots of tests to carry out about its reaction in beer.'

'You're really convinced something nasty is ending up in the beer, aren't you?'

'Yes, I had my doubts until Ben did his little experiment yesterday. Now I'm convinced. No proof, just the strongest of suspicions.'

Andy asked, 'Supposing you're right, supposing there is some horrible stuff present, why does it make some people aggressive and others just tired?'

Larry shrugged. 'I'm sorry, I just don't know.'

Derek took the chair. 'Right, team, it's decision time. I want a show of hands. All those in favour of continuing with this project?'

Two arms shot up immediately, Larry's and somewhat surprisingly Ben's. Andy's followed seconds later. 'Good, here's what we're going to do.' Derek looked at his watch. 'Today's Thursday. We've covered some ground in just a few days but basically our information and knowledge are pathetic and extremely limited. Larry, you want to carry out a whole string of further tests? How much time do you need and will you require any more samples?'

'About a week, and no, I'm all right for powders, thanks.'

'Great. Now Ben, first of all snap out of it. Last night's history all right? It happened. It's over.' Derek stared at him. It was a good job Ben was not being held by some foreign power – they would be laughing themselves silly by now. This pathetic young man would be singing his head off and the nation's secrets would be going down the pan fast. Derek focused back on the main topic. 'I want you to return to your base and with your computer find out all you can about any previous operations where illegal additives have been found in food and drinks. I don't care what methods you adopt or how you do it, understand?' Ben managed a small nod.

'And what will you and Andy be doing?' Larry asked.

'Visiting Union Mining and Minerals headquarters in Sacramento.'

'You'll need to make some travel arrangements.' Larry picked up the phone. In less than a couple of minutes a young lady knocked on the office door. They gave her their respective instructions. Ben to fly to San Francisco, Derek and Andy direct to Sacramento. Derek made one call. They all listened; it was the hot line to Hutton.

The conversation was stinted. 'Madden here, have a preliminary report for General Hutton. . . .Right, yes, will do, bye.' He slammed the receiver back. 'Somebody will pick the report up from your receptionist this afternoon, Larry.'

The young lady returned. There were no flights to Sacramento until Sunday, something to do with a music convention. They would have to join Ben and go to Frisco and then drive the remainder. Derek told her to book the flights and arrange car hire.

'Larry, can we use your telephone numbers again please? Thank you. Ben, if you come up with anything contact Larry immediately. I'll ring in at least once a day. Good luck, everyone.'

The meeting broke up. Andy made the only comment on the way back to the hotel. 'You'll only need one of Larry's numbers – his lab – he'll be tied to his bench for the rest of the week.'

They checked out and by early evening were in the Golden Gate City. Ben took his leave, his mood very sombre.

'He may be a genius with his computer, but he's still a very immature kid,' Derek summed up as they watched him disappear into the mêlée outside the airport.

There was no way Derek was going to drive all the way through the city in the rush hour traffic. They booked themselves in at the nearest airport hotel – the Holiday Inn. They beat the commuters pouring into the city the following morning. By six o'clock they were well on their way to Sacramento, with most of the traffic on Interstate 80 going in the other direction anyway. They stopped on the outskirts of their destination. Sacramento had the distinction of being the seventh largest city in California and was the state capital, the huge sign said.

'Never been here before, but if I remember my school history it's where the gold-rush started from,' Derek said as they entered the restaurant. He gave his breakfast order to the waitress and then went to buy a street map. In between mouthfuls of breakfast Andy read the brief history of 'Cow City' printed inside the front and back covers. Although interesting, it was the method of naming the streets that fascinated him. There were no 'Railway Streets' or 'Acorn Avenues' here. All the streets ran at right angles to each other, as if curves had not been invented. There was even a guide as to how the system worked. 'Each block represents one hundred street addresses. These addresses also correspond to lettered cross streets. For example 200 3rd Street intersects B Street, whilst 1700 C Street is on 17th Street.'

They found their target. It was downtown at 1701 C Street. The building was turn-of-the-century, solid, with about ten storeys. They parked opposite and watched the comings and goings for an hour. It was a busy place. There hardly seemed a moment when people were not being discharged from the revolving door. About a hundred metres to the right was a slope. The barrier to the underground car park seemed to be forever saluting the cars entering or leaving. Curiosity got the better of him. Derek crossed over the road and went inside. He returned minutes later and sat puffing in the driver's seat after his short burst of speed back across the road.

'Two security guards. They check everyone's ID. Eleven companies occupy the block. Union are on the fifth floor. Rest look like insurance outfits, but there's one that sounds like some sort of mail order concern.'

Andy asked the leading question. 'How are you at

breaking into places then? You know locks, safes, that sort of thing?'

'Hopeless, never really needed to, I suppose. Always use my charm to bluff my way in through front doors with the odd counterfeit card in my hand. And you?'

'Not bad with the old conventional locks but haven't a clue about any of the new electronic stuff. Mind you, I need certain bits of bent metal to help me along.'

Andy told his friend about the old burglar the Army had used to show them the ropes, and how his new skills had come in very handy on several occasions in Northern Ireland. Then the watching game continued in silence.

Derek broke the peace after an hour. 'What sort of things do you need?'

Andy gave several descriptions of bent bits of wire. Derek started the car and pulled into the traffic. He cruised for several blocks until he found a phone booth. Whatever he'd been up to had been successful. He returned wearing a broad grin, and sat. Another hour passed and then a car pulled up behind them. One man. Derek went to meet him. Andy moved the interior mirror and watched them. They talked and laughed for a good ten minutes. As they shook hands, a small parcel was handed over. Derek sat down in his seat and turned to Andy.

'Compliments of the CIA.' He handed over the package. It contained a selection of skeleton keys and other pieces of metal that looked as if they belonged to a dentist. He held up his hand. 'No questions please, I've got to leave them at a local address once our little prowl-around is over.'

They found a bar and whiled away several hours. By half past four they were back on watch outside their target building. On the dot of five, there was a mass exodus, people and cars pouring out of the two exits.

'The weekend starts now, eh? Well, at least for some folk anyway,' Derek said dryly. He drove away.

The first accommodation they came across was a 'Motel 6', which would do for the night.

Derek made a phone call from his room to Sales at Union Mining and Minerals. The security man said they'd all gone for the day. No problem, he replied, he would catch them tomorrow, Saturday. The guard almost apologised on their behalf. He was sorry, but they didn't open over the weekend. 'Then I'll have to place my order elsewhere.' Derek hung up.

The time window for their operation was now fixed even if their plan of campaign wasn't. A poster in the motel advertised 'The Fox and Goose Bar – a traditional English public house with lots of imported beers'. Derek thought it would remind Andy of his home. They spent the whole evening there. The music was good but neither of them felt like drinking any of the beers.

They were on duty in front of the building at 7.30 a.m. Several cars started to turn up just before eight. Andy felt uncomfortable in his suit and tie, but Derek had insisted they look 'commercial'. It was Derek who moved first. He urged Andy out of the car, locked it and ran across the road, briefcase in hand. He explained his new-found plan as they went. They ducked under the barrier, their eyes blinking at the sudden darkness of the car park. Yes, Derek was right, there was an elevator at one end. They split up and waited by separate cars. It didn't take long. Two cars arrived and parked. Three women walked towards the elevator. Derek followed them. The four stood by the double doors. One of them striped a card through a machine and the doors opened. They all stepped inside. Just as the doors were about to close, Derek pressed the hold button. 'Come on, Andy, late as usual.' Andy ran from 'his' car and joined the party. One of the women pressed three and Derek asked for seven, adding in a very chatty manner, 'Fancy having to work on a Saturday. Still, it pays the bills.'

They were soon on their own. The doors opened at seven; the corridor was deserted. They instructed the lift to take them down two floors. Andy peered out first. No people, no security cameras. 'Probably feel they don't need them with guards patrolling the building.'

Two huge glass doors etched with Union's name blocked their entrance from the corridor into a large reception area. Andy searched round the edges. There were no alarm systems visible. However, he warned Derek not to stand on the large mat they could see just beyond the doors. It might have some sort of pressure pad underneath. Derek cupped his hands and peered through the thick glass; again no cameras were visible. Andy sorted through his ring of new toys, selected one funny-looking key and within seconds he was beckoning a very impressed Derek through the open door. He locked it again once they were on the wrong side. Leading off from reception was a small corridor. They walked along it, reading names on all the office doors. They were so busy doing this that they had lost their sense of direction. In no time they were back in reception. They had walked round the entire four sides of the building. The elevator shafts ran directly up the centre of the offices.

'Let's start at the top.' Derek was standing by a door proudly stating that the vice-president of Sales and Marketing occupied the office. Andy unlocked it. What a disappointment it turned out to be. One large brown desk, a leather swivel armchair, six upright chairs round a glass-topped table and some photographs on the wall. There was not a single file or memo anywhere. Even the desk drawers were empty, apart from some unused writing-pads and envelopes.

'This gentleman believes in the ultimate delegation theory,' Derek said sarcastically.

'You mean he does sod all!' Andy translated.

They left what little there was as they had found it and moved down the corridor. The Sales Manager – Domestic Sales was next. The door wasn't even locked. Their spirits rose. This was more like it. A desk with 'in' and 'out' trays full of paper. One wall had four sliding doors running the full length of the room. Derek slid one back. Hanging on runners were probably hundreds of files, all in alphabetical order. Andy concentrated his search on the desk. He soon found out the manager was called McDonald, that he was married with two very young children and was obviously very proud of them – photographs in small frames almost covered the desk top. The one thing he couldn't find was any relevant information. He soon joined Derek and selected half a dozen files at random. They sat in silence for well over an hour. The inside cover gave the customer's full address, telephone numbers, main contacts and grades bought. There were letters of all descriptions, some complaints about deliveries, some about price increases, orders, even technical reports recommending the correct grades to use. But nowhere were there any lists of tonnages produced against grades.

Derek sighed and put back all his files. 'I've just read through all the brewery ones I've visited. A waste of time. It's impossible to even hazard a guess of what's happening from these general files. Even if we went through all of them we still wouldn't know the amounts made. Only the grades are mentioned.' He pushed the sliding door back wearily.

'What a slob!' Andy commented as he opened the door to the Export Manager's office. The desk top was ringed with coffee stains. Paperwork was half piled in one corner of the room and a large chunk of plaster was missing behind his chair where he obviously liked to lean back.

'One of the feet-on-the-table brigade,' Derek observed.

Empty cigarette packets and sweet wrappers littered the desk drawers. Everything had the stale smell of nicotine about it. His VDU screen was dirty, the off-white casing black in places. Derek opened his filing-cupboard. A set of golf clubs made as if to fall out. He caught them and propped them back up. Only one row in the centre unit held any files.

Andy started to go through the pile on the floor.

'Don't hold your breath waiting for an answer from this fellow, Derek. There's one letter on the top here dated four weeks ago from some poor bugger in Malaysia wanting an urgent reply.'

Derek went through the files, which were not in any order. He counted forty-seven and passed some across to Andy. Again details of the various agents and distributors adorned the inside pages. However, this time the man had added comments. Derek read one out from an Australian file: 'Rosemary, Colin's wife, shags like a rabbit,' Andy found two files he thought might prove interesting reading: Midland Trading and Union in Brussels. Nothing. Most of the letters referred to his visits and golf club arrangements. This export manager, Mr Stanley Carver, was more interested in other things than selling dry powder for filtration.

It didn't take them long. Between them they noted down all the names of the overseas people. But export tonnages, in fact any tonnages, still eluded them. The next stretch of corridor had numerous offices leading off. They were smaller, destined for middle managers. Andy unlocked the doors along one side for Derek to sniff about in and then did the same on his chosen side. It took nearly two hours before they reconvened. Both had the same weary look of defeat. Both had nothing to show for their efforts. Andy relocked the doors, feeling like a prison warder. They walked on past a storeroom – mainly samples and old invoices – and came to a small crèche and rest room. A vending-machine was humming away to itself in the corner. The coffee was free and tasted awful but none the less they drank it gratefully.

'What do you think then, Andy, my friend?' Derek was rubbing his stockinged feet.

'That it's a complete waste of time. The information we want is probably stored in the computer system. Every office I've been in has a terminal. You'd have been better off bringing Ben!'

'And who would have opened the doors for us?

You can't win, can you?'

Derek struggled to get his shoes back on. They completed the last leg of the trek. The whole side of this part of the building was one large general office. Bums on seats were concentrated in this area. They found some invoices, some shipping-notes and lots of bloody computer screens, but not one mention of production tonnages. They made their way round the corner back to reception. Derek hit the last VDU screen with his clenched fist. It served no purpose but made him feel a bit better.

They let themselves out and left the building via the car park. It was late afternoon and the street was bathed in bright sunlight. A parking-ticket was rammed under the wiper of their car. Derek tore it into shreds and threw them into the air. Andy stuffed his jacket into his case. At the first opportunity he would change into his shorts. Derek began to relax once again. He removed his tie and began the drive back to San Francisco unsure of what to do next, humming to himself.

They were back on the freeway before Derek broke Andy's concentration. 'What are you reading?'

'Union Mining and Minerals Inc. Annual Report!' Andy told him. 'I picked it up in reception.'

'Smart-ass! You hungry? Good, let's pull into the next service area. I'll phone Larry after we've eaten.'

Over the food Derek read the booklet. A lot was financial bumf. The company were into all sorts of diverse activities – all mining-related – having started out in 1860 with some gold claims. There were some small paragraphs devoted to the performance of the various operations. Favusite production and sales came out of it well, they contributed a good chunk towards the profits. The head office for this operation was in Sacramento – yes they knew that! Eight production plants were mentioned. Two had such pure deposits that the stuff was suitable for use as filteraid. the other six deposits went into insulation products, industrial fillers. . . the list went on. This side didn't matter. The book had considerably reduced their legwork, Derek thought to himself. Now there would be only two sites to visit. The tour round the office block had almost been a complete waste of time, but thanks to Andy, not entirely pointless.

Derek made his phone call and returned to the table, 'Everything quiet from Larry's end, he's just getting on with it. There is one thing he'd like us to do. You know Larry – "if it's not too much of a problem, of course", he'd like practical details about exactly how the Purflo is used at a brewery. How about this for our next few days of action? You do the brewery bit for Larry whilst I'll catch up on the latest report to keep Hook off our backs, then by next Wednesday we can split up and visit a Union plant each?'

'No problem,' Andy replied, doing his best to imitate Derek's accent, and volunteered to drive the rest of the way. He couldn't make his mind up about Derek as a leader. Yes, he could. Derek got his way not by being assertive but by asking people in a nice sort of way to do things, suggesting rather than ordering.

There were four breweries around San Francisco. He chose one at random and phoned them first thing Monday morning. He explained to the manager that he was over from New Zealand and amongst several other items had been offered an agency agreement with Union Minerals to sell their filteraids back home. He had a problem. He hadn't a clue as to how these products worked, apart from the fact that they were used to clarify beer. He asked whether it would be possible to visit and see how they worked. Even if they did not actually use this brand it didn't matter. He was just looking for the basic principles so that he wouldn't feel a complete idiot when he had his meeting with them later on in the week. Like all nations the Americans have their faults. Lack of hospitality is not one of them. Andy was told he would be welcome to visit any time on Tuesday. The manager would even ensure someone from the process side would be on hand to answer any questions.

Derek had not one card in his collection relevant to New Zealand but in the end it didn't matter. Andy was given the royal tour round the place with no questions as to his identity asked. It was his first brewery visit and he found it interesting. Some of the things he'd only heard about now made sense. He made a few notes on the more practical issues, particularly about slurry strengths of powder and dose rates. He hoped he had enough to satisfy Larry's request. The brewery did use Purflo – two grades. Andy drove back to the hotel. His free gift of six bottles of lager looked inviting. Derek and he would have made short work of them normally, but the word Purflo would ensure the crown tops stayed on the bottles.

Derek was pacing up and down in the foyer of the hotel. 'Andy, am I glad you're back early. We've got to shoot down to Los Angeles as soon as we can. I've already booked flights for 6 o'clock tonight.'

'Why, what's the panic?'

'Dunno. I phoned Larry earlier on this afternoon, just my daily call to see how things are. He sounded distressed, said we're to get down there as soon as possible. I rang him back with our e.t.a. and he said he'd meet us at the airport.'

Apart from his usual warm greeting, Larry only spoke once during the journey back to his laboratory. His voice was unusually sharp and agitated.

'General Hutton's waiting in my office. He's been there off and on for most of the day. No announcement or anything, he just arrived out of the blue. He's been helping himself to my notes. I feel quite intimidated. He said I was to get you all back as soon as I could. I haven't been able to speak to Ben directly. Left messages for him to ring me but nothing as yet.'

Larry rushed them through the signing-in formalities and led the way up some stairs. This was a part of the building they hadn't been in. He ushered them into a small conference room. Coffee was simmering away on a corner table but there was no sign of Hook or his prehistoric man. They sat and waited. It was almost an hour before he arrived. He was on his own and was wearing his full uniform, rows of medal ribbons adorning his ample chest.

'Sit down!' He went round to the end of the long table and remained standing. He began to thump the table with the palm of his hand. 'I'm very disappointed with you all. Firstly, no report until yesterday, secondly that it was out of date anyway and thirdly at the very slow progress you're making.'

Derek stood up. 'Wouldn't it be better to wait until Ben arrives before we start to discuss anything further?'

'Mr Hansen won't be joining us. He was killed last night.'

The room fell silent. Then questions were all asked in a rush. Ben dead? What was the General saying? The General held up his swagger stick until he got silence again.

'The young man was murdered, stabbed to death to be precise, at exactly 9.30 p.m. last night. Seems he was taking a short cut through some alleyway back to where he'd parked his car. The silly young fool always carried that computer thing of his everywhere he went. The local police think he was mugged for it. Some drugged hippy probably trying to raise some cash for his next fix. It certainly hasn't been found anywhere near the scene of the crime. I understand that he died immediately, the wound pierced his heart. Anyway, I did not come here to discuss his death, tragic as it is. I called you here to discuss the urgency of the project you're working on. First of all you send me a very negative report which concludes that you all feel there is nothing in this beer thing, and then I find out – find out mind you, I was not told – that you're all out and about pursuing possible clues because you *do* believe there is some truth in it. When I said I wanted reports I meant, and insist on, truthful and up-to-the-minute documents!'

Derek stood up again. He was polite but to the point. 'General, the report was accurate and expressed everyone's true feelings, including Ben's, up to a few days ago. We have not proved anything since that conclusively identifies there is a genuine problem. When we do then it will be reported.'

The General's face did not alter its expression one little bit. 'Fine sentiments, Madden, but the test on the mice was a few days ago and should have been included in the report, shouldn't it? But to the point. I want greater effort. If the problem exists, which you all seem to believe it does, then I want whoever's responsible identified and interrogated as soon as possible. I want greater commitment from you all. No more passing the time playing board games and the like. Now go to it.' The General's pep talk was over, he headed for the door.

Derek stood up and drew himself up to his full height. 'General, you are a cold, unfeeling sod. There are bastards and bastards, but you, sir, are the all-time arch-bastard.' Derek sat down again and could feel himself shaking. The General ignored the remarks completely and continued to leave the room.

The three of them sat staring at each other for ages. Larry made the first move. 'It's getting late and I know you haven't any accommodation fixed up, so I insist you come back to my house. If you'll give me five minutes I'll just check everything that needs to be is switched off in the lab.'

The Doc returned shortly. 'Millie, my wife, is expecting us.'

The journey up the coast road to Santa Monica was conducted in silence. Each man with his own thoughts about their dead team partner. Larry's house was on one of the minor roads that lead off Wilshire Boulevard. It was a typical middle-class property built in the late fifties, by no means as opulent as those further up at Beverly Hills but still expensive and proof of a good income. His wife opened the door as soon as she heard the car pull into the drive. She was as warm and friendly as Larry. For a woman in her mid-fifties she hadn't worn too well. Her face was covered in worry lines and her eyes had huge bags underneath them. She was also white. For some reason both Derek and Andy had expected to meet a black person and they had to conceal their surprise. She made them feel at home straight away. Neither daughter was at home at present, so between them the two guests had the choice of three bedrooms. It was obvious Millie was in charge of the decor, furniture and fabrics – everything was in pastel shades and reflected the female touch. Even Larry made the comment, 'Normally it's three women against one man in this house but tonight the tables are turned.'

The four of them sat in the lounge devouring a large platter of sandwiches. Millie asked Andy about England and, to maintain a balance, Derek about New York. Both places were equally foreign to her. After half an hour she discreetly bade them goodnight and left the room, saying she knew they wanted to talk. Larry disappeared into the kitchen and returned with a bottle of bourbon and two glasses. Before anyone could say anything he stated, 'It's not for me but I thought you might like some.'

The conversation turned to Ben. What a waste. He had only just started out in life really. They all felt a bit annoyed with themselves. They hadn't really supported him much at their last meeting, preferring to see him as an immature young man. Perhaps as the project gained ground they would have warmed to him more and helped him to become more worldly-wise. It was all too late now.

Derek raised his glass. 'To Ben.' Andy joined in the toast.

Larry just spoke the words and added, 'Thanks for helping with the problem.'

Larry said he was going to turn in but insisted they stay up as long as they wanted to.

Derek intended to and was well on his way to getting drunk. 'One day maybe I'll be able to piss all over that bastard General's grave.'

'I might just join you,' Andy added.

Derek was silent. He just sat staring out of the window. Andy browsed around the room. Photographs of probably every member of the Fletcher clan stood on every available surface: grandparents, parents, grandchildren. Generations of nameless people stared back at him. Derek started to hum. Andy went across and poured him another drink. 'Penny for your thoughts.'

'I was just thinking. How did that bastard Hook know about us playing Monopoly?'

'From your report?' Andy suggested.

'I never mentioned it.'

They both knew immediately what that meant: unless Larry had told him, then his office was bugged. They would ask him in the morning.

'And another thing.' Derek's voice was beginning to slur. 'Did you notice that he never said anything about all the other projects he's heading? The last time we were just an irritant to him; now that we might have the glimmer of something, we've become centre stage. I got the distinct impression we're the only ones with anything worth listening to.'

'You know what that means if it's true? He'll be hounding us for information at every available opportunity.'

By the time they went upstairs, Andy had to help his friend up to his room.

Andy was up early – too many thoughts going round in his head plus a strange bed and surroundings didn't encourage sleep. He let himself out and went for a run. A group of young women invited him to join them and they jogged along one of the beach roads.

Millie was out in the garden when he returned. She led him into the dining-room, where Derek and Larry were tucking in to scrambled eggs on toast. Derek appeared none the worse for his alcohol consumption the night before. Andy excused himself and went off for a shower first. Later, they all settled down around a plastic table in the back garden. Larry was anxious to learn about the practical aspects associated with filteraids.

'The filter I saw was described as typical so what I learnt is probably very true of all others,' Andy began. 'A coarse powder is put onto the mesh screens first. Only a very thin layer. This is to stop the finer ones going straight through. As I understand it, fine grades such as Purflo P5 clean up the beer, coarse ones will not. A slurry of P5 was made up in clean water and injected into the beer just before it was passed into the filter. The P5 powder and dirt are held back by the coarser material, clean beer passes through the lot. Once the gap between the plates fills up the filter is stopped, the muck washed off and it's ready for its first application of coarse powder again.'

'How long did the filter you saw run for?'

'A good question, I'll have to get some notes I made hang on.' Andy dashed back inside, returning moments later with his pad. 'I've written down that they filter 350 hectolitres per hour and they try and get a tank of 5,000 hectolitres through before they have to clean the filter off. Any good?'

'Perfect. Thanks, Andy. That's exactly what I wanted to know.' Larry sat back with a look of satisfaction on his face. He suddenly stood up. 'No, this is all wrong. Me thinking about stupid things like filters whilst Ben's lying in a morgue somewhere. It's not respectful. Let's drop the subject of Purflo for a while.'

Derek sat Larry back in his chair. 'I know it's all very sad. Nobody's more upset than myself. But I'm sure Ben would have wanted us to carry on. You've obviously got something going on in your head about Purflo. Share it with us, please.'

Larry composed himself. Derek was right, of course the show went on. 'I was getting nowhere because I was feeding the mice either neat Purflo or a slurry mixed in water added to their feed. As I've said before, the protein present in Purflo is not soluble in water, so no results; but it is soluble in acid.'

'In acid?' Derek queried. He exchanged glances with Andy. Perhaps it had all been too much for the good doctor. Perhaps he'd flipped. 'Larry, we're talking about beer – you know, good old-fashioned beer.'

'Precisely! Beer is an acid. There's a scale, seven is neutral – water. Anything above alkali, anything below acid. The beers we've got have all tested four – strongly acid. The protein is not immediately soluble in acid – it takes about twenty minutes. That's why Ben's test worked. If you remember he left the P5 sample soaking in some beer for about fifteen minutes. The powder had settled, but the protein must have dissolved – well most of it. That's why I asked you to find out about what goes on in a brewery. If the contact time is only seconds or minutes, my theory breaks down – but it isn't. The filter bed of Purflo builds up all the time, beer is continually washing out the protein over many hours. That's how it gets into the beer.'

'This is a major breakthrough. Well done Larry.' There was a sense of excitement in Derek's voice.

Larry refused to accept any praise, insisting that Ben had been responsible. He continued, 'There's something else we've unearthed. This protein, once dissolved in acid, breaks down into amino acids.'

'And what do they do?' Andy asked.

'They make the brain function normally. I must confess it's not a subject I'm an expert on. I may need to confer with a colleague at the university to find out exactly what they are and what they do. Have I your permission to do this, Derek – you know, go outside our small circle? I can assure you my friend will only know the absolute minimum, and he'll be discretion itself anyway.'

'Do it. You have open house to do whatever you think necessary. Okay? Can I use your phone please?'

Larry showed Derek a phone just inside the kitchen. He was gone for quite a while, and Millie made them some cold drinks.

When Derek returned, he sat down, let out a huge sigh and downed his lemonade in one. 'I've just spoken to an old contact in the coroner's office in San Francisco. They've already carried out an autopsy on Ben. One stab wound to the heart, attacked from behind, he reckons. He's going to find out the funeral details and call back. Andy and I have got to fly up there, anyway – it's *en route* to the production plants. The least we can do is pay our last respects to Ben. You're welcome to come with us, Larry. The project can wait a couple of days.'

Larry declined, asking them to buy a wreath on his behalf. Derek wrote down a number on Andy's pad, tore it off and gave it to Larry.

'This is a very secure number. Should you need to get in touch with us urgently then please feel free to use it day or night and leave a message. Try not to use your office phone if possible – you never know what sons of bitches are listening!'

While they were having lunch, the message came through. They had Ben's last and permanent address. They left to catch the four o'clock shuttle.

'What are you up to?' Andy asked as soon as they were in the taxi. 'One of the production plants is directly east from here, nowhere near San Francisco.'

'I know, but I've got a hunch – in fact, more than one. I've just got to get them out of my system before doing anything else. There's no need for you to tag along if you don't want to.'

'Try and stop me! Anyway, I do want to attend Ben's funeral.'

7

Ben's funeral wasn't until the Saturday, so they now had two days to click their heels in San Francisco. Andy would have felt better occupying his mind with something constructive, however, like an obedient servant, he followed Derek around from one Government building to another to find out more about Ben's death. None of Derek's friends came up with anything more than Hutton had told them.

When you live out of a suitcase, you try to pack for every eventuality, but neither possessed a black tie. Andy wasn't that bothered but Derek was, and even tried to hire black suits. The shopping expeditions wasted more time but in the end Derek had to be content with just buying ties.

On the Saturday Derek drove out of San Francisco across the bridge to Richmond. They'd allowed themselves plenty of time but kept getting lost. Roads weren't at right angles any more – Richmond must have been designed by the English, Derek commented. There were sweeping bends, dead ends, the lot. They saw the place twice over before they eventually spotted the chapel. Andy was glad to get out of the car. He was used to the American system of moving out right on a red light but his colleague was attempting to rewrite the whole bloody highway code single-handed, and his humming! The later they got the louder it became. They crept in at the back and slid into the last pew just in time to see poor old Ben's coffin begin its last journey to the hungry fires waiting somewhere in the crematorium.

There were only about twenty people in the congregation – all dressed in black. In the front row was one female. Everybody else was male. Andy couldn't take his eyes off her arse. It was a perfect example of what a female backside should look like wrapped in tight black material. He looked away ashamed. This was a funeral for God's sake, not some peep show. He caught site of Derek's face, open-mouthed and totally focused on the same piece of fabric. Derek caught Andy's eye and let out an imaginary whistle. The woman was about five foot four. Apart from her rear, she had shoulder-length natural blonde hair. The man next to her had his arm around her waist as if to support her in her hour of maximum grief. He was big – about Andy's height – but with athletic-looking broad shoulders, and blond hair as well. Their shoulders were moving up and down in unison as if sharing some joke, only this wasn't the time or the place. The music, something by Elton John, stopped. The silence seemed to last for ever and then the couple turned and walked back down the aisle. The woman was in her late twenties. Even with her red eyes there was no mistaking her classical beauty. To Andy she was the perfect specimen. The blond man was probably a few years older. He was handsome, there was no doubt about that. He had a rugged square chin and looked to be very much the outdoors sort – the all-American male. Andy made his mind up that they were brother and sister.

Derek tapped the shoulder of the man in front. 'Who's the lady?'

'That's Clare Hansen,' the anonymous face whispered back without turning around.

'Lucky old Ben,' Derek muttered to Andy. 'Fancy being married to that lovely woman.' He realised the futility of his words and shrugged. The rest of the black-suits began to file out.

Outside, the couple were doing their best to maintain some sort of composure and were shaking everyone's hands and accepting condolences for the umpteenth time. Andy and Derek shuffled along in the small queue awaiting their turn. Derek introduced them both as Ben's colleagues from work and began to fumble for the right words.

'Only knew Ben for a short time, of course, but he certainly helped us. He was very good at his job. Still, this is all small compared to your loss. We will miss him, as a friend as well, but your loss, the loss of your husband, well, we are both very very sorry.'

For the first time since they'd seen her she stopped crying. 'I'm afraid you've got it wrong Mr Madden. I am, was, Ben's sister, Clare. This is Simon, Simon Ryan. Ben and Simon lived together.'

Simon's sniffles turned into full-scale sobs and the poor man began to cry his heart out. Andy took Derek's arm and pulled him away so that the last few remaining guests could say their piece.

'Oh my God! Please let the ground open up and swallow me whole,' Derek pleaded.'That will go down in the *Guinness Book of Records* as the biggest balls-up of all time!'

Andy watched her from a safe distance and after a few minutes Simon left her and went to talk to a group of men about his own age. Clare looked around and saw Andy staring at her. She quickly averted her own gaze and then started to walk slowly over to him. Her hands were clenched behind her back and the very sight began to alter Andy's blood-pressure levels. He got his sentence in first.

'Look, I'm terribly sorry about our mistake. We haven't worked with Ben long and never got much of a chance to talk sociably so we just assumed – sorry again.'

Derek joined them and blurted out his apologies as well.

'That's all right, you weren't to know. Would you like to come back to the apartment? There's a small buffet. Some of our friends have travelled a long way and could do with a rest. Where have you come from?'

Andy told her Los Angeles. It was a bit of a lie as they both had hotel rooms just across the bay in San Francisco, but it had the desired effect. She insisted they both come back and that she would travel with them to show them the way.

Her composure held for most of the 35-minute drive

and they learnt a few general things about her. She lived in Seattle and worked as a personnel secretary to a marketing manager at one of the large aeroplane companies located there. She was not married not even engaged.

Derek kept his eyes on the road but muttered to himself, 'Jesus, what's the matter with fellas in Seattle?' He'd have married her then and there!

Ben's apartment was nothing special, probably typical of thousands used by young couples starting out on the ladder of life together, and if they'd expected it to be full of computers they were sadly disappointed. Apart from the usual hi-fi and television, that was it. They both circulated and made small talk with the other guests. Simon never let up on his grief, which occasionally had a snowball effect and set Clare off. One by one the guests drifted away, and when there were only the four of them left Clare suggested Simon go and get some rest. He needed no persuasion once she'd promised she would still be there later on. She also excused herself.

Derek was really quite house-trained when it came down to it; he began to tidy up the glasses. Andy had to do one thing first – he ripped off the black tie and stuffed it into his 'Sunday best' jacket, which he threw across the back of the chair. They were in the small kitchen when she returned. She had washed, touched up her make-up and changed into a white shirt and jeans. Andy wanted to reach out and touch her skin. He was having urges unlike any he'd had for years. Not raw sexual urges. These were different, these were protective desires. Given a free hand he would have cuddled the beautiful lady for hours on end. Derek made coffee and ushered the pair of them into the living-room.

Over the next hour they learnt she was now the last of the Hansen family. Her father had worked in Kenya but when she was old enough she returned to the States to attend Seattle University. In her second year her parents were murdered. She gave up her studies to run the small farm, but it was too much for her – too many memories as well. She sold it and returned to the States for good. Andy was having a hard time listening to all of this. How much did someone still so young have to bear in life? She started to sniff again, small tears appearing in the corner of her eyes. He didn't care if the whole world as well as Derek was watching. He moved across to her chair, sat on the arm and held her hand in both of his huge brutes. The gesture was appreciated and she settled down again.

'Tell us about Ben and Simon, please,' Derek asked. She stared back at him for a good minute before agreeing, but there was a condition – in return she wanted to know more about how they'd come to be working with Ben. At first Derek was suspicious. Did she also have a hunch about his death? She answered his doubts without any prompting. She just wanted to remember him working with two nice people. Derek obliged and invented a totally false story. Ben came out of it with flying colours – in fact, he was painted as the lynchpin of the whole operation. Andy was delighted. There was no mention of sulks or dead white mice. She would go back with good memories of Ben, the professional man.

Clare outlined her brother's short life. At an early age he had developed an interest in computers. There were few distractions out in Kenya and by the time he was fifteen he'd already designed several systems for US companies operating out there. On one occasion he was severely reprimanded at school – one of their telephone bills was enormous. In due course it came out that Ben was using the line to tap into mainframe computers belonging to some very important organisations. Later, he attended Stanford University, where he met Simon, who also shared a passion for computers. Once they qualified they set up home together in the Bay area. Simon had been accepted by the Treasury first and after about a year put Ben's name forward for a vacant position, and so for the last five years they'd literally shared every interest together.

'Ben's sexual preference, has he always been . . . ?' Andy had trouble saying the word.

'Homosexual?' she replied. 'Yes, well at least I had a good idea that he was. He used to take some of my underwear when we were teenagers, but fortunately our parents never found out.'

Andy felt he had to explain. 'I'm sorry, I didn't mean to ask you that question to embarrass you. Ben was murdered. Nobody knows why, except that he was possibly mugged for his laptop computer. Derek and myself would like to see justice done. You don't think it might have anything to do with his lifestyle, do you?'

'No, Ben and Simon never mixed with others. Their relationship was kept very low-key, they didn't go to gay bars or things like that.'

'Again, sorry to ask you.'

Her response was instant she put her other hand over Andy's and squeezed it hard. She understood.

Simon rejoined them, still looking awful. Try as he might, he said, sleep was beyond him at the moment. Clare volunteered to stay with him for a few days if he felt it would help.

'That's real sweet of you but I know you've got to get back to Seattle as soon as possible to sort your own affairs out. I've got to come to terms with living on my own. No, you go back. I'll be all right.' He wasn't, tears started flowing down his cheeks again.

'It's just the timing, that's all,' Clare explained. 'For months there's been a small market garden business up for sale just outside Seattle and it's finally coming up for auction tomorrow. Ben and I were going into partnership, at least financially. We have our parents' legacy. I was going to bid, and if successful run it on my own to start with. Ben and Simon talked about joining me in a few years' time – and now this.'

'Please go, Clare,' Simon said. 'You've got to think of your future, it's too late for Ben now.'

Andy insisted on driving Clare to the airport himself. He held a scrum-down with his partner. Derek would stay and keep Simon company.

There was so much he wanted to say to her but didn't; most of it would sound corny and the rest too pushy. In the end she leaned her head on his shoulder and the journey was made in near silence. It was as if they could both recharge their batteries just by touch. He checked her in, and before she disappeared through the numbered gate she kissed him full on the lips and gave him a slip of paper with her address and phone number on it. Her final words were that he must come and see her in Seattle. 'I will not need asking twice,' he told her.

Derek answered the door, rubbing sleep from his eyes. 'Thought you must have gone back with her! Come in, but keep your voice down. Simon eventually nodded off. Coffee?'

'How have you been getting on with him?'

'Very well, even surprised myself. I've never understood queers before – not when there's such a pleasant alternative – but he's okay, quite normal in every other respect. We've been getting along famously. Just like you and Miss Hansen!'

Andy could still taste the perfume on his mouth. He needed to change the subject quickly. 'And what's the master plan then?'

'If you don't mind getting some shut-eye in a chair, we'll spend the night here. Simon was beginning to tell me things about Ben. He already appreciates us staying, by the way. You can have the chair she sat in!'

They were all sitting around the small kitchen table by eight o'clock. Simon looked a lot better and, like Andy, stubble was appearing on his face. Derek, as always, had shaved, but was still wearing his black tie and suit.

'Simon, would you mind telling Andy what we talked about last night, please?'

'Okay.' His voice was still a bit croaky and his lips quivered in between sentences. 'For the last two days of his life Ben was very upset. Derek mentioned that the last time you saw him he was worried about some white mice, but it wasn't to do with them – he told me about them as soon as he got home on the Thursday. Don't get me wrong, Ben wouldn't tell me stuff he wasn't supposed to, he was very loyal, you know. No, he'd got over that. We went out for dinner on the Saturday and he was fine again. It was after that. He spent a lot of time working – I hardly saw him.'

The eyes welled up. Poor old Simon, Derek thought, he'd hardly seen his lover all week because of the beer project and now he was gone. He asked if he could get him anything but Simon waved his hand and continued his story.

'I asked if there was anything I could do but he just snapped at me and told me to mind my own business. It was so unusual. Ben and I never rowed. We were happy, a total item. He wasn't sleeping either. I heard him get up at least three times one night. He would come into the living-room and just sit for hours. He was worried about something.'

'This something, would he have made a record of it on his personal computer?' Andy asked.

Simon nodded. 'Sure.'

'And would he have kept any notes or anything in writing here?'

'No, when you're heavily into computers as Ben and I are, there's no need to. I use mine for everything, as a diary, for bank statements, addresses – the lot. There's no need for paper.' Simon realised he'd used the present tense with Ben and started to cry.

Andy and Derek gave him some privacy and moved rooms. Derek kept his voice to a minimum. 'The lad had something on his computer, something he was extremely worried about, so he's murdered for it and it's made to look like a street mugging for money. How's that for a resumé, Andy?'

'It's a very plausible theory but we've no proof, have we? We're doing a Larry here. We're fitting pieces into convenient slots to make the story suit.'

Derek didn't like the answer and the frown on his face summed up his feelings.

Simon joined them. 'Thanks, I feel a bit better now.'

'Tell me, did you or Ben ever do any of your investigative work here?' Derek asked.

'Never, too risky. It wouldn't take the authorities long to trace our phone number. At work we could tap into virtually untraceable lines. Do you know much about computer systems?'

Derek shook his head and quickly added, 'Don't bother, Simon, it'll be totally wasted on the pair of us.'

Simon became very serious-looking. 'What we do,

used to do, is illegal, of course. I'm not going to say any more. I don't know you people. You might be trying to catch me out, trying to trick me into revealing something I shouldn't when I'm at a very low moment. You'll have to talk to my boss if you want to know anything else.'

Derek made him sit down and began to talk to him in a quiet, reassuring voice. He stressed that they weren't out to trick him, they were as upset as anyone over Ben's death and wished only one thing, to bring his assassin to book.

Whilst this was going on Andy browsed around the living-room. The dining-area was bare except for an old swivel chair and a wall-mounted bookcase. There were no novels, every book was on computers. Andy sat in the chair, swung it round and read some of the titles. Four were on virus introduction techniques. They might as well have been in Latin as far as he was concerned. He picked up a beer-mat and twiddled it round in his fingers. There was what appeared to be a telephone number written on it: *Oakwood 8363*, and the printed word *Cola* on the mat had been circled many many times. Andy laughed quietly to himself. It was all right having these fancy laptop computers but you still needed something to scribble on quickly when a caller reeled off a number. He joined the other two and threw the card onto the coffee table.

Derek immediately picked it up. 'Your writing, Simon?'

He only glanced at it for a second and shook his head, 'No, it's, Ben's.'

Andy and Derek promised to contact Simon immediately should they have any news about the murder, then they said their goodbyes and left him standing in the doorway in his dressing-gown.

Andy drove them back to the hotel. They just hoped their rooms hadn't been relet and their luggage discarded in some junk room. Andy was getting to know this corner of the world quite well now. Derek took the beer-mat out of his pocket and propped it up on the dashboard. The humming started but he didn't speak during the entire journey.

After a typical hotel dinner they decided to enjoy an early night in comfortable beds. Neither slept well, although for entirely different reasons. At two o'clock Andy phoned his mother. She had just got up. She was all right but horrified with the news. He'd seen it on CNN four hours ago. The Tory Party were holding their annual political conference in Brighton on the south coast. Groups of protesters had started peaceful demonstrations outside several hotels where ministers were staying. As the night wore on, several people had tried to get inside the buildings. One thing had led to another and full-scale riots had broken out. One hotel had been burned to the ground. At the last count over forty police had been injured, five were known to have died from their wounds, and at least two hundred people had been arrested. There was no mention of the numbers of civilians killed but the pictures on the television were graphic enough. Bodies lay over the promenade as if it were a battle zone, and the Army in armoured cars now stood between the remaining hotels and the embittered crowd. He could tell by her voice she was upset. And it had happened only a few miles up the coast from where she lived. He would have to think about moving her somewhere else. Somewhere safer. But where?

Derek didn't sleep at all that night. At about the time Andy was speaking to his mother, he thought he recognised what the number on the mat was. But he wouldn't be able to confirm it until about six in the morning so he just sat looking at the clock willing the time away.

They had agreed to meet at nine for breakfast. Derek had finished his by eight and cursed Andy for not being early. He knocked on his door but there was no reply. He returned to the dining-room and was almost beside himself when Andy turned up with three minutes to go. He explained he'd been out jogging for a couple of hours and was about to go into detail when Derek cut him off in mid-speech.

'Never mind that now. I've found out what the number refers to. Phoned my uncle as soon as he got to his desk this morning. He works for the same outfit in Washington – in fact he got me my original job. Anyway, the number used to belong to an agent.'

'You mean, like James Bond 007?' Andy said sarcastically, still slightly annoyed with Derek's rude interruption.

'Not really, more like an army number. He said it was used for salary records and pensions. They were done away with over twenty years ago. I don't have one. Computers again, I suppose. Just as easy to put a name in now. Then it was all done by hand and cross-referenced with numbers. My uncle will try and dig out the name attached to this faceless number.'

'When?'

'Later on today, hopefully. Spoke to Larry as well. He sends his regards and sounds very enthusiastic. Says he's getting some very interesting results. He's asked us to bear with him – should be ready with some answers by this weekend.'

'Then that gives us at least four to five days to visit the Purflo plants?'

'I reckon that's our next move now.'

The phone call came through just before eleven. Andy was more relieved than anybody – there was only so much of Derek's humming he could take. The call didn't last long. His uncle knew the ropes better than anyone, and there were no 'whys' or 'what fors', just the information required – 'Roger A Schumacher, retired, current address unknown.'

'At least we now have a name,' Derek said enthusiastically.

'And now all we need to do is find this gentleman,' Andy said, and then a thought struck him. 'Hang on. Simon works for the Internal Revenue, Treasury, or whatever you call it. Perhaps he can find out where this individual lives, always assuming he's still alive. Perhaps he receives a pension?'

'Good thinking. I suggest we pay young Simon another visit.'

'We?' Andy queried. 'Wouldn't it make more sense for me to go and sneak around the plants?'

Derek shook his head. 'No, they can wait – they're not going anywhere. We're pretty sure that's where the problem starts but we don't know anything else as yet. We don't know who or what's behind it. Just supposing Ben was eliminated because he did stumble across something, we might need to change direction suddenly if we pick up the same clues – and we can't do that if you're in some God-forsaken place. If it's true, we might need to watch our own backs, and as always there's safety in numbers.' Derek rested his case.

'You're the boss – at least we don't have to drive halfway across the State to see Simon.'

Although it was early afternoon on Monday when they arrived, they knew Simon would be home. He'd already told them he intended to take a week's sick leave from work. Simon answered the door still in his dressing-gown. The beginnings of a beard were now very evident and his hair needed a good wash and brush. He was delighted to see them again and took a step towards Derek. Derek in turn recoiled a step – he didn't know if he was going to be hugged or even kissed. It was no good, Derek couldn't get to grips with the fact that he was gay.

'Just called to make sure you were all right. You were pretty low yesterday and we didn't want to think you'd do anything dramatic. How are you feeling now?'

'Slowly coming to terms with the situation, but I don't think I'll ever get back to normal, not with such a gap in my life now. But don't worry, I'm not going to do anything suicidal, I promise you. Thanks for your concern, anyway. Please come in – it's very rude of me keeping you on the doorstep like this.'

They sat and talked and drank coffee for about an hour. Derek was itching to ask his question but knew the timing had to be right. In the end he brought the conversation round to the relevant subject matter.

'Simon, I don't know what you remember about yesterday's conversation? We mentioned that Ben was helping us out, using his expert computer knowledge. We are working on a project which might have worldwide repercussions. Both Andy and I work for our respective governments. I must emphasise that this is a straightforward project and that nowhere along the line was there any danger to Ben. And then this tragedy happens. Of course, there is every possibility that his death had nothing at all to do with it. They may be right, it may have just been an unrelated mugging. But just suppose it wasn't? Simon, we need your help. Unofficially, of course, we need you to take over where Ben left off. Andy and I are hopeless with computers. Will you help us, please?'

Simon stood up and paced round the room, his eyes staring only at the floor. He stopped and faced them both. 'Yes. I will help anybody who helps bring Ben's murderer to justice.'

Derek let out an audible sigh of relief. 'Thank you. We have something we need your help with right now. We need to know the whereabouts of a Roger A. Schumacher – an ex-government employee. If he's alive then he'll be retired. His very old government number was 8363. It was on the drip-mat Andy found here yesterday.'

If Simon felt he'd been set up he showed no signs of it. The fact that he might have the opportunity of tracking down his lover's killer took precedence over everything at the moment. He picked up the phone and dialled. It took him ages to get through to whoever he wanted, all the intermediaries *en route* were obviously offering their sympathies. 'Hello, Roger . . . yes a lot better thanks, . . . next Monday. Listen I want you to do something. Check the records for me and find out the details on a Mr Roger A. Schumacher.' He spelled out the last name. There was more small talk, then he hung up. 'It'll take one of my colleagues til about eight tonight. He'll phone back here later on.'

Andy thought fresh air would do Simon good so he encouraged him to get showered and dressed. They would take him out to dinner. There was also an ulterior motive in his suggestion: he didn't want to listen to Derek hovering over the phone humming all night.

Derek phoned Larry while they waited for Simon. 'Larry, does the name Oakwood mean anything to you?

I've heard the name before and thought if might be a university or something.' Larry obviously had an answer. Derek stood there listening while his face got paler and paler. He started to bite at a fingernail. 'Thanks. Oh, nothing, so don't go and start reading anything into it, it's just that someone mentioned the name, that's all, and it's been bugging me ever since . . . Yes, see you soon, bye.' Derek replaced the receiver as if it were made of glass. A whistle came from his lips. 'That word on the mat – Oakwood; well, it's the United States Chemical Warfare Experimental Laboratories based in Maryland.'

'My God,' Andy exclaimed. 'What on earth was Ben delving into?'

Simon found his appetite and the trip out did him the power of good. They were back in the apartment by eight. As expected, Derek patrolled around the phone, humming. It was nearer ten by the time the message came through. Simon wrote it down on Andy's notepad.

> Roger Austin Schumacher, born 1928. Government employee. Retired 1989. Pension of $37,000 per annum. Paid monthly into the Pismo branch of the Bank of America. Tax deducted at source.

Simon thanked his friend and hung up. 'I hope it's what you want?'

It was just what they wanted. Once again, they took their leave. Back in the car, Derek outlined the agenda. 'Before we visit this pensioner, I'd like you to visit the *San Francisco Chronicle* archives tomorrow, see what you can dig up on Oakwood, will you? If the old memory is not playing tricks, there was a lot of media coverage in the late eighties – that's where I remember the name from.'

'What will you be doing?' Andy asked. 'Writing another report to Hook?'

'No, stuff him for the moment. I'm going to make some discreet enquiries within my own organisation.'

Andy started at 1990 and worked back. The records were literally scattered with articles on Oakwood. The news stories peaked around 1987–88. He spent a good four hours reading and making precise notes in his pad. Some of the accounts must have been over-embellished by the reports – things like that just didn't happen.

At dinner, Derek ate and listened, but Andy let his food go cold, he had so much to tell. He finished off by saying he couldn't believe all the stories were one hundred per cent true.

Derek put down his glass and looked his friend straight in the eye. 'Andy, everything you have related did happen, I can assure you. Some of the things I've found out today confirm it most definitely.'

Pismo is situated almost midway between Los Angeles and San Francisco. Derek drove and kept to both the coast road and the speed limit. Andy could see the attraction of the place: a gently curving bay made up of almost white sand stretched away into the distance for at least twenty miles. The small town of Pismo lay in a dip between the rolling hills stretching back inland. It was 'resting' at this time of the year, anticipating its summer influx of visitors. Some of the wooden buildings were receiving a lick of paint. Slap bang in the middle of the town was the usual multi-storey Holiday Inn, and Derek headed straight for it – it was thirsty work driving! They sat in the bar, scanning through the local phone book, but there was no mention of any Schumacher.

'He could have been dead for years, of course,' Andy said. 'Perhaps we should have made some more enquiries before we set off on the long journey.'

If looks could kill then Derek would have murdered his colleague. 'Not my style, old son. I like to work things out *in situ*, so to speak. Don't worry, if your man's in the area I'll find him. Just you relax – have some lunch or something.' He left Andy to his own devices.

Derek's mind was working as flat out as it could. He couldn't ask at the local bank, that would be too much of a giveaway. No, he had to find the address by more subtle means. He distracted the hotel receptionist just long enough to reach over and grab an unopened envelope from her desk. He then had the cheek to ask for a plain self-adhesive label, copied down any old address from the wall map on it, stuck it over the original writing and called her over to point out where the post office was on the town plan. It was within walking distance of the hotel. He approached the post office teller with confidence. 'This came today, wrong address.'

The man went off and came back with a sheaf of papers. He crossed out the false address and neatly wrote alongside the correct one. Each word was registered clearly inside Derek's brain. He even offered to take the package to its rightful owner, saying he was going that way. The teller thanked him, but insisted it would have to be sent officially. He returned to the hotel, checked the wall map, finished off what was left of Andy's sandwiches, and within minutes they were back inside their rented car.

Their Mr Schumacher lived about eight miles out of town along the northern coast road. No doubt this would have been the only road to and from Pismo decades ago. Now it was deserted, long overtaken by the newer inland bypass. When people who live in a large sprawling country describe a property as detached, they mean it! To Andy's mind, isolated was a better description of the Schumacher property. Derek drove slowly past it. About two hundred yards further along the road was a small dirt-track which started to climb away. Without warning Derek swung the car into the wrong lane and reversed into this ideal parking-spot. He climbed until they had a panoramic view of both the road and the chalet-style house on the other side of the road. It was set in about two acres of garden and in its heyday if would have caught every driver's eye. Now it was run-down. Paint was beginning to peel off weatherboards, the lawns were running wild and the swimming-pool was empty and carpeted in rotting vegetation. One thing wouldn't have changed over the years and that was the magnificent view. The house was on the edge of hundred-foot high cliffs overlooking the Pacific and the sweeping expanse of Pismo bay.

Derek explained his plan. He would go and talk to

Schumacher, Andy was to stay in the car as lookout. If anything untoward happened he was to blast the horn twice. Derek reached back and took his briefcase off the back seat.

'Did a bit of shopping as well yesterday,' he said casually. He opened the lid up and handed his friend a small pistol and a pair of binoculars. He slipped a similar weapon into the waist band of his trousers and stuffed a small cassette player into his jacket pocket. 'I know it's a bit over the top, but better to be this way than end up like Ben.'

Derek crossed the road, and after a quick glimpse behind walked down the old drive. Andy put the glasses to his eyes. Derek's brown-suited back leaped into focus – he was banging on the front door with a clenched fist. He was so close Andy even imagined he could hear the noise. Nothing happened. From his more violent hammerings Derek was obviously running out of patience. Andy bet he was already humming. In the end, he gave up at the door and started to investigate the far side of the house. After about ten minutes he hadn't returned so Andy assumed he'd at last found his quarry. He slid down into the car seat and pulled down his newly acquired baseball cap, a tourist taking a short rest from driving.

Derek found a side door next to a large patio area at the back of the property. No expense had been spared in building the house. Everything had been done properly, using the best raw materials. It was a shame, Derek thought, to let it just rot away like this. He repeated his drumming on this door, but still nothing. Perhaps the man had died years ago – the place certainly had the appearance of being empty. Then he heard the noise, a stick or something hitting a hard surface. A shadow appeared behind the glazed door. Bolts were drawn back.

'What do you want?' This was said with a great degree of irritation. Derek stared at the man. He was in reality sixty-eight years old but looked more like ninety. He was bald, apart from a few strands of yellow-looking tufts, and his small unkempt beard was white, completely the opposite colour of what teeth he had left. In his prime he would have been well over six feet tall, but he was now so stooped he looked Derek eyeball to eyeball. He was emaciated, his skeleton was starting to show through. Again he asked what Derek wanted. He started to cough, and Derek made a small move forward. Immediately, the walking-stick came up, as in self-defence.

'Mr Schumacher? My name's Bill. I'm from the White House – may I come in please? I would like to ask you some questions and what I have to say is not doorstep conversation.' He handed the old man a card. He fumbled in his old shirt pocket for a pair of reading-glasses and studied the writing. Derek had actually had this card for several years now – it was an old favourite of his: *Bill Littlejohn, Inspector, Department of Internal Affairs, Washington DC.*

'Follow me, but don't rush me, I've got rheumatoid arthritis.'

The hunchback shuffled along the corridor. Room after room led off. Derek glanced into every one. They were all furnished.

They reached the room nearest the ocean. It was a mess. Books and yellow newspapers were piled on a table. An old bureau was spewing out letters several dozen unopened. The walls were covered in framed photographs that no doubt chronicled his life. He knocked some magazines off a chair and instructed Derek to sit. With a great wheeze he lowered himself onto a single unmade bed. He had given up on the rest of the house, this room was his whole life now. It was stuffy, the air stale. Derek slid back the patio door. His guest didn't seem to mind or care. He looked blankly at Derek, waiting for him to start.

'It's to do with Oakwood,' Derek said abruptly. There was not the slightest sign of acknowledgement on the gaunt face. 'As you will be aware, if you watch or listen to the news, there has been a lot of publicity recently about Oakwood. A lot of reports in the early nineties were not only confusing but downright detrimental to the Government of the United States. There are several further court cases coming up soon, and once again the subject will be on the front pages, some of the truth will be distorted and there will be more bad feelings across the nation. The President wishes to make a clean start on the subject and go to the people first with the truth, and then if necessary, and with a clear conscience, answer any criticism. Unfortunately, some of the records are missing, perhaps deliberately to conceal some of the facts. However, I am instructed by the President to obtain as much information as possible from people who were directly involved at Oakwood.'

Schumacher may have been physically falling to pieces, but at least his hearing was working. He nodded as Derek progressed, indicating that he was both receiving and understanding. Derek reached into his inside pocket and handed the man a white envelope. His claw like hands couldn't open it. Derek did the honours and handed him an official-looking letter. It was on official White House paper and handwritten. Derek knew the contents off by heart. It was one of his better efforts. It was addressed to 'Roger' and contained three paragraphs. The first repeated what Derek had said; the second asked for his fullest co-operation, with just a hint that untold damage could be done by parties not sympathetic to the Government if the truth was not treated in the strictest confidence; the last paragraph was bullshit. It thanked 'Roger' for all his efforts, and hoped he was well and enjoying his retirement. It ended with 'God bless America' and was signed by the President of the United States of America. A personal handwritten note from the most powerful man on earth. Even Roger was now impressed.

'What do you want to know then?'

'Perhaps you'd be good enough to run through all the events during your time at Oakwood.'

Derek reached into his pocket for his tape recorder and placed it on a corner of the table. Schumacher looked puzzled but Derek didn't give him a chance to say anything. 'Don't forget you will be speaking to the President.' The old man sat upright and at one point Derek thought he was trying to stand up. The weak voice had gone, somewhere he had tapped into lost inner reserves or perhaps he was just about to relive his days as an officer in the 'service'.

'Good day, Mr President.' Schumacher began. 'This is indeed an honour and a privilege. Please excuse me if my memory lapses from time to time, but I'm not as active as I used to be. Throughout our history, I suppose we as human beings have always been looking for ways to be one step ahead of our enemies. The Germans brought things to a head during the First World War when they used mustard gas to try to wipe out tens of thousands of their opponents at the Somme and Ypres. Various American committees were set up in the thirties to discuss the potential future of chemical warfare. As a direct result of their reports the Government of the day set up Oakwood. It was to employ all the best chemists of the day to work on the development of products which could be used as weapons of mass human destruction without damaging any of the infrastructure. Of course, the other side of the coin was not forgotten and teams of people started to investigate ways of protecting their troops from other countries' products. I suppose Oakwood reached its zenith around the time of the Second World War.'

The old man had a coughing fit. Derek pounced on the recorder, stopped play and then brought in a glass of water from the kitchen. Schumacher drank half of it, reached under the bed, produced a bottle of rum and topped the glass up with it. Derek's stomach turned over, rum and water! They sat staring at each other for a minute or two.

'Okay I'm all right now. How am I doing – too much, too little detail, what?'

'Just fine, Roger, just fine.' Derek rolled the tape again.

'In the early forties they manufactured large quantities of weapons containing a whole range of chemicals, viruses, anthrax – you name it, Oakwood produced it. They were stockpiled all over the world ready to be used if the Japs or Nazies resorted to such tactics. Fortunately they were never used; well, not in large quantities anyway. Such weapons were outlawed by the early fifties – all the superpowers and leading world countries saw to that, and numerous treaties were signed to that effect.'

Again a pause. Again more diluted rum. He had spoken more words in five minutes than he would normally do in a week.

'In the mid-fifties a big purge was carried out at the place. After all, we were now into the space age. Out went all the old "mustard" scientists with their old-fashioned ideas, and in came a new breed of technical men – people who knew about drugs and gases that would alter the state of mind. The expression "mind-bending" was first heard within the confines of buildings in Maryland. All these new products were tested on animals to start with, but the results proved inconclusive. After all, you can't really ask primates and goats how they feel, can you? I don't know who or how it was first decided, but the army "volunteered" three thousand men to take part in various experiments. It was at this time – let me see, 1958 – that I was posted there as an observer for the CIA. I had to witness these human tests and suggest to my bosses the best ways of introducing any of these products into theatres of war.' He hesitated, his eyes just staring straight through Derek.

'You okay? You want to take a break?'

'No!' Schumacher picked up his thoughts and carried on. 'Some of what I saw was obscene. The tests got out of hand but were still allowed to continue. There was one particular drug that had been dreamed up by the boffins, a very powerful hallucinogen called simply BZ – forerunner to LSD. It was injected into dozens of soldiers. Please remember, Mr President, that it had never even been tested on animals. This drug altered the minds of these men dramatically, it seemed to tap into and release their base anger. Some behaved like savage animals and had to be physically restrained and left to come down off their own "highs". Once they were back to normal they couldn't even remember what they'd done. But some tests went even further. New, totally untried drugs were coming out of the laboratories almost daily. Some soldiers were tied down and made to swallow these compounds, they had them literally forced down their throats. They died horrible deaths in only a matter of hours. I remember seeing one young man, he couldn't have been more than eighteen, foaming at the mouth before he passed away. As soon as they were dead there was a rush to grab the body and dissect it to see what damage had been done to the vital organs – there was no finesse, three or four people would hack the body to bits in seconds. Once they'd finished, the left-over bits were burnt, there were no military funerals. Of course, as all of this was top secret, any leaks were categorically denied by the Government right up until 1975. The volunteers, those who survived, were warned off taking any further action in civvy street. They were threatened by big brother not to make waves, otherwise their lives as well as their families would be in danger. You also have to remember that by the time these men were discharged from Oakwood they were well and truly hooked on drugs. Who was going to listen to a drug addict's ramblings about something as awful as Oakwood? Nobody would believe them. A few brave souls did persist, though. God, those men had some courage – more than I had, I never dared to protest, not once. They did manage to find sympathetic ears in the legal profession and started to file compensation claims against the Government, but it took nearly ten years before they were heard in court. The amount of red tape the Government put up as a smokescreen doesn't bear thinking about.'

There was silence. Derek watched the man opposite. He was worn out and physically weary but his brain was still active. Perhaps it was some form of punishment for what he'd been involved with.

'And that's the story?' Derek switched off the tape.

'Good God man, no!' Schumacher almost shouted back. It was as if the old man would not be satisfied until he had unburdened himself of the whole sorry tale.

'Give me a second to turn the tape over, and then again in your own time, please Roger.'

Schumacher took another sip of rum and water and

resumed. 'What I've told you is just the beginning. The Vietnam War saw to that – that war, the war everyone wants to forget about. Oh, there was great national fervour and pride in our forces in February 1965 when President Johnson ordered the bombing of North Vietnam. It would all be over soon, everybody thought, the might of America against a few slit-eyed commies. How wrong they all were! The more we bombed the North the more determined they became to fight and discredit us. At one time there were over half a million American troops stationed in Vietnam. I was sent over to take part in several covert operations and everywhere I went morale was at rock-bottom. The troops felt let down and betrayed by the folks back home; after all, it was the time for peace rallies and flower power. The news media were mainly to blame, they made the GIs out to be the bad guys. Napalm raids on villages full of women and children, the summary executions of untried opponents, the stories of horror committed against an innocent population were rife in all the papers. The American military machine was not very good at self-publicity either – if force failed then more force was their only answer, or so the folks back home thought. Morale had to be raised.'

Derek was listening but his mind was also working overtime. Yes, he remembered the period well. He was at university and had organised many a protest march where he'd ended up sticking flowers down the barrels of rifles. He'd had long curly hair in those days. He ran a hand across the large expanse of bare head now. Schumacher finished off the last of his drink and launched himself back into his story.

'The Oakwood experiments had until that time been confined to the complex. It was suggested that the war offered the perfect opportunity to test the chemicals in the field. Again, I was told to monitor the results of the trials. They began to test their new wonder drugs on apes first. I still remember the early tests – it took about half an hour before anything happened and then gradually they all started to snap at each other. Within the hour most were dead, they had literally pulled each other to pieces. I had to shoot one – there was little of its guts left intact. The drugs were then modified and retried, and at last after three weeks of working day and night the chemists reckoned they had the most suitable drug – one that would cause aggression but not towards members of the same team. It was tried out on prisoners of war – they were all condemned men anyway. Half were given clean shirts so that they could be recognised and given this newest drug in their food. The dirty shirts were to be the control. It was all low-key stuff to start with; the drugged men just started to row with the others and then fights broke out. Seven out of the nine non-drugged prisoners were killed – stoned, kicked or stabbed to death – and the two survivors were in such a mess that they were shot later in the day to put them out of their misery. But the experiment was deemed to be an outstanding success and beer flowed late into the night, I can tell you. The tailor-made aggressive fighting man had just been born.

'Stockpiles of this new drug were hastily manufactured and it wasn't many weeks later that the opportunity arose to try it out on a grand scale. Reports started to come in that the Vietcong were about to launch an offensive. Our troops defending that section were secretly given the drug over a period of a few days, again in their food. Everyone in the know was convinced that a major victory was about to happen – not only would we repel the enemy but we would drive forward, taking many hundreds of miles of new territory. The tide of war would then swing in our favour and the American people would start believing in their military once again. But the experiment failed dreadfully. In the heat of battle confusion set in and our troops started firing at each other. Remember, they were all hyped up and on very short fuses. They fired on anything that moved. Those who were not killed by their own side were soon disposed of by the enemy. The Vietcong offensive worked, they gained the ground that day. Of course, post-mortems went on for weeks afterwards, debating what had gone wrong, and it was eventually concluded that the troops, unlike the prisoners, were under pressure and this had resulted in them being out for self-preservation – anybody firing a gun was their enemy.'

Schumacher stopped and took some deep breaths. The amount of talking he was doing was draining him; soon he would be totally exhausted. Derek had to keep the pressure on him, he still wanted one or two more answers.

'Did the experiments stop after this fiasco?'

'On humans, yes.' Schumacher answered. 'At least until anything new had been thoroughly tested on animals first.'

'That implies that more trials went on, using approved substances. Did they involve the use of a cola drink as a carrier?'

The old man's eyes bulged. Derek's guess had hit the mark. Schumacher started to cough and look terribly uncomfortable on the edge of the bed. 'But how did you know about that? There was only a handful of people involved, this was an ultra-secret project.'

'Oh, the President knows there was some work done using a soft drink but doesn't have any details.' The fact that the President was the recipient of the tape made the old man sit up straight and gather his wits once more.

'Who was involved in the project?' Derek pressed.

'No, I can't, I took an oath – anyway, they're all dead now.'

Derek knew it was not worth pursuing this line. The man might be old but he wasn't going to reveal names. 'Okay, what about the drink then?'

'It was the staple drink amongst all the troops, alcohol was strictly forbidden when on active duty. The drug selected was, I believe, heroin based, again to promote anger and a lack of fear in the fighting man. It had to be tested at Oakwood for a month before anyone would consider field trials in Vietnam. The method was quite simple really. In those days – might still be the same, for all I know – a cola concentrate was shipped out in drums from the States, then diluted and bottled locally. The drug was put into the concentrate and had an accumulative effect. It worked after a fashion but the trials were abandoned after five or six weeks. The product was only stable at low temperatures and the effect of the drug was lost when the bottles were stored hot for a week or so.'

'Did the drinks company know you were tinkering with their product?'

Schumacher shook his head. 'For goodness sake, of course not! The drug was added at naval warehouses once it was *en route* from their factory to the Far East.'

'And then what?'

'The war drew to a close shortly afterwards – I suppose on the face of it we lost. It's taken a quarter of a century to hold our heads high again, thanks to our success in the Gulf conflict a few years ago.'

'And afterwards,' Derek persisted. 'Were tests still carried out looking at ways of adding these mind-blowing drugs to people's food and drink?'

'Only for a short time, as far as I know. There were some other trials held in South America but then I suppose the scientists moved on to other projects.'

'You suppose – don't you know?'

'No. After the war I was transferred back to Europe,' Schumacher explained. 'The Cold War had started and I spent my remaining years with the service collecting information from contacts in East Germany and Poland.'

'You retired early – why?'

'Health reasons.' There was a long pause. 'You have to remember that when I was in Nam I was a young impressionable person. Perhaps it was bravado, but we all took some of the drugs, we were curious to see how they worked. I've paid the price. I suffered on and off ever since.'

The old remains of a human being were spent. He handed Derek his glass and requested some water. When Derek returned from the kitchen he was already asleep, flopped sideways onto the bed, stick still in his hand. Derek put the glass down onto the table and stared at the relic, his anger starting to mount. They had both worked for the same outfit, but this old bastard had stood by and watched men die as guinea-pigs to satisfy some scientists' curiosity and had done nothing to stop it, he had obeyed his orders no matter how distasteful. Derek refused to admit to himself that he might have done exactly the same. He went outside and tossed the glass over the cliff. The more he stood gazing out to sea, the more angry he became. He returned indoors, gathered up the envelope and stuffed it back into his pocket. Then very coolly and calmly he took the old man's pillow from his bed and pressed it against the old wizened face. Within minutes the heavy laboured breathing had stopped. Derek returned the pillow to its original position and turned to leave by the patio door. Of all things, he'd forgotten the tape recorder. He cursed and stuffed it in with the letter. Perhaps it was morbid curiosity but he stopped by a group of old photographs arranged in a vertical column on the wall leading into the kitchen. He wanted to see what this old and now dead man looked like as a young CIA agent in Vietnam. One showed a group of six men standing in a jungle clearing; all were dressed in combat uniforms but he couldn't make out their ranks or insignias. Schumacher stood out, he was the tallest and was grinning from ear to ear. It was the man standing next to him that caused Derek to expel the word 'shit'. He was short, thin and had a mass of black hair, but one feature stood out more than anything else – a huge hooked nose. There were no two ways about it, standing in Vietnam next to Schumacher was Hutton.

Derek walked quickly back to the car. Andy saw him coming and got out to greet him and to stretch his cramped legs.

'Another half an hour and I was going to come and see if you were all right.'

Derek looked at his watch. He'd been in the house for nearly two hours. 'Sorry, took longer than I thought. Everything okay out here?'

'Yes fine, very quiet in fact. Only been about six or seven cars went past the whole time.'

As Derek drove them back to San Francisco, he explained about the state of the house and the condition of the old man and then asked Andy to listen to the tape. The rest of the journey was spent in silence, as if in respect for all those unfortunate soldier guinea-pigs. Derek parked in the hotel grounds but before Andy could make a move to get out he grabbed his arm.

'Something I must tell you. In the house there's a picture of General Hutton with Schumacher. They were both in Vietnam together. He may have been thirty-five years younger but it was his nose – nobody else has one that big!'

Derek didn't tell his friend he'd suffocated the old man – after all, it wasn't necessary for him to know everything. 'I suggest, that if it's okay with you, we don't tell Larry about any of this,' he said instead.

Andy agreed. 'We're in it up to our necks by choice, whereas Larry was drafted in on a temporary basis. Anyway, it would probably only just worry him and he's got enough on his plate as it is.'

Derek liked his new partner from across the water – they both thought along similar lines. Andy would have also killed Schumacher, he concluded.

Andy found Derek sitting on the small beach next to Fisherman's Wharf the following morning. He was aimlessly throwing pebbles into the water.

'You all right? Couldn't find you in the hotel. How long have you been sitting here?'

'Not long. Just thinking things over. We're all like termites, I suppose.'

Andy looked at him in surprise. 'I beg your pardon, termites?'

'Yes, termites! Years ago when I was married we went on vacation to Australia. I remember on one occasion we drove out into the bush. Must have been a bit careless with some bits of our picnic, I suppose, but these termite things appeared and started to carry away the scraps of food. They'd formed themselves into a column. The bigger termites, the soldiers, stood guard on either side of the line. I disturbed their organised little world with a stick, but within seconds normality had returned and my bits of food were on the way to their larder. I even stamped on the column and broke the black river, but again it rejoined itself as if nothing had happened, they even walked straight over their crushed ex-fellow workers. Some time later I read that termites have the most ordered and structured society of any living creature, every one of them is born to perform a preset function. For years I thought that the soldiers were solely there to protect the workers but they're not. They're also there to keep them in order, to stop them wandering off and doing their own thing – at least until they've learned the error of their ways and become true society members. Perhaps that's the long-term goal of our Government's, to ensure that the masses fall into nice preset categories so that a well-structured and organised world exists. It would certainly make life a hell of a lot easier for the powers that be.'

'An interesting theory, my friend, but it would take thousands of years to get rid of that independent streak in humans.'

Derek did not reply but continued to throw his stones and Andy could hear him humming. He suddenly stood up. 'Enough of this. I reckon old Big Nose is up to his fat, little neck in this latest episode. Wouldn't surprise me if he's still working for Oakwood. I think it's about time we paid him a visit to learn some home truths for a change.'

Andy followed his friend into his hotel room. Derek was in too much of a hurry and his stubby little fingers misdialled the Washington number. He was very short with the innocent party on the other end. He tried again and asked to speak to General Hutton.

'No, I can't leave a message and I haven't got a report to leave. I want to see the General personally. What I have to tell him is by word of mouth only.' There was a pause. 'Thank the Lord, you're getting the hang of it! Yes, I want a face-to-face meeting with your boss.' Another pause and Derek slammed the phone down on its cradle. 'Arrogant bitch! She must think we're the scum of the earth. She's coming back with some instructions within the hour.'

Andy raided the minibar for soft drinks and kept insisting Derek drank some. At least whilst he was drinking he wasn't humming. Exactly one hour later the phone rang. Derek acknowledged the message and relayed it to Andy. 'We're to meet the old bastard tomorrow morning at eleven o'clock, Holiday Inn, Oakland Metropolitan International Airport, Room 1236.'

'Where's that?'

Derek spread out the map of San Francisco and its surrounding area. He pointed. 'Here on the other side of the Bay – on Ben's side.'

'Ironic, isn't it? We chose the west coast so we could be at least three thousand miles away from the guy and yet every time we've met him it seems he's staying over on this side.'

Derek listened to Andy's comment. 'Struck me as well. Perhaps he's following us! Still, we've nothing else to do today, let's go and see something of the city. Have you ever been to Chinatown? No? Good. I"ll show you the best chow mein in town.'

As agreed, they met in the foyer of the hotel at six the following morning. It was Andy's idea to move out, their current address would now be known in Washington.

They sat in the nearest Denny's restaurant and over breakfast worked out their strategy. They would arrive at the Holiday Inn at least an hour early and give the place the once-over. It was always possible that the General had posted some of Albert's brothers or sisters around and about, but they would be fairly easy to recognise. People on watch in hotel reception areas were never at ease like normal tourists; their heads were never still, for a start. After what had happened to Ben, Derek was not going to take any chances, especially not with Hutton, so they would go armed and ready; Derek would concentrate on Hook, Andy on his minder. As Derek had said, 'If the big bugger gets too much for you, shoot him in the kneecap or somewhere similar but not in the head – the bullet won't go in!'

Dead on eleven Derek rang the bell whilst Andy stood several yards down the corridor, ready for any sudden action. The intimidating Albert opened the door slowly. He was dressed in navy trousers and a short-sleeved white shirt. Every size was far too small on him, but perhaps that was deliberate to show off all his extensive steroid work. He directed them to a table and chairs in the middle of the large room. It had always been a mystery to Derek why these people never actually spoke; surely they were capable, with some tuition, of stringing a few words together! Hook was reclining in an easy chair by the window, reading a newspaper. He threw it down and stood up. For once he was sensibly dressed in sports shirt and slacks – in fact, he looked as if he'd come straight off the golf course. His manners hadn't changed though and he was still as blunt as ever.

'I told you before I didn't want to be disturbed unless it was absolutely necessary, so I assume it is and I'm waiting to hear about your breakthrough.'

Derek wasted no time on formalities, 'Oh yes, we've had a breakthrough. How will Oakwood, drugs, Schumacher and Hutton do for starters?'

'What the hell are you talking about, Madden?'

Derek produced his gun from his waistband and pointed it at his adversary. With jerky movements of the barrel he indicated that he wanted Hutton to sit on one of the dining-chairs.

Albert decided to make his move towards his boss but Andy quickly moved round and cut off his path. They were about the same height but Andy was skinny by comparison to this muscle-bound hulk. Albert came forward with outstretched arms. His huge hands reminded Andy of mechanical digger buckets, and were aimed at his throat. Andy stopped suddenly and looked up; the other man did the same, breaking his concentration for a few milliseconds. It was enough. Andy raised his leg and kicked the protector hard in the balls. He dropped like a falling brick chimney onto his knees. A quick rabbit chop to the neck finished him off and he was out like a light.

Andy went over to the wardrobe but it was empty. 'I don't think these people intended staying long,' he shouted across to Derek. He found what he was looking for in a suitcase – two of the General's best silk ties. He dragged Albert into the bathroom and tied his hands together round the toilet pedestal; he would have to bring if off the wall to get free.

'Nicely done, Andy.' Derek was impressed by the ease with which the big man had been reduced to a heap on the floor.

'I don't go around making a habit of it, but these muscle men are all the same – no quick reaction times.'

Derek checked the General to see if he was armed but he was clean. He produced the tape player from his jacket pocket and put it on the table. Hutton kept trying to speak but each time Derek held the muzzle to his lips and the General eventually gave up. Derek made Hutton listen to his interview with Schumacher. On several occasions Hook tried to interrupt but Derek warned him in no uncertain terms, 'You either keep your mouth shut or you'll leave me no alternative but to gag you, understand?' The General decided to keep quiet.

When it was all over, Derek switched the tape off. 'Well, Hutton, you've been stringing us along, haven't you? All this time you've known exactly where the source of this problem lay. You didn't need us to investigate it, we've been used as a smokescreen, haven't we? Why? Did you hope we would do our bit and come up with nothing and then the matter would be dropped? Well, we nearly did, but you made one big mistake. You shouldn't have taken on someone as clever as Ben, should you? He found out all about you and Oakwood with his computer, so you had him killed, you bastard.' Derek started to circle round the table and chairs, his eyes never leaving the General's. The silence was becoming unbearable.

Then the General started to shake his head, totally undaunted by Derek, his gun, his words. 'My God! How do they let brain-dead people like you join the CIA? Don't you ever think before you speak, Madden, or is it too much trouble for you? As usual, you've got everything ass about face and gone off on some totally unrelated tangent. Oakwood has nothing to do with any of this, I can assure you. Sure I worked at Maryland and yes, some unpleasant things went on there, but we were at war, remember? But all that was decades ago. I left in

1976, not that it's any of your business. Don't you think that one of the first organisations we asked was Oakwood? They're as equally mystified by what's going on as we are . . . '

Andy stopped the arrogant monologue in midstream. 'If you're telling the truth and you're not involved then what do you know about Ben's murder? You certainly got to hear about it quickly enough.'

'Correct, I do know more than you as juniors are privy to, but if it makes you come to your senses I'll bend a few rules and tell you. Ben was a young fool. He wasn't professional enough for the job – emotionally, that is. Too much of a conscience. He was obviously extremely good with computers, however, because he managed to do the impossible and gained total unlimited access to the mainframe computer at the CIA headquarters in Langley. This piece of equipment cost the American taxpayer billions and was supposed to be foolproof, so it was a good job he was on our side – otherwise he could have altered or destroyed all of this country's official and highly secret records. I can tell you one or two heads have already rolled over it. He got hold of the records about Oakwood in the fifties and sixties and even took a copy onto his personal machine. He called me in Washington and told me that such information should be made public now, to ensure it never happened again. I had a job understanding him at times as his voice was trembling so much. In the end he said that if the Government hadn't made its mind up in forty-eight hours he would send copies of his disk to the newspaper and television companies. You both know, at least you should, that some things are best left buried. Can you imagine the outcry if this sort of information was made public? The people would never trust the Government or their security agencies ever again. No, the disk had to be recovered.'

'So you sent your friend out to retrieve it even if it meant Ben had to be killed in the process?' Andy asked, pointing towards the bathroom.

'No!' The General's voice was firm and steady. 'I did my duty, no more. I reported my conversation to my superiors and pointed out who had taken the information from the computer. The situation was immediately taken away from me – your lot saw to that, Madden.'

Derek's mind was in turmoil. Ben killed by his own organisation and Hutton not involved in the current plot? It was all going wrong. By now he'd hoped to have had a full confession from the General on the blank tape still in his pocket.

'You swear that you never had any part in Ben's death?' Andy asked as he watched his beaten colleague slump into a chair.

'Absolutely none, and that goes for Albert too.' The General took command once again. 'Now that this little mutiny is over I suggest that you start making a real effort to find out exactly who's behind this beer-poisoning affair. I have to say once again how disappointed I am with you both. You were selected from your past records for being very good at pursuing leads, so it's about time you proved it to me. And don't forget reports, Madden. I must be kept up to date with any news – please drum that into your thick skull. Now, if you'll excuse me, I'm going to see how Albert is.'

Hutton stood up and was half-way to the bathroom when he stopped and turned. 'Leave the tape where it is on the table when you go – and by the way, Lockwood, I'll forget what you did to my chauffeur.'

Derek snapped out of his lethargy. If the General was lying and they left the tape, where would they go from here? 'The tape stays with us as proof of Oakwood's goings on.'

'If the tape is not on the table after you've left then I will have no option but to inform the FBI that two days ago you, Madden, murdered Mr Schumacher – and I'll make sure that you're put away for at least fifteen years with some very unpleasant people. As for you, Lockwood, I'll involve you as an accessory to the crime.'

'I don't know what you're talking about, General,' Andy said in all honesty.

'Then I would suggest you talk to your friend on the way out.'

The tape stayed on the table and Derek nodded to Andy that they should leave. They walked down the stairs and left the hotel in silence. The fresh air felt good in Andy's lungs. 'What was all that about murder? I think it's your turn for some explanations,' Andy began.

'I don't really know,' Derek lied, making sure Andy couldn't see his face. 'I told you Schumacher was old and frail – the interview must have been too much for him, he must have keeled over and died.' He shrugged his shoulders and got into the car but was annoyed with himself on two counts, firstly he'd lost his bargaining tool – the tape – and secondly Hutton already knew Schumacher was dead. Perhaps Andy was right, perhaps their movements were being monitored.

8

As they drove south down Interstate 880 on the east side of the Bay, Derek asked, 'What did you make of all that? Is the General telling the truth or not?'

'It may sound strange, but I believe him. He desperately wants to get to the bottom of this thing. From his answers, I don't think he knows more than we do. I get the impression somebody higher up is putting pressure on him for results. Mind you, I wouldn't trust that bastard as far as I could throw him!' Andy added.

'As soon as we find a hotel, I'll phone around a few colleagues and see what's been going down lately. Something like Ben's scandal – if it's true – will have been whispered down all the corridors by now. While I'm doing that, can you phone Larry and see how he's getting on? It's a bloody shame if our fat friend Hook is not involved – I was looking forward to seeing him nailed to the door.'

They found an out-of-the-way motel on the outskirts of San José. By the time they met for dinner Derek had made seven phone calls, whilst Andy had made just the one but had used the swimming-pool several times. The weather was warming up nicely, Andy thought – he could soon get used to this climate, especially if he could wear shorts and teeshirt all the time. Even Derek seemed to be making an effort; the shirt he wore had short sleeves.

Derek was anxious to divulge his news, 'Good old Ben, he's caused absolute pandemonium back at headquarters. Any and everybody connected with the computer section has been as good as castrated. Memos stating that this would happen have been appearing out of the woodwork most with the ink still not dry even though they're dated years ago! Twenty per cent of the personnel have been downgraded. Everybody's trying to blame the next man. Good! It was about time the complacent buggers had a shake-up – I should know, I was one of them for nearly fifteen years. Some bad news though. The General was right, the incident was handed over to Department Eight. Poor old Ben didn't stand a chance with that lot, they're hooligans and misfits the lot of them, except that they work on the so-called side of law and order. Your turn. How's Larry?'

'Sounds fine.' Andy replied. 'Says he's nearing the end of his work and would like to see us in about two days' time. I suggested he came up here – at least Hook won't be able to listen in if Larry's office is bugged. I don't know about you, Derek, but the more we try and stay one step ahead the better I'll feel.'

'Couldn't agree more, and it's a good idea to bring Larry out of his lab for a change. I bet you he hasn't been home all week.'

The General would have been annoyed if he'd known that his two field men did precisely nothing for the next two days. Andy was quite happy to go and visit one of the Purflo plants but Derek would hear nothing of the sort. Andy reached the conclusion that Derek's brain only worked on one thing at at time and anything that either changed the routine or the order of events was a bad idea and dismissed abruptly. They spoke to Simon, mainly to see how he was and to tell him that the Schumacher business was totally unrelated to anything connected with Ben's death. He sounded a lot better in himself and was still prepared to help them to bring Ben's killer to justice – that was the bit Derek wanted to hear.

Derek waited in the car while Andy met Larry in the airport concourse. He was smartly dressed in a good-quality light blue suit, white shirt and his trademark red bow-tie. He was carrying a small overnight bag and looked different, since they had last seen him nearly two weeks ago. He had lost weight, his eyes were red and very tired-looking, he had several blemishes on his chin and his hair desperately needed a cut, but his enthusiasm was still the same.

'Nice to see you again, Andy. Where's Derek? Please tell me how did Ben's funeral go?' Andy took the bag from him and answered his questions as he led him to the car, hoping the good doctor was not back on the bottle. Andy could tell from Derek's stare that he had the same thought.

Derek drove south from San Francisco for the next hour and a half. He had taken Andy's suggestion to keep on the move to heart and booked them three rooms at one of the older hotels at Pacific Grove, using one of his many pseudonyms so nobody would know where they were headed. The view from all the rooms was magnificent – Monterey Bay in all its colours and glory. The fresh-smelling sea air with just a hint of ozone and the warm ocean breeze encouraged a more relaxed way of life. Although only early evening, Derek suggested Larry have an early night and a good sleep, as soon as they'd finished dinner.

Once he'd retired Derek confided to his friend, 'He's no good to us if he drops dead from exhaustion! Look at the man, he's absolutely worn out through hard work and lack of sleep. That's why I thought coming to somewhere like this would give him a chance to recharge his batteries.'

Andy felt a pang of guilt. The Doc was dead on his feet through hard work while he'd done sod all for days now.

The tonic was working. Larry looked more like his normal self when he came down for breakfast. 'I love the Jacuzzi in the bathroom, it's so relaxing I could wallow in it for days! Tell me when you're ready to start and I'll explain what I've been up to and what I've found out.'

'No rush, Larry,' Derek replied. 'We'll find somewhere nice and quiet in the hotel grounds. Did you manage to get any help from your university friend?'

'Yes, Professor Wakeman's been really helpful, but I have to admit some of this is even pushing his knowledge to the limit.'

They found a vacant table and chairs at one end of the garden, where several large trees would keep the sun off them as the day progressed. Derek ordered coffee and tipped the waiter thirty dollars to ensure they had peace and quiet for a couple of hours. To start with Larry just sat and looked at them both.

'Are you all right?' Andy asked with some concern.

'Yes, I'm sorry, it's just that I don't know where to start. I don't mean to be rude but a lot of what I have to say is technical and I'm just trying to work out the best way to describe it to both of you. Please bear in mind that what I'm going to tell you has all been running concurrently over the past eight days, and I'm going to split it up into sections to make the explanations easier. But first to recap a bit. Ben discovered the key to the whole thing, that the protein present in the Purflo was only soluble in acid and that all beers are very acidic. I carried out some preliminary tests to start with and decided to add Purflo to just acidic water as I felt it would give more consistent results. After all, I didn't know how the beers varied from make to make. Remember that the beer itself is just the carrier, the vehicle chosen by whoever's behind this to get humans to ingest the protein. But there was not the slightest signs of anything untoward happening to the mice. Then I learnt something from talking it over with Bill Wakeman – the alcohol and the acid state are both vital. Later on when I talk about the protein this will become much clearer. Ben, of course, went way over the top on his dosage levels. What I have tried to do is keep it consistent with what happens in breweries. From all the information we've got they use between 100 and 200 grams of powder per hectolitre filtered, so I've taken the average figure. We also know that there's 0.3 per cent by weight of the protein in the powder. This means that there's approximately 50 milligrams transferred to every litre of filtered beer, and our human results showed that the effects became quite apparent when about two litres of beer had been drunk. Therefore in all the tests we carried out from now, on these figures, were adhered to. For the next series of tests I used a standard five per cent acidic ethanol solution – this is the alcohol in beer and the one responsible for getting you drunk! I made up quite a large stock solution so that there would be no more worries about anomalies coming from different beers now. We, that is my two assistants and I, went through all the powder samples again. All very controlled stuff this time, proper weighed amounts mixed into set volumes of my stock solution. Once the powder had settled we analysed all the clear solutions on the machine I showed you in the lab, Andy. The peaks produced this time were in a different place to the original ones produced from the protein removed from the powder, and I must confess I couldn't interpret what they were at all. I showed them to Bill and he came to the rescue once again. He knew straight away that they were things called amino acids but even he didn't know exactly which ones.'

'Sorry to butt in, Larry, but you keep mentioning these things in the plural. Does this protein break down into more than one of these amino things then?' Andy asked.

'They can do, but the main point here is that there are two distinct and separate peaks, which means that we are dealing with two different proteins and each one is producing a different type, or maybe types, of amino acid. Bill has some very sophisticated equipment at his disposal so he's going to try and identify them from their original proteins. I've given him some of the Purflo samples so he can extract his own. I hope that's all right?'

Derek nodded and added, 'Of course.'

'As the results were catalogued we divided the Purflo samples up into their two respective groups and that's where the problem lies. In each separate pile we have samples with the same code number. For instance, we've got two different samples of P5, both collected by you, Derek, from two American breweries and both have different proteins present.'

'What about the samples I sent back from Europe?' Andy asked.

'All the ones from England contain the same protein,

but the ones you collected from Brussels are . . . ' Larry dived into his notes piled on the table. 'Ah yes, here we are, four have a different protein to the English ones and two have the same. In fact, it's a similar picture with all the American samples. There's no definite pattern.'

Andy asked for a break as he needed to visit the gents. Derek stood up and stretched his legs and walked away from the table. He had a lot of new information to absorb, but the main thing was it didn't matter a damn what these things were called – they now knew that there were two of the buggers.

'Having established that there were two products' Larry resumed, 'we then set about examining the behaviour of mice injected with solutions of both. We had hardly started the work when we had a stroke of luck. One of my colleagues from the lab opposite had a mishap. He was about to start some behavioural test on monkeys to see how a new drug affected them but the drug hadn't arrived, so he was delighted to offload them onto me. These primates are much like ourselves and have individual characters to match. I was quite excited at the prospect of watching them, their reactions would be far more realistic than mice's.'

'We used the two different Purflo P5 grades mixed separately in our stock solution. For the purpose of the trials we had to identify them so we simply called one X, the other Y. Two of the monkeys were injected with X, two with Y. With time the two who had X became very restless and one in particular kept pulling at the bars on his cage. The other found a small knot-hole in the wooden base and kept picking at it and got quite annoyed when he realised it was not getting any bigger. Of course, none of them could see what the others were doing. The two who had been given Y went the other way. One just held onto the bars and stared out of its cage with a very blank expression, the other spent most of its time in a corner nodding off. I gave the four of them a day to recover and then reversed their injections, and their behaviour changed around completely. The very quiet one nearly drove me mad this time, he just wouldn't stop making an ear-splitting shriek – one day if you're both interested I'll show you the videos we took. Now we were totally convinced about the effects of these products on their behaviour. I must tell you about one particular fellow. After the first day I'd obviously had a chance to study all the remaining creatures in their normal state. One was a real exhibitionist. We put him on X to start with and what a furore he caused! He managed to knock his cage onto the floor by jumping from side to side. After the initial tests we decided to make things a bit more complicated by pairing two together in the same cage. The couple on Y were no problem and spent most of their time huddled together in a corner asleep. Their cousins on X however were a real handful. At first they just started playing together, all harmless stuff, then one started to pull their water-bottle off its fastening but the other one wanted it. A squabble broke out and they started to hiss and go for each other. I had to separate them to stop them injuring each other. But what a difference when they were put on Y – as quiet as lambs! There's one other test we did which I must tell you about. It was not that scientific, I suppose, because we'd jumped several stages – but time wasn't on our side. So far I'd discussed all the results with one of my technicians and he mentioned that to date we'd only given the monkeys the equivalent intake of drinking two litres of beer – he had a lot of friends who drank far more! So we decided to up the rate, in fact double it, and give one monkey X another Y and put them in the same cage. X started picking on Y, who put up no resistance at all even when X started jumping up and down on its head! Again we had to separate them very quickly. I got this as a result.'

Larry held up his hand. There was a nasty red bite-mark near his wrist. It was a good point to break, and Derek suggested that they go back inside the hotel for lunch.

After the meal Larry excused himself, saying he needed to return to his room to make a telephone call. He was gone for a good hour and was full of apologies when he rejoined his friends outside. They didn't ask who he'd called or why; presumably if the phone call concerned the project he would tell them in his own good time.

Andy asked the first question. 'All your trials have been on Purflo. When we last met you were still analysing various other products. Any news on them?'

'Yes, Purflo is the only product that contains these proteins – in fact, only in the bottom half of their range, the fine grades; there is absolutely no organic matter present in their coarser products.'

They all sat for a while letting their digestive systems get to work on the meal. The temperature had climbed steadily all morning and Larry had followed Andy's example and changed into shorts and deck shoes. Derek had made some sort of effort – his jacket was nowhere to be seen. A large cold beer would have gone down a treat but Andy dismissed the temptation from his mind for obvious reasons, as well as to keep a clear head to absorb Larry's next chunk of information. There was obviously a lot more to come, from the reams of paper he was sifting through.

'I'd like to give you a little insight into how proteins and amino acids work on the body if that's okay. It should help you understand what's happening a bit more.'

His small audience nodded together.

'The brain is the key item. It may only account for 2 per cent of our body weight but it uses up over 20 per cent of the total energy consumption of the body's requirements. It's not able to store very much itself so it needs a constant supply of its own food, and one of its main requirements is protein. As you know, the brain controls everything and every minute of the day and night it's thinking, deciding, planning and judging things. It never switches itself off even when the rest of the body is asleep. It is always ready to control our moods and our physical actions, and decide what reaction to take to anything thrown at us. However, if this status quo is disturbed or if the balance of certain chemicals is upset then all our functions can suffer as well as our behaviour and mental health. All these decisions happen in a part of the brain called the limbic system, located right at the core of the brain and associated with the cerebral cortex – the thinking part, or what we commonly refer to as the nervous system. This area receives all the various messages and instructions from all over the body and makes sure they're actioned. The nearest analogy I can think of is to imagine a telephone system. Suppose you dial a number from New York wishing to get through to me in Los Angeles. An electrical impulse speeds along the wire to an exchange containing millions of different numbers. The exchange sorts out the right connection and sends the impulse down to the right receiver. It's the same with the brain. Inside the nervous system are literally billions of units called neurons, which are designed to communicate with one another constantly just like the telephones. They receive and transmit messages through little filaments linking them all together – the telephone wires. The messages pass along the "wires" either by chemical or electrical impulses called the neurotransmitters. But what happens if you change the receiving telephone number? Of course the messages can't get through any more, and it's the same with the brain – alter the neurotransmitter and you have the same problem.

'Now for the crunch. These transmitters are all derived from proteins and are, as I think you might have guessed, called amino acids or, when they're in groups, polypeptides. Add different amino acids and you alter the message. It may not get through to where it's supposed to go and it ends up as a wrong number delivering its message to the wrong place. With a wrong telephone number the outcome is fairly harmless, but not with the brain. It will act on the "foreign" message and as a result a person's behaviour may be altered.

'Whoever's behind all of this certainly knows his subject. When you ingest proteins, or amino acids in this case, they are absorbed into the bloodstream and before they can get into the brain they have to cross something called the blood–brain barrier. This is one of the brain's lines of defence and has been specifically designed to block the entry of any harmful or unwanted chemicals. However, it is known that some products can pierce this shield by just floating through the molecules of fat that it's made of – some of the well-known ones are nicotine, cocaine and alcohol. We think that our nasty little amino acids are getting into the brain by riding on the back of the alcohol in the beer.' Larry stopped, his mouth dry after all the talking.

'So that's why you didn't get any results with just your acidic solution? You needed the alcohol to carry these things into the brain,' Andy remarked.

Larry let out a huge but unintentional sigh of relief. They, or at least Andy, had been listening to his story. He had tried to keep the scientific detail to a minimum and was grateful his friend Bill had suggested the telephone angle. 'Well done, that's exactly right. By the way, the phone call I made was to Bill Wakeman. He has identified one of the amino acids and hopes to finish his research on the other one by tonight. Do you want me to continue or wait until the rest of the information is in?'

Derek had had enough chemistry lessons for one day so he suggested they wait, he had no questions to ask and said Larry had more than adequately covered any earlier queries. Whether this was true or not only he knew.

'Just one more thing,' Larry asked. 'I know you have to send a report in to Hutton so I've written out a *précis* of the work so far. I've taken the liberty of excluding Bill from the work. I didn't see any point in involving him.' Larry handed the three typed pages across. Derek let out his own sigh of relief. Now he wouldn't have to spend half the night trying to unravel his illegible and almost non-existent notes.

The following morning the weather had changed. A thick Pacific sea mist covered the hotel with a white shroud. By midday the sun would have burnt it off but this would be too late for Derek's meeting in their quiet garden location. He started it three times in the lounge and three times he moved them to different corners, convinced that other guests were eavesdropping on their conversation. They eventually settled down in a remote corner of the conservatory, Derek relaxed again and asked Larry to continue.

'Bill phoned through the information regarding the composition of our amino acids late last night. The first one, X, is an excitatory type – to put it in a nutshell, it rings up all the telephones it can and triggers off a reaction that makes the body feel aggressive. It's a very complicated derivative of something called phenylalanine. This substance then makes tyrosine, which in turn is converted to the amino acids dopamine and adrenaline. You'll have heard of the latter, of course. It's present in the body and controls a person's survival instinct. Yes, Andy?'

'You mentioned yesterday that there was only 50 milligrams of this stuff present in your tests. As I understand it, a milli's a thousandth of something, isn't it? How can such a small amount of this amino product produce such a dramatic effect on the body?'

Larry smiled. Some of yesterday's complicated facts and figures had been thought about overnight. Andy was a good student. 'Remember I said that these compounds had to pass through the blood–brain barrier?' Andy nodded. 'They're in direct competition with lots of other things, of course. How can I put it? It's like seats on a bus. There are only so many places on the transport – in this case the fat molecules. Once these places are taken no more can hop across into the brain. There are many types of amino compounds. Some are neutral, others alkaline, but ours are acidic. They are the bully-boys, they jump the queue at the bus-stop and get a ride across. Once inside the brain this tyrosine sends out its own message asking for more of itself to be made, so the problem spirals out of control. The more of X you drink in the greater this effect becomes.'

'Is this a permanent effect? I mean, does this tyrosine stay there?'

'No, not this one. After a while it is broken down and the brain returns to its previous non-agitated state. I'm afraid that this is not the case with the other one, Y. This one is an inhibitory amino acid which produces something similar to a beta amyloid but Bill is not sure of its exact make-up. It kills off nerve cells and as a result cuts down on the level of serotonin.' Larry spelt it out for them. 'A low level of this neurotransmitter leads to depression, lethargy and a general feeling of being tired all the time. Every time this one makes its phone calls it permanently destroys the wires.'

'So eventually too much of this one would zap your brain to nothing?'

'Only after many years, Derek. There are billions of wires and phones, as I've said, so the process would be a very gradual thing.'

They broke off whilst a waiter brought them some morning coffee. It was Andy who took up the conversation again. 'I'm still having trouble coming to terms with the fact that 50 milligrams can do so much damage. It can't be any bigger than a pinhead?'

'I understand your dilemma. People like me are quite used to working with such small amounts and appreciating the effects they can have. Let me tell you how effective some drugs can be. You've both heard of Valium? It used to be prescribed as a sleeping-pill. Millions of people took it – some in very high dosages. It contained a drug called nitrazepam, and like our two products worked on the brain in exactly the same way. This one sent out messages demanding a tranquillising effect on the body. People were and still are addicted to this product, having taken only 30 milligrams a day – so you see you don't need much to become hooked on it.'

'Do drugs, the hard type as I know them, work on the brain in a similar way?' Andy asked.

'Yes, exactly the same. Take cocaine for instance. Earlier on I mentioned the neurotransmitter dopamine. When cocaine or one of its derivatives is present this dopamine level is disturbed and instead of making just one phone call it keeps the line permanently open with the message continually going both ways. Now multiply this by the tens of thousands of lines involved. The result is a massive shot of adrenaline production and an instant but short-lived high for about twenty minutes. Then comes the downside and Catch 22 enters the equation. The dopamine levels drop because the cocaine blocks the mechanism that recycles this neurotransmitter for future use. The only thing to do is to take more cocaine – and now you're hooked, it's taken you over. The cocaine provides the dopamine all right, but because the brain wasn't meant to receive such high levels the amount going back and forward down the wires tends to drive you insane. When the next lot of cocaine wears off the dopamine levels drop even lower. The brain just cannot replace them any more. In time there is so little of this neurotransmitter on reserve that the continued use of drugs doesn't even produce any more pleasure – there is no one left around to make the telephone calls. The chemical inbalance makes you go into a deep depression and then it's downhill all the way to the end. Sorry about that, got a bit carried away – after all, this is my pet subject. I must emphasise that our protein problem is in no way as serious as the hard-drug problem.'

Larry realised what he'd said and corrected himself. 'Well, not in terms of damage to the brain, but the consequences are more horrific. After all, what a cocaine addict does is self-inflicted, whereas X and Y are being consumed by an unsuspecting public worldwide.'

'What would happen to a drug addict taking X and Y?' The question came from Derek and made Larry sit back in his chair with his arms folded behind his head. It was several minutes before he spoke.

'I have no practical information to hand and I would hazard a guess that total confusion would exist in the brain and that the person concerned would not be responsible for any of their actions. I can also do some laboratory trials to—'

Larry didn't get a chance to finish his sentence. Derek had held up both hands. 'No, Larry, give the monkeys a break this time.'

Several more questions were raised. Some Larry had answers for, most he didn't. He didn't even know where these new products came from. Were they naturally obtained from plants or were they synthetically manufactured? If so, by whom? What sort of chemical company would produce things like this? He would have to ask around; discreetly, of course.

They moved into the dining-room and helped themselves to a carvery lunch. Two businessmen on an adjoining table were drinking glasses of cold beer. Derek found himself staring at the light amber liquid. He had no idea he was doing it until one of the owners made some remark about there being plenty more behind the bar and why didn't he buy his own goddam glass instead of coveting his. If only the man knew what was going on in Derek's head!

Derek drove them all back to San Francisco and Larry asked to be dropped off at the corner of Fulton and Baker, saying he was going to visit his brother-in-law. Derek's paranoia rose to the surface again. He insisted Larry leave all his notes with him – he would make sure they were sent back to his laboratory by registered mail. He explained that they were too valuable to carry about on the streets and reminded both of them what had happened to Ben. Larry handed his file across without the slightest argument and they all said their farewells.

After they had booked themselves into a central hotel, Derek summoned his colleague to his bedroom. Spread out on the only table was a detailed map of the western United States.

'Time for our next operation. I would like you to start crawling all over Union Mining and Minerals' production sites.' He pointed to two locations circled in black ink. 'Sod the General and sod the expense. Get what you need, and for Christ's sakes be careful – they could be guarded like Fort Knox.' He folded the map and shoved it into Andy's hand. 'You've still got the pistol? Good.'

'And what will you be doing in the meantime?' Andy enquired.

'As you know, we originally planned to do a site each, but I've come to the conclusion I'd be better off in "the office". We've got to start figuring out who's behind all of this and where fucking X and Y are coming from. But promise me one thing if you need help then shout. I'll drop everything and be there with the goddam cavalry if necessary.' Derek wrote a telephone number down on the map cover. 'Day or night, ring me with anything relevant. Oh, by the way, there's a three-hour time difference with California so just keep ringing until I answer. I have to sleep sometime!'

9

Andy had studied the map for less than a minute when he made his mind up how he was going to tackle this latest assignment.

One of the plants was in Oregon near a place called Melford; the other was on the California – Nevada border south of San Francisco, north of the Panamint Mountains but south of the Yosemite National Park, at a place called Bullen. This was the nearer plant so he would start there. Derek had described the sort of terrain he would encounter, repeating his dislike of the wide open spaces – 'Give me skyscrapers anytime.' According to the map there were no major airports anywhere near Bullen, so Andy decided it would probably be quicker to drive the four hundred or so miles. But not in a hire-car, this time. No, this time he was going to blend in as a tourist. He checked through the Yellow Pages and found a suitable company.

The size of the car lot amazed him – there were literally hundreds of units up for sale. One sign swinging in the breeze read RECREATIONAL VEHICLES. Andy walked up and down the rows of campers several times, unsure of what he was looking for, so vast was the range. He had to make a decision soon otherwise the day would be wasted, so he decided on one at random. It looked reliable, was definitely used and would blend in nicely. He called across to one of the salesmen and was given the standard used-car man's patronising spiel. 'A very good choice, sir. It's one of our better models on display, and as you can see has been very carefully looked after by only two owners from new. If you care to step inside you will see it's fully loaded and a real bargain at only $7,435.'

Andy did as instructed and indeed was impressed with the interior. It had two swivel chairs in the driving-area, whilst blackened side windows would keep prying eyes from seeing two bunk-beds either side of a narrow corridor. At the back was a small wash sink, a fridge and a single-ring mini-cooker. Various cupboards were attached to the sides of the van above the bunks. Both the walls and floors were carpeted. The salesman also pointed out that the four and a half litre engine block had only done 58,000 miles and as such was just about run in. The laugh that followed was so false Andy cringed. He stepped outside, checked the tyres and handed over his gold Visa card. It was snatched out of his hand. Perhaps the norm was to haggle but he couldn't be bothered, not with a man who insisted on breaking up every word into its correct number of syllables when he spoke. Andy had already unpacked his belongings into the various cupboards and changed into shorts by the time the cowboy hat appeared around the door with his receipt and card.

The first stop was the nearest gas station, for fuel and for some soft drinks to stock the fridge with. He pencilled in his intended route. He would drive due east, cross through Yosemite Park and over the Sierra Nevadas, then drive south down Highway 395. With any luck he should be in or around Bullen by nightfall.

After about an hour he'd fully mastered the different driving technique necessary with the biggest vehicle he'd ever handled. The van was running well but nobody could just drive through such scenery without stopping to admire the views; just the scale of it all took his breath away. He laughed out loud. He was wrong, there was one person who could sleep through it all – Derek Madden.

The temperature started to drop dramatically the higher he climbed, so he stopped, put on a thick sweater and stood outside. The spring air was cold but clean and refreshing on the lungs. The RV had climbed nearly fourteen thousand feet without missing a beat.

He was pleased with his purchase – or rather the British Government's. Anyway, he would sell it back once the exercise was complete and in the end it would probably work out cheaper than hiring. He was also saving them hotel expenses – but what the hell, he really couldn't care less what they thought.

Andy pinched his nose, blew his mouth up with air and his ears popped. He was leaving the mountains behind now and the countryside was starting to flatten out. The temperature began to climb and climb and climb. On came the air-conditioning, off came the sweater. The views were still staggering but were the complete opposite to the tree-lined mountains and fast-running streams he'd been used to for the last few hours; now everything was desert and he could see for maybe twenty or thirty miles across great plains. He stopped the van at a junction in the road called Two Pines and jumped out to check a signpost. It was like stepping into an oven and he had trouble breathing. He jumped back into the van, slammed the door shut to ward off the heat and consumed two cans of soft drinks one after the other. Already his clothes were starting to stick to him. The sign was useless, he couldn't find any of the three local names on his large-scale map. He decided to follow his own sense of direction and turn off the highway anyway.

After two hours his patience was wearing thin. He was hot, the roads were little more than dirt-tracks and he'd twice passed the only signpost declaring that the Death Valley National Monument was only forty miles away. He wasn't even sure if he was still in California or had crossed the stateline into Nevada. He carried on, taking a different track this time, and after half an hour crossed a railway line. He stopped just off it and looked down the shiny rails which shimmered in each direction as far as he could see. The tracks looked as if they were in permanent use – and then the thought struck him.

'I bet they ship the Purflo out by rail,' he said aloud. 'It would take too long on these roads. Bullen must be that way to the right, I've covered every bloody inch the other way.' He drove alongside the track for about ten miles until it crossed over a metalled road, which he turned on to, cursing. Somewhere he'd totally misjudged the road off the main highway and had wasted a good three hours. A few miles further down the road was a sign. He slowed down to read it properly: BULLEN TOWN, STATE OF CALIFORNIA, POPULATION 1,098.

The road he was on ran straight through the middle of the town, with now and again some smaller dirt-tracks leading off it. Bullen centre consisted of a few shops, a large farm-equipment store and a long single-storey motel building. Several bars were open, with clusters of four-wheel drive vehicles parked outside. He wondered how much it had changed over the last century. Get rid of the cars and put horses in their place and you could be back in the old pioneering West. He wondered why some of the settlers had decided to stay here and not carry on to the fertile, cooler coast. He drove on and realised that the road was offset to the main part of the town. To the right lay the majority of houses, scattered on a small rolling hill. All had front porches and there was a certain age about them. Within minutes the town was behind him and he was surprised to find field after field of crops growing. He couldn't identify what the green crop was but it looked healthy enough. He shook his head in amazement; he just couldn't believe anything could grow out here, let alone anyone wanting to plant it in the first place.

He nearly overshot the sign, looking at the crop. The paint has suffered under the sun and several large blisters had fallen off, making the words illegible. Even so, it was what he had come to see – the Union Mining and Minerals plant was somewhere off to his right. He drove on and parked in the first available dirt-track off the main road. It would be several hours before it was dark. He would put his head down for a while.

It was well after midnight when he woke up and much later than planned. He blamed the heat and opened the driver's door, bracing himself for the sudden inrush of hot air. When you least expect it the opposite happens – it was cold. He looked up at the heavens. Bright stars twinkled back from every direction and he remembered his school geography – all deserts have cold nights because there's no cloud cover to keep the heat in. He liked this temperature better and inhaled several large lungfuls of the night air. He reversed back onto the main road, headed towards the town, turned left just after the flaking sign and drove slowly down the concrete road. It started to climb, gradually at first and then quite steeply up a small rise. At the top he did an emergency stop and turned the lights off. There in the next small valley was the Bullen plant. It was about a mile away and totally bathed in light. He jumped out of the van and surveyed his immediate area. He decided he would park the camper somewhere off the road and go the rest of the way on foot. He bent down and grabbed a handful of earth; even in the semi-darkness it showed up white. He looked at the plant. It was white just as it looked on the Purflo brochure. He would blend in better with what he already had on, white shorts and sweat-shirt.

Over the ridge he crossed a railway line. There wouldn't be two out here, he thought, this had to be the one that had guided him into Bullen in the first place. It went straight into the works. About three hundred yards ahead the road forked. The left section disappeared into the night whilst its counterpart curved round and ran parallel to the rails. He walked quickly along the side of the tracks. As he got nearer and his eyes adjusted to both the dark of the night and the glare of the floodlights, he made out a car park with about twenty to twenty-five vehicles in it. Behind the lot was a long low whitewashed building with several lights glowing from office windows. The roof was made from corrugated material and several solar panels were scattered along its entire length. He could also hear the distinctive noise of heavy machinery groaning away somewhere beyond the offices. The only signs of life he could see were two men operating fork-lift trucks. Every so often they would disappear behind the white building and return with a pallet of bags each and load them into a rail car. As far as he could see, the whole site was open-plan and there were no obvious security fences nor any security guards; it was all very peaceful and laid back. Andy moved into the car park and remained hidden behind a company sign and watched and waited. After an hour nothing in front of him had changed but he was beginning to feel the cold. It was time to formulate some other strategy. He moved around the sign, stopped and almost burst out laughing. Large black letters spelt out UNION MINING AND MINERALS INC, BULLEN PLANT but hooked onto it was a smaller notice *Vacancies – Casual Workers Wanted. Apply Reception.* Andy walked quickly back to his camper with a smile on his face and muttered to himself as he crossed the track, 'Better get a good night's sleep if I'm going to work for a living!'

He was up at six and could feel the outside temperature coming up fast. He couldn't remember when he'd last seen sky as blue. He finished off the last of his bread rolls with some pâté. Then he pulled on his one and only pair of jeans, not the coolest of clothes to wear but the most suitable. He walked around the outside of his dusty van, which had almost changed colour. The dark blue paintwork now looked powder blue; it all blended in with the image of a passing traveller very well. Andy had to admit that Derek had been right in his description of the area – hot and hellish, or words to that effect.

The reception opened at eight o'clock. A sign in the window said so. He sat in the van and waited. Several workers arrived, all with a distinct lean Indian look about them. He patted his belly. It was still hard from the bit of jogging and swimming he'd done the last few weeks. He just hoped to God that he hadn't gone too soft or, worse, looked soft and would be refused work. A middle-aged woman arrived just the wrong side of eight and unlocked the reception door. He followed her into what looked like the general office. She probably did everything from rail shipments to making the coffee, he thought. The first thing she did was switch on two large fans.

'All those lazy buggers in the big cities with their air-conditioning, money's no object for them, yet all we get is these. What do you want?'

'I'd like to apply for one of the vacancies.'

'Wait here.' With that she shuffled away towards a door at the far end of the office and was already pulling her dress away from her sweaty overweight body. She returned about five minutes later, accompanied by a short young-looking man who was dressed in light brown shirt and trousers, both of them too big. Across the breast pocket were the letters UMAM. To accompany the outfit the man wore orange boots, a matching baseball cap and sun-glasses. The receptionist left them to it.

'I understand you're looking for work?' The surprise on Andy's face was evident. The voice that had just spoken was female. Andy re-examined her quickly from head to foot but it was very difficult to tell.

'It's hot, heavy and dusty work,' she continued. 'Mind you, you look as if you're fit enough.' It was her turn to look Andy up and down. 'Hourly paid. The company will provide you with protective clothing.' She tugged at her shirt. 'And free soft drinks.' Her examination had reached Andy's feet. 'You'll need some protective footwear, got any?'

Andy shook his head. 'No problem, I'll get some from that hardware place in town.'

'You're Australian, aren't you? What you doing in these parts then? You'd better get some sunblock and shades as well whilst you're in town.' She was looking at his arms – pale in comparison to her dark brown tan.

Andy didn't deny his new origins. 'Yes, I'm on a working holiday across America. Thought it the best way to see everything without it costing a fortune.'

'What do you do back home then?'

'Fireman.' It was the first thing that came into his head. 'Well, I was. Had to take early retirement. Got too much smoke. Get a medium-sized pension from the Adelaide City Corporation. That's why I've got time to do these sorts of things now.' It would also explain his very slight breathing difficulty in this zero humidity climate. 'You always got vacancies then?'

'Not in the winter months but we're coming up to our busy season about now and need all the stock we can make. The trouble is it's also the busy season in Las Vegas and casual work there pays much better rates than we can, especially if you add on the gratuities. A lot of casuals drift across the border about now. Shouldn't tell you this, should I? You'll be off after them. By the way, I'll need your green card – no card, no pay! You know the rules by now, I expect?'

Andy had planned and schemed for most eventualities but not actually working at the plant. 'My old employer still has it,' he lied. 'I promise you'll get it in the next couple of days if that's all right.'

'It's your money on the line. By the way, I'm the process manager around here, responsible for the day-to-day running of the place. I'm the one with the big whip! Name's Maureen Bradley.' Andy stared at her. 'What did you expect, Billy Jo or something?' She turned and walked away. 'Be back here in an hour,' she shouted back. The shirt and trousers were still too big from the back to give any idea of the body underneath. What he could see of her face didn't do much for him either. She certainly didn't strike him as attractive, the jaw was too thickset, for a start. Andy guessed she would be in her late twenties.

The first stop in town was at a telephone kiosk. Derek answered immediately. There was no problem, a green card was as good as posted, made out for some Australian with wanderlust – he might even throw the passport in with it for good measure!

She was waiting for him when he got back. He had to fill in and sign some forms. She threw him a bundle of clothes. 'What the well-dressed Union employee is wearing these days. Follow me.'

She led the way to a locker-room. 'Don't leave anything valuable in it, the company can't be held responsible.' She hovered by the door whilst Andy changed. The shirt fitted quite well but the trousers were far too short.

'Sorry about them,' she said, pointing to the half-mast legs. 'We weren't expecting someone as tall as you. Still, it shows your posh new boots off!'

They walked to a long shed. Above the opened

double doors was the letter 'A'. She shouted at him to watch out for stacker trucks. Inside, it was even hotter. They walked the full length of the building, which was stacked floor to ceiling with pallets. All contained white bags bearing the Purflo trademark.

'What do you make here?' Andy enquired.

'Filteraids,' came the reply,

'Filteraids? What are they?' Andy asked innocently.

'Used to clarify water – anything else, for that matter. Make a hell of a lot for treating swimming-pools. As I said, the season's just about to start – that's why we're busy. That's why we want your help, sir!'

At the end of the building and running across the full width was an automatic bagging machine with one man operating it.

'Juan, can you teach this new man the ropes?' She looked at her watch. 'It's all eight-hour shift work here: six to two, two to ten, etc. Most of the guys do a back-to-back. There's very little else to do around here and they all want the cash. You should have mastered this little lot by two o'clock. Can't afford to have two of you here after that so I'll move Juan on to other duties. I'm assuming you'll be staying after two o'clock?' The last sentence was said sarcastically.

'Yes, need the loot as well, Blue,' Andy replied living up to his new-found nationality.

Juan showed him the machine. Things were demonstrated rather than spoken about. A twelve-inch pipe came through the wall and fed powder into an enclosed hopper. Underneath it a machine with suckers took an empty bag, forced one of its corners into a filling nozzle and seconds later the bag was full. A hydraulic arm then pushed the bag onto a conveyor belt and the process was repeated. Andy had somehow imagined all bags were filled through an open top and then stitched or glued shut – he had already learnt one thing new. He picked up a bag from a pile on the floor and examined it. The empty bag was already sealed. Then he saw the valve in the corner. It worked like a mouth opening and closing.

The filled bags then passed through a series of ever-decreasing rollers; they went in looking like rugger balls but all came out the same flattened shape. Labels bearing the grade and batch number were added by a much smaller piece of equipment and then bags were automatically stacked onto a pallet and shrink-wrapped. Somebody else was on hand with a stacker truck to take the finished pallet away to join its brothers further down the shed. As far as he could see, his jobs were to make sure there were always sufficient empty bags in the feed to the filler and sufficient labels in the code shute, to replace the pallet at the end of the machine and ensure rolls of shrink wrap were in position. The last was the most complicated operation and it took him three goes before he got the hang of it. Juan showed him an emergency stop button and the telephone to call the process manager, and that was it, the teach-in was over.

Andy was on his own but it was going to be difficult finding out anything doing this job. It was like the spinning-plate syndrome. No sooner had he replenished the labels than the bags got low, then the rolls of plastic ran out. He would have to organise himself better so he had some time to snoop about the place. There were only four other men in the shed, as far as he could tell: his fork-lift driver, two more down the end taking finished goods out and one guy filling much bigger bags one at a time. They looked as if they held about half a tonne; his bags held only kilos, according to the label. Throughout the day the grade never changed, Purflo P30. If memory served him well this was a coarse grade not used by the brewing industry. He was glad of the half-hour's break at six o'clock. He could feel the dust in his hair and his face mask was wet with condensation from his breath. He went outside and was grateful that the air was cooling down. He found a mess-room, grunted greetings to its few occupants and swallowed pints of cold orange squash. Across the yard were some very large revolving pipes standing about twenty feet off the ground. They were at least two hundred feet long by about twelve feet across and he could see the fierce heat haze coming off them. He walked across and stood underneath one and his back started to burn. But there was not much else to see except a few large silos. Still, it was early days yet.

When ten o'clock came round, his muscles were aching and he was thankful his bed was in the car park and he didn't have to drive anywhere.

He arrived just before six the following morning. A bear of a man in his early sixties was unfurling two flags on the company's flag pole. Andy was tall but this guy was a good six-six and built to match. Andy stood still until the second flag was up and flapping and the ritual was over. The big man turned and faced him.

'Thanks, son, not many people left who do that any more.'

Andy asked about the second flag. 'State of California,' came the reply. 'You must be the Australian who started yesterday.' He held out his massive hand. 'Clay Steadman, production manager, pleased to meet you.'

As Andy shook hands he realised the situation was crazy. Here he was at the very plant that was supposed to be poisoning the world's beer production and the man who ran it was the very epitome of everything decent – crazy.

Maureen put him back on to the same job in shed A. Again Purflo P30. He learnt two more things by the first mess-break, firstly that P30 was the main swimming-pool grade and accounted for a great slice of the plant's capacity, and secondly that Maureen was out to reintroduce slave labour! It never let up all day. Same routine – no sooner had he sorted one area out, than something else, somewhere else, ran out. The sweat poured down his back. No wonder none of his workmates were overweight, it was a permanent sauna. Perhaps some of the obese people he'd seen on the west coast should pay to come here, he thought. It was better than any health farm – if you could stand the pace. But he wasn't here for his health, he was here to ferret about with a special purpose. On one occasion he asked his stacker driver what went on in the other large shed, but only received the curt reply, 'Same as in here.' He decided this building would have to be his next venue, either officially or unofficially.

Just after six in the evening, new faces started to take

over. Maureen had conned him. Nobody seemed to work sixteen-hour, back-to-back shifts as she had said. She certainly got the most out of her itinerant workers. Andy made up his mind, this would be his last double. He had to have some energy left to prowl round the area. He was dead beat when ten o'clock came round, clocked off and did a small recce. On the side of the office block was a shower-room. He didn't know if it was for the likes of mere workers, but he spent five glorious minutes under the cold water.

He was obviously very good at what he was doing. Maureen put him back on the same boring routine the following day and he told her he was only going to work twelve hours from now on. She didn't seem to mind and just shrugged her shoulders and walked off. He met one other new face late morning. Well, he didn't actually meet him officially. The man walked slowly through the shed with a clipboard, wearing an oversized full-length laboratory white coat. He stopped at each row of pallets and jotted figures down. As he passed close by, Andy nodded and said hello but received not the slightest acknowledgement in return. The very thin and surprisingly pale man looked as if he should have retired years ago.

Andy finished his shift, showered, walked back to his van and changed into his shorts and a cool fresh cotton shirt. Tonight he would drive into town, report to Derek – although he had nothing new to tell him – and then find a restaurant that served large steaks. His calorie intake definitely needed a boost. By nine o'clock he was replete and felt much better with a glass of iced whiskey in one hand and the sounds of country music washing over him from speakers scattered around the restaurant.

'Fancy buying your boss a drink then?' The voice came from behind him.

'Sure, sit down.' He called the waitress over. She ordered a beer and a bourbon chaser.

'So you escaped early, as you said you would. Cheers!'

She looked so different out of her work uniform. The square-jawed face could still not be considered pretty, but with the sun-glasses off big brown cow eyes stared back at him. And now her hair was on show. It was in good condition, light brown, thick and curly and it rested on her shoulders. She was wearing a bright short-sleeved floral-print dress that was loose fitting and in Andy's mind slightly old-fashioned – his mother would have called it a 'catalogue dress', bought unseen because it looked good in the photograph.

Maureen took up the conversation. 'Well, what do you think of our little town then?'

'Haven't seen much of it. Some woman with a large whip has been making sure of that!'

She laughed, finished her drinks and ordered some more for them both, and insisted on paying for them there and then.

'You a local?' Andy asked.

'Good Lord no! I'm originally from Fresno, about a hundred miles west of here. I did an engineering degree in LA and I've been out in Bullen for about six years now.'

'And how do you like it?'

She shrugged. 'The work's great – I enjoy that side of things – but socialising's out the window.'

Andy could understand that, looking around the near-empty restaurant. 'Do you live here in town?'

'No, I rent a small ranch house about three miles the other side, right in the middle of alfalfa country.'

'Alf what?'

'Alfalfa, the green clover-like plant. You must have seen it growing in the fields?' Andy nodded, but was not expecting or indeed ready for her next sentence.

'Fancy coming back to mine for coffee? You can leave your camper near the ranch and see the alfalfa in all its glory in the morning.'

In all his life Andy had always had to make the first moves when he'd fancied a certain female, and yet here was this young woman, still in her twenties, reversing the role. He tried not to let his surprise show. He'd had other plans for tonight, but what better way to obtain information than befriend the process manager of the plant itself? He accepted her offer, settled the bill and followed her old Ford pick-up truck out of town.

If Bullen was remote then the ranch house was definitely isolated. They drove in convoy past field after field of the clover and there was not a sign of human habitation. He parked behind her truck, leaving a cloud of dust to settle in the night air. She waited until he'd joined her on the porch steps.

'Used to be pure desert out here until the migrant farmers moved in seventy-odd years ago – this is one of their old converted ranch houses. Now the land is all irrigated. Come in, let's have a nightcap.' Throughout her little speech she didn't pause for breath once. She switched on the light to reveal one very large room that doubled up as living and sleeping-quarters. She disappeared into a smaller room at the far end and returned with a cold bottle of wine and two glasses.

They sat on the porch and talked. The night air had a nip about it but was pleasantly refreshing after the earlier inferno. She wanted to know more about him, so he obliged, making up his Australian heritage as he went. She listened intently, only breaking off once to fetch another bottle of wine. Andy sat on the only chair whilst she perched on the top step hanging on his every word. She stood up and looked at her watch. Andy took the hint that it was time to leave. She rubbed her arms.

'Let's go inside, it's getting chilly now.'

Andy followed and looked round the room while she disappeared into the kitchen. If he was expecting coffee he was in for a disappointment. When she returned she was completely naked.

'Take me to bed and screw me.' The words hit his ears but didn't sink in. He was staring at the most perfectly formed female body he had ever seen. Her deep tan was universal and there wasn't a body hair to be seen anywhere. Her job had toned her to perfection: her stomach was flat, her arms and legs athletic-looking. But it was her breasts. Andy knew he was staring at them. They defied gravity, they were solid with two very dark brown erect nipples pointing straight at him. As the initial shock wore off he refocused on a mark. It looked like a birthmark. It ran from under her left armpit across one breast and stopped at her navel. Such a body and it had to be spoilt by a blemish, he thought. Then he realised he was staring at a tattoo. It was a series of flowers on a vine-like stem. The focal point was one large flower on the side of her left breast. It was a stupid question but all he could think to ask at the time. 'What's the flower?'

'Honeysuckle!' She came across the room, took his hand and led him to the bed. He knew from what was happening to his own body that even if he wanted to it was too late to turn back. He just stood there while she undressed him. He lay back on the bed. She gently rubbed his penis but if she had wanted to make it even harder she was going to be out of luck, he was at maximum revs and had been since she'd stepped through the door. She unrolled a condom onto his manhood and mounted him. She was good. He could feel her internal muscles pulling at him. The sight of this body riding him like a jockey with the breasts and tattoo only inches from his face was too much. Within minutes the pair of them were shouting out the pleasures of orgasms. She got up, removed the protection and disappeared into the end room. On her way back she flicked a switch. Country and western music filled the room. She climbed back into the bed and put Andy's arm around her neck. They lay there in silence for many minutes. They knew it had been good – very good.

Andy's brain was full of all sorts of thoughts. It was usually the female spy who slept with the potential informer not the other way round. He smiled. He wouldn't go for overkill on their first night, though. He sat up and looked around the floor for his shorts.

If he'd thought their night of passion was over then he was in for a big surprise. What he'd sampled was only the *hors d'oeuvre*; the main meal plus dessert were still to come. She reached over and yanked him back onto the bed. Within seconds she went down on his penis with her mouth. The pleasures that followed were unlimited and he remembered eventually falling asleep at three o'clock.

She woke him at five with a cup of coffee and the

remark, 'Told you I'd invite you back for some decaff!'

Fortunately, she was dressed in her work clothes so Andy felt in no danger of a further attack. When he stood up the pain from his genitals hit home and he realised just what a session it had been. He pulled on his clothes, swallowed the coffee and very gently and painfully headed towards the camper. She shouted that she would see him at the plant. He was pleased with last night. Providing he could stand the pace, he could start asking her some questions soon. Mind you, to get any answers he would have to catch her when her mouth was not full.

It was all very businesslike back at the plant and no mention at all was made of their activities just a few hours ago. She asked if he could drive a stacker truck, adding that he really needed an official certificate but she was short of drivers, so what the hell. Andy lied. She sent him off to shed B to report to a supervisor. Before she left, she winked and said, 'and you'll be sitting down all day!'

Andy watched her walk under the revolving tubes. The bitch. She knew, she bloody well knew, he wouldn't be able to survive the day standing up. But fate works in mysterious ways. This was more like it. This was the shed he wanted to see and he wasn't disappointed. It was full of the names he knew, P3,P5, P7 and so on, row after row of pallets of the stuff. The filling-line was exactly the same as the other one but this time his job was to move the finished pallets off the end and stack them in a column. The grade was P5. Two other drivers were rapidly emptying a row further down the shed and were gaining on him. Business must be good, he thought. The old boy in the white coat made several visits and wrote down batch numbers from his ever-growing stack.

During his breaks Andy walked round the outside of the shed but couldn't spot anything different except on one side was a very large storage tank. It didn't have any markings on it. He decided to work late, mainly because he'd snap in half if he had a repetition of last night and also to crawl over the plant during the evening to find some answers without wasting any more time. She caught him walking about during his evening dinner-break.

'Lost, are we?'

'No, just stretching the legs and getting some fresh air. The mess-room smells like an ashtray. Anyway, I'm fascinated by all this lot, never seen anything like it before. I suppose I must be curious by nature. I like to know how things are made. After all, I spend all day filling the bags and moving them about, but know nothing about the product itself. I'm sure most people would work better and take greater pride in their job if they knew more about the process. You know what it is and what it's used for, but take me, at the moment I just think the bags are full of some dirt out of the ground.'

If Andy had hoped to reach a soft spot he was wrong. 'The majority of people who work here don't give a shit. They're only interested in the money. In fact, the people at the top don't either, for the same reason. It's only people in the middle, people like me, who have to be interested. Okay, Andy, if you're that interested as well I'll give you the personal tour myself. It's my day off on Sunday. You can either forgo your day shift or I'll put you on at night. Mind you, the personal tour's going to cost you – and how!'

Andy knew exactly what she meant. Still, Sunday was two days away. He should be fighting fit again by then, but he would need a great deal of patience to stop the two days dragging by. He was anxious to get on with the detective work but knew that if he asked too many questions too soon or was seen in the wrong part of the plant they would probably assume he was some sort of industrial spy gathering information for a competitor. Yes, patience was now the name of the game and Maureen Bradley was the way forward – even if he had to knacker himself in the process! He decided to work as much as possible so that the time would pass quickly. It would also avoid an interim night with her. She kept him on the same job for the rest of the week; perhaps, he thought, she was resting him in readiness. On Saturday she waved him down and threw an envelope onto the cab. The postmark was San Francisco. Inside was an Australian passport.

'I've kept your green card. You didn't tell me you'd worked as a waiter at Salomon's.'

He didn't know he had! Derek's little sense of humour, no doubt, and he spent the rest of the day wondering where the passport photograph had come from.

Half-way through the afternoon the grade was changed. They were going to pack Purflo P9. Maureen moved him back onto the bagging machine, where he changed the labels and code numbers while she got covered in powder readjusting some valves on the filling hopper. She handed him a small plastic container full of powder.

'Before we can start the run the laboratory has to check that it's all P9 and not mixed in with some of the previous P5 grade. Can you take the sample up to them please.' She pointed in the general direction of the lab and told him to wait for the result.

The technical department was certainly not like Larry's. It was situated in a small portable cabin. Two large fans made very little difference to the temperature inside. Equipment was sparse and the whole room was covered in a film of dust. A man in his early twenties took the sample. As far as Andy could see, he carried out three tests and it was all over in ten minutes. He handed Andy a signed official-looking chart. Andy walked back to the shed reading the piece of paper. It was titled *Purflo P9. Batch 765, Code 1538*. Three columns, *Density, Permeability and Mesh Size*, contained figures, and the word PASSED was stamped diagonally across the sheet. He had to skirt round the large circular tank outside his own shed, and made a mental note that shed A didn't have a similar one.

Andy arrived at the ranch house at nine o'clock on the Sunday morning, sat in the camper and blew the horn. For some reason he half expected a semi-clad male to open the door. But he was wrong. She came bounding down the three steps wearing baggy white trousers, a blue denim shirt and scandals, set off by a wide-brimmed yellow hat and sun-glasses. There was not the slightest hint of any make-up. Andy thought of the body hidden underneath the material. It was going to be difficult to concentrate on anything else. She climbed up into the passenger seat, plonked a white baseball cap on his head and asked, 'Can you give me a hand please?' Andy followed her indoors, where she pointed to a large cool-box. It weighed a tonne and he struggled to carry it out to the van. She shouted after him, 'Have you got your sunglasses?' He half turned and nodded.

'You drive, I'll navigate.' It was almost an order as she plonked herself down in the seat. She fiddled with the air-conditioning until she got it to her satisfaction. They drove past the plant and on up the other fork in the road for about ten miles, passing two enormous tipper lorries heading in the other direction. She reached across and sounded the camper's horn. Both drivers acknowledged, flashing their lights and sounding air horns.

'Bringing the base ore from the quarry, forty tonnes at at time!' she explained.

The concrete road ran out. From now on it was just a crushed rock highway. She told Andy to stop at the top of a small rise, and opened her door first. The heated air rushed in and hit them full in the face. They got out and walked to the edge of the outcrop. Even with his shades on the glare hurt his eyes.

'The Favusite deposit!' She said it with her arms outstretched and genuine enthusiasm in her voice. 'Formed nearly twenty million years ago, spewed out of the ground during some enormous earthquake.'

The area was brilliant white. In the bottom of the quarry a bulldozer was scooping the stuff from the side and loading it into a lorry. They stood and watched the ritual in silence then she continued her tour-guide bit.

'Hundred feet deep and enough here to last for the next fifty years.' She bent down, picked up a piece about the size of a fist and tossed it at him. Andy braced himself to catch it but overreacted – it was no heavier than a sponge.

Maureen burst out laughing. 'I told you, it's Favusite. *Favus* is Latin for honeycomb. It's full of holes.'

She was still laughing as she walked back to the van. Andy examined it more closely. It crumbled easily and left his hands chalky white. He caught her up.

'Are there any other deposits around here?'

'Some, but this is the best one. It's the only one we use for filteraids. The others are not so pure so they wouldn't get approval for food use. They're used as fillers and things.'

Andy looked around him. He was standing on the spot where Purflo began life. It was all so tranquil and innocent. Yet if they were right, this was where a major world problem also began. He was having trouble associating the two extremes.

They went back towards the plant, then took a small partially used track which led off to the right and climbed towards a spur. She shouted for him to stop at a group of three large rocks and to reverse in between two of them. The ground bore the signs of tyre-marks.

'My favourite spot. Always come up here for a recharge.' With that she dived into the back of the camper.

Andy got out and admired the view. He could see twenty miles or more to the horizon. In the foreground was the plant, with Bullen a few miles off to the right. The rest of the panorama was a patchwork of either desert or green fields. The sky was a rich blue, cut into sections by several vapour trails. He heard her voice and turned. The view this side was more breathtaking. She was walking towards him with a glass of wine in each hand and was wearing nothing but a pair of white shorts. The transformation was quite incredible – at least he now knew how she got her tan!

'There's a rug next to the hamper. If you spread it out over there we can have lunch.' She pointed to a sheltered spot currently out of the full glare of the sun. They ate their picnic of cold chicken and salad, but as far as Andy was concerned it could have been rabbit and nettles! His concentration was wrecked. As hard as he tried he couldn't take his eyes off her body. Everything about it was perfect. He hadn't smelled it before but every now and again he caught a whiff of perfume. His blood pressure was rapidly coming to the boil.

This time he made the first move and she responded immediately. He couldn't remember if he'd ever made love outdoors before, but he certainly couldn't remember a woman who approached lovemaking with such enthusiasm or vigour. The colours on the tattoo took on different hues as the sun picked them out. It was going to be a long, long day if every item of interest they came across resulted in such rewards.

They tidied up and sat in the shade of one of the rocks. She had put her shirt back on so at least Andy's brain was multi-functional again. Another bottle of wine was opened.

Reluctantly he returned the conversation to work. 'Good view of the plant. You can see sheds A and B quite clearly from here. What's all the rest do?'

As usual the answers came in an enthusiastic voice. 'See that big stockpile over there?' She pointed to it. 'That's where the ore from the quarry is dumped. There's usually enough stock there for two months. It's then taken by conveyor to a crusher and at this stage ends up about the size of a split pea.' She made a small gap with her finger and thumb. 'Any impurities like sand and pebbles are taken out. It's all done by weight. The lighter Favusite passes over mesh screens whilst the heavier stuff falls through. Very effective – most simple things are. Then the clean material is crushed again, depending on what it's going to end up as, and passed through the rotary kilns.' Again the finger identified the long tubes. 'These are heated to above a thousand degrees Celsius to burn off organic matter.'

He let the last comment go. She was in full flow and he didn't want to break the continuity.

'From there the various grades are fine-tuned by passing up that tower thing that looks like a rocket with side pieces coming off it. It's actually called an air classifier. The lighter particles are blown to the top whilst the heavier pieces are taken off at the bottom. It's very accurate. We can manufacture very reproducible grades each time – seventeen different grades, to be precise. Once the grade is made it's stored in one of those eight silos, as you know, it's filled off into bags. Mind you, these days a lot more goes straight out in bulk rail cars.'

'So there are two categories of powder then, the coarse ones in shed A and the finer ones in shed B?' Andy asked.

'We actually talk about three, a medium range as well.'

'And which shed do they go to?'

'All depends whether the medium grade is coarse or fine!'

Andy didn't know whether she was winding him up or not. She started to laugh so he knew, and acknowledged her flippancy with a rude gesture. She pounced on him and pinned his arms down. She was strong. It would have been extremely easy to lie back and enjoy her, but he had to keep the flow going – hers! He deflated the moment with a serious question.

'So what's that tank for?' He nodded in the general direction of the plant. 'You know, the one near shed B.'

She climbed off him and sat on the edge of the hill with her knees tucked up to her chin. 'That's for the fine grades. Favusite contains silica. The dust is not deadly but can irritate the lungs. We started to receive a lot of complaints from end-users about the amount of dust released when the bags were emptied. Anyway, our technical manager came up with the answer. When the fine grades come out of the classifier they are still at a temperature of about fifty-five degrees and very dusty, so they are sprayed with a fine mist of water to clump the small pieces together. Not permanently, of course – as soon as they are made into a slurry the stirring action of the agitator breaks them up into their original particles. Neat eh?' Maureen stopped and poured more wine into their glasses.

'So the tank holds just water?' Andy tried to hide any disappointment coming through. 'I suppose out here water's a valuable commodity. That's why you have to store it, so you always have a constant supply?'

'Too right, a glass of good water's more expensive

than beer out here. Hang on a minute though, it's not pure water, so don't go drinking it, will you! The finished powder-clumps are not sent out wet – most of the water evaporates – but it does contain some moisture. So what had we gone and done? Got rid of one problem, but given ourselves another. Some customers, mainly in the warmer countries, reported that they'd found mould growing on the powder. We couldn't have that, not with a food-approved product. Again the technical manager came to the rescue. He added some food-approved fungicide to the water in the tank which would prevent any future growth and the problem disappeared overnight.'

'So was this water-spray device worth all the aggravation?'

'Oh yes, the mould growth in the bags was only in isolated cases but the removal of the dust problem was a mega breakthrough, and because of it we've more than doubled production of the finer grades.'

'This technical manager, is he the old fellow in the white coat? You know, the really chatty one!'

'So, you've met our Doctor Tom Allsop then? Miserable old bugger he is. Don't take it to heart though, he's like it with everyone. If you're not a fish he doesn't want to know you.'

Andy looked puzzled.

'His only interest in life is fishing,' Maureen explained. 'He has a small boat and spends most of his spare time on it, so I'm told.'

'A boat. Here?'

'No, you daft Australian, give me strength! Not here, on one of the lakes further north!'

Andy had never got to grips with the Yanks' ideas of distance and travelling. They would think nothing of driving five hundred miles for a picnic. He could imagine the reaction he would get if he asked his mother to go to Edinburgh for the day!

Maureen broke in on his thoughts. 'Tom's been here ever since the plant started up nearly forty years ago. He invented the first grades and knows as much about filtration as anybody. He's part of the furniture now –

looks after all the technical side for Union. Fortunately, he only spends just over half his time at Bullen. The place cheers up when he's away. Roll on next week, it's his turn to annoy our Oregon plant.'

Andy expressed surprise. Another plant at Oregon? Hadn't she said there was only one deposit used for filteraids?

'In California!' came the terse reply. 'Anyway, their deposit is not as good as ours and neither are their products.' The statement was made with a definite amount of bitchiness attached to it.

Andy changed the subject. 'This fungicide idea sounds very clever, did Allsop develop it himself?'

'You've seen our little old plant we haven't the resources to make something like that. No, we buy in a concentrate and just dilute it further with water.'

Andy had so many more questions to ask but he was getting to know Maureen Bradley more by the hour and knew that if they were rushed she would probably get bored and his information source would dry up. He would have to spread them out and bring them in gently. It was time for a break now. He fetched some more wine and asked her where she'd like to have dinner. For the next hour the talk was kept to neutral items.

'So what's the capacity of this plant?' he asked when he judged the time to be right to start again.

'In round figures we're budgeting for about 300,000 tonnes this year. About two-thirds coarse and roughly 120,000 to 130,000 tonnes fine end.'

'And the other plant, the one at Oregon, is it the same size as yours?'

'Oh no, it only makes about 150,000 tonnes total per year, split almost down the middle between coarse and fine grades.'

Andy excused himself, pretending nature called and dashed to the van. He quickly found pen and paper and wrote the figures down before the wine vapours dulled his brain. He was already asking his next question before he sat down next to her.

'Tom Allsop travels between the two plants then keeping an eye on quality and making sure there's no mouldy bags produced? Mind you, I'm assuming the stuff at Oregon has the patented Allsop spray treatment.'

'Sure does. It was installed several months after ours.'

'Do you get to Oregon very often to meet up with your counterpart and discuss production problems, mould and the like? Sorry! Lack of mould!'

Maureen shook her head. 'I've only been there twice in six years. My boss Clay Steadman does all that sort of thing. They have a group managers' meeting in Sacramento once a month.'

'Does Tom Allsop live by his lake and commute between the two plants then?'

'No. Born-and-bred Bullen man. Some people wish he'd died here like about ten years ago!' She thought it was funny and giggled away to herself.

'Why don't you spray the coarse grades?' Andy continued.

'No need to. The pieces are much bigger so they don't create the dust problems the finer ones do.'

Andy mentally kicked himself. It was a stupid question and had used up more of the quota of time before she got bored with the question-and-answer session. She stood up, stretched. The look on her face told him that her loins were beginning to stir once again.

'Enough of the life history of Union Mining and Minerals. There's more enjoyable things to do on my day off.' She moved closer and Andy's view of the valley was now framed between two brown well-muscled legs but he persevered.

'Just one more question. Why do you need all these different grades? It's all the same stuff, after all.'

The front of the shirt fell open and the flower enjoyed some more of the sun's rays. She stood defiantly with her hands on her hips.

'What you trying to do, put me out of a goddam job? The classification into the different grades is my main job responsibility – you know, process manager!'

'Sorry!' Andy bowed his head in mock disgrace.

'The different grades are necessary because, believe it or not, you've got different sizes of solids to be removed from liquids.' Her voice was full of sarcasm. Andy looked her up and down, the urge to grab her there and then was almost overpowering but he bit his lip and resisted. He had to hear this bit out – his body was going to have to be patient no matter how much it hurt.

'Okay, rocks, let's give this mentally challenged Aussie some examples, shall we?' She kicked Andy's bare foot with her own and he found it difficult not to smile. This woman was beginning to grow on him. 'Imagine that you have a box full of soccer balls. What would happen if you dropped golf balls on the top and shook the box?'

'The golf balls would work their way to the bottom,' Andy answered.

'Very good! And what would happen if you dropped, say, tennis balls into the box?'

'They would probably get stuck between the footballs.'

'Correct again! Now empty the box.' She went through the motions of emptying an imaginary box. 'Now fill it up with baseballs, okay? Now drop the golf balls in the top and rattle it. What happens now?'

Andy hazarded, 'The golf balls get stuck between the bigger balls?'

'Great. And that's why you need different sizes of Purflo. The gaps between each piece holds the dirty solids back. The smaller the solid to be removed, the smaller the gap has to be. Of course, the balls are not solid in practice, they're full of holes to let the cleaned-up liquid flow through. Happy now?'

Andy gave her a round of applause.

'It's all very clever, thank you for taking the time out to explain it all to me. I didn't realise what I was packaging before. I shall resume work with renewed vigour tomorrow!' He received another sharp kick on the leg for his sarcasm, ignored it, and added, 'Beer has small impurities to be removed, so requires a fine grade like P5. Very clever, very clever indeed.'

'And wine,' came the reply. 'The stuff you're knocking back now. We sell more fine grades to wineries than to breweries.'

Andy sat up. Fortunately, she was looking past him at the camper and couldn't see the look of horror on his face. Christ, they had only uncovered half of the problem, he had to get an urgent message back to Derek. He suggested they start to pack up but she would have none of it. She moved forward, straddled his legs and with one simple finger movement undid her shorts and let them fall to the ground. The sight only inches away from his face was overwhelming. Derek would have to wait. What he didn't know yet wouldn't hurt!

It was two hours later when he dropped her off at her place and made the excuse that he had to go into town and book a table for dinner. She thought he was mad, the place was never full. She was probably right about him being mad. Creeping back to the ranch along dirt-tracks had been all right; driving into town after all the wine he'd drunk was asking for trouble, but it was the only place with a phone. He dialled the number and it just rang and rang. Andy's palms were so damp the phone slithered about in his hands. 'Come on Derek. Of all days, answer the bloody thing,' he muttered.

He did, in due course. Andy reeled off the figures about production tonnages, explained about the fungicide spray and then dropped the bombshell about the wine. Derek merely said 'yes' four times and then gave out a new number he could be reached on as from today. He was either remaining very cool about it all or was speechless, it was difficult to tell from Derek's phone voice.

Andy made his mind up to take the night off mentally and enjoy himself. He would give Maureen a taste of her own medicine and play the aggressive, dominant-male role in bed and to hell with it. If he had to go straight into work tomorrow at six in the morning having made love all night, then so be it. He was going to remember this day for a long time to come. Then the thought struck him. Did he feel in this mood because Maureen had turned him on so much throughout the day or was it because he'd drunk quantities of wine laced with that bloody X amino acid thing? He would never know.

It took him until Tuesday evening to recover properly and to find what he'd been searching for. So far, he'd riffled through every scrap of paper in the laboratory without success. Now it was Allsop's office's turn. Even though the technical manager was off-site for a week his door was unlocked. The delivery note was in a pile of papers stacked on a filing-cabinet. Thirty-five tonnes of a thing called Fungicide G500 had been delivered on 12th April – about three weeks ago. It had come from Sarius Chemicals, Bakersfield.

Andy's work at Bullen was drawing to a close. He rang Derek from town. Derek's message was brief and to the point: 'Meet you on Friday in the car park of Circus Circus, Las Vegas.'

He broke the news to her on Wednesday. There were tears. She knew he would leave sometime but hadn't expected it to be so soon. Her passion reached a new high that night, it was as if she wanted the future now, all in one frantic session. Andy waited until she was sound asleep and slid quietly out of the house. It was three o'clock in the morning and still dark.

He found Tom Allsop's bungalow, drove past and parked on the main street. He ran back, using the darkness as much as possible but he had to be careful. People in these areas were good neighbours, the slightest noise or a dog awakened and they would be out investigating. As it was, he would have to be long gone before sunrise. The rooms smelt of dust and old furniture and as his eyes adjusted to the small amount of light he could see that everything looked shoddy and old-fashioned. It had been at least a decade since Allsop had bought anything new for his home.

The personal paperwork was in a kitchen drawer. He had just over a thousand dollars in a savings account and his bank balance showed a moderate salary going in every month. One large standing order wiped out almost two-thirds of this. Andy continued his search through the man's papers and found the answer. He was paying off a loan on his boat and more went on insurance. Basically the guy was poor, not much to show for a lifetime's dedication to Union Mining and Minerals. He certainly wasn't being paid vast sums of money to spike Purflo products, not from the information Andy had read so far.

He returned to his camper and drove away from Bullen. He would remember the town and the plant where he'd worked – but most of all he would always remember a young woman called Maureen Bradley.

10

Andy crossed into Nevada and headed south on Highway 95. After miles of parched desert the gambling city appeared on the horizon. It was totally out of place. Skyscrapers erected in the middle of nowhere! The Circus Circus hotel and casino was equally easy to find. The building just seemed to go up and up into the sky. Even the car park took him by surprise, it was so enormous you could have held a grand prix in it. There were literally thousands of cars, campers and coaches parked there. Meet you in the car park, Derek had said – it could take days to walk around all the vehicles. He paid his overnight parking-fee, found a space about half a mile from the main entrance and parked up. He walked across to the main entrance and found a bank of telephones just inside the reception area. The phone connection was poor and he had to raise his voice to pass on the message, but at least Derek now had a parking-lot number and a clue as to where to find him.

He wandered through the casino, which was almost as big as the car park. Row after row of one-armed bandits ran as far as the eye could see. They were probably called something else these days, he reckoned – something more psychologically friendly. Every machine was occupied. There were old ladies wearing white gloves and cowboys complete with boots and spurs. He looked at his watch. It was only three o'clock in the afternoon. He imagined it didn't take long to become an addict lured on by the possibility of multimillion dollar jackpots. It was all so different from Bullen's one-horse pace of life. Maureen would hate it –

there were no windows and no clocks. It was designed to do away with the concept of time altogether. No day, no night – you were not supposed to know how long you were playing the machines. He was approached by a young waitress, her body squeezed into a skimpy corseted outfit. She asked if he would like a drink and added that they were free if he played the silver dollar machines. He declined and left the place smiling, just glad he didn't have to pay their electricity bill.

Andy decided to tidy up the camper, sort through his clothes and have a very early night – he daren't count up the few hours' sleep he'd got over the last week.

He'd heard the knocking sound several times but ignored it. Now curiosity was getting the better of him. He rubbed the sleep from his eyes and looked at his watch. It was ten o'clock, he'd been asleep for only two hours. He listened to the sound again, trying to orientate himself, and decided it was from the back of the van. He sat up, pulled on his shorts and was still fastening the top button when he opened the door.

'Not interrupting anything, am I?' Derek stood there grinning from ear to ear. As always, he was wearing a suit, but this time the colour had changed from brown to blue.

'Derek, nice to see you again. Come in. Welcome to my – our – property. Make yourself at home.'

'Take these and then get dressed properly, I've a taxi waiting.' With that he handed over his well-travelled suitcase and a black briefcase.

They were driven to the casino entrance – no point in walking, Derek said. They found a bar and tucked themselves into a corner seat. There was just enough piped music to prevent them being overheard. Derek summoned a waitress. She made a point of stooping low to take their order and Derek helped himself to an eyeful of very tight cleavage. He asked for a bottle of bourbon and two glasses and made some rude comment about the Grand Canyon as he focused on the fishnet-covered cheeks when she went off to get their drinks.

'I thought you said we'd meet on Friday? I know

some strange things happen in this part of the world but by my reckoning it's still Thursday,' Andy said, showing his confusion.

'You're right, it is only Thursday, but I've been dashing around like the proverbial blue-assed fly so I'm running a day ahead of my plans.'

'So you've come in straight from the East then?'

Derek shook his head. 'No, I've been on this side of the country for three days. I've seen Larry and Simon and I was at Vegas Airport when you phoned earlier.'

Andy was totally lost.

'I've joined the modern world, my friend,' Derek explained. 'I've bought a combined mobile phone and facsimile machine with coast-to-coast reception. It's going to cost the taxpayer lots of dollars, I can tell you. It was Simon's suggestion really. I objected at first – you know me, I'm an old traditionalist and set in my ways – too used to phone boxes on street corners ringing at such and such a time and all that other cloak-and-dagger stuff. Then I thought, why not? If you can't beat them, join them.'

Andy laughed. Yes, he knew exactly what Derek was talking about – he held the same viewpoint. The drinks arrived and they toasted the electronic age – whatever that meant.

'Both Larry and Simon send their regards. Lots to tell you about but first I want to hear all about the Bullen plant. By the way, you're looking very fit and mean, was the suntan part of the brief as well?'

They both laughed. Andy recited all the main events that had happened but only referred to Maureen as 'the process manager' he'd befriended in a bar. No mention of her gender was made. If Derek had known only half the truth Andy reckoned he would have a coronary on the spot. Andy summed it all up by saying, 'There's no way anybody at the plant knows what's going on. The production manager is John Wayne personified, the technical manager is worn out, nearly broke and only interested in fishing. The quality-control methods are so slack it's not true. They don't check incoming raw materials, they just take it as read that what they get is what they ordered. They all honestly believe in the good of the company. Someone else has slipped this protein thing in right under their noses. If it's masquerading as a fungicide then Sarius Chemicals are my number one target.'

'Did you manage to get a sample of this fungicide?'

Andy shook his head. 'No. It's delivered by tanker and pumped straight into a storage vessel which doesn't have any sample points. There wasn't even a retained sample in the laboratory. I suppose I could have climbed onto the top of the tank and lowered something through the manhole cover, but I would have looked bloody obvious thirty feet up and right out in the middle of the yard. Oh, nearly forgot, the other plant, the one in Oregon, they spray their finer grades as well – that's confirmed.'

'So what do you think? Bullen gets one type, Melford, Oregon, the other?' Derek asked.

Andy shrugged. 'Who knows? Bullen's last delivery was something called Fungicide G500. Next time they may get the other variety. What's in a name, anyway? As I said, nobody's checking incoming raw materials. Hopefully we'll find out more once we've visited Sarius – I take it we'll be heading in their general direction soon?'

'Too true, old son. Now let me give you my news. First of all, I've spoken to our beloved leader. Can't say he passed on his best wishes – he didn't! And although he didn't say it in so many words he sounded pleased with our progress. He still wants all the answers by yesterday, of course, but it's as near as we're going to get to a thank-you all the same. I saw Larry on Monday – he looked as rough as hell, I don't think he'd slept over the weekend. He's done some more tests on his monkeys. You remember his first trials, when he injected them directly with 50 milligrams of his solutions and said it was the equivalent of drinking two litres of beer? Well, he decided this was a bit drastic as it would take about one to two hours for a human to consume this volume. So he gave them smaller amounts over a set time. It made no difference in the end with Y, the creatures just took longer to get depressed. Larry said they looked as if they were waiting for the executioner to come along! It was a different story with X, though. To start with, he used pairs of them in the same cage, but instead of fighting each other they became hooligans together and nigh on broke their home up. Then he put three in one box, two were on X, one on Y. The couple on the aggressive stuff beat the shit out of the depressed one – not very nice, is it! Larry reckons that they acted as a team because their mental states had gradually been changed in each other's company. In his earlier tests they developed this state immediately and just turned on whatever was about. Anyway, that's the drift – he explained it much better. He's still doing some more trials and I have to get him some more powder.'

'You should have let me know,' Andy replied. 'I could have let you have tonnes of the stuff at cost price!'

'Only we don't know whether it's X or Y, do we, my friend?'

Derek observed. 'Larry's also been speaking to his friend at the university, who has definitely confirmed what he originally told us. The effects of Y are cumulative, X is not. He also reckons the speed and the way people are affected will depend on things like age and diet. In fact, if people are prone to some sort of existing protein problem then it's anybody's guess how they will react. Larry suggested that's why your fellow countryman in Cyprus went off the rails so quickly. He had gout, didn't he?'

Andy looked thoughtful. 'Seems a long time ago since we saw him. You know, I've even forgotten his name!'

'Larry hadn't. He reminded me about our Fred Clarke. Well done about the wine-filtration discovery. I could have kicked myself, I never even gave it a thought.'

'Neither did I,' Andy added as some form of consolation.

'Yes, but you don't have vineyards stretching for hundreds of miles back home so there's no reason why you should have thought about wine. This idiot here has driven through most of them in the last few weeks. Still, better late than never I guess, I spent all day Tuesday with Simon. You should see the equipment he's got at work – it's like mission control. It took him precisely ten minutes to find out the world's wine production figures for last year!' Derek referred to his diary. 'Two hundred and ninety million hectolitres.'

'Well, at least it's only a third of the beer production, and anyway you don't drink as much wine as you do beer,' Andy observed.

'I'm afraid there is a problem,' Derek told him. 'I went to a winery yesterday and found out that wine is filtered using about three times the amount of filteraid as beer. It's either filtered several times or much more powder is added to stop the filters blocking. I also found out that wines are also acidic so our bloody amino acids are alive and well in all the plonks.'

Maureen's words came flooding back into Andy's brain. She'd been quite insistent that Union sold more fine Purflo to wineries than breweries. 'So you could become more mixed up on wine – the whole thing's getting worse by the day!'

Derek waited until Andy had recovered from the shock of the latest news. 'That's not the end of the story. Simon went through the drinks industry with a fine-tooth comb. You can also add the cider products to the list – they contain alcohol, are acidic and are filtered, so our proteins will split into their lethal little offspring. But there's some good news as well. You'll be pleased to hear that the stuff you've got in your glass is not filtered. Seems distilled spirits are manufactured clean enough from the start.'

'Thank God for minor miracles!' Andy raised his glass and drained the contents.

'Simon's been working on the tonnage figures you obtained from your process man.' Derek continued. 'With sixty per cent of the world's beer sewn up, this accounts for 105,000 tonnes of Purflo. He's had to estimate on the wine, but assuming Union have fifty per cent of the market this gives them about 70,000 tonnes, making the total not too far removed from the 200,000 tonnes of fine grades manufactured from both plants.'

'You have got a lot of gen and there was me working my fingers to the bone thinking you had your feet up in some snug little office!'

Andy's remark brought a smile to Derek's face but it was very short-lived.

'Not far from the truth, old son. It's all come from Larry, Simon and you. I haven't found out a fucking thing! Remember eleven days ago? I was going to tear the world apart looking for the culprits. Well, I've personally found out nothing – absolute zero. There's no whispers, no news from any of our field men nothing from any of the other agencies. There's no money coming in anywhere that could finance it. I've drawn a complete blank. At the moment I couldn't disprove that the man on the moon is behind it all! All I've got is a goddam map of the world with areas shaded in where Purflo is used – and Simon drew that up?'

'Any clues there?'

'Yes!' Derek said sarcastically. 'Union don't supply the Middle East or Russia, which is a fat lot of good. The Arabs don't drink and the Ruskies haven't got any hard currency to buy food let alone Purflo. No, I'm afraid there aren't going to be any short cuts to the top with this little enterprise. We're going to have to do it the hard way. I'm ready for my bed. You going to invite me back to your place or do I have to force myself on you?'

Andy woke just after eight. The smell of a cooked breakfast wafting across from the next camper had roused his taste buds. He looked across the van at the other bunk. Derek was lying on his back snoring, trying to imitate the sound of a bath emptying. Andy decided to let him sleep on. He obviously needed it. He searched around the camper looking for some clean clothes. Things were getting desperate, he was down to his last shirt. He rammed the dirty pile of clothes into his holdall. Perhaps the hotel had a launderette for the camping fraternity. A piece of paper stuck out of a shirt pocket. He retrieved it and swore out loud. The paper was covered in dust and had been creased along the same line many times, and he had nearly washed it into oblivion! He walked briskly to the hotel. In typical American fashion the man behind the counter said that the laundry service would have his garments clean in two hours' time but he would have to pay up front as he was not a hotel guest. When Andy got back Derek was up, if not fully awake. He had a saucepan of water on the boil on the small stove and was looking through all the cupboards for some coffee. It was agreed they would go back to the hotel in about an hour, have breakfast and then pick the laundry up.

Andy handed across the piece of paper. 'Forgot to mention this last night, in fact to be honest I had forgotten all about it and it nearly got washed with my shirts.'

Derek studied the scruffy page, which was covered with the names of countries of the world.

Andy explained, 'It's all the places Purflo from shed B Bullen is sent out to. I took the names from the shipping-documents for all the containers sent out over the last six months, I'm pretty sure I didn't miss any.'

Hangover or not, Derek suddenly sprang into action and almost knocked Andy over in an attempt to get to his briefcase. He spread out a map of the world on his bunk. Most countries had been criss-crossed with blue lines.

'These are all the countries Purflo is delivered to. I used the information we got from that slob's office in Sacramento. Just for the sake of it, let's suppose that

Bullen always get the same ingredient. We could then superimpose your information on the map to find out where it goes and then by a process of elimination find out where the other one ends up. We'll need another couple of coloured pens.' Derek ransacked his case but could find nothing suitable. The humming started as his frustration mounted. Over coffee there was some respite for Andy as his partner showed him how the fax and mobile phone operated.

On the way over to the hotel Derek remarked, 'I like your camper. It makes a good little headquarters. I suggest we hang onto it and use it as our permanent base. Even the bunk-bed is more comfortable than some of the motel ones I've stayed in!' Andy had no objections to this at all, the van brought back some vivid memories for him.

By the time they sat down for brunch they were both ready for the full menu. Derek shovelled the food into his mouth as if he hadn't eaten for weeks. As soon as he was done he disappeared from the table and returned clutching a fistful of pens, markers and highlighters. Andy reckoned he must have bought the kiosk's entire stock. He sat there playing with them, willing Andy to eat faster. It was no good, Andy couldn't stand the fidgeting any longer. He tossed across the van's keys. He would see Derek back there in about half an hour after he had collected his laundry.

'I've just sent these,' Derek said, thrusting two sheets of paper at Andy as he was still in the doorway. One was to Larry, asking him to check out which ingredient was present in an assortment of wines. The other was to Simon, and more cryptic. It asked him to try and find out where 'the fine varieties' from Melford go.

As if to pre-empt any comment, Derek added, 'They'll know what to do.' He sat down again and carried on shading in countries on his map with a huge red felt pen. He called Andy over when he'd finished and they both sat and studied Derek's work of art. Red and blue areas covered North America, Europe, South Africa, China, Australia the Indian subcontinent and one or two Far Eastern countries.

'I think we can assume that the other areas, the ones left in blue, are where the second ingredient, perhaps Y, is sent,' Derek said proudly.

'I'm sorry, Derek, but I beg to differ. Look at the States. It's red at the moment yet we know from Larry's tests, on samples that you collected, that both types of ingredient end up in Purflo grades here. No, I don't think we can draw any hard-and-fast conclusions at this stage. We'll have to wait until Simon comes back with any news; failing that, I can always go and visit the Oregon plant.'

Derek stared back, his face expressionless. He threw the pen down and carefully folded the map up. Slowly his face broke into a smile. 'I'm getting carried away with it all, aren't I? If I start to do it again, do me a favour, will you? Kick me up the ass! I guess I'm trying to make up for my disastrous week. Right, enough of this colouring-book stuff, I think it's high time you and I paid a visit to Sarius Chemicals.'

Andy suggested Derek drove, to gain experience of how the camper handled. Andy checked the map. It would be a relatively straightforward journey to Bakersfield, about two hundred and fifty miles west all along the one highway, US 466. There was no point in arriving on the Friday night. The weekend was going to be the best time for what they had in mind, so Derek took it leisurely and kept his speed within the law.

The fax machine made both of them jump. They had parked up for the night in the Mojave Desert, and with glasses in hand were watching a red sun disappear across the Butes. The neatly handwritten message was from Simon.

> Latest message received and avenues are being explored. For your information, Union Mining and Minerals was owned by TACIT until 1989. It was under chapter eleven for two years prior to this.

Eventually sold off to the litigants, who in turn agreed to sell out for cash to a management consortium plus several finance houses. The claims were to do with Union's asbestos-manufacturing plants in the late forties and fifties.

Underneath he had tabled some figures of the number of people currently employed, plus last year's published annual turnover. The fax ended, 'Best regards, Simon.'

Andy handed it back to Derek. 'I've heard of TACIT before. It's one of the world's biggest chemical companies, isn't it? But what's this chapter eleven thing about?'

Derek reeled off the words: 'Trans American Chemical Industries And Trading – now that's a biggy. I'm glad Union are no longer part of that outfit otherwise we'd be searching their goddam premises for the rest of our lives. Dates are wrong anyway. You said that Bullen didn't introduce the watersprays plus fungicide until the early nineties, after they'd been sold off from TACIT. So we can forget the connection permanently. Great!'

Again, Andy had to ask for an explanation about what sounded like some chapter in a book.

'Chapter eleven. It's a form of legal umbrella against bankruptcy. Sounds as if Union had a lot of claims slapped on them. I'm only assuming now, but suppose a lot of their employees caught cancer after working in their asbestos plants. Their lawyers would slap in massive claims for compensation – even for their next of kin. They would argue that the workers had been exposed to the dangers without being properly warned or provided with suitable protection. You know the size of claims awarded here in the US – too many in at any one time and the company's broke and out of business. Chapter eleven stops this. The claims are spread out to give the company a breather; it can keep trading, make some money and pay off the claims. If after a set number of years it's not doing so, then all the litigants end up owning the outfit. They don't want it, they want the cash, so they sell if off to the highest bidder and divide up the proceeds.'

'Wouldn't the parent company be responsible as well?'

'No, not necessarily. They probably bought Union before asbestos became a headline but long after they stopped making the stuff. Why should they be responsible? No, as I said, Union would be very much on their own. I suppose TACIT could have bought them back from the litigants if they'd been that bothered. The buck has to stop somewhere. This is your van – but you're not responsible for my fax stored inside it, are you?'

Derek was up first and woke Andy with a cup of coffee. It was only seven in the morning and the heat was already soaking into the metal of the van, yet Derek was still dressed in long-sleeved shirt and suit trousers.

'Sorry, couldn't sleep, my mind's been working overtime all night. If there's 200,000 tonnes of fine Purflo knocking around, then we're looking for 600 tonnes of protein. That's one hell of a lot. That should be easy enough to spot in Sarius's warehouse. Twelve tonnes a week. They can't hide that, can they? There must be some stock ready for the next delivery.'

'And how did you arrive at all this wonderful mathematics then?' Andy asked, sitting up and stifling a yawn.

'Larry's figure that there's 0.3 per cent by weight in the powder.'

'It's not right. There's something wrong somewhere.'

'What?' Derek shouted out the word.

'For Christ's sake, Derek, let me wake up properly before you snap my head off, will you!'

Derek apologised. He knew he was beginning to flap again. He went outside in order to give Andy some space and it was a good five minutes before

Andy joined his partner.

'I've remembered what's wrong.' Andy confessed. 'The protein is not delivered in dry form. My contact said that they dilute the bought-in concentrate with water, so what we're looking for is already a liquid. Depending on its strength, it could be double or treble your figure, or even more. I should have got a sample whilst I had the opportunity. That was my fault, so it wasn't a completely flawless week for me, was it?'

They packed up and continued their journey and drove through Oildale and Oil City, just on the outskirts of Bakerfield. The sights they saw whetted their appetites for Sarius. Everywhere were chemical complexes and refineries with lots of steam and bright steel glinting in the sunlight. It took them a further two hours to find their intended destination and their jovial moods dropped as soon as they entered the Redhills Industrial Park.

'Looks more like a military base than a place where chemicals are made!' Andy stated with more than a hint of disappointment in his voice.

'Probably was, a lot of young men had their first introduction to military service in places like this. Camps such as these were thrown up all over the States during the early forties,' Derek replied.

They drove into the estate. The original two-storey buildings were of breeze-block construction, inset at regular intervals on each floor with sets of small metal windows. The various detached buildings – some small, others of considerable size – were now separated from each other by metal fencing. Large signs advertised a car repairer, a printer and a timber company . . . They drove slowly round the old base. An attempt had been made to add some greenery to the stark surroundings by planting young trees and flower-beds at the corners of road junctions.

They both saw it and pointed together: SARIUS CHEMICALS INC. Beyond the familiar chain-link security fence was a car park marked out for maybe thirty vehicles. Beyond it stood an old two-storey military block which resembled an old barracks. Some of the small window frames had been replaced on the first floor with modern single panes and the building had been painted from top to bottom in matt cream finish. To the left of this building and almost at right angles stood a new warehouse with green corrugated side panels. They kept following the road. Another fence separated the warehouse from another older building which had nothing to do with Sarius, and then the road swung off to the right. Another right turn and they were at the back of the two companies. A third and smaller building had been added to the warehouse. Together the three buildings almost made the letter 'U'. There was no rear entrance. They turned right again. They had circled the premises. Two companies on their own little island. But where were the smoking chimneys and mass of pipes and tanks?

Derek drove round the block again but they could only see three storage vessels tucked between the two newest buildings. One lorry was on site and had backed up against an open roller-shutter door. Two men, maybe three, were loading boxes by hand. The fence had signs posted at intermittent intervals: *Premises protected by Total Guard. Warning – Loose Guard Dogs.* Derek parked for less than a minute at the front and to a casual observer it would look as if he was trying to find an address. He pointed at the piece of meaningless paper while they both took in the entrance. The two chain-link gates were open, whilst several feet beyond two hinged barrier poles bearing the word STOP were in the down position. The bottom corner of the old barracks had been altered and large windows added to create a security office which now had an unrestricted view of the entrance and the factory yard. They could make out some sort of movement inside this office.

Derek looked at his watch. 'Three o'clock on a Saturday afternoon. Hardly a busy operation, is it?'

They drove away to look for a motel and to prepare two contingency plans for tomorrow: the first and easier one if the place was totally devoid of guards and dogs, and the second if they had to deal not only with these but also some of the workforce as well.

'Doesn't look like anyone's coming to work today,' Andy said, breaking the silence.

It was just after half past nine on a cloudy Sunday morning and they had been watching the premises for well over an hour now.

'And still just the one security guard on site,' Derek replied. He deliberately didn't mention anything about dogs. They made him nervous at the best of times. He tucked his automatic pistol into his trouser pocket and added, 'Time to get the show started.' Still, people must have been working somewhere close by, theirs was not the only vehicle parked on the road, and the others had been there when they arrived. He reached in and grabbed the cardboard box.

Andy watched him walk towards the closed outer gates. He looked ridiculous, blue suit trousers, long-sleeved red-striped business shirt, sun-glasses – and the crowning glory, a bright green baseball cap pulled firmly down onto his forehead. Both Derek and Maureen had a lot in common when it came to dress sense! He examined the handgun Derek had left for him; it was a huge weapon – an Israeli Desert Eagle automatic pistol. He shook his head. In Britain you would have been locked up for possessing such a lethal piece of hardware, but not here in the States. Here you could buy one, and cheaply at that, in any outdoors type of shop. He threw it down on the passenger seat and returned his attention to Derek, who was rattling the closed chain gates and shouting.

Derek's heart was working flat out. At any moment he half expected vicious-looking dogs to come bounding out from the shadows, but so far there'd been none. A couple of minutes went by. Once, he turned towards the general direction of the van and shrugged. Then a guard came into view and started a slow walk towards the gate. He was dressed in a uniform of pale blue shirt and trousers and was very tall but built like a beanpole. Derek guessed he was in his early twenties. They spoke through the chicken-wire.

Andy watched the pair of them. On several occasions Derek again shrugged his shoulders, and at one point looked as if he were about to spin round on his heels and walk away. Then it happened. The guard unlocked the gate and opened it just enough to accept the package. Immediately, Derek's hand whipped out the gun and in seconds it was against the other man's head. Derek slid through the gap and both men started walking towards the security office. He'd said the urgent-parcel scam would work and it had.

The side mirrors showed Andy the road was still deserted. Then he glanced into the rear-view mirror. Derek was right about their appearance: a baseball cap pulled well down and dark glasses did make recognition difficult. He grabbed the gun, leaped from the camper and sprinted across the road. Within seconds he was through the gate. He closed it and replaced the chain but not the padlock. He vaulted the stop barrier and ran towards the office, taking the four steps in one go. He was in a small corridor, the glass door at the end was open and Derek had the young man sitting down with his arms outstretched on a table. An ancient black and white collie dog sniffed at Andy's trouser leg. He quickly shut the door to stop it escaping and bent down to pat it. It responded by lying down and rolling over.

'Please, please don't hurt me. The dog's my father's. He won't attack you or anything, I promise. Please!'

'What's your name, son?' Derek asked.

'Sam, Sam Gregory. I'm a student. I only do this job at weekends to help pay my way through college. Please don't hurt me. I'm not armed.'

'Where are the other dogs?'

'There aren't any, honestly, just the signs. This company only wants the cheapest security package going, to satisfy the insurance company. Please believe me, there aren't any dogs.'

Derek checked Sam's body for weapons. He was telling the truth and his whole body was trembling with fear. Andy checked the office. The corner site had good visibility down the road but their van was out of sight. Below all the windows were worktops, good old-fashioned wood which showed many years of abuse. There were also two television monitors which showed black and white views of the back of the buildings, three telephones and a device with three buttons for raising and lowering the security barriers. In the far corner was a tray containing a kettle, some old china mugs and a jar of coffee, and underneath it a small refrigerator. On the bench by the door was a microphone on a stand, presumably for calling people on some form of loudspeaker system. The rear and only solid wall had one calendar hanging from it and a small glass-fronted box containing sets of keys.

'Where are the cameras placed?' Andy asked in his best Australian accent.

'In the yard on the two new buildings – there's a blind spot.'

'Okay,' Derek said. 'Tell us about your day. Your routine. How many times you have to report in. Everything. Got it?'

Sam nodded. 'I start at six in the morning and work a twelve-hour shift, then somebody comes and takes over for the night. I have an emergency phone number to ring but that's about all. I don't have to report in hourly or anything like that. Please, what are you going to do to me?'

Derek reassured him, 'Nothing, if you keep on doing what you're told. Do you patrol inside the buildings?'

'No, at weekends they're all kept locked – it's not part of my instructions. I do go for a walk round outside every now and then, mainly for the dog's benefit and also to stretch my legs. I bring my own lunch box and stay in here most of the time studying.' Sam gestured towards a neatly stacked pile of textbooks at the far end of the table. 'But what do you want? There's no money here. There's nothing of value.'

'How do you know that?' Andy asked.

'Because you've been told to say it, haven't you?' Derek interrupted.

The look of fear on Sam's face intensified. Again he nodded.

'Well, that's where you're mistaken, Sam. We have it on very good authority that there's some cocaine stashed here, hence our little visit. Now stand up and show us which keys open what.' Derek prodded Sam with the gun, towards the glass box. He needn't have bothered, all the key-rings bore neatly typed labels.

'Very considerate of the company,' Derek said, stuffing set after set into his pockets.

In the meantime Andy switched off the television sets and pushed the table and chair into the far corner, well away from the telephones. Derek broke open his cardboard box. Its sole contents were half a dozen large plastic ties. He beckoned Sam to sit down again at the repositioned table and chair and tossed the ties across to Andy. Within a minute Sam had both legs firmly secured to table legs and his trouser belt to the back of the chair. Derek walked the few yards to the microphone, switched it on, checked it was working and turned the volume control up full. He placed the now empty box at the very far end on one of the television sets.

'Sam, my friend and I are going cocaine searching. In the box over there is an explosive device. If we hear as much as a cough from you over this mike then *boom*! So be a good boy, forget we are here and get on with your studying.'

The dog insisted on going with them, so Derek just shrugged his shoulders and let him. They walked round the back of the old barrack building towards the two new warehouses. Sam was right, it was a blind spot from the road. Two security cameras hung from the corner of each structure. Alongside the wall of the smaller building drums and pallets of chemicals in bags were stacked neatly in rows. Andy shouted out the names while Derek wrote them down in his black diary. On more than one occasion he had to spell out long, complicated chemical names. The three large storage tanks had a four-foot wall built around them. The first and biggest one had the words FLAMMABLE – WHITE SPIRIT written on it in large black letters. A smaller label stated that the tank capacity was ten thousand gallons and the wall bore several *No Smoking* signs. The second tank held a detergent concentrate and its capacity was five thousand gallons – the same size as the last one which held methanol. Further along the wall were more signs stating what to do in case of spillage or ingestion. Like trippers to the zoo, Andy and Derek stopped in turn to read about the beasts behind the wall.

The side door into the first warehouse opened into a finished-goods area and the smell that greeted them was unmistakably chemical. It reminded Andy of an old-fashioned hardware shop he'd visited many times with his father. They split up and examined the boxes stacked neatly on pallets. These contained plastic bottles labelled turpentine substitute, window cleaner, hard-surface cleaner and oven cleaner, all bearing the name of a well-known store. They joined forces again and walked down the length of the building. The central section was taken up with various filling machines, and in between, pallets of empty plastic containers were randomly placed. At one bench somebody obviously made up cardboard boxes from a stack of flat ones. Their walkabout was temporarily halted by a heavy-duty plastic ribbon door. They pushed it aside and entered a small manufacturing area. A mezzanine floor contained five stainless-steel mixing tanks. Andy climbed the open stairs to take a closer look. Some had lids, all had stirring devices. At the far end a hoist was used to bring up drums or pallets. Pipes came through a neat hole in the wall, presumably bringing liquids from the outside storage tanks. All the pots were empty. They returned the way they had come, and once back at the finished goods area Derek helped himself to a sample of each of the cleaners and felt it necessary to justify his actions by saying, 'I bet I'm not the first. Theft must be rife in places like this.'

They crossed the yard and unlocked the main door to the smaller second building. This time they'd entered at the manufacturing sharp end. There was no distinctive smell this time but there was a fine coating of dust on everything. The equipment was more complicated this time and they came to the conclusion that they were powder blenders with small silos on the top. Whatever was made in here did not contain water or require stainless-steel mixing pots. There were a lot of bags stacked on pallets in one corner.

Derek started to write down names and shouted out, 'Why can't they use goddam English names instead of telephone numbers!'

Andy went across to see what the fuss was all about. Derek was right, though. The only markings that stated what the contents were read either P18963 or V3366, but they had one thing in common, they were all from the same supplier – the Decker Pharmaceutical Corporation. Andy left Derek to it and wandered into the rest of the plant. Again he had to negotiate a plastic curtain wall. The filling machines were also of a different type now, designed to cope with powder products. The containers were also different, white opaque pots with large screw-cap lids. They also came in a range of sizes from two hundred and fifty grams up to two kilos. In a corner of the plant was a very unusual-looking machine. Andy hadn't a clue what it was for. Derek joined him, shrugged again and together they continued into the finished-goods end. The boxes were more substantial this time and instead of being left open were heavily sealed down with tape. The word *Leviathan* was stamped on the front of each carton, and another name went into the diary. At the end of the building was the roller door where they'd seen the men loading the lorry yesterday. Andy opened up one of the boxes and shouted for Derek to join him. He handed him a plastic jar.

Derek sat down on a pile of unmade boxes and shook the jar, which rattled; it was full of tablets. He read the words out loud: '"Leviathan 2000. Extra Strength Amino Acid Tablets. Contents 150 Tablets".' He turned the jar round in his hands and continued reading from the label: '"Leviathan 2000 – now with a full two grams of protein as peptide-bonded amino acids per tablet. Made from the best pharmaceutical grades of whey protein and egg white protein. See catalogue for further details and also other products available in the Leviathan range. Sevenstar Nutrition, Miami, Florida. The leaders in sports supplementary diets".'

He put the jar down and smiled at Andy. They both knew that this part of the operation was beginning to look extremely promising. Andy went through all the pallets of brown boxes with renewed energy. Every time he came across a different code, he passed it to Derek to examine. One box was much heavier than the rest. It was full of Leviathan catalogues. On the glossy front cover was the photograph of a grotesque body-builder posing in the briefest pair of swimming-trunks. A caption read: *Stay ahead of the crowd. Vince (The Bear) Kramer recommends only Leviathan products*. Andy slung Derek a copy and they sat reading the drivel. Mr Kramer had written the foreward himself.

> When you're training, when you're building muscle, when you want strength and endurance, your body needs every edge it can get. When I was training for the IFBB World Pro Cup I lost six pounds of fat and gained three pounds of muscle. How did I do this? By using Leviathan products. Right now I'm training at a body weight of 205 pounds with only 5 per cent body fat! I've never been this big in my life. Body-building has never been so much fun, thanks to Leviathan.

Derek broke the silence, 'This crap goes on for

another five pages. Talk about conceit!' He flicked back to the front cover. 'Didn't make his prick any bigger though, did it?'

Andy laughed 'Have a look at some of the products on offer.'

In all there were some thirty products listed. Most were the '2000' range, designed for weight gain without fat, available in capsules, tablets or as a powder – in vanilla, chocolate or strawberry flavours! There was also a range of drinks.

'Do people really believe in all this bullshit, Derek? It's a giant con, surely? No sooner have you taken one mouthful of pills than you have to take something else to stop a side-effect from the first lot.'

'I guess some of my fellow countrymen – and women – are gullible enough to swallow anything. As for me, I'll stick with my T-bone steaks for protein.'

Their relief was obvious, they had found an amino acid connection. For the next half an hour they tried to outdo each other by finding the most absurd claim for a product in the catalogue. Derek won with something called Leviathan 7000 – it did everything to the body except make you fly! It took him over five minutes to read out the ingredients, most of which he couldn't pronounce. His attempts made Andy crack up with laughter. 'I'm so glad it's got the last one in it,' came his sarcastic reply. 'Wouldn't buy it if it hadn't! You need a science degree before you can even attempt body-building!'

'And a good bank balance,' Derek replied. 'Have a look at the price list on the inside back page. Seventy-nine dollars for a hundred tablets. Further down there's something called carnitine, one capsule costs one dollar. More money then sense, these dick-heads.'

They collected sample jars of all the different products and hid the open boxes at the back of some pallets.

'There's a small office by that weird machine back there. Let's go and see what's in it,' Andy suggested.

The machine turned out to be a tableting press – it said so on a small manufacturer's label. Inside the room they found a well-thumbed loose-leaf file containing the various recipes. Between them they had them copied out in fifteen minutes onto a pad some kind soul had conveniently left. But there were no formulations for any liquid preparations and Derek concluded that some other contract filler must make them.

They returned to Security, leaving their box in the outside corridor. Sam was deeply involved in a book but sat bolt upright when they entered. The dog started to lick his wrist.

'I'm doing as you told me. I haven't moved, I promise you.'

Andy inspected the ties. They were not cutting into his flesh – after all, there was no need to make his life too miserable. He had just been in the wrong place at the wrong time.

Derek hung up the keys they'd already used and took several more off the hooks. He led the way out to the front and unlocked the door into the office complex. It opened directly into what looked like a general office.

'I need to find a computer terminal so I can attach this.' From his trouser pocket Derek took out a small black box no bigger than a cigarette packet. Attached to it was a long length of cable that had come unravelled. Andy hadn't seen this little gadget before and asked what it was for.

'Simon invented it,' Derek explained. 'We have to plug it into the back of a terminal and then put the jack lead back into here.' He pointed to a recessed hole in the little box. 'This lead goes straight into a normal telephone socket, it's got an adaptor so the existing phone will still work. On Monday when Sarius switch on their software Simon will be able to enter their records as well. Clever little thing, isn't he?'

They found what they were looking for, a machine in a corner but at an angle to the wall. Derek fastened on the box whilst Andy got down on his knees and found a suitable phone socket. The dog thought it was a great game playing under someone's desk and licked his face all over. It then decided to fall asleep and Andy made a mental note not to forget it later on.

Whilst Andy was putting the finishing touches to concealing the wire, Derek went for a walk around the place. He returned with two cups of coffee and some bars of chocolate. 'Lunch? Found some vending-machines in the corridor and a clocking-in machine. The place employs thirty-seven full-time staff, most of them women. How many do you reckon in here?'

They counted up the desks – another seven. They sat and drank the very welcome liquid and from their position they could see the camper through the small window panes. It was all very quiet outside.

Derek rested his elbows on his knees. 'I'm a bit disappointed we still haven't found any large stocks, or references to the famous ingredients X and Y.'

'We haven't done the place completely yet.' Andy reminded him. 'There's still corners to look into. Tell you what, you go and have another coffee and I'll go and talk to Sam, the security guys must keep a record of all the lorries and tankers coming and going, there must be delivery notes somewhere.'

Derek sat up again. 'Delivery notes, of course! You go see Sam, I'll look around here.' His enthusiasm was immediately restored.

'All right, Sam? How you feeling?' Andy asked as he entered the security office. 'Anything happening out there? Good. You comfortable, do you need the lavatory or anything?'

Sam nodded then shook his head respectively to the questions.

'Is this your lunch box?' Andy poured what looked like soup from a flask into the cup and removed the box lid, leaving them within easy reach of Sam's hands.

'Tell me, Sam, delivered goods, do you keep records?'

'Yes, there's a book. It's got a blue cover. All goods either leaving or being delivered are recorded in it. But I don't know where it's kept – I never have to use it on Sunday. The regular weekly security people look after it.' Sam's voice possessed less of a tremble now. He had decided that the big man wouldn't hurt him if he answered the questions.

Andy glanced out of the window again. 'Looks like an old military establishment, this park.'

'It was,' Sam answered. 'My father worked at the camp until it was closed in 1988. This site we're on, he says, was the transport area.'

Andy rushed back to find Derek but he wasn't in the office. He found the blue book without too much trouble. It was stacked neatly between others on a desk. He worked systematically and methodically back through the pages. There it was! On 3rd April, a twenty-tonne tanker of fungicide G500 was delivered to Union Mining and Minerals, Bullen, California. There was another in March, in fact, one a month going back at least two years when the book had been started. The word *Melford* caught his eye. Deliveries to Oregon. The were less frequent and didn't form a regular pattern but as near as damn it one every two months. He closed the book and let out a huge sigh. After all these weeks, after all the balls-ups, after all his experiences at Bullen, they had at long last found where the elusive X and Y ingredients came from. A feeling of warm satisfaction flooded into Andy's body but was short-lived.

Derek returned carrying some small sample bottles. 'I found a laboratory,' he said, sounding fed up. 'They test all the incoming raw materials for the household products but as far as I can see none of the protein stuff, they just rely on suppliers' certificates of analysis and conformity. There's a great pile of them stashed in a drawer but I still can't find anything of any goddam use.'

Andy gave him the book, opened it for him and pointed. The look on Derek's face was worth waiting for. He let out a great whoop of joy and hugged

Andy. 'Got the bastards! Well done, my friend. We're going to get well and truly rat-assed tonight, I can tell you!'

Derek found a photocopier and switched it on. He hadn't a clue how it worked but somehow every single page of the blue book was leaving with them. Andy handed him the individual loose-leaf pages, making sure they were kept in strict order. They each glanced at the pages before feeding them into the machine, and it was Derek's turn to make a discovery.

'Have you noticed that several days before this G500 stuff goes out there are tanker deliveries coming in? Look here and here.' He pointed to the various entries. He was right. Two products were involved, '50% stabilised solution P1818' and '50% stabilised solution P1414'.

Then the penny dropped. 'That's our X and Y coming in!' Derek's excitement was now uncontrollable. Even his voice had taken on a higher note. 'Yes, yes, look again, here, P1414, two days before a drop to Melford. Fantastic!' Then his voice dropped back to normal. 'No manufacturers' names are mentioned. It all comes in using contract tankers.'

'Pound to a penny it's from Decker Pharmaceuticals?' Andy challenged. 'Listen, somebody has to get paid. Simon will sort out the invoice side on Monday when he breaks into the accounts.'

'But where do they put it? Is the white spirit tank just a cover or what? No it can't be, we saw all the finished packs of product,' Derek answered his own question.

Andy tapped the floor with his foot. 'Somewhere there are underground tanks around here – Sam said this area used to be the army's garage. We need to find them.'

Derek willed the copier to work faster. It didn't and his patience was wearing very thin when the last page went through.

'What are we actually going to look for?' Derek asked, as they went outside.

'I really don't know,' Andy answered, 'but there must be some outlet pipes that the tankers can connect up to plus some sort of pumping mechanism.'

There was nothing obvious outside any of the buildings, neither were there any manhole covers in the yard which might offer a clue. Derek found two external slatted doors at the far end of the old building but they were locked. Andy ran back to Security and returned shortly, waving the key. The room was only about four feet deep by six feet long. On the floor were two large pumps and on the far wall two large gauges were calibrated in gallons. A small electrical panel was screwed to the left-hand side wall. There was a master on/off switch and four green 'on' buttons, together with four red 'stop' ones. Four pipes with screw-on covers rose in pairs from each pump and were labelled *Tank 1 In* and *Out* and similarly for Tank 2. Andy flicked the master switch and pressed both green buttons marked *Tank Levels*. The buttons lit up and the gauge needles stirred but settled on zero, the maximum they could go up to was fifteen thousand gallons.

'Probably wash them out after each delivery to hide the evidence,' Andy said as he switched off the power and relocked the doors.

'As far as I can tell, the company is run by a Victor Warren – at least he signs all the main memos and notices around here. Let's go and pay his office a visit,' Derek suggested.

Warren's office was on the first floor, directly above the security lodge. They had to pass several other rooms including a print room to get to the end of the corridor. None were of immediate interest. Warren's room was big and airy with its new large windows. They riffled through his desk drawers and a stack of paperwork on top and came to the conclusion that Warren kept a very watchful eye on finances and worked out selling prices and costs himself.

The inevitable VDU stood on a side desk. Derek patted it. 'Simon will expose this little beauty's secrets tomorrow.' In one corner stood an old safe.

Derek pointed to it. 'Do you think you can open it?'

Andy crouched down to examine it in more detail. The plate read *Hollingsworth 1952*. He turned the tumblers. There's two inches of hardened steel surrounding the contents. I'll need some form of stethoscope. Where's the laboratory?'

Derek directed him in the general direction and when Andy returned he had a strange-looking piece of kit round his neck, consisting of bright orange rubber tubing and a small plastic funnel. Derek stood to one side and watched. It took Andy the best part of ten minutes before the combination yielded to his fingertips, and he was sweating heavily as he opened the door and invited Derek to inspect the contents. He went off to find a washroom and return the bits he'd borrowed.

Derek removed a cash box containing two hundred dollars in assorted notes and a company cheque book. Underneath was a pile of certificates. Two were from the Food and Drug Administration approving Sarius's plant and methods as meeting their standards. There was one from the University of Stanford. Victor was obviously a very clever fellow. He'd been there from 1974 to 1977 and had obtained a doctorate in petrochemical research. There were a few personal letters, mainly from end-users praising the company's products. There were some title deeds to a house; Derek noted down the address. There was also the leasehold agreement on the factory. It had eighty-one years to run and had been signed in 1987 by Warren himself. Next came an old brown envelope. Inside were official-looking letters from US Immigration and a certificate, dated 1976, declaring that a Bogdan Masaryk known as Victor Warren had been granted citizenship of the United States of America. His place of birth was given as Prague, Czechoslovakia. Derek put this lot to one side to photocopy. At the bottom of the pile was an innocent-looking file. Inside were dozens of newspaper clippings referring to various conflicts going on around the world. The oldest dated back to 1993, the newest last week's news about the near war going on in South Africa. Neatly written across the inside cover were the words *Special Reserve Lives On*. Again Derek wrote this sentence down.

Andy read the various copies as Derek ran them off, then they returned everything in its correct order to the safe. Andy swung the door shut and spun the tumblers. They had exhausted their search of Sarius, it was now time to retrace their steps. They stopped off at the general office, Andy scooped up the coffee cups and Derek's samples and stirred the dog. Derek searched round and found a large brown envelope and stuffed it full of screwed-up paper to make it look very padded. Every door back to Security was relocked. All the samples and paperwork joined the others in the box outside Sam's door. As they entered the office Derek made a great point of displaying his envelope and saying, 'Knew we would find it eventually.' Andy hung up all the keys and removed the empty 'bomb box'

Derek offered Sam two choices. 'As you can see we got what we came for. We can leave you either all trussed up like you are or free – it's all down to you, son. You can forget we were here, get cleaned up before your relief comes on – or stay like you are, in which case the police will spend days questioning you. You'll lose your job and you'll be the laughing-stock at college.'

Sam was undecided, so Andy reached the compromise for him. He cut off his leg ties. All that restrained him now was the trouser belt to the chair.

Derek left first. Andy watched him until he'd reached the camper and dumped the cardboard box inside, then he ran to the gates and re-padlocked them before joining Derek.

'I think we're earned a long, hot bath in a good hotel tonight,' he suggested wearily.

11

Andy had to put his thoughts about clean sheets and hot water on hold. No sooner had he climbed into the driver's seat than Derek wanted to go and look over Warren's house. He pointed out it was only twenty miles away and it was still only two thirty in the afternoon.

'Warren lives in Kern County near a place called Isabella. It's due east of here,' Derek said, with the map perched on his knees.

Outside Bakersfield the road followed the course of the river Kern and started to climb into the Sierra Nevada range. Andy stopped the camper and asked to look at the map. His curiosity had proved right. If they kept going east in a straight line for another sixty or so miles they would eventually come to Bullen on the other side of the mountains. He had come round in one gigantic circle. The scenery was magnificent with mile after mile of citrus groves, cotton plantations and green fields of what he now knew to be alfalfa – and all grown in a former desert. They parked at a viewing-point overlooking lake Isabella. The air was cooler up here and Andy took in deep breaths of the stuff to give his lungs a treat. A large notice-board showed places of interest around the picturesque lake, claiming it was the largest man-made freshwater stretch of water in southern California. Now he understood how they were able to grow so much in the valley downstream.

If Derek had imagined they would drive straight to Warren's front drive, he was sadly mistaken. It took them nearly two hours to find the property. Dirt-tracks and small roads lead off the main highway every couple of hundred yards. People were prepared to pay lots of good money to have privacy and Warren was no exception. The split-level expensive-looking log cabin overlooked the best part of the lake.

Derek went off to carry out an initial observation of the place but was back in less than a minute. 'We'll have to wait until tomorrow when hopefully, he goes to work. The place is crawling with people at the moment, there's at least three cars parked at the top of the drive.'

Andy would get his hot water after all! They booked into the biggest tourist hotel and were given lakeside rooms. Over dinner Derek requested a favour. He said he would like to tackle Warren's house on his own. Andy could only assume his partner was having another attack of the blues about all the important clues being found by somebody else – even the blue book at Sarius. If it was going to boost Derek's confidence finding something of earth-shattering significance at the house then he had no objections at all. In fact, he would welcome it. The more cheerful Derek was the sweeter life in the confined space of the camper would be.

He dropped Derek off at the bottom of the driveway and as agreed said he would return in about ten or fifteen minutes just in case there were any problems. He watched as the short man, dressed in full blue suit and carrying a Gideon Bible stolen from the hotel room, climbed up the steep incline. Three times Andy drove past the entrance in the next thirty minutes but each time it was deserted. He wished Derek well out aloud. 'Please let him find something important for all our sakes!'

As agreed, he gave Derek two hours to have a good look-round, then drove slowly past but there was no sign of the 'Disciple of God' on the stretch of the road. He left it another hour. Some bushes moved as Derek climbed down onto the road and waved.

'Another five minutes and I was going to come looking for you,' Andy told him.

'It's nice to know you're wanted!' Derek replied, throwing his jacket into the back. He was smiling and seemed much happier in himself.

Andy drove off. 'Well, I'm all ears. How did you get on?'

'Easy, piece of cake really. He leaves a key under a plant-pot by the front door. It was the first thing I noticed, all the different marks where it had been moved so many times. He's a dirty little bugger is our Victor, I can tell you. The inside of that house is just like a bordello. The master bedroom is something else – the bed alone would sleep six, although I don't think that's what it's there for! He's got a porno video collection which must run into hundreds and one of those big-screen televisions to view them on. Some of the videos are signed by those who took part in them. He's not kinky or anything like that, just very red-blooded. He likes ladies, the more the merrier. He's not married, so I guess he's free to do what he likes.'

'How do you know that?'

Derek shrugged. 'Just a hunch, but there are no female clothes hanging up in the numerous wardrobes – at least not the sort a wife would wear! The bedroom is on the first floor, connected to a bathroom and a study. Incidentally, he has a two-way mirror between these two. Bet he's seen some rare sights! His study is littered with photographs, nearly all of them poses with young women.'

'What's our Victor look like?'

'Mid-fifties, tall, built like a beanpole but still got a full head of black hair cut short. Must be fit still. There were some papers on his desk and he's just passed his annual medical to renew his pilot's licence. Has his own plane, a single-engined job parked at Bakersfield's municipal airport. There was a receipt – it's just cost him four thousand dollars to have it serviced. Mind you, he can afford it. He pays himself fifteen big ones a month, although most of it goes straight out again. There was a pile of plastic-money receipts to places in Las Vegas – hotels, casinos and escort agencies. To sum up, I would say Victor lives his life to the full and what he earns he spends right away on the nicer pleasures in life.'

'Anything connected with the protein business?'

Derek had been savouring this moment. 'Remember we found the file with *Special Reserve* written in it? Well, his desk diary for the Friday after next, had "meeting of Special Reserve" entered in it. The rest of his social calendar makes very interesting reading as well, I can tell you!'

'Any clues where the meeting's to be held?'

'None, but we can keep him under observation and follow him,' Derek said confidently.

'What about his plane, supposing he uses that?'

Derek slumped into the seat and started to hum.

Andy continued, 'I'm driving about aimlessly at the moment – any plans?'

'Yes, let's head for Los Angeles and give Larry all these samples. No, hang on a minute, they're not relevant any more, are they? Larry has enough on his plate without spending all night ploughing through this lot. Anything we've got has powdered protein in it, we didn't get any of the proper P1818 or P1414 crap, did we? Keep heading towards Bakersfield and pull in at the first shopping-mall. I need to buy some bottled water or something to quench my thirst.'

Andy did as he was instructed. Once parked, Derek decided to write the General a report; it had to be done sooner or later. Andy left him with his head bowed over his note pad and went shopping. He was gone for less than an hour. Derek was lying on his bunk-bed reading a magazine.

'Thought you were going to write a report?'

'Done it! Not wasting too much ink on that bastard. Told him what we've found and suggested he keeps his distance until we find out more about this proposed meeting. Knowing Hutton, he'll send in the Cavalry and have Sarius surrounded and frighten off whoever else is behind this. He said he'd get back to us soon.'

The phone beeped. The call only lasted a few seconds and Derek didn't actually say anything. He switched the machine off and slung it back on the bed. his light-hearted mood had gone.

'Problems?' Andy enquired.

'The voice in Washington says we are to remain here. Somebody will pick up the photocopies in less than an hour's time. Everywhere we go, they're close by. I don't like it.'

Andy changed the subject. 'What's the magazine?'

Derek passed over the journal. It was titled *Muscular Bodies*. Andy flicked through it. Page after page of advertisements claimed that their range of products could work miracles with your body. Derek interrupted. 'Turn to the centre pages.' He started to laugh.

Andy unfolded the requested pages and turned the magazine round and round. 'It's difficult to know whether it's male or female; the latter, I guess, considering it's wearing a bikini top, although what for, is beyond me. The picture does nothing for me at all, in fact it's a total turn-off.'

'Nor me – I much prefer Victor's taste in women. You know there were seventeen different mags on bodybuilding in that mall shop over there? Somewhere near the front it says that the market is worth something like two point eight billion dollars a year!' He found Andy the relevant page and pointed out a full-page advert for Leviathan products whilst doing so.

Derek broke the silence first. 'Do you want to call Larry to see if he's got any news?'

Andy was on the phone for a good ten minutes. The conversation was heavily one-sided and Derek sat on the edge of his bunk like a schoolboy waiting for the lesson to start.

At last Andy reported, 'Larry's tested over two dozen bottles of wine from all over the States so far. He said that without fail they all contained the equivalent of about 160 milligrams per litre of protein and that in over seventy per cent of cases it was the X variety. He also confirms what you told me – that although you drink less wine than beer, the amount of poison taken is near enough the same. In fact, he said heaven help those people who drink a lot of wine! He's also been working with his monkeys again, giving them X and Y alternately. He was coming around to the conclusion that Y was the dominant one until he opened the cage of one depressed specimen and it went for him. Larry said it had just been pretending to act dopey waiting for its moment to escape. He's now got four stitches in his hand as a reminder. He says he's now convinced that it doesn't matter which protein you start with, X always comes out on top. He's also followed up the hard-drug line that we discussed. Basically, things like heroin are far more powerful than our two chemicals and override them. He's also been talking with his friend at the university. Both X and Y are totally acid-soluble and are absolutely colourless and odourless; it wouldn't matter how much you shovelled into wine or beer, you'd never taste them over the normal flavours present. His friend also reckons they're both synthetically and very cleverly made. The amino acids have things called side chains attached to them which make them very resistant to further break down by enzymes in the body. I said yes, but I haven't a clue what he's talking about.'

Derek shrugged. 'Nor me!'

'In short, this professor guy doesn't know exactly what they are because he's never seen anything exactly the same before. He's left Larry a list of people who are more knowledgeable in this field, and as you heard I gave him our number. He'll fax them through now.'

Derek plugged the machine lead into the cigarette lighter and switched on the ignition – there was no point in draining its batteries. They both sat and waited for it to ring. It did, but the message was from Simon:

Dear Derek and Andy. As requested, a breakdown of the export tonnages shipped out of Union Mining and Minerals, Melford, Oregon. Drawn out below in neat columns were all the fine grades of Purflo and tonnages sent out against country of destination. The fax finished with the words *Hope this is all relevant and you can understand it, kind regards to you both, Simon.*

Derek scrabbled about looking for his map and briefcase and busied himself for the next twenty minutes. Andy left him to it. The fax rang again and he watched each line come through from Larry but decided to wait until Derek had finished colouring in the world before confusing him with the latest information.

The look on Derek's face showed that he was very satisfied with his handiwork. 'There's just over twenty-seven thousand tonnes sold in the States. The rest of it is mainly exported to Mexico, South America, Europe and Japan, although there are also some shipments to South Korea, Kenya and New Zealand. I've marked off all these places in green.'

Andy stared down at the map of the world. Large areas were marked off in red and blue whilst others were covered in green and blue. Whole continents like North America and Europe were criss-crossed with all three colours. As if waiting for something to happen, the former Soviet Union expanse remained colourless, as did several other areas. He pointed to half a dozen places. 'All these countries are in some state of chaos and it's probably being fuelled by the people drinking laced alcohol.'

Derek added to Andy's list. 'If only we knew which colour was definitely X or Y. Hang on a minute! Have you still got that man's letter from Cyprus?'

Andy nodded, eventually laid his hands on it and passed it across.

Derek sat patiently reading it and then let out a tremendous yelp. 'We've cracked it! We've fucking well cracked it! Fred Clarke said the Japanese beer made him feel lousy and depressed. The only relevant colour on Japan is green – Purflo from Melford. The Y stuff goes to Melford!'

'Congratulations!' Andy said, patting his friend on the back, genuinely impressed with his detective work. 'From now on I'm going to call you Sherlock!' At last Derek's luck was beginning to change. This would help make their lives together in the close confines of the van more tolerable and would keep the humming down to a minimum!

Andy let him reflect on his latest success for a few minutes before showing him Larry's list. There were five names on it. Four were meaningless but the one half-way down caused Derek to exclaim, 'Doctor Charles Wilenius, Decker Pharmaceuticals, Stockton, California. Things are getting interesting! That's the second time we've seen that name and I think it's more than just a coincidence. As soon as Albert or whoever has picked up the papers then we're definitely going to hotfoot it to Stockton.'

Derek reached across for the map and found Stockton. It was about two hundred and fifty miles north of Bakersfield on the same latitude as San Francisco but about fifty miles to the east.

Albert was indeed the messenger boy and arrived exactly on time. No words were exchanged as the report was handed over. He placed it in a very secure-looking leather case and was out of the shopping-mall car park in less than a minute.

Derek volunteered to drive the first stint. They made good time on Highway 99 and by late afternoon were on the outskirts of Fresno. The name rang a bell inside Andy's head until he remembered that this was where Maureen was born and raised. The surrounding countryside was certainly more fertile and pleasant than where she currently resided.

The fax machine rang. It was on automatic and set itself in motion to receive the messages. Andy turned his seat round to watch as the special paper spewed out of the black plastic unit like an unrolling toilet roll. The message was in Simon's writing and looked very complicated. Derek suggested they find a suitable off-road diner and read the long screed over a meal.

The message began with Simon's usual greeting and then ploughed straight into the facts.

> The device at Sarius worked perfectly and I have managed to obtain some other details from the IRS department. I have all the full details back at base, what is given below is just a resumé. Sarius is wholly owned by a Mr Victor Warren. He started the company in 1983, outgrew the original premises rapidly and moved to his current address in 1987. Listed as a manufacturer of both a range of household cleaning products and, as from 1990, a range of nutritional food supplements (strange combination?). Turnover in 94/95 was $8.83 million, making a net profit of

$0.149 million. Some of the figures don't add up though. Sarius buy many hundreds of tonnes of liquid proteins from a company called Decker Pharmaceuticals at a price of $32 a gallon. However, according to their records, the only liquid that leaves the premises is invoiced at $5.7 a gallon. The products are delivered to a company called Union Mining and Minerals. More tonnage leaves Sarius than is bought, so I can only assume that the products are diluted down with something else as part of a finished formulation. To be exact, last year Sarius bought just over 600 tonnes split between two code numbers and delivered nearly 1200 tonnes bearing one different code. On such a transaction the company are making a loss of nearly $2.5 million. I suspect someone has made a mistake and a figure of 32 should read 3.2. I will recheck this. Also buy powdered protein from Decker – 200 tonnes last financial year at $9.6 per kilo. Also vitamins, 150 tonnes at $12.4 per kilo. Chemicals such as white spirit and detergent bought from Noble Oil at $4.3 and $8.9 per gallon. Numerous other prices if required. The company employs thirty seven full-time and six part-time employees. All tax has been paid for last year. I have a list of salaries and names and addresses of all personnel if required. Please let me know if more info required. With all good wishes, Simon.

They passed the fax back and forth over the table, each trying to take in another fact. At the moment some of it didn't make any sense, even Simon had admitted it. Warren made a loss of nearly $2.5 million by selling on X and Y solutions to Union at a ridiculously low price, and yet all the facts so far showed that he was not being financed externally by some third party or by foreign money coming into his firm. How then did he manage to keep his company afloat and continue his rich lifestyle?

Derek suggested they park up for the night where they were. As soon as he was inside the camper he made a beeline for the body-builder magazine, tossed

Andy his calculator, found the page with the Leviathan advert on it and studied it for several minutes.

'You crafty little bastard, Victor. He's offsetting X and Y against these!' He hit the page with his palm. 'Work it out on the machine, will you? He buys 200 tonnes of powder protein at $9.6, and 150 tonnes of vitamins at $12.4 what's the total?'

Andy furiously tapped the keys and Derek passed across a pen. He double checked the figures and wrote down $3.78 million.

'Now let's suppose he sells his finished goods on for $25 a kilo. Knock off $5 for labour and the packaging. It's a fair price, after all – Leviathan are retailing the stuff at anywhere between $45 and $60. So, 350 tonnes at $20 a kilo – even I can work that one out – $7 million. He's making about a $3 million profit on the body-building powders themselves – which is more than he's losing on the Union deal. I know I'm only guessing at these figures, but they almost add up. One cancels the other out. He's selling cheap products expensively to Leviathan to offset the loss of selling expensive X and Y to Union for next to nothing. Union get their "fungicide", and whoever's ultimately behind all of this gets their nasty little products into the filteraid.'

Andy put down the calculator and gave Derek a round of applause. 'Brilliant! You're certainly having a good day. Even if Sarius only break even on this, Warren's still got his household side to make money from and keep solvent.'

'And the body-builders of America are unwittingly financing the whole nasty business,' Derek added.

Derek was up early. His recent discoveries had indeed worked wonders for his soul. Andy watched him as he made the coffee. He looked far more relaxed and was even smiling for the first time in days.

'I've made out a checklist,' Derek began, 'and as far as I can see we still have four things left to do. Establish if there's any connection between Victor Warren and Charles Wilenius; find out if both are Czechs and if there's anything in this; get some background on Wilenius and, finally check out Decker Pharmaceuticals. Of course not necessarily in that order. I've a friend in Immigration in San Francisco – after we've been to Stockton we'll pay him a visit. Any other ideas or thoughts?'

Andy couldn't think of any so early on in the day, and anyway Derek was making a good job of it all on his own.

Derek phoned Simon while Andy drove. He thanked him for his Sarius report and agreed there must have been a decimal point wrong on the $32 figure. It wasn't important anyway, he lied. Simon said he would do his best once again to obtain any information about Decker Pharmaceuticals. Derek had no sooner put the phone down than it rang again. Derek had to hold it away from his ear – even Andy could hear the voice.

'General Hutton here. Where are you, Madden?'

'Heading towards Stockton.'

'Exactly, I mean, numbskull!'

Andy shouted out that they'd just passed a sign saying 'Chowchilla'.

There was a pause and then the voice started up again. 'Now hear this! I want you to turn round and head for an air force base called Edwards near Rosamond. Obeying the speed limit, it should take you no more than four hours. I will expect you at two o'clock this afternoon. Ask for me at Security.' *Slam*!

Andy hadn't a clue where he was supposed to go. Derek dived into the back and came back with the map, uttering obscenities.

'That bastard wants us to drive back almost to Los Angeles! Turn round when you can. It's back to Bakersfield on the 99 and then on to Mojave. If the idiot knows where we are all the time, or at least we suspect he does, why couldn't he arrange a meeting up this end of the road?' The good mood Derek had started the day with had now gone.

It took Andy another five miles' driving north before he could find a suitable exit to change carriageways. The fact that Hutton had been able to locate their mobile phone number both annoyed and niggled Derek.

He hardly spoke on the entire journey south except to mouth off swear-words, all aimed in the direction of Oliver Hutton. Andy was getting used to this stretch of road. Bakersfield was very familiar, but try as he did, he couldn't make the time allowed by the General.

It was half past two when they announced themselves to the officer on duty at Security. To make matters worse, this smartly dressed young man insisted on a full vehicle search before letting them into the base. How much longer he would have detained them if he'd found the pistols was anyone's guess. He instructed them to park just inside the perimeter fence, and no sooner had Andy switched off the ignition than a sergeant screeched his Jeep to a halt next to them. He jumped out, saluted and asked them to climb aboard his vehicle. He drove them at high speed along a runway, then turned off along a recently repaired concrete road and did an emergency stop outside a one-storey row of concrete buildings with antennae poking through the flat roof. The short journey had been a nightmare and both were glad to get out of the boneshaker. Either the driver was chasing the land speed record or he was a total idiot.

'I reckon this bum had two glasses of wine X for lunch!' Derek whispered to Andy.

The driver led the way into the block and knocked on a door marked *Private*, the unmistakable voice of Hutton rang out. 'Enter!' He was standing by the only window, wearing his best dress uniform with rows of dubious medal ribbons sewn onto it. If anything, he was putting on more weight and the thread holding his jacket buttons was taking a tremendous strain.

'You're late. It's not good enough! Two o'clock, I said.'

It was not worth arguing with the bloated fool but nobody could have made it in less than four hours, Andy reckoned. It was all part of the rude man's humiliating tactics so that as soon as they walked into the room he had them at a disadvantage.

In the far corner sat a man dressed in an obviously very expensive suit.

'I want you to meet Commander Jeremy Young,' the General continued.

'Derek, Andy, it's nice to meet you at last.' The voice was cultured English. The man was in his sixties, in good physical condition and had a mass of black curly hair. He stood up, came across and shook both their hands warmly. 'The General and I have been following your exploits with the greatest of interest. Let me explain, I'm the British end of the operation.' He glanced across at Hutton. 'Of course, as all the action is happening on American soil, Oliver's in charge of the whole operation.'

The General's face reddened and his neck strained under the tight collar. He looked absolutely furious. Once again he'd been called 'Oliver' in front of junior staff. As if to rub it in, the Commander did it again.

'Oliver and I are looking forward to hearing all your news. Of course, we've read your report from yesterday. Come and sit down and tell us everything you know about Sarius and Mr Warren, plus your views on the whole situation.'

Andy and Derek took well over an hour to relate all the facts and satisfy the other two men's questions. It hadn't been rehearsed but everytime Andy stopped, Derek took over, and vice versa. They performed well as a double act. Young's questions were always polite and either began or ended with the word 'gentlemen', Hutton's were not! They broke off all conversation when an orderly arrived with coffee and sandwiches. Again, this had clearly not been the General's idea. His methods would not run to such close fraternisation with mere mortals.

Young resumed the interview. 'We are all concerned about you unearthing possible links with something called "Special Reserve". I – we – thought it would be in order to give you some basic background on this topic so that you will have a better understanding should you run into it again. As they say, forewarned is forearmed and all that. The story starts on our side of the Atlantic, Andy.'

The General made a move as if to interrupt, but the Commander cut him off short before he could speak.

'What you're about to hear is, of course, very highly classified and for your ears only. I know you're working closely with Larry Fletcher, but he does not have the necessary clearance – I think you know what I'm implying.'

Andy and Derek nodded.

'Special Reserve, gentlemen, is not as you may think some vintage port but a very frightening organisation set up by the KGB. It was fully born in 1968. In that year our country and Belgium expelled something like one hundred and fifty KGB and military intelligence officers known as GRU. Most of these men and women were attached to their embassies and – you know the usual sort of thing, all pretended to be diplomats. Let me assure you none of them were, they were all spies. Anyway, these expulsions neutralised the Soviets' activities in these two countries, and back in the Kremlin alarm bells were beginning to ring. What would happen if all countries worldwide started to expel anyone with known KGB links! Before long their vast rivers of information would dry up and they would be totally cut off from world events. To such a manly organisation as the KGB it would be worse than castration. So they got their heads together and came up with the concept of a special reserve organisation. This body of people would be such a secret group that they would remain undetectable and so could remain in foreign parts even if all the regular KGB agents were sent home in disgrace from every single embassy.' Young paused and took a drink of water and even passed the jug around. Hutton refused his offer.

'With the full approval of the Politburo,' the Commander continued, 'the KGB set up a new department, known as "R" at its Moscow headquarters and began to select its new "ghost" personnel. People from all professions were interviewed – genuine diplomats, engineers, economists, scientists – basically, anyone who travelled as part of their existing job or who was prepared to emigrate and start a new life on some distant shore. None of those finally selected had any previous connection with any intelligence organisation. All were clean. They were put onto the KGB payroll and paid normal KGB salaries whilst still continuing their normal jobs, all of this unbeknown to their regular employer. They all went to special training sessions at night or at weekends. It took about a year to induct them satisfactorily into their new roles and once they were considered ready they were sent to all corners of the planet. Some already had predetermined jobs to go to, others had to start from scratch in their newly adopted homeland. But they all had to report back to a known contact with any scrap of information which might be valuable to the Soviet Union – anything that could be turned to its advantage in order to make it richer, stronger and more powerful. Yes, Derek?'

'Were they still paid by the KGB once they'd been sent abroad?' He was casting his mind back to Victor's bank statements. He certainly was not receiving any extraneous monies.

'Some, presumably: others would have chosen to have it paid directly to their families. The spy-masters gave this project a lot of thought, I can assure you. They recruited heavily from the student population. What better way to capitalise on your investment than to choose people who would rise through the management systems in foreign organisations. Some would also marry and get information from their partners or in-laws. These young people were not motivated by money, they'd never had any at this stage in their lives anyway. No, they were turned on by the sheer challenge of starting new lives in places like America, France or Australia. The one thing we don't know is how many people they recruited over the years – it could run into many thousands. In a matter of years the old-style KGB was made almost redundant and in its place was a very effective and secretive organisation called Special Reserve whose tentacles spread into all the world's activities, from basic items such as an engineer passing on some scrap of computer technology right through to a senior diplomat eavesdropping on world leaders. In fact, we know that some young men joined the army just so that they could report back on the number of troops and the type of military hardware at their disposal where they were stationed. We don't know, of course, who they were and what rank they might have reached now.' It was unfortunate but Commander Young's gaze fixed unintentionally on Hutton.

Both Andy and Derek were itching to ask the same question. It fell to Derek.

'If this Special Reserve is so secretive, how come you know so much about it?'

'A stroke of good fortune. In the late eighties a General Vitaly Makarov of the KGB decided he'd had enough of the Russian way of life and came across, as they say, – first to Britain but I believe he resides here under a new name and identity. He blew the whistle on the whole thing. Neither our government nor our allies had the slightest idea of what he was talking about at first. He gave us a lot of names of diplomats but was vague about the lower order of things. That was the whole point of the exercise: no one man knew exactly who else was involved. Anyway, we checked up on his story and found that numerous Russian chambers of commerce spread throughout the world were not exactly what they should have been – all of this was just before you joined us, Andy, so you missed the fun. We, that is, the Western Alliance countries, took Makarov's news very seriously indeed. We all began to investigate the extent of this organisation and make plans to infiltrate it or in some way undermine it. Either way it had to be stopped. Then it started to self-destruct. Everything started to go wrong for the hard-line communists in the early nineties – the Berlin Wall came down, Germany was reunited and the old Soviet Union started to collapse. A new world was emerging with a new-style leader – Boris Yeltsin. The old days of the KGB were over, their undisputed former power was taken away and Special Reserve appeared to go with it. We have no further mention or news of it from any source until your report yesterday, hence this hastily gathered meeting and obvious concern. Thank you for your attention. I have no more to say so I will hand you back to Oliver.'

'What's your next plan of action?' he stormed.

Andy jumped in quickly, knowing that Derek would only make himself angry talking to the General. 'To establish the connection between Victor Warren and Charles Wilenius and to find out what happens at Decker Pharmaceuticals. After that, we're going to look into the Czech connection.'

'Right, get on with it – and again and for the umpteenth time report back the moment anything happens. I want to know immediately, understood?'

Commander Young added, 'Good luck, gentlemen, on your next mission. Oh, by the way, leave the Czech connection business to me, will you? One of my colleagues knows Eastern Europe well. I'll get him to sort this one out. Mind you, it'll be like looking for the proverbial needle now – a lot of records disappeared after the invasion of 1967. He'll do his best, though, I can assure you.' He shook their hands again.

'Will you check out Charles Wilenius as well?' Derek asked.

'Certainly.'

The sergeant was slouched down in the Jeep but sprang to attention as soon as he saw them. Andy had a few words with him and the drive back to their camper was far more sedate than their outgoing journey.

Derek started to drive the camper north. 'What did you say to that sergeant?' he asked.

'I told him you were a four-star general on an undercover mission and that if he didn't drive you back safely you would have his stripes!'

Derek laughed and the van nearly veered off the road. 'Tell me, you've never met the Commander before, but do you ever get to meet any of your other senior people?'

'No, never. It's a bit like Special Reserve, isn't it?'

'Well, I know one thing. I would rather work for your faceless lot, if they're all like the Commander, than for a little shit like Hutton. I don't suppose there's any chance I could "come across", as they say?'

12

They sat in silence watching the same countryside roll by that they'd seen several times already. Skirting around Bakersfield, Derek mused, 'It would be interesting to know what our friend Victor Warren did with himself before he started up Sarius. According to the dates, there's a good six-year gap since he left university.'

'That's what I've been mulling over, along with a whole series of things,' Andy replied.

'Such as?'

'This Special Reserve outfit. Young said it had virtually collapsed. I was just wondering how all the thousands of agents must have felt. They would be stuck in some foreign country unable to do anything because officially they didn't exist.'

Derek laughed. 'I'd have gone out and got smashed! Genuine freedom at last! I think I'll fax our young friend at the Treasury and ask him what he can unearth on Warren's past. While he's at it he may as well include what's his name, Wilenius.'

He pulled the van over and they changed driving positions. Andy left his friend to potter about in the back and was mentally miles away when he felt a hand on his shoulder.

'Had a fax in from Larry. You carry on driving and I'll read it out to you:

"I have now concluded the last of the studies on the monkeys, observing their difference in behaviour when just injected with alcohol and then with alcohol plus X or Y. The tests were carried out to see if their reactions were in the main due to just being inebriated or controlled by our two additives. The findings are conclusive and show that irrespective of the original behaviour it can be dramatically changed around by both X and Y. For instance, a happy-go-lucky drunk beast can be reduced to a tired and lethargic creature in a short space of time by giving it Y. This work concludes all I have on at the moment. Please do not hesitate to forward any more items you might think relevant and call in and see me either at home or at work anytime you're in Los Angeles. Good luck in all your efforts. Larry."

'He's a good human being, Larry,' Derek commented. 'I'll send him a note back thanking him for all his efforts. We've been lucky having someone as dedicated as him. I just hope he'll be able to get some sleep from now on.'

It was approaching midnight when they neared Stockton. Derek reckoned they had about another fifteen miles to go and then would start to see signposts advising them to leave Highway 99. The night sky ahead of them grew brighter and brighter.

'Probably some oil refinery.' Derek suggested.

Andy turned off the first slip road signposted Stockton. The refinery grew larger by the minute.

'Now that's what I call a proper factory – look at all the steam and chimney flues.' Derek was so immersed that he was not prepared for Andy's sudden left-hand turn and was thrown almost off his seat. 'What the hell are you doing?'

'Decker Pharmaceuticals! We're here,' Andy replied, slowing the van down to almost a crawl. On their right was a car park where over a thousand assorted vehicles were parked. On the left was the enormous production complex. High-security fencing ran along all sides, and security cameras, including infrared devices, were placed prominently on high poles spaced every two hundred yards or so. Floodlights illuminated everything, including the road. It was tempting to go even slower but Andy knew that they would already be on some monitor, and a camper cruising past after midnight might be sufficient to arouse someone's curiosity. A footbridge crossed over from the car park, but at each end turnstiles prevented outsiders from entering.

'The employees probably have personalised plastic cards to let themselves in,' Derek observed.

Half a mile down the road was a vehicular entrance. Two large signs either side of the road boldly stated DECKER PHARMACEUTICALS – MAIN ENTRANCE. There were another half-dozen smaller signs scattered around but the print was too small to make out. The entrance to the internal factory road was separated by a large futuristic-looking security building. Through the glass they could make out at least four guards on duty. A container lorry stood on the exit weighbridge. Further along the main road the production facilities began to peter out and were replaced by a well-manicured lawn planted with flower-beds. Set way back from the road and with its own private car park was a very grand building. Derek gave a low whistle. There was something definitely colonial about it, Andy thought; it looked almost like an English stately home. A large fountain was set in the half-moon of the lawn in front of the 'palace' and even at this time of night was still playing its programme of water movements.

On the other side of the road there looked to be some sort of sports and social club. They could make out the start of a golf-course behind it.

'Certainly know how to look after their—' Derek didn't get a chance to finish his remark.

'Did you see that?' Andy interrupted.

'What?'

'I'll turn round.' Andy was half inclined to do a U-turn but decided there were too many cameras about. He drove on for about a mile back into the night and blinked sharply as his eyes got used to the darkness again. He retraced their steps, approached the spot where he'd shouted out and slowed down to a mere crawl. 'Now! Look at the flag by the fountain.'

A green and white company pennant fluttered in the

night air. In the centre were two words, the top one much larger than the one underneath.

'Got it!' Derek replied. 'TACIT Corporation. My God, that's the lot who sold off Union Minerals!'

'This whole thing's getting more involved by the day. Somewhere in all of this lot we reckon X and Y start life, and just to make things even more interesting a Mr Charles Wilenius, one of the world's leading authorities on amino acids, also works here. Now we know that Decker Pharmaceuticals are part of the TACIT Corporation, one of the world's largest chemical outfits, and as you correctly stated, the lot who sold off Union Mining and Minerals. What on earth are we uncovering here?'

Derek sighed. 'One thing's for sure, getting into this place is going to be no pushover. It's like goddam Fort Knox. Where do we even start? It's a small town in its own right!'

They were both too tired to formulate a decisive action plan. Andy found a suitable piece of scrubland miles from the plant and both of them were asleep in minutes.

The morning air had a chill about it. As soon as Derek turned on the engine to provide some warmth from the heater the fax machine started buzzing. The message was from the Commander and written like a telegram.

> Charles Wilenius. Arrived USA 1971 from Zagreb. Original name Zoran Vladimir Radelk registered with US Immigration. Born 1944. Applied US citizenship 1975. Granted 1977. No US university attended. Decker Pharmaceutical employee since arrival. Now Vice-President of Research and Development.

Derek made only one comment, 'Your Commander is actually helping us! Did you hear that, Hutton, you ass-hole!'

There was enough coffee left for a cup each and some bread, which although stale didn't taste too bad thickly spread with blackcurrant jam. They both sat staring at each other, waiting for inspiration.

Derek stood up and stretched. 'Let's head for

Stockton itself. I'll go visit the local newspaper office and see what I can dig up on Charlie boy. How about you finding out where he lives, and let's see if we can make a start searching his house first? I certainly don't relish the thought of breaking into his works!'

They drove past the factory again to see it in daylight. Derek was right, to get into Decker Pharmaceuticals without being seen was going to be not far short of a miracle. Andy dropped Derek off in the centre of town and agreed to pick him up from the same spot at four o'clock – in six hours' time. He parked in a municipal car park and struck lucky, County Hall was situated only one block away.

The young male clerk went out of his way to be helpful. Not only did he give Andy the address he also showed him where it was located on the district map – after all, it was not every day someone from Europe wanted to pay his cousin a surprise visit!

It took Andy about thirty minutes to reach Framlingham. He was already impressed. There were no large chemical factories this side of town. This area was reserved for the rich homeowner. The houses were big and set in many acres of land, and the countryside was beautiful – rolling hills and forests plus the odd small lake.

The Willows was no exception. Like its neighbours, the house stood back from the main road and had a sweeping in-and-out driveway. The main building was of old-fashioned brick construction and the double front doors were entered by means of four imposing stairs. To Andy it had a definite European look about it. To the right of the house stood a detached garage that would hold at least three vehicles. On a hard standing area between the two buildings stood a Jeep Cherokee four-wheel drive and a new-looking powerboat on a trailer. Mr Charles Wilenius had certainly done all right for himself.

Andy drove on, turned round and slowed down for his second pass. His heart sank. Smaller details missed on the first sighting now registered. The two main gates guarding the driveway were electronically controlled and security devices were everywhere. Intruder alarm boxes were stuck onto the two buildings and at least four security cameras were situated in all the best vantage positions. He ground the van almost to a halt. He couldn't be one hundred per cent sure, but some sort of trip-wire seemed to run along the top of the ranch-style fencing surrounding the property. Whoever had installed the security arrangements had done a very professional job. Someone appeared with a wheelbarrow. The hired help was about to start tending the flowers and shrubs in the front garden.

Behind the house, Andy could see that the land started to rise quite sharply into a small ridge which was covered in various species of deciduous trees. About half a mile along the main road a dirt-track headed off in this direction. It didn't say it was private or anything, so he turned off and drove slowly along it deciding he would just act the lost tourist if challenged. A small clearing greeted him at the top of the ridge. He parked and climbed down from the camper. The view across the valley revealed the rooftops of all the properties, each one at a discreet distance from its neighbours. The clearing had been visited quite recently, by the look of it. The grass bore the signs of tyre tracks and some of the longer growth had been trampled down into nests. Andy laughed, he'd found the local lovers' hideaway, probably where the sons and daughters of the rich families experienced their first fumbling moments of sexual encounter. The undergrowth needed beating with a stick but it only took him twenty minutes to walk along the ridge level with the back of the Wilenius house. If the front was impressive then so was the unseen side. Two tennis courts and a large swimming-pool were set in a large lawned area. A patio area complete with barbecue was attached to the house. An eight-foot-high mesh fence surrounded the whole back garden and again there were signs of sophisticated security devices. Shrubs planted in front of the ugly fence would make it invisible from the lower levels of the garden – after all, it was not meant to be viewed from Andy's peeping-Tom vantage point.

He settled himself down to watch and wait but it was nearly two hours before anyone appeared. A dark-haired woman began to lay out lunch on a table on the patio and then erected a large umbrella to keep the hot sun off the spread. The patio doors were suddenly flung open and the air filled with shouts of children's voices. In all Andy counted five females: a woman in her mid-fifties, a much younger woman – under thirty, he reckoned – and three young girls. He was hopeless at guessing ages but they seemed to be about four to five years old. He cursed. He was just that little bit too far away to make out detail. They all sat and ate lunch and he was impressed with how well-behaved the three small girls were at the table. At the end of the meal some sort of argument followed, the girls were ushered indoors and peace was restored to the garden.

The two older women drank coffee and just talked for the next thirty minutes, but as far as Andy was concerned they could have been miming. The maid cleared away the last remnants from the table and the younger woman lit up a cigarette. Andy gave them all a pecking order. Mrs Wilenius senior, her daughter or daughter-in-law and her three grandchildren. The question was, were they just visiting for the day or did they all live together? Apart from the gardener tending to his duties in the far corner of the estate, nothing else happened.

Andy picked Derek up and explained the situation, adding there was still plenty of time for a night sortie if need be.

'Charlie's quite a local celebrity,' Derek announced between great mouthfuls of steak, and handed some photocopies over the table. 'The local press like people like him. He arrived penniless from some downtrodden European country and through his own efforts has worked his way to the top, it's the all-American dream!'

Andy flicked through the articles. For a start, Wilenius was a tenor in the town's operatic society. Then there was a picture of him holding up a large salmon plus a headline stating that it was a record weight caught from a Lake Tulloch. He was even Santa Claus last year at the county hospital. This was not the sort of reputation they wanted the man to have.

Derek looked at his watch. They could be out at the ridge by seven at the latest. There would still be enough light left for him to see it at first hand. They stopped once *en route* for Derek to buy a good pair of binoculars. Andy parked in the same spot and put towels over the inside of the front screen. At least it looked like the real thing should somebody visit the clearing! Derek found it all highly amusing and walked into the undergrowth with small mincing steps and one hand on his hip. They settled down in Andy's previous hide. The young mother and her brood were all in the swimming-pool and it looked as if she was teaching them to swim. Safety was paramount. They all wore armbands, whilst the maid hovered on the side, clutching a long pole with a metal hoop on the end. The older woman lay on a sun lounger. Andy pointed out all the security devices and described what the front of the house looked like. However, his colleague's mind was on other matters and his new glasses firmly focused on the younger woman's swimsuit. A little while later a grey-haired middle-aged man whose stomach was proof of his good life appeared. He kissed the women in turn, waved to the girls, then disappeared into a small outhouse and came back wearing swimming-trunks. His very hairy chest only emphasised his D-shaped belly. He dived straight into the pool and the children played and fooled around with him in the shallow end and the shrieks of laughter cut through the wooded area. On the patio the maid busied herself setting out the table for dinner and it was served an hour later. By ten o'clock the garden was quiet once again. As darkness intensified, Derek and Andy received a further shock. Lights were being turned off in the house, but *on* in the garden. Within minutes the outside of the house and its surrounding area were bathed in brilliant light.

'We don't stand an earthly chance of breaking into his fortress undetected,' Derek stated. 'Apart from all the electronic gadgetry, there were seven people inside and those three girls will probably be the excitable light-sleeping type who would hear a pin drop in the middle of the night! Plus we don't know what other little surprises are waiting for us inside. I think we will have to pursue other avenues of investigation regarding our Mr Wilenius. Come on, let's get out of here.'

It was becoming a habit but neither spoke much on the drive to find a suitable camp-site for the night. Both men were having their own private doubts about a middle-aged family man and grandfather being involved in a plot to alter the personalities of most of the world's beer and wine drinkers. After all, they had seen him drink two or three glasses of wine himself. Perhaps their lines of communication were wrong? Perhaps the man at Sarius added something to innocent products he bought from Decker and Wilenius was just an innocent party? There were still too many pieces of the jigsaw missing.

Andy got up early and went for a run. The countryside seemed too nice to miss out on and he hoped it might clear his confused brain a bit.

Derek was awake when he got back. 'Well, any further thoughts then?' he said, rubbing his eyes furiously.

'Afraid not. I can think of at least half a dozen ways of getting into both Decker's plant and Wilenius's home, but all of them would bring the law down on us – something our beloved leader insists we shouldn't do. What's his expression again? "Low-profile blended surveillance". No, we'll just have to hope that the whole Wilenius tribe plus staff go out shopping or away for the weekend and there's a power failure at the same time!'

'It's going to be a long bloody wait, it's only Thursday today!' Derek moaned.

'Well take up jogging!'

Ignoring Andy's remark, Derek looked at his watch. 'Make me some coffee, please. I'll phone Simon and see what he's come up with on Decker.'

Andy did as he was bade and left Derek to it. He'd passed some primitive-looking showers on the camper park so he decided to put one of them through its paces. He returned fifteen minutes later to find Derek sitting on the bunk-bed with the cup of coffee still untouched.

'Problems?'

Derek looked up. 'I've spoken to Simon. Had trouble getting hold of him in the first place. Normally I call him at work but some woman answered his phone and said he'd resigned his position. Managed to get him at his apartment. He wants to see us as soon as possible, says he's some news for us and wants to explain it personally.'

'All sounds very mysterious.' Andy commented. 'We can't be that far from San Francisco, according to all the road signs around here.'

'We're not. It would take us about an hour to get to his apartment. We might as well do something more useful than sitting around here with all this nature!'

Derek was right. Exactly one hour later they met Simon in the lobby of the block of apartments.

'Thanks for coming to see me so quickly,' he greeted them. 'I was afraid I might miss you both. I've resigned my position at the IRS and I'm moving up to Seattle at the weekend. You remember Ben's sister? Well, she's invited me to move in with her to help start up her garden nursery business. She bought the land and four large greenhouses at an auction and there's plenty of room for expansion. We're going to rent out and maintain indoor plants at offices and the like. Anyway, come on up to the apartment.'

'Great news!' Andy told him. 'We're very pleased for you. It's probably the best thing you can do, start again with a new challenge and a new outlook on life.'

Derek nodded in agreement.

Inside Andy's head his brain was working overtime. Were Simon and Clare going to live like brother and sister, or would he see the light and they become lovers? There again, perhaps she didn't fancy men and knew that she was safe with Simon – but he didn't think so, remembering her kiss. But he couldn't ask, even though his curiosity was burning him up.

Derek snapped his thoughts back to the real world. 'What news have you got for us, Simon old son?'

'Before I left I managed to obtain these tax returns.' He reached into a drawer and handed Derek a sheaf of papers. They all sat round the small kitchen table whilst Simon took them through the pile.

'These show the earnings of Charles Wilenius over the last twenty years. He's always been at Decker Pharmaceuticals, as I said in my fax. As you can see, his salary has steadily increased over the years and he now earns a little over three hundred thousand dollars a year.'

'No wonder he can afford his nice house and trappings!' Derek said with just a hint of jealousy attached.

Simon added, 'He's also a shareholder of Decker Pharmaceuticals.'

'Any signs of any other money coming into the equation – you know, from abroad?' Andy enquired.

'Absolutely none, all his affairs are dealt with by Decker accountants, everything, and I mean everything, is down in black and white and every single penny of tax is paid.'

'And Victor Warren?' Derek asked.

'He's beginning to catch Wilenius up on his earning power. Mind you, he owns Sarius Chemicals, so on paper at least he's the wealthier man. But it wasn't always like this. In the early eighties he almost hit rock bottom and his tax returns and payments were miserable.'

Derek scanned the papers. 'What about before this, Simon?'

'Nothing. There are no records at all on file for 1979 through to 1982 but there was some tax paid in 1977 and I think 1978.'

'What do you think then?' Derek persisted. 'Was he fiddling the Government by not declaring his income?'

Simon shook his head. 'Oh no. The department would have checked into that. No, I don't think he worked permanently during those years, maybe did a bit of moonlighting – casual or seasonal work – but definitely nothing legit. I also managed to obtain this,' Simon added as he handed a glossy brochure to Andy. 'It's TACIT Corporation's annual report. There's a small piece on Decker Pharmaceuticals which I thought might be of interest to you. I've also got some disappointing news. I can't break into Decker's Computer System. Sorry.'

'Do you mean you need one of those little black boxes installing – like we did at Sarius?' Derek enquired.

'No, it's more complicated than that. Getting into their system *is* possible. However, they've built in a security scrambler and unless you have the right code the screen is just one mass of assorted numbers and letters. I can get all their records but unless I can obtain the password it's all meaningless garbage.'

Derek asked, 'And can you get the code?'

'No, it's computer generated.'

'I don't understand. How do the operators at Decker translate what you've seen into English then?'

Simon explained, 'It doesn't work like that. On authorised terminals at Decker it will always be in English. It's only unauthorised ones like mine that it will react to and reverse into code.'

'You mean the master computer at Decker will know all by itself that it's being impregnated by some foreign operator!' Derek wanted to know.

'Yes. In fact, it even goes one step further. Once it knows you're fiddling about with its security system it actually stops transmission. A bit like a car radio where you get so many attempts to punch in the code and if it's still wrong the radio becomes permanently useless and has to be reset by the manufacturer.'

It was Andy's turn for a question. 'Will Decker's all singing and dancing piece of kit know it was your computer that tried to gain entry?'

'No.' Simon assured him. 'Mine has a built-in security system of its own to throw it off the scent.'

'*Touche*!' Derek added shaking his head in total bewilderment at all these silicon chips and bits of wire playing chess with each other.

'Simon, this is a delicate question,' Andy began. 'We understand that during the course of his work Ben managed to enter the CIA master computer and yet you can't get into a device run by some pharmaceutical company. Why?'

Simon was not in the least offended. 'It's a good leading question and perhaps when you've read that brochure you'll understand the problem more. Of course the nation's security details are important, but the big business these days is in industrial espionage. Imagine a Decker competitor being able to steal the formulation for some new drug about to hit the world market or getting hold of years of research work. It would be worth billions. If anything, the CIA ought to learn about security systems from companies such as Decker.'

'Anything else to tell us?' Derek asked, anxious to stop Simon going into any technical mode on computer security.

'No, that's about it all.'

'Right then. I think Andy and I will make tracks back to Stockton. Thanks for all your help over the past few weeks – we've really appreciated it. In fact, without it we wouldn't be half as advanced as we are.'

Simon hesitated before speaking again. 'Thank you. Look, please come and see me and Clare if you're anywhere near Seattle. You'd both be made very welcome.'

He handed them both a printed address card and then added, 'Is there any more news about Ben's death?'

Derek had been hoping to escape this question. 'Yes, we know who it was and it's only a matter of time before he's brought to justice. Can't say any more, as I'm sure you will appreciate, but the case is as good as closed. Go and start your life again with a clean sheet.'

They all shook hands, left Simon sitting in the kitchen and let themselves out.

'And then there were only two!' Derek said as soon as they were out in the street.

'Why did you tell him we'd found Ben's killer?' Andy asked.

'Precisely for the reason I said – so that he can forget all about this episode and start rebuilding his life from scratch again.'

Andy volunteered to drive back whilst Derek sat with his head engrossed in TACIT's book. Every now and again he read out extracts relevant to Decker Pharmaceuticals.

'They make everything! Listen to this: insulin, vitamins, proteins, ultraviolet protectors, headache pills – the list goes on. They had a turnover of nearly eighteen billion dollars last year and contribute seventeen per cent to TACIT's worldwide operations. Wouldn't mind some shares in the company myself!'

'You said that Charles Wilenius was mentioned a lot in the local paper,' Andy remarked, not really listening to Derek. 'Just a suggestion, but why don't we arrange to visit him as reporters from some obscure magazine? We could make out we're doing profiles on people who started with nothing and who are now at the top of their particular professions. With any luck we could be invited to his house, especially if we pushed the family man bit. Once inside we'd at least have a good idea what we're up against. You can do the interviewing, I'll be your photographer.'

'And while I'm doing all the talking you'll be taking candid pictures of his daughter by the pool! Only joking, I reckon it's a good idea. I'll ring his secretary first thing in the morning and arrange an appointment.'

By mutual consent they booked themselves into an hotel. As Derek pointed out, the camper didn't have either a restaurant or bar.

Andy was studying the map of western America when Derek joined him for breakfast.

'Planning our next moves then, are we?'

'Just studying where we've been. If Decker sends both proteins down to Sarius at Bakersfield and one of them is then shipped on to Union at Bullen, then the route is quite logical, it's basically a straight route south. But it's the other Union plant at Melford that doesn't make any sense. It's in Oregon, about four hundred miles north of here, which means that our ingredient Y travels from Stockton two hundred-odd miles south to Sarius only to return six hundred miles north again.'

'What are you suggesting?' Derek asked. 'There may be another Sarius operation north of here – a Sarius two?'

'It's crossed my mind but I don't think so. After all, we found written proof of material leaving Bakersfield *en route* to Oregon. No, the more I look at it the more I think the operation is not flawless. I bet it's costing Victor Warren a small fortune sending product Y from Bakersfield to Melford.'

Derek changed the subject. 'Well, there's one thing for certain. Today's Friday. We have exactly one week to find out where this Special Reserve meeting is taking place – and who's coming to it.' He polished off the cooked breakfast and had hardly finished the last mouthful before he pushed his chair back and went off to find the nearest telephone.

Andy knew the call hadn't been successful as soon as Derek walked back into the dining-room. His expression spoke a thousand words.

'That goddam guy starts his holiday tonight!' he said dejectedly. 'I spoke to his secretary and even put on my best West Coast accent as well. He's away all next week and seemingly always has the same week off every year. She was very nice, even apologetic about it, and suggested we call again when he gets back, but that's a fat lot of good to us.'

'Did you ask her where he's going?'

Derek nodded. 'Of course. Wanted to find out if the house will be empty next week. No such luck, I'm afraid. He's off on his own – fishing! I said that it would make good copy writing about a top scientist who relaxes by fishing and she opened up a bit. She told me that his daughter and children always come to stay at this time of year to keep the old lady company. We couldn't have picked a worse time! He's off and there's still a full house. We need a break, Andy, and we're not getting it, are we? I told the secretary to fix us up with an appointment week after next, it was all I could think to finish our little chat off with.' Derek sat down and let out a huge sigh.

'Where's he usually go fishing, did the woman tell you?' Andy asked.

'Yes, some place on Lake Tahoe. As I said, he's been

doing it for years now and always goes with the same people, probably work colleagues, I dunno.'

Andy stood up suddenly. 'Can you settle up the bills, Derek? I need to get back to the camper to phone someone and the number's out there.'

'No problem. But something's stirring in that head of yours . . . what are you thinking about?'

Andy said dismissively, 'Just a hunch at the moment – I'll know more after the call. It'll probably not come to anything.'

The woman at Union Minerals couldn't find Maureen as she was out on the plant as usual. She suggested he phone back in ten to fifteen minutes. Derek was back in the camper when he tried again.

'Hi, Maureen, it's your Australian friend Andy here . . . Yes, yes I'm fine. How's the honeysuckle keeping? . . . Great! Look Maureen, I'll be coming back through Bullen again in a few weeks' time – any chance of some more casual work? . . . Really? Great! . . . Yes, I look forward to it as well! How's things on the plant, still as busy as ever?' There was a long pause as Maureen relayed the answers. 'And how's everybody? . . . Good, and how's your favourite person on site, old misery guts himself? . . . Oh, is he? For a week? Well, that's good news for the rest of you. I hope he's going too far away to drop in on you.' Again there was another pause as Maureen did her share of the talking and then Andy finished off the conversation, 'See you in a few weeks' time . . . Yes, so do I. Bye.'

He switched off the phone and looked across at Derek, who was grinning from ear to ear.

'You crafty bastard! You didn't tell me that your "process manager friend" was female did you? Nice is she? Now I know why you looked so well after your stint at Bullen!'

Andy ignored his jibes and quickly got down to the crux of the matter. 'We've got our first break. You remember Tom Allsop, the technical manager at Bullen? Well, he's away next week, and guess where? Fishing on Lake Tahoe with an old friend as well! Both Allsop and Wilenius have worked for their respective companies for decades, so at one time they were both part of TACIT. It's all too much of a coincidence, isn't it? The man who makes X and Y meeting up with the man whose products it goes in!'

Derek rubbed his hands together. 'Excellent, at last something positive. Where's your map? Let's work out the route to Tahoe, for God's sake. You said Allsop had a boat. Whose will they use, his or Wilenius's? We're going to need some help, we'll never hear what's going on if they're stuck out in the middle of some stretch of water. What if—'

Andy stopped him in mid-flight and grabbed him by the shoulders. 'Stop getting yourself all lathered up, will you? Maureen said Allsop doesn't leave until tomorrow morning so we've got a whole day to get organised and I don't want you dropping dead on me just yet. I might need your help!'

Derek raised one arm and acknowledged Andy's comments but he couldn't help himself, it was in his nature to panic. It was agreed they would phone the General – it was going to hurt their pride, but now they needed his help; after all, they had not expected any possible future meeting to take place on a boat in the middle of a lake!

Derek did the honours and explained the situation to him. The General said he would call back in twenty minutes, and to the second, the mobile phone buzzed. All Derek said was 'yes' three times and 'understood' once.

'Sends his love!' he said sarcastically after turning the phone off. 'He wants us to find an old airfield near a place called Munden. Somebody will meet us and give us some electronic gadgetry so we can listen in on our fishermen. The General says he will be very cross if we don't succeed, he wants every word, fart and splash recorded for posterity!'

The map came out and after a bit of a search they found Munden. It was just over the state line in Nevada, about ten miles from Lake Tahoe, and nearly a hundred miles away. Andy drove, and the further east they went the hotter it became and the higher the terrain got. He stopped and changed into his lightest shorts and sweat-shirt, and reckoned it must have been over forty degrees. He found it strange that Derek, overweight as he was, didn't seem to be affected by the heat. He just sat there quietly in the passenger seat, wearing his suit trousers, white long-sleeved shirt and tie, waiting for Andy to get on with it. He wasn't even sweating.

They checked the map again. In front of them lay a mountain range and beyond it the lake. Somewhere before was Munden. The first signs appeared five miles down the road but there was no sign of any airfield, so they pulled into a gas station on the other side of the road. Derek jumped out to ask the old woman on duty for directions, and returned with a small book.

'Detailed map of the lake area. The woman said that the only strip around here is now used by a gliding club. It's somewhere over in that direction.' Derek pointed over the garage.

At first Andy thought they were birds, but the closer they got, the more obvious the outlines of four gliders became. A fifth was being towed into the air by a single-engined biplane. They followed the aerial activity and turned off the main road.

The Munden Gliding Club consisted of two buildings, a hangar and a small brick-built office-cum-clubhouse. Andy opened the camper door and the hot air flooded in. He jumped down and in no time at all the ground started to burn through his deck shoes. There were no signs of life. They walked around the corrugated sides of the hangar and stopped dead in their tracks. Parked facing them was a large black helicopter. It looked evil, like some giant wasp about to pounce on them. Three men were lounging about, trying to keep cool in its huge shadow. They all wore vests and shorts but not standard army issue, the assortment of colours looked more like you'd see in Malibu. The 'beach boys' spotted them and lazily got to their feet. One of them spoke, offering his hand as he did so.

'Hi guys, I'm Sergeant Greenhaugh. Guess you've come to have your new stereo system fitted? Bring your wheels over here and my guys will sort you out.'

'How long will it take?' Andy asked. The way he was dressed at the moment, he could have been taken for a fourth member of the helicopter team.

'Australian eh? Nice place. Stationed there on an exchange visit, gee must be five years ago now. You know Adelaide? Some classy broads in that place. I reckon this'll be two to three hours.'

Derek brought the camper round and handed the keys over to Greenhaugh.

'Suggest you guys get out of the sun while you're waiting,' the sergeant said, and pointed across to the clubhouse. 'There's a cold drinks machine in there – leave us some!'

A woman sat in a small office adjoining the clubhouse-cum-waiting-room, totally engrossed in a pile of paper. She heard the door close and looked up. 'Sorry, didn't know you'd arrived. You'd be surprised at the amount of work involved running a small club like this. Make yourselves at home. There isn't much to do – unless you want to try gliding?'

Derek shook his head furiously – the very thought made his stomach churn. He turned to Andy. 'You go if you want to, I'll mind the fort.' Andy was tempted but didn't feel the time was right to start enjoying himself, so he also declined.

The next three hours passed very slowly. Derek dozed in an old armchair, Andy read through some of the dog-eared magazines on flying and looked at some charts and maps pinned on the wall. He was not surprised Munden was hot – it was on a desert plain six thousand feet above sea level. Eventually, the sergeant returned, wearing a towel round his neck.

'We've finished. If you'd like to come and inspect our handiwork, I'll explain what's what.'

The three of them walked back to the camper. The army team may have been very good at their jobs but they were certainly not house-proud. The inside of the van was a tip. All their personal belongings had been piled up in a heap near the driver's seat and one of the side cupboards had been ripped off its brackets. One bunk-bed now rested over both front seats. In the gap created stood a large black metal box about the size of a small domestic refrigerator. Six wires ran from it up to the roof and out through a newly made hole, the jagged lining hanging from it.

'Sorry, we had to make a few modifications to get the kit in. I'll show you how it works.' The sergeant opened the door to the box, which almost touched the other bunk as it swung open. The contraption looked like a stacked music centre. 'You only have to bother with this top bit here. Forget the rest underneath – it's the receiving part of the gear. You turn it on here.' He turned a knob and a red light came on. 'To record messages you press these two switches.' Again there was a demonstration. 'The machine takes nine-ninety-minute cassettes. Once one's full it automatically records onto the next one underneath, and so on. It's on a continuous loop, so you guys have got to remember to replace the full tapes with blank ones, otherwise you'll just tape over your original juicy conversations, right? If you want to hear the news firsthand you can adjust the volume with the on/off switch. The speakers are inside this box, so you'll need its door open, of course. We've labelled all the switches for you. Simple, isn't it? On the roof is a directional aerial. It's got to be pointed towards your intended target to get the best reception.' Greenhaugh pointed to a small wheel sticking through the roof. A red arrow hastily painted on the inside of the roof recorded the direction the aerial was supposed to be pointing to.

They all went outside and stared at the roof. A large streamlined travel box had appeared. Then the sergeant continued his teach-in. 'The aerial's in there. Now for the bad news! To run all of this little lot takes some power. The unit's got its own batteries so we've put them under the bunk. But these will only last maximum three hours and then they'll need to be recharged from the RV's engine for at least six hours a day. We've put a switch to the alternator. Once the van's batteries are fully charged, one flick and it will change over to the receiver ones. We've put a little gadget on the dash so that at any one time you'll be able to tell what the state of play is. Right, demonstration time, folks!'

They all went back inside and he pointed to Andy. 'Like to have a go, sport?'

Andy nodded.

'Okay, point the aerial towards the clubhouse and switch on the machine.'

The van was suddenly swamped with the loud conversation between the woman and one of his men. The sergeant rushed forward. 'Volume control a bit too high, I think!' He turned it down. 'Unless you're both deaf, of course!' He bent down and handed Andy a small cardboard box. Inside were about thirty small metal cylinders no bigger than the flat batteries used in pocket calculators. Some had blue bases, others red. Derek went to pick one out but was reprimanded.

'Careful! They're delicate. Pick them up by their sides. These are the transmitters. The red ones are the most important; they're mono-directional – that is, they'll pick up direct conversations. The blue ones are omni – they will add on any background noise, for instance a third party joining in the discussion but some distance away. They need to be placed about ten feet apart for the best results, but alternate them. We've put three reds and two blues in the clubhouse. You've seen the size of the place, so it gives you some idea of the scale. To fix them, just peel off the coloured identification sticker and press them into place – they're self-adhesive. Don't forget to keep them out of sight and don't press them too hard on the top.' The last remark was directed straight at Derek.

'And what happens if you put them much closer together?' Andy asked, thinking about a boat's enclosed confines.

'No problem. In fact, the more the merrier – just like Adelaide Sheilas eh? I wouldn't go closer than about four foot, though otherwise you might start to pick up some static.'

One of the men called out the sergeant's name and passed in a small black box about the size of a car radio.

'This, folks, is "mother" – she's the key to the whole

thing. It's the main booster transmitter. It receives its electrical impulses from its babies and sends the signals back via your aerial into this pandora's box.' He lightly kicked the bottom of their new 'refrigerator'. 'If this box is left near its offspring, it will give you a range of about eight miles – a bit more, the higher the ground the aerial is on. You switch it on and prime it with these two buttons. The box is weatherproof and can go outside if necessary. If there are no air-conditioning ducts or false ceilings available then we usually sling it in a gutter or attach it to some garden creeper, just as long as it's not more than twenty feet away from the first bug. For this demonstration we just put mother on the coke machine. Be careful with this box, you're rationed to only one.' Greenhaugh handed the box across to Andy, along with half a dozen plastic ties.

'Right, that's about it. If you folks are happy, me and my men will leave you to it. Happy eavesdropping! Oh, there's an envelope, marked *fragile*, for you on the driver's seat. So long.'

Derek found the padded package and ripped it open. It contained two small hypodermic syringes secured into a sheet of foam padding. A brief handwritten note pinned to the foam stated, *One needle to be injected into any drinks bottles found.*

'What do you reckon's in them, Andy?'

'I would guess something to make conversations flow more readily – but if the General's behind it, God only knows. I'd better put them away in a safe place.'

The helicopter roared past shaking the van.

'Just look at this goddam mess,' Derek said, kicking his loose bunk-bed. 'Even my lot go easier when they're looking for something!'

'Well, we can't go anywhere until we've done something about it,' Andy replied. 'Come on, give me a hand. It'll take us less than ten minutes.' With that he picked up loose bits of wire and other dross left behind by the technicians. They decided the bunk-bed would have to live on the floor at the back of the van. Derek found a sealed cardboard box by the passenger seat. It contained twenty-four blank cassette tapes labelled

Property of the United States Army. After a visit to the club's washroom to remove the dust and sweat, it was time to get on the move again.

Andy had no problem retracing his steps back onto the main highway, then he followed the Tahoe signposts and turned on to Highway 207. This road started to climb immediately; they were beginning to cross the mountains separating the desert from the lake. At first Andy thought there was something wrong with the van's engine; the power had gone. Then he realised that all the extra weight they were now carrying was too much for the vehicle. The climb became steeper, the engine and gearbox complained bitterly and the noise and vibration began to get on their nerves.

At the summit, two things changed their world. Firstly the van was happy again free-wheeling down the road, and secondly the view ahead took their breath away. The lake was like a sheet of blue glass surrounded by tree-covered mountains, and there was no doubt in Andy's mind that it was one of the best panoramas he'd ever seen. Even Derek the confirmed city-lover remarked on the beauty of it all. The temperature had dropped to a much more bearable level, so he switched the air-conditioning off, wound his window down and breathed in great gulps of cool air.

Without any warning or prior announcement Derek started to quote. ' "Lake Tahoe is twelve miles wide and about twenty-two miles long. With nearly two hundred square miles of surface area it is the largest alpine lake on the North American Continent, it is 1645 feet deep and its water is 99.9 per cent pure. There is a spectacular seventy-two-mile drive around its perimeter".'

'That's a very detailed map you bought!' Andy quipped.

Derek thought Andy was serious until he looked up and caught him smiling. 'Smartass! The map folds inside a little information booklet.' He held it up for Andy to see.

At the bottom of the mountains Andy turned left onto Highway 50, which ran parallel to the lake. He was not prepared for what he drove into a mile or so down the road though, enormous hotels and casinos with bright lights burning even in the middle of the day.

'This is a place called Stateline,' Derek said. 'According to the map, we're still in Nevada, where gambling is legal. Pull into that car park over there so that we can get our bearings.' Andy did as instructed and turned into Caesar's Hotel. The car park must have had spaces for five, ten thousand vehicles; it was anybody's guess.

Over some sandwiches Derek passed on more information from his guide. 'We're at the southernmost tip of the lake and it looks like this whole area we're in is known as South Shore. The border passes straight through the middle of it all. The other half of the town is in California and is known as South Lake Tahoe.'

Suitably refreshed, it only took them a matter of minutes to cross into California. There was even a white line painted across the road, signifying the boundary. Over the border, both the style of buildings and pace of life immediately changed. The hotels, houses and restaurants were more subtly designed and blended in better with the environment.

Derek started to hum. Andy knew the sign by now and said, 'What's the matter now?'

'Didn't expect the area to be so big. How we going to find them in all this expanse? And anyway we don't know what we're looking for, do we?'

'Yes we do – a boat!' Andy replied. He hadn't expected the area to be so big either but he wasn't going to let it show.

'Or two boats. We don't know if they're using Allsop's or if Wilenius is trailing his own across here.'

Andy conceded, 'No we don't, but we can eliminate one. Phone up the General – he seems to be all-powerful. Get him to organise a small chopper to fly discreetly past the Wilenius house to see if the boat's gone or if it looks like he's getting it ready.'

'And if he isn't? We still don't know what sort of boat Allsop has. We don't even know its goddam name!'

'I'll recognise the name when I see it, it's something

like *Doh Ray Me*, according to the information I saw in his house.'

Derek stared at him almost in disbelief and then reached for his guidebook and furiously flicked through the pages. 'It's not *Dat So La Lee*, is it?'

'The very same. You psychic or something?'

'No, it's in the book here. It's the name of a squaw from the Washoe tribe who used to live on these shores during the last century.'

While Derek phoned the General, Andy walked the few yards to the water's edge and splashed his face with the clear water. It was freezing cold even in mid-May.

'That's organised. Any more bright ideas then?' Derek said when Andy returned.

'Let's concentrate on our man Allsop, at least until we hear about Wilenius. He's a quiet man with no real friends in Bullen, so I don't think he'd like the glitzy Nevada side of things. He'd much prefer to keep his boat moored in the peace and quiet of this lot. So if you agree I would suggest we continue driving around the California side of the lake and start checking out all the marinas and jetties we come across.'

Derek's confidence returned and he even began his next sentence without the word *if*. 'When we find the boat, we're from an insurance company giving it the once-over – should anybody start poking their nose in, okay? I've got a business card somewhere that'll pass inspection.'

They continued their drive on up the west shore. Once again the road began to climb steeply. A camper park had been built on a promontory at a place called Emerald Bay State Park. They both studied the map. They were near Mount Tallac, the lake's tallest peak. Below them was Emerald Bay itself, which contained a small island with a large castle on it. The late afternoon sun brought out all the colours nature had at her disposal and Andy had to bring himself back into the real world and remind himself that they were here to hunt down a bunch of conspirators.

During the next seven miles Derek started to get edgy

again as the road took them through a state park high above the water line.

'There's nowhere to keep a boat in this lot. Let's turn around and try looking over the Nevada coastline near Stateline.'

Andy didn't reply but just kept on driving. By now, he reckoned, the best thing to do with Derek's little panic attacks was to ignore them. In five minutes' time his mind would have moved onto something else, the original outburst forgotten. In fact, Andy didn't have to wait that long. They had just passed a place called Sugar Pine Point and within seconds the road was back at the water's edge – literally. A sign came into view – 'WELCOME TO TAHOMA'. They parked in a small shopping-mall and walked onto a jetty. Derek almost ran round the three sides looking at the names on the twenty or so boats moored side by side, but returned with a crestfallen face.

'That bloody squaw's not here.'

A voice shouted out, 'You guys need some help?' It came from the direction of a small boatyard. Derek had been so eager to find the craft he hadn't noticed the old man varnishing the upturned hull of a rowing-boat.

'Yes please, we're looking for a craft called . . . ?' He had to turn to Andy to call out the name 'We're here to give her the once-over for insurance purposes but damned if we can find her, though.'

'Old Tom's boat? You'll find her just up the road at Homewood. You'll have a wait though, he never gets here till Saturday morning.'

'Thanks. We're in no hurry – too nice a place to rush around anyway.' Derek turned to Andy. 'I could kiss the old beggar!'

Andy didn't reply. He just found it strange, almost unreal, that Derek had survived all these years as an undercover man.

Allsop may not have been too fond of his fellow man but he certainly treated his boat with love and attention. It wasn't new but it was in superb condition. Everything from the blue hull to the white superstructure gleamed; the varnished handrails reflected back the sun's rays. The stern area was open and occupied about a quarter of the boat's thirty-foot length, whilst the enclosed wheelhouse area was dead centre. It was moored in a marina alongside a more glamorous modern cabin cruiser and an old open fishing-boat. None of the other thirty or so boats showed any signs of life. They were overlooked by a restaurant verandah, which was also deserted at the moment.

'Must be all eating inside, lucky things!' Derek said jealously. 'I think we'd better wait until it's dark before we do the deed.'

'No,' Andy disagreed. 'You've just said it yourself – everybody's eating. Later on, those jetties could be awash with people. It'll be best to do it now, and if I can get behind that bigger boat nobody in the restaurant will see me anyway. I'll also need some daylight to position our little bugs – a torch beam would really be obvious. Put everything I'll need in your briefcase, will you please, whilst I change.'

Andy was gone for thirty minutes.

'Everything okay?' Derek asked.

'Yes, managed to place about twenty of the little blighters. Every corner's covered, including that open bit at the back. See that wooden rail? Underneath, it's got a groove up the middle – tailor-made for bugs. It's all very cosy inside. Through the door from the open deck there are three steps down into the main cabin, which has four berths, a galley and two toilets that double up as showers. I put the black box down the back of a locker and stuffed all the original ropes and things back on top – I doubt if he'll find it. The boat is spotless, smells of new paint and all the upholstery looks new as well. I reckon all Allsop's money goes on his Indian squaw. There's not the slightest trace of any food or drink on board though; he must bring it all with him.'

Derek slapped him on the back. 'Well done. I watched you move along that jetty you were like greased lightning. I'd still be trying to fathom out how to get in through the door! Let's see if the system works, shall we?' He opened the black door, switched on the equipment and fiddled with the aerial, but there was nothing on the speakers. Andy turned the volume up. They could hear what sounded like footsteps and then muffled voices. They both peered out of the camper window and saw two men walking down the jetty about twenty feet from Allsop's boat.

Derek let out a low whistle. 'God, you cut it fine!'

'Fancy some dinner in the marina restaurant?' Andy asked. 'We'll be able to see the boat from a different angle.'

'Do I! I might even have one or two very large whiskeys as well. I'll sleep on the bunk on the floor tonight, so at least if I do get drunk I won't fall out of it!'

13

It was just as well there was little to do the following morning as both of them suffered king-sized hangovers.

By lunchtime Derek was having another attack of the doubts. 'What if Allsop doesn't come? What if he uses Wilenius's boat launched from somewhere else? We're buggered, we haven't got a spare master transmitter, have we?'

'Stop panicking, will you? If necessary we'll retrieve the one from Allsop's craft. It'll still be empty if they use the other boat won't it?' But his colleague had a point they weren't sure which boat was to be used for the meeting. In fact they didn't know for certain it was to be held on the water. Andy kept this last thought to himself to stop Derek completely losing his marbles. Instead, he suggested Derek went off and did the shopping. They could do with another pair of binoculars and a whole stack of provisions – they might have to spend days away from bars and restaurants. Derek reluctantly agreed but was back in ten minutes in a taxi.

'Apart from a few restaurants, there's not much in Homewood. I've asked around and the locals say there's some great outdoor shops which sell optical equipment in a place called Truckee, about fifteen miles north of here. See you later.'

At last Andy had a few hours peace to look forward to. But it was soon shattered. The phone buzzed. The reception was poor as it was being patched through from a helicopter.

'Boat still on the premises at Stockton but black Jeep left sometime between six and eight this morning. Message out.'

It had started, and thank God it looked like they'd backed the right boat!

The taxi returned after three hours, and at first Andy wanted to burst out laughing but bit his lip so as not to offend his partner. Derek was standing there looking like a lumberjack. Gone were the city shirt and trousers; instead he was wearing a checked short-sleeved shirt and red shorts and his black polished shoes had been replaced by a pair of lace-up walking boots. From the colour of them it looked as if it was the first time his knees had ever seen daylight. The taxi driver kept unloading bags from the trunk.

'How long do you intend staying here?' Andy asked.

'You never know, can't have us woodsmen going hungry, can we now?'

Andy broke the good news about the boat and it had the desired effect. He also suggested they move the van. 'There's an authorised camper park about three hundred yards down the road. We'll be less obvious down there than in this small marina one. I reckon we'll still be able to see the marina, and anyway our new ears will tell us when things start to happen.'

They found a prime site by the water's edge and sat outside reading the newspapers Derek had bought. It had been months since Andy had seen one and he wasn't impressed. Every headline was bad news. The world was just one antagonistic place at the moment, country after country was at each other's throats. He read one story about French and German leftist organisations blaming the lack of employment on migrant workers. They wanted them out, and were turning to violence. He threw the paper down, wondering if those involved had drunk spiked beer and wine. His frustration mounted so he decided to lose it by going for a run. Derek asked where.

'Probably the three or four miles back to Sugar Pine Point. Thinking of coming with me?'

Derek laughed. 'I think I'll pass this time, thanks anyway! No, I was just thinking, somewhere along the line we might need a boat. Can you check for a place that rents them out? Mind you, the very thought of stepping into a small boat gives me the willies. Can you handle one?'

Andy was noncommittal. 'We'll manage if needs be.'

He returned two hours later and waved a small bunch of keys under Derek's nose. 'Your ship lies anchored one mile down the road at Tahoma, Captain! Sorry I couldn't get you a parrot to go with it! It's not as big as Allsop's by any stretch of the imagination, so don't think I've hired out some liner, will you?'

'Shouldn't we – you – bring it up here so it's ready and waiting?'

'No, I thought of that, but don't forget Allsop might recognise me. It's best left at Tahoma until after the party's started. It'll take me less than fifteen minutes to run back and get it.'

By late afternoon the park had begun to fill up. Derek went back into the van and emerged carrying two bottles of beer. The look of horror on Andy's face made his day.

'Don't worry it's not filtered! It was recommended by the store in Truckee, where it's made. It's naturally produced or something. Read the label for yourself.'

Andy swigged from the bottle. It was good; there were times when there was nothing better than a long cool beer. Suddenly there was a loud undefinable hissing noise coming from inside the camper and they nearly knocked each other over in the rush to get back inside. The volume control on the listening device was on full throttle.

Derek turned it down. 'Didn't know if we would hear anything outside,' he explained. 'What on earth is it?'

Andy grabbed the binoculars and peered through the back window.'Allsop's arrived! He's testing his engine.'

Derek found the other pair of glasses. 'We won't be able to hear any voices above that din. You didn't put a bug next to the engine compartment, did you? Sorry, I'll withdraw that comment, you're not that stupid. That's the sort of thing I'd do!'

'He's over-revving at the moment. It'll be much quieter when he's engaged the propeller and is on the move.'

As if to order, the noise dropped away to a distant hum in the background, so Derek turned the volume up again. Allsop was in a good mood and was whistling. After all, he was about to embark on his favourite pastime. From their position, they watched him carry three boxes of provisions from his four-wheel-drive truck, disappear behind the restaurant and then reappear on the jetty. It was a different story on the fourth journey down the jetty. His pace was slower and he watched his footing more carefully because he was now carrying his pride and joy, his fishing-rods. He spent the next hour on board and then he locked the boat up, moved his pick-up to almost the same spot Andy and Derek had originally used and disappeared into the restaurant. He resurfaced some two hours later and walked slowly back down the jetty. Within minutes snoring came through the speakers, so they decided to turn the machine off.

'How many of our little coloured bugs have we got left?' Derek asked.

Andy rummaged in the box. 'Thirteen – five blues and eight reds. Why?'

'I was just thinking. Suppose they discuss the nitty-gritty in the restaurant and not on the boat, then we're sunk – sorry, no pun intended. The spares are not doing anything, so how about you and me distributing them around the place?'

'Do you think we'll hear anything?' Andy asked. 'The black box on his boat is a good hundred feet from the restaurant.'

Derek persisted, 'Let's experiment anyway. We'll go in separately – you first, and then when I see where they've sat you I'll make for the other half of the room.'

The restaurant was nearly empty at that time of night. Anybody the slightest bit interested would have thought Derek had a weak bladder. He visited the toilet three times, each time using a different route through the tables. Derek, being Derek, rushed his food down, anxious to get back to the van to see if his idea had worked.

'I didn't know you slurped your coffee, and you never said pardon either when you made that belching noise!' he said to Andy when he got back twenty minutes later. He played the tape back and they both laughed. The reception was a bit crackly but good enough to make out conversation. Derek put his new sleeping-bag onto the remains of the bunk-bed on the floor and from his cocoon muttered, 'Either Wilenius is a bloody slow driver or he's stopped off somewhere in a hotel.' In a few more seconds, he too had joined the fraternity of snorers.

Andy woke up suddenly. Derek was shaking him furiously. 'Wake up, wake up, will you? Allsop's gone!'

He looked at his watch – it was six thirty. 'Don't panic, he can't have gone far. Its a lake not the bloody Atlantic Ocean. What's happening on the listening equipment?'

'Nothing.'

'Have you fiddled with the aerial?'

Derek hadn't, so he reached up and turned the wheel slowly. The sound of a humming noise filled the camper. Andy dressed quickly, grabbed the glasses, walked to the water's edge and scanned the lake. There was no sign of Allsop's distinctive boat.

When Derek joined him, Andy pointed south. 'I reckon he must have gone round Sugar Pine Point into Emerald Bay. We'll drive round and see. We'd be better getting onto higher ground, anyway; we'll be able to observe more, and this little box of tricks should function more accurately.'

The ten-mile drive back to Emerald Bay totally topped up the batteries. The trailer park was almost deserted, so Andy reversed the van as far as he could to the edge of the rocky cliff. the view was unlimited and Derek spotted the boat almost immediately. It was directly beneath them, going round the island.

'He's probably checking out the best fishing areas,' Andy commented.

No sooner had they set up camp than Allsop began to move off. He seemed to be heading back to Homewood, his deed for the day complete.

Derek was unsure what to do next, and once again Andy provided the calming influence. 'Look, if every time he moves, we move, we'll meet ourselves coming back! The best thing to do is stay in one place. There were some parking-spaces back at Sugar Pine Point, so I suggest we set up a permanent base there, and then we'll be able to see all of the southern area of the lake, including Homewood and Emerald Bay. At the same time we'll be able to hear what's happening on the boat.'

'What about the restaurant?' Derek asked.

'We can only hear what's going on there through his boat moored in the marina, and he's hardly likely to leave it somewhere else and walk back, is he?' Andy replied somewhat flippantly.

Derek was not entirely convinced but went along with the plan. Once they got there, they saw that the Sugar Pine Point camper park offered some additional benefits. It was amongst pine trees so would afford some shade; the next camper would be at least thirty yards away, so they could run the engine without annoying their neighbours; and nobody could park in front of them, ruining their view. As Andy manoeuvred into the prime spot in an otherwise empty park, Derek watched Allsop's boat turn into Homewood marina.

The rest of the day passed without incident. Both sat outside reading and enjoying the sun but both were bored rigid. They took it in turns to listen into the receiver and left the tape running just in case. The only sounds they heard resembled burnt toast being scraped and it took them a long time to figure it out, but they reckoned Allsop was sanding down some wood. He didn't even play any music they could listen to. Both were desperate for something to happen, just to prove that, after all this time, the big meet was about to take place.

It did. Just after eight o'clock in the evening Derek shouted for Andy to join him quickly. They sat there as if listening to a play on the radio.

'Hi, Tom. Nice to see you again. How have you been? I must say the boat looks nice. They've done a good job on the gel coat for you.'

'Chas! You're looking well. I do believe you've lost a bit of weight. How's the family?'

'All very well, thank God.'

'Good. Pass me your rods first.'

'Be careful with that box. I managed to get a case of your favourite Zinfandel wine.'

'Thank you. Have you eaten? I can always rustle you up something or we can use the restaurant.'

'I think the restaurant, Tom. You know what I think of your cooking!'

Like two avid listeners tuned to the latest episode of their favourite serial both Derek and Andy sat with their heads close to the speakers in case they missed a word. The equipment made a clicking noise as the small spools recorded each and every word. The two fishermen pottered about for another twenty minutes without saying very much and then left the boat. The sound of their shoes on the jetty could be heard getting fainter and fainter. Derek turned the volume up to nearly maximum and what had been only an irritating background noise converted itself into voices in the restaurant.

'Interesting.' Andy said. 'Because the main transmitter is on the boat it preferentially picks up noises there first and overrides anything else. That's why we couldn't hear the restaurant when they were talking on board.'

'Well, let's hope they don't split the meeting up!' Derek replied dryly.

Long eating intervals were interspaced with the most boring talk on where the best fishing-sites were likely to be at the moment, and the eavesdroppers found it extremely hard to concentrate on their quarry as far more interesting conversations were being picked up as well. By ten o'clock the two men were back on board and by half ten the sound of snoring echoed through the equipment once again.

Monday through to Wednesday followed exactly the same pattern of 'activity'. Allsop and Wilenius always got up at six, had a light breakfast and then motored to Emerald Bay, where they spent the whole day fishing. There were always squeals of delight when one of them caught something, followed by endless questions from the other about what fly was used, which rod, what strain of line. They behaved more like schoolboys who had skipped lessons rather than two men nearing retirement. In early evening they always headed back to the marina, spent a good hour preparing their beloved tackle for the next day's fun and games, then after a shower they went off to the restaurant. They didn't seem to bother much with lunch on board, a couple of glasses of wine seemed to suffice – the fishing took precedence over most things. They didn't even bother to keep their catch, which annoyed Derek. 'I'd have the goddam thing in the skillet in seconds,' he'd said on more than one occasion.

By Wednesday Andy and Derek were beginning to get on each other's nerves. The routine had become monotonous and Derek had taken up humming once again. Andy decided to give them a break from each other. He'd hired the boat for a week, so he felt he might as well get some use from it. He ran the two miles to Tahoma and had a very pleasant day learning how the thing behaved. It was only an eighteen-foot-long cruiser but it was reasonably nippy.

He returned to find Derek totally pissed off. 'I think we've ballsed this one up, Andy. There's no way they're going to talk business. These guys are on holiday.'

Thursday morning got off to a bad start. Derek was sitting outside the van wearing only his vest and shorts and reading some mild girlie magazine whilst Andy was doing some step exercises with the aid of an old tree stump. The sound of the speakers could just be made out through the open van door over the noise of the running engine.

Without any warning a voice shouted out, 'I'd have thought you two would have applied a greater amount of commitment to the job but I should have known better. Again I'm disappointed.' General Hutton stood only yards from Derek, who dropped his magazine and stood up.

'You try listening to this load of crap every day and see if you're not bored rigid.' Derek replied, angry that the man had crept up on him. 'You should have called first –we'd have baked a cake for you!'

Andy looked over Hutton's head. On the main road he could see a parked white car. Albert was standing outside watching them, no doubt ready to rip trees asunder should his master call out for help again.

'I've decided to move closer to the action. After all, tomorrow is supposed to be the day for the Special Reserve meeting. I shall be staying at the Horizon in Stateline. Call me the moment any news breaks.' Hutton turned, his visit over.

'How the fuck did he know where we were?' Derek asked, still nonplussed by the visit.

Andy shrugged. 'Apart from Albert searching every camper park on the shoreline, who knows?'

Derek had a very bad attack of humming, which soon got too much for Andy. 'Come on, let's have the rest of the day off. Nothing's going to happen and there's some nice little restaurants in Homewood – I'll buy you lunch.'

Friday morning started out no differently. On the dot of six the anglers set sail for their usual spot and fishing commenced. However, around midday the sound of engines starting up came through the speakers.

'Probably bored the fish round here to death!' Derek said.

Andy trained his glasses on the boat and watched as it steamed away. But instead of heading in towards Homewood it ploughed on into deeper water in the middle of the lake.

'They're going to meet Victor Warren!' Derek shouted, with panic in his voice.

'Go and listen!' Andy demanded. The last thing he wanted now was Derek wetting himself if they were heading for some remote spot out of listening range.

'Apart from the engine noise nothing's happening,' Derek shouted out from the door.

Andy continued to watch the ever-diminishing craft. Slowly it changed course and headed north, and then after a couple of miles stopped. He could just make out a splash as an anchor went over the side. He called out to Derek. 'They've stopped. I think you were right, the fish have moved or somebody's told them that there's bigger and better hunting over there.' Any explanation would do at the moment to stop Derek throwing a wobbly.

They got the map out and estimated that the boat was anchored about three miles out from Tahoe City, which by road was some eight or nine miles north from their current position.

Perhaps the fish weren't there, after all. By four o'clock the boat was under way again, heading towards Tahoe City.

'I'm going to call up the General,' Derek said. 'If they leave the boat we're in the shit. He can sort it out – he's supposed to be in charge.'

Andy kept listening and heard a bump as the boat manoeuvred into a jetty. A third voice asked them how long they would be staying and Allsop shouted out, 'Overnight.' A mooring-fee was requested and paid for. The engine noise disappeared, the toilet flushed a couple of times and then there was silence.

There was a knock on the camper door. Derek opened it and was pushed out of the way by the General.

'Update now!' he demanded.

Andy obliged, turning up the speaker volume so that Hutton could hear for himself that nothing much was happening.

The little fat General looked ridiculous; he was dressed in a one-piece pale blue tunic that was at least one size too small. The central full-length zip fastener strained to keep the fat underneath in control. If it had been his intention to emulate Winston Churchill it had failed abysmally – he looked more like a house painter. They all sat listening to little more than a hiss coming from the speakers. The atmosphere was uncomfortable, especially for Derek. He didn't like the General at the best of times, let alone sitting next to him on a bunk-bed in their camper. Almost an hour passed before sounds were heard from the boat again.

'What time did you book the table for, Tom?'

'The usual, eight o'clock.'

Hutton got to his feet. 'I'm taking over total command of all field operations as from now. You stay put until you hear from me, and make sure that your damned phone line is kept clear. Be ready to move at a moment's notice.' He pushed past Andy and left.

Derek laughed. 'I bet old fatso's really annoyed the meeting's going to take place in a totally unbugged restaurant and there's nothing he can do about it.'

They settled back to wait and the time dragged by. The phone rang just after ten o'clock. As expected, it was Hutton and he wasn't wasting words.

'Three people leaving restaurant, heading back to boat. Third man wearing leather flying-jacket. Ensure machine operative. Returning to your base.'

'Better smarten the place up, Derek. The boss is coming back for coffee!' Andy warned.

Derek stood to attention and saluted. 'Yes sir! How about I put both hypodermics in his coffee?'

Andy wouldn't have put it past him either.

The General missed the first sounds. The boat was unlocked, lots of footsteps went down into the main cabin and drinks were poured. Then came Allsop's voice.

'I still can't agree, It's not working, is it? Either the Double A is too weak or we're still not reaching enough of the population. Only this morning I heard on the news that there were riots once again in Canada. We're certainly not making the world a less hostile place as we set out to do. I'm all in favour of scrapping the entire project now.'

At this point the General walked into the camper. Derek held his finger up to his month and the three of them sat there in absolute silence whilst the airwaves continued their story.

'And as I was saying earlier, my dear Tom, please be a little more patient. Some of the product has only been in circulation for little over two years and you've said yourself that it can take up to a year before it is used. But I have some good news. As from July of this year the Double A will be supplied in a much more concentrated form. One day, Tom, one day very soon, your wish will be granted and the world will be a much safer and quieter place to live in. Let us toast that day.' There was an audible chink of glass. 'Now, let's have some more of that excellent wine and then we can take Victor across to his dens of iniquity.'

Apart from some shuffling about and drinking noises, no more could be heard. The next noise, the boat's engine starting up, made Hutton visibly jump. Then a new voice spoke.

'Please remember, Tom, nice and slowly. You know how I hate boats and water.'

'Victor Warren?' Hutton asked. The others nodded.

Andy went outside and studied the dark night in the direction of Tahoe City. Derek handed him the binoculars and after a few minutes he spotted the green and red lights of Allsop's boat slowly heading out into the lake. More conversation started up, and they went back inside to listen.

'I'll go and stand outside for the crossing and concentrate on smoking this excellent cigar you bought me.' Warren's accent had a slight European twang to it but it would be difficult after all his years in the States to pinpoint exactly where from.

'If you're all right for the moment Tom, I'll also join Victor in the stern for a breath of fresh air,' Wilenius added.

A door was opened and closed.

'Stupid old fool. I see him twice a year and all he ever does is complain. He still does not suspect anything I suppose? Still thinks we're tying to save the world from Armageddon does he?' The European voice cleared its throat and spat.

'Maybe a fool, Victor, but an important one. Without him our whole project would never have been possible – please remember that. I saw your proposed new site yesterday. It's perfect and will save enormously on transport costs. When do you hope to have it operational?'

'In about six to eight weeks' time if the contractors don't let me down. This story you told Allsop about sending out a stronger material in July, is it true?'

'Yes, but only for one of the products at the moment, I'm afraid.'

'Which one?'

'P1818. It will not only be stronger but far more lethal. I estimate its aggressive power to be 2.7 times that of the present material. I have great hopes that by the end of the year I will be able to improve on P1414 as well.'

'And no doubt this new one will be more expensive! I can't afford to keep Sarius solvent if it is, I'll go bankrupt.'

'Patience, my dear Victor, patience. I have numerous contacts in the industry, as you know. One company requires some cosmetic preparations – someone will visit you shortly. They are anti-wrinkle products for the fading lady; all contain cheap proteins but sell at very high prices.' There was a brief laugh. 'Money is no object to our female friends when they are losing their youth! Your profit margins will again be very handsome indeed. Now, if you'll excuse me I'm going below.'

Andy peered out of the door, binoculars already at his eyes 'The boat's headed this way, looks like they might be coming back to base at Homewood. No hang on a minute he's just correcting his course. The boat's turning away, it's now heading out into the lake.'

From the map it looked as if they were making a direct crossing for Stateline in Nevada.

'Of course! They're taking Victor Warren to the casinos so that he can lose some more of his money,' Hutton said with an air of self-satisfaction. 'I've heard all I want to. I think it's time we paid our three sailors a visit. I want one of you to commandeer a boat now! Use my car. Move!'

'All ready and waiting, we've already thought of it.' Derek savoured the moment.

'My God, you've shown some initiative at last! Well, what are we waiting for? Let's go.' He stepped outside and blew a whistle. Immediately a car engine started up and headlights flooded the camper.

Derek tugged at his shirt. 'I'm not going onto any water dressed like this. Give me a few seconds to grab a sweater.'

Andy searched for the boat keys and his water-proof jacket. Derek threw across the camper keys and said, 'you've got more pockets. by the way, I've got your gun.'

The General chided them to get a move on and asked Derek to turn the listening device off. They piled into the car and Andy relayed instructions to Albert, who neither acknowledged nor turned his head round.

At the Tahoma jetty Hutton told his minder to wait in the car. Andy led the way. There was no finesse employed in getting the boat out, he just untied it, pushed it clear from some others into open water and started the engine. They shot off into the darkness and Derek's face took on a look of despair and bewilderment.

Hutton gave out the instructions. 'No lights! Go alongside and make out we've got some sort of engine problem and need their assistance. I want to be able to get aboard quickly. And remember, leave all the talking to me. Lockwood, you watch my back – they seem reasonable men but you never know with these commies.'

Derek exchanged a quick glance with Andy and they both smiled, having reached the same thought – if only the men on the other boat would shoot him!

Andy's total lack of seamanship brought about a disastrous coming together of the two boats. He came up from behind and at a slight angle and rammed the other craft amidships. His prow dug in, and until he killed the engine his greater speed caused a great ugly scar to appear along Allsop's hull. Derek did well though, he reached across and hung on for all he was worth to the nearest cleat. The other boat slowed down and people appeared in the open stern area. Andy started to tie the two boats together.

'Are you crazy! What are you trying to do? You've rammed us! Where are your Navigation lights?' Allsop's voice was frantic and high-pitched as he inspected the damage. 'My boat, look at it! This is going to cost you, so I hope you're heavily insured.'

'I'm so terribly sorry,' Andy shouted back. 'We've got

no steering – something's snapped. The power's gone down as well. Can you give us a tow back to the shore and we can sort it all out?' Throughout his dramatic lies Andy made sure he kept his head down. The last thing he wanted was for Allsop to recognise him.

'Sure we can,' Wilenius said calmly. 'After all, it is the number one rule of the water to help a sailor in distress. Throw some ropes across and we'll tie you securely alongside.'

They did as requested, whilst Allsop ran about like someone half his age, slinging protective buoys over the side. From the instructions he was shouting out he was both very angry and on the point of hysteria. Somebody had appeared out of nowhere and attacked his life's most precious possession. He wasn't finished with his threats, either. 'As soon as we're ashore I'm going to call the sheriff's office. You're madmen, all of you!'

'No you're not!' Hutton attempted to board their vessel but had trouble negotiating the three-foot difference between the two boats. Derek reluctantly gave him a leg up. 'Allow me to introduce myself, gentlemen. I am General Oliver Hutton and represent the Government of the United States of America. My two men down there are armed, so I wouldn't attempt to do anything foolish.'

'And why should we do that, General?' Wilenius asked.

'I think you have a good idea why, Dr Wilenius. You, together with Dr Victor Warren and Dr Tom Allsop here, are responsible for adding two different types of chemical to Union Mining and Minerals' filter powders, which are used in the world's production of beer and wine. By doing so you intended to change people's personalities and behaviour patterns.'

For several seconds the only sound heard was the slapping of the small waves on the two hulls.

It was Allsop who spoke first. 'Your information is wrong, there is and only ever has been one product. Its purpose is to stop people being so aggressive in order to help create a better world, a more peaceful world. You board us in the middle of the night as if we're criminals, whereas you should be pinning medals on us instead.'

There was a sharp rebuke from Warren. It was the first time he'd spoken and his accent was quite pronounced. 'Shut up, you old bugger! Don't say anything else! We demand to have our lawyers present before any more is said.'

'As you can see, we're not in the most convenient situation at the moment for you to have legal representation, are we, Dr Victor Warren? Or should I say Mr Bogdon Masaryk, or even Anatoly Petrolkch Fedyakin? Yes, we know a lot more about you than you think,' Hutton replied.

Derek looked across at Andy and the face said it all. The bastard Hutton had been holding out on them. He knew Warren's origins and hadn't bothered or thought it necessary to tell them.

Warren again repeated the earlier request. 'I'm not saying one word until I have my lawyer with me.' With that he lit up his huge cigar.

'Fine, well, in that case, Victor, I think we'll hold you in Special Reserve, shall we?' Hutton answered.

The cigar fell out of his mouth, which remained open. Hutton's last remark had definitely struck home.

'Lockwood, look after our friend here, will you?' Hutton indicated that he wanted Warren on the smaller boat and then added, 'If I were you, I'd find something to tie him up with. He looks like a slippery one to me and I wouldn't put it past him to jump overboard and swim for it.'

The passenger was transferred. Andy ushered him forward into the small half-open cabin and tied his feet together.

'Right, your turn, Dr Allsop,' Hutton announced. 'I would like you to stay in the wheelhouse and steer your vessel due north at minimum speed please, whilst Charles and I have a little chat below. And don't forget my men will be watching you the whole time.'

Allsop put the boat into gear and glanced across at Andy. The recognition penny dropped. The glass made it impossible to hear the words but the look on the old man's face was venomous.

Derek adopted a sitting position at the top of the cabin's three steps, silhouetted against the bright light streaming out. He turned to face Andy and gave him the thumbs-up sign. Andy reciprocated, pleased to see that at least Derek was half out of the cold night air. He moved forward a few feet and peered through a port-hole on the other boat. Hutton and Wilenius had taken up sitting positions on opposite sides of a table, and he was just in time to see the scientist offer his guest a glass of wine.

The time passed slowly and Andy stamped his feet in an effort to keep warm. He hadn't realised how much colder it got on water at night. The noise of Allsop's boat in low gear drowned out any other sounds and his immediate surroundings were bathed in an eerie green glow thrown off from the starboard navigation light.

Suddenly and without warning Warren tried to slither past him but he wasn't interested in Andy. He reached the side and vomited.

'Is there anything I can get you?' Andy asked.

'My jacket please, it's on the other boat.' He started to shiver so Andy helped him back inside his hideaway and then caught Derek's attention. In due course a leather jacket was passed and draped around the sick man's shoulders.

Warren was violently ill twice in the next hour, but he was well house-trained and made it to the handrail first. Andy had the greatest sympathy for the man. He was beginning to feel bilious himself. A combination of cold and the constant yawing of the little boat strapped to Allsop's was beginning to get to him. Another half an hour elapsed before there was any movement on the other craft, then Derek warned him the General was about to come up the steps.

Hutton reappeared and shouted across, 'Lockwood, I want you to take me back to shore. There are several things to arrange before these men can be taken into custody and sent on for further interrogation. Bring Warren back across.'

Andy undid the very loose binding round the sick man's legs and had to almost carry him.

'Allsop,' Hutton shouted, 'I want you to turn around and head back to Stateline, where a reception committee will soon be waiting for you. Madden, you stay on board and keep an eye on these three and make sure Allsop keeps his speed down. Come on, Lockwood, things to do. And Madden, make some coffee for our guests, will you? They look frozen.'

Andy untied the ropes and the current took them away from the bigger boat. He started the engine but couldn't feel his hands; they were numb. Hutton asked for maximum power and pointed towards the general direction of Tahoma. Andy hadn't a clue where he was and desperately scanned the shoreline. It was going to be almost pot luck where he came ashore to start with, and then he would have to cruise up or down until he found Tahoma. He just hoped that there wouldn't be any rocks *en route.'*

Suddenly there was a single loud dull thud. Andy's heart missed a beat. Seconds later he felt a shock wave through the boat and braced himself, totally confused as to what was happening.

Hutton turned and screamed over the wind, 'Oh my God, I think Allsop's boat has just exploded. Turn round quickly! Quickly, damn you!'

Andy swung the boat round and made up the mile gap in a matter of minutes, but there was no boat. At first he thought he'd gone to the wrong spot. But there were no boat's lights anywhere to be seen. They had the lake to themselves. On Hutton's furious commands Andy made several passes over the area but found no wreckage, no survivors, no bodies, nothing.

'Poor bastards, what a way to die!' Hutton said, sitting down. 'Somebody must have left the gas unlit. We got away by the skin of our teeth, Lockwood. Another few minutes and it could have been us as well. There's nothing we can do about it now, so continue towards shore as originally planned. I will have even more reports to write now!'

Andy was in a state of semi-shock. Only minutes ago he'd waved to Derek as the boats separated and now he was dead, lying at the bottom of some deep lake alongside his quarry. Admittedly he'd been a pain in the butt at times but he didn't deserve to meet his end like this.

Hutton interrupted any further thoughts. 'Wilenius was behind it all from the start and confessed the lot. No real motive except that he didn't like his fellow man very much – he was going to tell me more later. Well, it looks like it's all over now, so everything can be put back to normal as soon as possible. A blessing really, it's certainly saved the taxpayer the cost of some very expensive trials. Perhaps they took their own lives and sacrificed Madden's to avoid all the disgrace. Who knows?'

Even so Andy thought, Derek hadn't deserved to be included in their pact.

'Would you slow the boat down a bit,' Hutton requested. 'I'm beginning to feel the effects of being on the water.' He added, 'You realise that because of what has now happened we won't be able to get involved with the local police. Too many questions will be asked about what we were doing here in the first place. I think we should just let it take its natural course. The boat will be reported missing and found to have sunk with the loss of all on board.'

After straining his eyes for over half an hour Andy recognised the outline of the small marina and slowed down to a crawl. The last thing he wanted to do was ram the jetty, so he switched the engine off and glided in and let out a huge sigh of relief when the boat was finally tied up to it. Albert flashed the car lights on and off, presumably to signal that he was still awake after all these hours.

The respite seemed to have done the General the power of good. He leapt from the boat and held out his hand. 'I'm sorry about your friend, Andy – a good man lost. Thank you for all your help, you have carried out a most satisfactory campaign. Look, if I were you I'd have next week off. Sell that pathetic camper, see a few sights, relax – forget about this whole thing. I'll tell your people to expect you back in England next weekend. Oh, one more thing, I'll arrange to have all that equipment removed from your vehicle and I'll also arrange to have Madden's belongings returned to his next of kin, if you'd be good enough to pack them up. There's an airfield north of here at a place called Truckee. Shall we say later on today – four o'clock this afternoon?'

Andy watched as Hutton headed for the car. It was probably his imagination but he was half convinced the General had a spring in his step. Albert went round the car and held the door open for his illustrious boss. His hair looked wet. Perhaps he'd been for a run or doing some muscle exercises to pass the time, Andy thought.

He went back on board the boat, retrieved the gun and looked around to make sure there were no signs to show that it had been abused or used much. In the small cabin Warren had left his jacket. He picked it up, put it on and then walked up the jetty and posted the keys through the office letterbox. The run back to the camper warmed his body up but his mind was still numb.

14

Oliver Hutton sat back in the limo. A huge supercilious grin began to spread across his fat face. Inside, he was glowing with a huge sense of pride. He opened up his small attaché case and took out a silver hip-flask, poured a capful, swallowed it and decided to have another. Why not, he'd deserved it. He raised the small cup to Albert, who acknowledged it with a slight nod of his head. A neat, successful operation. He would certainly get some pats on the back for this one when he was wined and dined by his bosses – perhaps even another star to help complete the set. After all, they had allowed him nine months to reach a satisfactory conclusion and he had done it in three. He was proud of his tactics – always intimidate your subordinates and don't ever praise them, that way it keeps the pressure on them and makes them work harder. Perhaps one day they might even name the method after him, he thought, and the smile took on new proportions. He reached inside the case once again and found his notebook; its spine and corners were decorated in the same silver as the flask. He slid the pen from the hinge and ran down a check-list.

Dr Larry Fletcher – negative risk. There was no problem there. The man was nearing retirement age and had not been privy to all the information anyway. A permanent move away from any more investigation would be best. Against the name he wrote, 'university teaching post?'

Ben Hansen's name had a black line already running through it. He did the same thing through Derek Madden's without giving any further thought to the man who had helped bring the case to a satisfactory conclusion and who now lay at the bottom of icy waters. Andy Lockwood's was next. A good man, fairly obedient, strong, worked well on his own initiative. Yes, he would have made a good member of his small team, but no he wouldn't consider him further. The man was slightly too emotional and seemed to have a conscience, and he was also a foreigner. He tapped the pen several times on his chin. After a few days, Lockwood would have forgotten about all about it. After all, he was a professional and had come highly recommended. Anyway, he would be gone in a week, if not sooner, and the Brits had agreed never to return him to the States again. So with one stroke of his pen he crossed Lockwood's name off his list and out of his mind. Both Tom Allsop's and Victor Warren's long and complicated lives were eliminated with two more lines of the pen. Charles Wilenius's name deserved and got special treatment and was circled three times in rapid succession.

Hutton laughed out aloud at the next entry, *Sarius Chemicals*. What a bonus! Victor Warren had no known relatives or heirs to pass the business on to – one would be found! For the moment they would hang on to Sarius, but whether it would be needed in the future required further consideration. If it were sold off, minus its little secrets, it would probably fetch between five and six million dollars – more than enough to finance this and future operations. Indeed an unexpected bonus! *Union Mining and Minerals* came next. This was a more tricky situation – not the replacement for Allsop; that was the easy part. No, it was head office that worried him. Some of the personnel might need replacing.

Decker Pharmaceuticals was the last name on his list. Someone to replace Wilenius was going to be difficult – although not impossible. From what he now knew, no manufacturing changes would be made, so there was no hurry. He put the book down and told Albert to wake him just before they arrived at the airfield.

Andy arrived back at the camper just after three in the morning and made straight for the bunk-bed. He was exhausted. However, as much as he wanted it, sleep would not come. One word kept knocking on his brain – revenge. Hutton had said that Wilenius, like Allsop, was out for revenge against society, but the pieces didn't fit together properly. He'd heard for himself that Allsop had wanted the reverse – he had wanted to make people nicer to each other. Andy sat up, removed Warren's jacket and flung it across the van in a fit of tired annoyance. It hit the listening-equipment, and the red light flickered on for a split second. He switched on the small light above the bunk.

All thoughts of sleep suddenly vanished and adrenalin started to consume him. He reached across and touched the black box. The equipment was still on. Derek had turned the volume down, but in his rush for his sweater had not switched it off. He rushed forward to the driver's seat and switched on the ignition. The needle on the ammeter gauge didn't move, the equipment's batteries were totally exhausted. He flicked over the little switch and the needle climbed slowly to the central position. Thank God, at least the van's engine would start.

Andy sat down again to reassess the situation. Had Derek inadvertently taped all the conversation on the boat, including his own death, or had he deliberately left the machine on so that they had their own version of events? There was one thing for sure – Derek couldn't care less now. Hutton had told them to switch it off before they left with him. Why? Wouldn't he have wanted all the evidence he could get, especially the way it turned out? Then the thought struck him and he froze rigid in the seat. Perhaps they weren't the only ones listening in to the conversations on the boat; somebody, somewhere else, might have been keeping records for the General. Perhaps their black box in the van had hidden secrets and they had been used as a staging-post. Whatever they did with their equipment, somebody else could listen in, even override it and use it independently when they wanted to. 'They' might even have been able to listen in to all their conversations in the van. Andy turned and looked at the large black box. They had only been shown how to operate the top piece. Like an iceberg the majority of it was unknown territory. Then another thought hammered home. Had

Hutton also heard every word in the restaurant, using some small piece of software and the van as a relay station? He cursed his lack of knowledge. and decided not to do anything remotely suspicious until all the gear had been removed.

As tired as he was, he needed to get away from their old base camp and headed back down to Stateline. He found a suitable electrical shop which opened at ten o'clock and decided to wait and become a normal customer. He was tired and liable to make mistakes if he burgled the place, and the last thing he wanted at the moment was to be caught red-handed stealing a cassette player. He managed to fall asleep eventually but was woken at eight by the sirens of police cars dashing past the casino car park. He sat in the van and tried to behave as normally as possible, convinced someone was listening in to his every sound. He whistled and even talked to himself about his imaginary small losses on the gaming-machines so that any eavesdropper would think he'd just shrugged last night's events off as part of the job. He used the hotel's shower, felt much better and walked across the road. He was the first one into the shop after it opened. More sirens went by outside.

'Hi, I'm looking for a portable cassette player,' he announced to the male assistant. He was shown several and selected one. Whilst the man fitted batteries Andy chose some prerecorded tapes from the country-and-western section and a packet of four blank tapes.

'What's all the fuss about outside?' Andy asked.

'Some boat's been reported missing on the lake. I've been listening in on the police frequency. Seems somebody telephoned the Rangers early this morning and said they thought they'd seen a fishing boat explode and disappear.'

'Sounds like too many beers last night if you ask me.'

The assistant nodded, 'That's what the law originally thought. but then some boat didn't arrive at a booked mooring at the marina here so they've got to check it out.'

Andy drove the camper to a remote spot he'd seen on

one of his runs. Carefully he removed all the tapes from the van's equipment and kept them in order, then stretched out on a large rock so that he would look like a tourist sunning himself and listening to his favourite music if anyone passed by. Derek had always looked after the tape side of things and had been quite meticulous about labelling the full ones with the date and time and putting them back into the box the wrong way up to the new unused ones. Somewhere there might be just over two and a half hours recorded on two or three tapes. This was a big maybe though. The batteries might have faded out long before.

He sat bolt upright. It was certainly a small world! The country song being played was the same bloody one that he'd heard over and over again whilst being eaten alive by Maureen – he even remembered most of the words. He turned the volume down, removed Maureen's song and inserted tape one from his small pile. Nothing. He turned it over. Again nothing on it. The same happened with tape two, but three was different – voices came through the small speakers. Wilenius and his cronies had just got back from their meal and he was inviting them to join him in a glass of wine. Andy punched the air. Good old Derek, efficient with the tapes as ever. He left it playing and walked back to the van to check that the volume was low enough and was happy that any eavesdropper using the van's gear would only pick up the sounds of mother nature herself. He rewound the tape, ripped off the Cellophane from one of his bought blank tapes and inserted it into the other half of the machine. The man in the shop had showed him how to record from one tape to another but it took him several attempts before he got it right. Now he was ready.

He sat, elbows on knees, listening to the events of last night. For the best part of fifteen minutes he'd either heard the information before or very little was said. Then he heard Warren arranging their next meeting in July and assumed he was talking to Wilenius out on the deck as he was not being very polite about Allsop and kept calling him a 'silly old bugger'. Warren tried to convince his friend to spend the weekend with him in Stateline – he knew some incredible women – but Wilenius was not interested. For many minutes there were only engine and water noises. And then there was a large bang. Andy had just rammed the other boat. Allsop's panicky voice came over loud and clear, as did Wilenius's offer of help, plus all the noises associated with the frantic tying together of the two boats. Then Hutton's commands, the denial and excuse from Allsop and the transfer of Warren after he demanded his lawyer. All of this was followed by the sound of footsteps as Hutton and Wilenius went down into the cabin. The tape started to slow down and clicked.

'Don't run out on me now batteries, please.' He realised he'd spoken aloud – it seemed the natural thing to do even in a near wilderness. He turned both tapes over and sat quietly, hardly daring to draw breath in case he missed the next unknown passages.

'Dr Wilenius, it's nice to meet you at long last. I've been following your exploits for some weeks now. Please sit down over there. I must congratulate you on your little venture – I'm very impressed, a most ingenious plan.'

'General Hutton—'

'Oliver, please.'

'Oliver, thank you. Yes, I must say I'm very pleased with the way it's turned out. May I offer you a glass of wine? It's a very nice Zinfandel which I get from a small company up near Sonoma in the Napa valley. No, really, it's okay, it's not filtered, if that's what you're worried about, just left to clear in the vat naturally.'

There was a pause on the tape and then a *clink* as glasses were joined. Andy had actually watched them carry out this ritual.

'You seem to know quite a lot about us, Oliver. I would be most interested to learn what, if I may?'

'My pleasure, Charles, if I may call you by your latest first name? You were born Vladimir Pavlovich Parastayev, in 1944 I believe, and came from the small Russian town of Arzamas. Your parents were poor. However, you did well at school and won a scholarship to the scientific academy in Leningrad, where you studied chemistry and biology. You were almost a star pupil, so you came to the attention of your intelligence people. You were offered several choices, so I understand it, either to work in one of your country's secret scientific cities north of the Arctic Circle or join a special, newly formed organisation and be sent abroad to work in the West – sending back any information which might be relevant. The temptations of the later scheme won. But you didn't come very far west to start with. You had to be groomed a bit more first. You were adopted by a Croatian family living in Zagreb – official records show you to have been their third son. In 1966 you attended the university in Zagreb and went through the whole three-year scientific course again, and quite naturally you turned out to be the outstanding pupil of the year. We believe you came out via Ljubljana in Slovenia –you might like to clarify our records in due course. Coming to the West as a citizen of Yugoslavia was obviously a damned sight easier than as a Russian during the Cold War period. And so as Zoran Vladimir Radelic, armed with the best degree and glowing testimonials, you arrived in San Francisco late 1970. You spent a few months perfecting your English and started work as a humble quality-control chemist with Decker Pharmaceuticals. That same year, 1971, you met and fell in love with Elizabeth Whitehead and were married a year later, three months before your daughter, Sandra Jane, was born. You were granted American citizenship in 1977. You had well and truly arrived, as they say, and since then and through your own efforts and hard work you have risen through the ranks to your present job as director of research and development. Your talents were recognised early on and your ideas listened to, and you came up with several lucrative new products. As Decker prospered so did you. In addition, you are one of the world's leading authorities on several specialised scientific subjects.'

There was a pause followed by the glug of more wine being poured.

'No doubt a lot of the valuable information you had

at your disposal was passed back to your Soviet masters. Then they took advantage of your exalted position and asked you to come up with some scheme to destabilise the world by adding chemicals to the food chain. so you knuckled down and thought how to set about it. You already knew Tom Allsop from the old days and still occasionally met up with him to go fishing. You also knew that he looked after the quality side for Union Mining and Minerals and that his filteraids went all over the world to filter alcoholic drinks. You had your potential carrier, so you began work to develop suitable mind-altering chemicals that could be added to the powder. In fact, you came up with two: one that would make people aggressive and angry, and another that would produce a submissive effect so people would just accept the inevitable. If the two sets of people came together then the result would be obvious. The compounds you developed are amino-acid-related, so I understand – part of the very structure of life itself. If detected, it would be assumed they were some sort of natural material. Of course, you couldn't be seen to be doing the dirty work yourself, so you recruited Victor Warren to the project. Like yourself, he is from the Soviet Union and was recruited into Special Reserve. I don't know the connection between the two of you as yet but time will tell . . . I must agree with you the wine is excellent.'

Again there was silence on the tape. Andy sat through the lull in activities, cursing. All this information had been denied them and yet they were the people carrying out the investigation. Why? Although he hated to admit it to himself he was impressed with Hutton's summary. He certainly hadn't gone on board with any notes, so everything he'd said so far had been memorised.

Wilenius broke the silence. 'Congratulations, Oliver, your information is excellent. You obviously have some very thorough people in Eastern Europe.' There was another sound of glass clinking. 'Unfortunately, some, in fact a whole lot, of your information is wrong and misinformed. I can see you're itching for some of the answers, so please allow me to fill in some of the missing pieces.'

Andy switched the tape off. He needed a beer before

he could listen to any more of this and knew Derek had stashed some away somewhere in the camper. More than anything else at the moment, he was confused and puzzled. The two of them sounded like some mutual admiration society. Why was Wilenius being so co-operative? Warren certainly hadn't been! Hutton was being extremely pleasant, which made a change, but why Wilenius? Perhaps Hutton had added something to the wine and was prepared to drink it himself? Maybe Albert had done the deed when they were all in the restaurant? No, Andy didn't believe that. The only conclusion was that Wilenius wanted to talk, that he was such an arrogant man that he was actually proud of what he had done and had found both a sympathetic ear and kindred spirit in Hutton. He switched the tape back on.

'As you are not recording any of this I shall of course deny it all later on, and if necessary I shall let Victor stand the rap. Have you considered the mayhem of making such news public? Imagine world headlines declaring that all beer and wine is unfit to drink. That is why I don't mind giving you some answers. They will be just between you and me, eh?'

The General's voice boomed through the speaker, 'Madden! Madden! Good, he can't hear us. Please continue, Charles.'

'Your early information is spot-on. Yes, I was recruited by the Soviet Government, as were thousands of other students during the late sixties. We never met or even knew any other members – or were not supposed to. When I was at university in Leningrad we would travel down to Moscow twice a year to play chess with the students at the academy. It was always an honour to be chosen, especially if we could beat their Moscow team. I played Victor twice and that was it – you could hardly call it a friendship, could you? I forgot all about him, of course, and then more than ten years later I got a phone call out of the blue. He was here in the States and needed my help. He'd recognised me from a picture in the papers – I'd just caught the heaviest salmon ever pulled out of Lake Tulloch.

'It was totally out of order but I met him. He was a

mess, almost a down-and-out. He explained that he'd come through Czechoslovakia, he'd been to university there and obtained a degree in petrochemistry. He'd landed a good job with an oil company in Bakersfield but the corruption of the West was too much for him. He'd started to drink, gamble and womanise heavily and in a short time had been sacked from his job for persistent bad time-keeping. He'd started to drift and at the time I first saw him he was something like a part-time fruit-picker. His Soviet contact was quite rightly becoming annoyed with him, and gave him a final warning. Failure could take on many different forms of punishment; relatives back home could have all their privileges taken away, right through to Victor being found dead. I told him he was a disgrace and had let the side down badly. He was terribly shamefaced about it all and promised to mend his ways.

'I belonged to various chemical societies and rubbed shoulders with lots of other technical people and I'd heard that there was money to be made manufacturing own-label goods for some of the chain stores. To his credit, Victor did the initial legwork. He secured a small contract repacking white spirit into bottles. He did it all by hand to start with, working round the clock. I lent him the money to pay for his first purchases and in due course he paid me back with interest. But what mattered most was that he got his self-esteem back.'

'And so Sarius Chemicals was born. It all sounds highly commendable, Charles, but repacking solvents is hardly going to please the Kremlin. What did he do to appease his controller?'

'I fed him various bits of information to pass on. I was accepted by my fellow chemists by then and they talked freely about their work – in fact, some of them even invited me to have a look around their plants. Sometimes it was very embarrassing how much they took you into their confidence – believe you me, Oliver, there was enough for both of us! Anyway, Victor and Sarious grew and had to move to bigger premises. I continued to advance at Decker and the amount of key information available also rose. By now people were even sending me their research papers so that I could give my professional opinion on their work!'

'And you passed all this information on. Did it benefit your country much?'

'I honestly don't know, we were never told. I suppose we must have been doing something right, otherwise we'd have been told.'

'And then your masters decided to do something far more positive and dramatic to screw up the rest of the world. How were you first told about this and how much leeway did they give you?'

'No, this part of your information is all wrong, Oliver. Our Soviet bosses didn't dream up the idea – I did. Until 1990 I was perfectly happy to carry on as I had been. Everything was running like clockwork. I was attending seminars all over the world and even I couldn't keep pace with some of the discoveries. No, 1990 went wrong for me – the Soviet Union collapsed. After seventy years under the yoke of communism, Russia was a free country again. The world breathed a sigh of relief and then sat back and did absolutely nothing to help, it was just left to stew in its own juices. Oh yes, promises were made, but very little money or aid actually materialised. Russia already struggling against bankruptcy went further and further down the pan and its people, my people starved. Inflation spiralled and the situation grew worse. Then the huge military machine started to be dismantled and soldiers in their millions – men who had selflessly defended the country for years – found themselves thrown out onto the streets, reduced to begging for scraps of food. Armament factories were closed down and a further ten million people were flung onto the scrap heap and left to fend for themselves. By 1994 over one hundred and fifty million people existed on less than eighteen dollars a month each.

'Then the idea came. I have to be fair – it was something Tom said that started me thinking. He and I go back a long way and as you can tell we both enjoy fishing. We usually do this trip twice a year. Tom's all right – another clever man. He's shy by nature and he hates all forms of violence. I believe he was some sort of conscientious objector during the Vietnam war. In all these years I've never seen him kill a fish; he always treats them gently and throws them back over the side and insists I do the same. Anyway, years ago now, we were sitting in a restaurant and some of our fellow drinkers were watching a major league baseball game. The programme was interrupted to bring news of riots in Los Angeles. I remember it very clearly, Tom turned to me and said that as scientists it was a pity we couldn't come up with a pill or something that could be dropped into people's drinks to make them more peace-loving. Nothing happened, of course. Then months later I got a phone call from him. He was in a panic, which was most unusual for him. He'd introduced some sort of water spray into his process which had something to do with keeping dust down, but residual moisture was making the powder go mouldy. He asked me what could be added to the water to prevent it happening, so naturally I recommended a suitable food grade of fungicide. You have to remember that Tom's a mineralogist, so this kind of stuff is way outside his field of knowledge. I told him about Sarius and their facilities and that they were almost on his doorstep. I didn't realise at the time that Union had another plant in Oregon, Tom only mentioned the Bullen one.'

Some sort of crashing sound came over the tape, as if somebody had dropped something. Derek must have heard it as well and gone down to the cabin to investigate, because Hutton told him brusquely to resume his position at the top of the stairs. There was a *pop* as another cork left a bottle; it was thirsty work confessing. Wilenius continued his story.

'Let's see, yes, this was the same year we lost all our contacts – they just disappeared. We even tried to get in touch with our embassy staff in Washington but were given the cold shoulder. Victor was over the moon, I can tell you, and we had some terrible arguments. I could see him slipping back into his old habits as he considered himself a free man again; and especially now he had learnt to fly, all his old vices were much closer to hand.'

Andy stopped the tape. He could hear background voices so he rewound it and played it back at a higher volume. It was his voice asking Derek to throw across Victor's jacket. The tape continued to unravel the story and Andy was convinced of one thing – Charles Wilenius liked the sound of his own voice!

'Tom's idea would not go away – not for a peace pill though; to me the world was far too peaceful already. It was overcrowded it would not be long before food supplies would start to run out anyway, let alone all our oil reserves. Throughout history wars have culled the population to manageable limits. What was needed was a "war pill", if you like. I am sure that during your long and distinguished career, Oliver, various papers have come to your attention concluding that by nature *Homo sapiens* tends towards aggression and is happier when doing so.'

Andy didn't stop the tape but heard himself say out loud, 'Yes you probably wrote most of them, you bastard Hutton!' He calmed down and continued to listen.

'So the thought began to germinate; make mankind aggressive again, let frontiers go back up and put countries back on a war footing, like the old days during the cold war. Then Russia would have to re-employ the soldiers and open up its munitions factories again. I already had ideas, of course. I knew exactly what would happen if there was a deficiency or a surplus of certain chemicals in the brain.I discussed the idea with Victor first, but he was worried about the financial angle. He could see Sarius going bankrupt and all his peccadillos coming to an end, but he wasn't using his brain, I'm afraid. You see, the product I had in mind was going to be very expensive, far more than Tom's company would consider for a "new and improved" fungicide. But the answer was staring Victor in the face – his food supplement business. The proteins he bought from Decker were quite frankly very low grade and cheap, yet the finished products he made were sold on with a terrific mark-up, so this healthy profit would subsidise our "fungicide". In the end I almost had to blackmail him before he agreed, and the first deliveries of fungicide were made to Bullen in 1992.'

'With Tom Allsop's knowledge?'

'Of course, and with his blessing. It was *his* peace solution, after all! There, Oliver, I think that's enough, I've really said too much anyway – far more than I intended to.'

There was silence on the tape and then Andy had trouble making out the next sounds. They were applause! The bloody little General was clapping Wilenius's speech as if it were some stage play!

'Charles, once again I must congratulate you. We may have started out on different sides but I totally endorse everything you have said about the pitiful state of the world at present. You, sir, are a man I both admire and feel a close bond with. Please continue your story.'

'I don't think so. However, I would like to ask you a question. What do you intend to do with me now?'

Andy noted 'me'. Yes, Wilenius and Hutton were getting on well together because they were totally selfish people.

'If it were left to me I would do as Allsop suggested and pin a medal on your chest. As it is, you are right about one thing. None of this can ever be released to the public. God knows what panic it would cause. I have already spoken to my superiors and it has been agreed that all the information will remain classified. As for you Charles, I can assure you that no harm will come to your goodself; you have my word on that. Now please be so good as to finish your most interesting tale.'

There was a lull in the activities. One of them had been to the toilet, the pump-action flush system could be heard, and it took about two minutes before Wilenius resumed the conversation.

'I have given it some careful consideration, Oliver, and because you are an officer and therefore a man of honour, I have decided to continue. You have to understand that it takes many years to perfect complicated chemicals like this and the first one sent to Bullen was, I suppose, very crude by comparison to the current material. We are now on our fourth derivative and it brings on aggression very quickly, for some reason more so in wine than beer.'

'And would you be able to produce even stronger substances?'

'Definitely. I already have. In a few months' time it was the intention to substitute the Bullen liquid with a far more powerful concentrate.'

'Back at Decker Pharmaceuticals, doesn't anybody realise what's going on?'

'Of course the factory process people know that they are making proteins and amino acids – after all, that's the official title of their plant. They have all the recipes for making the numerous chemicals but don't know technically what the end results are or indeed what they will be used for eventually. Should any fine-tuning be necessary then it is left to me. How can I put it? They make the tree and I can come along and add the leaves. It's the same with the quality-control section. They are looking for certain reactions and criteria from a product, and as long as it meets them it is passed and accepted. They are not employed to carry out elaborate tests to discover if it has hidden applications. Incidentally, I set the various quality-test methods to be used. The changes I've made to Double A, as I call it, have been very subtle so far – altering the type of leaf on the tree. The latest version, however, will be very different; it's almost a totally new product, but as long as it meets my specifications it will be passed without any argument.

'You might like to know that in the three years we've been conducting this experiment Union have not received one single complaint from their customers about traces of organic matter being present in the filteraid. These days, products are sold on the understanding that they conform to a previously agreed quality standard, and as long as they are delivered with a certificate of conformity then an awful lot of companies don't even test their incoming raw materials. Everyone assumes that the other company is doing its job properly.'

Wilenius said something else which Andy couldn't decipher as the tape ran out. He looked at his watch: it was one o'clock. He was going to have to get a move on. He set up tape four and a blank in their respective slots. The first part of the next question was missing.

'. . . also little mention of Melford so far?'

'It wasn't even mentioned until about six months later. At that time nearly all the fine grades, the ones that got the water-spray treatment, were produced at Bullen. The new products sold very well, according to Tom, and sales started to outstrip production. Union's commercial boys decided converting some old plant at Melford was cheaper than installing brand-new kit at Bullen. The fungicide caused Victor and me a major headache. The transport costs into Oregon would be crippling. All I could come up with was a much cheaper derivative, and offsetting the increased road haulage costs. This was to be a stopgap measure until Victor could find suitable premises north of Stockton and *en route* to Melford.'

'And this derivative, the one that goes to Melford, is the depressant one, right?'

'Yes, at the moment. But once we get the site and finances sorted out I'll change it for something more potent and aggressive. I haven't decided what yet, as Union Mining have been up to some tricks lately.'

'In what way?'

'Originally all the fine material from Melford was destined for export to Third World countries, then somebody in Union changed the rules. Instead of keeping the good stuff for the domestic market he decided to get a bigger slice of business by undercutting the competition with the cheaper Melford grades. Now we have a mixed market.'

'But isn't that better for your plan to work, one aggressive lot of drinkers against others who don't care what day of the week it is?'

'Maybe, but we've lost total control. The plan was to manipulate the situation as we saw fit, not to be in the hands of some greedy salesman. For the catalyst to spark off a situation it might be better to have two aggressive sides coming together. Tom keeps me abreast of where the products are going now, and once the pattern had settled down, I would have had a rethink on what to put into the two fungicidal products.'

'And Tom still thinks there is only one product?'

'Of course.'

'And you set out to do this in order to help the Russian people? Incredible. The concept is brilliant and I have to agree with all your sentiments. I salute your enterprise. Three people. Just three people trying to alter the whole world's behaviour. I am right there is no one else involved?'

'No one. You said three – in fact, only two. Tom is not aware of the scope of the project. Thank you for your compliments. The project is not without its faults, of course.'

'And whilst you were creating all this mayhem, Russia would appear to the world as a responsible and calm nation for the very reason that no Purflo was bought, due to the lack of money. Brilliant!'

'Right again. Neither Russia nor the majority of countries in the Middle East use our materials. I have said that the project was not perfect. One day I might have dreamt up some other method for the Muslims – who knows? After all, I've spent many years and a lot of Decker's money researching into all types of food additives; colours, flavours, anti-oxidants and enhancers are big business. I think there's something like three thousand additives now which are allowed to be added to foodstuffs to either preserve them or make them look good on the supermarket shelves. Yes, I've plenty of thoughts what I could do . . .'

'What were your time expectations for the scheme to start taking a strong grip?'

'About five to six years. The new material which will be sent to Bullen in July is the key. It is not only stronger but will have an accumulative effect; in other words, the aggression will never go away and will always be built on.

'It's been a most informative meeting, Charles, but it's very late. I have to go ashore to make arrangements for you and your colleagues to be taken somewhere – but please don't concern yourself, you will be treated fairly and kindly. Madden! Madden! Call Lockwood, I'm going ashore, and help him get Warren onto this boat – now, for God's sake!'

Andy heard his own name being called out by Derek and the General saying that he wanted to go ashore, the bumps and Derek's heavy breathing as they manhandled Warren from one boat to the other, the instructions to Derek to make the three collaborators some coffee and then the command to Allsop to steer a slow course towards the town of Stateline. Finally, the sound of the boat Andy was steering faded away into the background and then there was a lull. He imagined Derek boiling up water for the hot drinks, Allsop muttering to himself in the wheelhouse, Warren feeling sick and Wilenius sitting in the main cabin beginning to feel the effects of too much wine. Andy was not prepared for what happened next.

'What the fuck! Where did you come . . . ?'

There was the sound of a gun being fired and Derek's voice never finished its startled sentence as his body hit the deck with a solid thud. Two more shots were fired and again there was another crash of bodies onto deck. Whoever was doing the shooting switched the boat's engine off. Then Wilenius's voice came over loud and clear and full of horror.

'What do you want? Oliver said he would treat us with due consideration. What are you doing?'

'Expose your arm, now!' It was the first and only time the unexpected visitor had spoken but it was enough for Andy to recognise the gruff tones of Albert.

There were no more words recorded on the tape just footsteps and scraping noises. It sounded as if Albert was dragging the two dead bodies into the main cabin and there was the sickening thud as heads hit each step. More footsteps were followed by heavy breathing and scuffing sounds as Albert did something that took him several minutes. Then the distinctive sound of a zip fastener being opened followed by the sound of water rushing in, some clicking noises, more footsteps, moving more quickly this time, followed by more heavy breathing and a dull thud. Then an outboard motor was started. The loud engine noise rapidly decreased,and all Andy was left with was the sound of gushing water. For nearly thirty seconds. Then there was nothing, apart from a very faint whirring sound from the tape itself.

Andy felt sick and sat staring at the tape player, stunned by all he'd heard. Albert had killed three of them – by the sound of it Wilenius was either drugged or unconscious – and had then scuttled the boat and blown it to pieces underwater, where it would create maximum damage but attract minimum attention. If the device had been placed on or near the bodies there would be nothing left to identify. Andy picked up a large rock and hurled it at the nearest tree.

He collected together his two pirate tapes and put them in the printed country-and-western boxes – he would destroy the genuine tapes later. Now came the difficult bit. Somehow he had to wipe off all conversation on the government tapes after they had left the camper to fetch their own boat. He found the exact spot. What now? It had to sound just like blank unused tape. Then the idea came, record from one of his unused tapes onto the government one. He tried it on fast-record for a minute and played it back. It was nearly there but still had a slight 'woosh' to it and somebody might just know it had been used and then wiped clear. He tried it again on the normal-record speed; it was much better. It was going to take over two hours to erase the two tapes – he was going to be late for his appointment at the airfield.

He returned to the camper and tipped the contents of Derek's case onto the bed. It was mainly old used clothes and there was nothing he thought he should keep. He stuffed them back in again, folding the shirts and jacket – he didn't know why really, but perhaps because Derek himself had always been so smart and tidy. He ran outside, checked the tape and then set about tidying up the van. He found several further items of Derek's in some of the cupboards and put them in the case, but decided to keep his box of business cards and his notebook. There was nothing in the briefcase containing the phone and fax machine he wanted, so he sat down and sorted through the various messages they had received. It occurred to him that they'd never had a written message from Hutton, he had always telephoned them. He took out all the reports from Simon; there was no point in involving him any more. The rest, along with Derek's world map, he left in the briefcase. He piled all his spoils onto Warren's leather jacket, took them outside and dumped them next to his tape machine. As soon as he knew the explosion on the second tape had been wiped clear he left it to run for a further minute and then went to fast record. Satisfied the wooshing sound had been eliminated and that nobody would suspect the tapes had been used, he put them back in the right order in the government box. The set was complete again. With all his tapes wrapped in the jacket and with cassette player in his other hand he headed into the woods, found a suitable spot, scooped out a large hole in the soft peaty earth and buried the lot. After a quick wash he was ready. They could pull the van to bits now if they wanted to. He rechecked the map; Truckee would take him about thirty minutes to reach. He would be late but he didn't really care.

In fact, he was very late. The airfield, for a start, was miles out of town, and secondly he was not concentrating properly on the road signs and got lost a couple of times. Too many thoughts were distracting him. Hutton had wanted the boat slowed down, claiming that he was feeling ill. The bastard. This was just an excuse to make sure Albert got back to the car with Wilenius before they did. And the flashing car lights? A signal to let his boss know that the mission had been achieved?

Andy felt angry. He and Derek had been used. They had done all the legwork and then been discarded as surplus to requirements. But at least he was still alive. Poor old Derek had been given the ultimate pay-off. He drove straight for the helicopter. The same crew jumped down from inside.

'Nearly giving you up for dead, man,' the sergeant shouted out.

'Sorry, had a very late night on the town and spent most of the day sleeping it off, it's put me all behind. I'll be glad when you take all this crap out of the van, then I'll also be able to do more than five miles per hour!'

'Was she worth it?'

'Oh yes, most definitely!' Andy lied. It might get back, indeed somebody might be listening now, and would be pleased to hear that he'd shrugged off last night and was already back enjoying himself.

'You go amuse yourself for an hour or so, we'll have this little lot out in no time.'

Andy had nowhere he wanted to go so he sat and watched them from a distance. The three army men worked hard and even pop-riveted a small plate over the hole left in the roof.

The sergeant shouted across, 'She's all yours, as good as new – well, almost.' He looked down at his clipboard and added, 'Says here there's a suitcase or travel bag to collect and a mobile phone machine. You guys certainly know how to travel, don't you? Where's your partner? Still sleeping his whore off?' He started to laugh.

Andy joined in, walked across and handed over the items requested.

'Great, we'll be off. So long. You boys take it nice and easy, you hear.'

Andy shook his hand and added, 'Give my regards to General Hutton when you see him.'

The sergeant frowned and turned to his two companions. 'Did you hear that, guys? The man here knows a general!' There was more laughter. 'Too rich for us, my friend. We never see anybody that exalted. A captain's about our top contact. Guess you're heading back for another session then?'

'Might just do that. I'm on leave, so I might as well enjoy myself.'

The van drove well now that it was back to its designed weight, and Andy reached his deserted spot in the woods in under thirty minutes. He retrieved his leather bundle and flung it onto the passenger seat, drove back to Stateline, found the biggest hotel casino he could and parked the van amongst dozens of others. He managed to put back the bunk-bed and cupboard without too much trouble and had forgotten how big it was inside now that everything was back in its original slot. But he'd had enough of it and all its memories, so he decided to sell it at the first opportunity.

Tonight, however, he would treat himself to some luxury. He would book into one of the better rooms in the hotel and have a long hot bath, his first meal of the day and an early night.

Next morning he retrieved his tapes from inside the leather coat. The coat intrigued him. It was of excellent quality and hand-stitched, but he hadn't realised how heavy it was before. He checked the pockets. The top one contained business cards, *Victor Warren – President, Sarius Chemicals.* The left pocket held a small leather wallet and contained two gold credit cards and list of addresses whilst the identical pocket on the other side contained a small bunch of keys. The fob said *Cessna* and was embossed with a small picture of an aeroplane. In the inside pocket was an envelope with *Caesar's Palace, Reno* printed across the bottom. He ripped it open. It contained two equal stacks of hundred-dollar bills. So Victor Warren had won at last; how ironic, and nobody knew Andy had them. As far as anyone who was bothered knew, they were now shredded in pieces somewhere in the lake.

It was time to start discarding a few items. He stuffed the jacket in the bag, quickly followed by old clothes, the cassette player, and the rest of the unwanted blank tapes. He double-checked what was left. The plane keys would have to be abandoned somewhere else. He found his two illegal tapes and put them with the money whilst the original country-and-western ones ended up in the bag. Andy found an incinerator on the lower ground floor, and watched until the bag and its contents were reduced to ashes. Bits of metal from the player remained but nothing that could be linked to him.

He asked the same question in every small and large hotel he walked past and received the same answer from all the receptionists: 'I'm sorry, sir, but no one with the name Oliver Hutton has stayed in the hotel over the last week. Have a nice day.'

He sold the van later on in the day at a used car lot. A mechanic walked into the caravan office as the cash was changing hands.

'This yours?' It was the brown padded envelope containing the two syringes. He'd forgotten all about it.

'Yes, thanks. I've been looking for that for days. Where did you find it?'

'In the icebox!'

On Monday he sat over coffee and reread all the faxes but there was nothing. The only number was in Derek's diary. He rang the Washington DC number and asked to speak to Hutton.

'Good morning, State Department, how may I help you?'

'Good morning to you, I'd like to speak with General Oliver Hutton please.' He just hoped his dodgy accent would pass inspection. He had to repeat the name and ended up spelling it out, then there was long pause.

'I'm sorry, sir, but we have nobody of that name on the staff. Are you sure you have the correct number? May I ask who's calling?'

'Major Freshwater from Edwards Air Force Base.' The name was real enough – he'd seen it on one of the doors where they'd met the commander.

'Thank you, sir, I'm sorry I can't be more help. Goodbye.'

Next he rang Maureen. She was over the moon to hear from him but her voice dropped when he said he wanted to come down and see her as soon as possible. She said 'okay' but there was no real conviction in her voice. Perhaps he wasn't giving her sufficient time to get rid of the new guy.

Andy remembered Larry had said he'd met Hutton once before – he might know where he'd slithered back to, but when he rang he was told Dr Fletcher was on vacation for the next three weeks. Andy declined to leave his name.

He was rapidly running out of ideas and his anger was quickly turning into frustration. It seemed that Hutton surfaced when required and then slid back into the ooze afterwards. As a bonus he had the biggest military outfit in the world to hide in, so what chance did a stranger and an outsider have of locating and tracking down the bastard? Simon! He would have to ask Simon one more favour.

A cheery voice answered the phone, 'Summertime Nurseries, how may I help you?'

Andy gave his name. Simon was out on a job at present but would be back in the office late afternoon. There was no point in hanging around the lake area any more so he decided to start the journey down to Bullen. He'd been driving for some hours when a thought struck him. What if Hutton had decided to check out Sarius for himself? He found the map; instead of turning off for Bullen he could continue further down the road to Bakersfield first. He stopped and tried Simon again.

'Andy, how nice to hear from you. Are you coming to see us? We'd love to show you round the nursery and we can put you up overnight without any trouble at all. When are you going to arrive?' Simon's voice was full of excitement.

'Simon, I need one last favour.'

The voice dropped its happy edge. 'But you promised, please don't ask me. I told you before, I've given up the horrible rat race, but please come and visit us.'

'Well if you won't do it for me, how about one last special favour for Ben? Please don't forget that it's to get justice for him that we've been working so hard. Some of us can't opt out quite as easily – we have commitments to fulfil.' Andy knew there was no need for the last bit but it did the trick.

'Okay, if I can. What is it?'

'Thank you, Simon. It's quite simple. I need to know where I can locate a General Oliver Hutton.'

Simon read back the spelling of the surname then added, 'You'd better give me a couple of days on it.'

It was agreed Andy would ring back on Wednesday evening, and he could almost hear the sigh as Simon put his receiver down.

Andy continued his drive on down to Bakersfield. He dropped the aeroplane keys down a grating near the Sarius place. If they were ever found it would look as if Warren had been careless sometime in the past.

Everything seemed normal at the factory for a Monday. People were going about their daily tasks like any other day and there were no large cars parked in the visitor slots. One thing was different though, the small flag was now flying at half-mast. He was wasting his time here.

It was after nine when he pulled up at Maureen's ranch house. It was still light but there were no signs of life and her truck was gone. He knocked on the door nevertheless, but got no reply. He decided to go back into town, have a meal and a drink and come back later when the ten o'clock shift ended.

He saw the dust cloud turn up the track and stood by his car and waited. She parked her old battered pick-up alongside and almost fell out of the driver's seat. She was a complete mess. Her hair was matted and covered in powder, her eyes sunken and tired and her company overalls shed dust with every movement she made.

'Hi. I'm sorry, I must look a real mess. Come in,' was all she managed to say.

Andy grabbed his new travel bag and followed her indoors. The usually spotless room looked like a bomb had hit it. She flopped onto the bed and more dust rose from the sheets.

'I've just finished at the plant,have to be back by six, I must get some sleep . . . .' If she had intended saying more then the words were lost for ever.

Andy tried one of the chairs but decided the car seat was more comfortable to sleep in. He had coffee on the go by five thirty and the smell bought her round. She sat up, looked at the clock, groaned and collapsed back on the bed again.

'Sorry, honey,' she said, still in the prone position.

'That's all right. What the hell have you been doing to get into such a state?'

'Work, work and more goddam work, that's what. Tom Allsop had last week off, you know – I told you over the phone that he was going fishing. It always means more work for Clay Steadman and myself as we have to take it in turns to keep an eye on the quality-control department. Well, that's not so bad in itself, but would you believe it, that old bugger Allsop's gone and drowned himself? Clay, who was supposed to be on duty this weekend, was summoned up to head office on Saturday afternoon to attend some hastily called panic meeting and I've now been running the place on my own for the last forty-eight hours solid. Look, I'm sorry about all of this, Clay should be back sometime tonight so we can catch up on things as from tomorrow. Oh for a long hot shower. Dream on, girl!' She got to her feet, threw some water on her face, drank two cups of black coffee and in the same clothes as last night headed for the door. 'Make yourself at home, I'll try and be back by nine.' She blew a powdery kiss and left.

Andy finished off the coffee. No wonder her voice had sunk when he'd said he wanted to come and visit.His timing had been lousy and it was all Hutton's fault she was having to work herself to a standstill. He began to mope around and the more he thought about the whole episode the worse his mood became. He had to snap out of it before it took a firmer hold on his life, if not he would end up humming like Derek. He walked around the ranch. It needed a good clean; housework – something practical – would take his mind off things and help him lose some of his pent-up anger, so he set to with a vengeance. The sweat poured off him. Even the sheets were washed, hung out in the hot sun and back on the bed in a matter of hours. He hadn't done so much around a house since he was a boy and then it had been a form of blackmail so he could increase his pocket money. There was one locked cupboard which he had open in seconds. All Maureen's personal belongings were contained in an old cigar box; a university certificate, a passport with no stamps or visas in it, her Union Mining contract of employment and this year's salary slips. Like Allsop, the company didn't pay her that well for all her efforts, he thought, and she only had just over one thousand dollars amassed in the local bank. There were a dozen or so old photographs from her college days and that was it. Maureen Bradley didn't look as if she had any hidden secrets or complicated past attached to her; what you got is what you saw.

Andy put all the bits back in the box and relocked the door. Across in the far corner stood an old Welsh dresser, its shelves piled high with music tapes. She must have one of the largest selections of country-and-western music in California, Andy thought, and toyed with the idea of leaving his two tapes amongst them, but quickly decided against it. He continued to look through all the remaining cupboards and drawers as he went about his chores, but she led a very straightforward existence.

The temperature climbed throughout the day. He showered, got into shorts and surveyed his handiwork – his mother would have been proud of him. The association of ideas reminded him, he would go into Bullen, find a phone and organise his flights back to Europe and let her know he was on his way back.

The temptation was too great, Edwards Air Force Base's telephone number was actually listed in the directory. His American accent was lousy but hopefully would pass over the line. 'General Oliver Hutton please.'

'May I say who's calling please?'

'State Department.'

'And what name?'

'Hutton will know who it is.'

There was a long pause the other end and the male voice was replaced by a female one. 'Sir, I'm sorry but we have no one with that name currently on the base.'

'Damn! He's never where I want him when I want him. Who am I speaking to?'

'Sergeant Helen Crombi, sir.'

'Do me a favour, Sergeant Helen Crombi, check when he was last there and when he's due back, will you please?'

'Certainly sir, please hold on.' Several seconds ticked slowly by. Andy's palms began to sweat and the phone squirmed in his hand. Perhaps they were tracing the call; he hadn't a clue how quickly modern technology could do this nowadays. He hung on. He had to see it through.

Crombi's voice returned. 'Our computer records

show that General Hutton was here ten days ago, sir, but I'm afraid we have no forward visiting date for him at all.'

'Thank you, Sergeant Crombi, your manners are most charming. You are a credit to the Air Force. Goodbye.' Andy hung up the wet receiver. The last bit he knew was patronising but would be typical of some of the pompous senior officers in Washington. Ten days ago – that was when he and Derek had been summoned for their briefing with the Commander – well, at least Hutton did exist and it all wasn't some horrible dream he'd wake up from, although right now it felt like one.

She arrived home at half past nine and stood in the doorway admiring her once again tidy home. 'Thanks, it looks great, but I'm sorry, lover, I'm going to have to get some sleep.'

Andy moved towards her, pulled her indoors and shut the door. 'Oh no you're not, not yet at least.' He led her by the hand to the bathroom and she left a trail of powder behind her. Andy turned on the shower taps and started to undress her, and as he undid the band holding her hair up a dust cloud formed as the thick tangled locks tumbled down onto her shoulders. He carefully removed her boots. Her feet were black. Her shirt and trousers created more mess as they hit the floor. He helped her under the warm water and she let out a low purr. He shampooed and rinsed her hair – that was the easy bit – washing the tattoo and the rest of her body with a soapy flannel wasn't! He tried not to look at her but to think of a real turn-off. He thought of Hutton and it worked. Occasionally the flannel snagged on spiky pubic hair, she hadn't bothered about herself for a week he reckoned. Her body was so tempting, she was in magnificent shape, honed to perfection by all the physical work she did. He dried her off. Hutton, Hutton, he had to keep thinking. He was glad when at last he slipped a cotton robe over her body and the temptations were hidden. Again he took her by the hand and led her past the bed, which she looked at with longing eyes.

'Where we going?' She yawned.

'Food next! What have you had to eat today, in fact, for the last couple of days?'

'Coffee and candy bars out of the vending-machine, why?'

'I thought so.' Andy sat her down on the chair on the porch; the evening air still blew warm. 'Don't fall asleep, I'll be back in a minute.' Some of his barbecued food was a bit burnt, but with coleslaw and salad it looked appetising enough. He was surprised, he'd half expected her to just pick at it but she ate the lot.

'Andy, I feel like the Queen of England. Thanks, I owe you one, you're one hell of a good guy.'

'Didn't get the chance last night, but sorry to hear about old Allsop. Is there any more news, you know, on the drowning?' Andy replied, slightly embarrassed by her comment.

'Spoke to Steadman this afternoon – he won't be back until much later tonight now – he said that the local sheriff reckons the three of them on board were drunk and had forgotten they'd switched the gas on in the boat and it exploded.'

'Three of them?'

Maureen shrugged. 'Know more when I've talked to the bossman.'

'Allsop didn't strike me as a drinking man.'

'Me neither, but you can never tell what people get up to in their own home or boat, can you?' She winked. 'Listen lover, I've got to get to my bed. Tomorrow I'll try and get back by six and then I'll take all day Thursday off, how's that?'

It was fine by Andy – his flight wasn't booked until Friday night. In fact, she was back by noon the following day, when Andy was in the middle of some press-ups on the porch.

'Save some for me!' she said with a wicked smile on her face. 'Can't stop, must get back but thought you might be getting bored. Steadman brought all these out-of-town papers back with him.' She dropped them on the boards and went back to work. She was looking a lot better, Andy thought, life had returned to her body again.

There were six daily papers, all dated the previous day, and all carried the story in some form or another. 'FISHING BOAT TRAGEDY' or 'THREE KILLED IN BOAT DISASTER' was the general style of the headline.The articles told the same story. Three friends had been on a fishing trip and had enjoyed a good meal in a local restaurant – with the suggestion that they'd had more than their fair share to drink. Back on their boat one of them had left the gas on but hadn't lit it. Later on, a spark from a lighter or from the engine had. The boat had exploded and sunk, and although a thorough search of the area had been made, no wreckage or bodies had been found. The *Stockton Gazette* devoted almost half its front page to a tribute to Charles Wilenius and titled its article 'PROMINENT LOCAL FIGURE LOST IN TRAGEDY'. It virtually gave a potted history of the man's life and achievements and ended with, 'Dr Charles Wilenius, who will be sadly missed by the local community, leaves behind a wife, daughter and three grandchildren.'

Andy slung the papers inside, locked up and drove into town. He had to get the phone number from enquiries.

'Hi, my name's Captain Parker, State Police. Just read your article on the boat tragedy at Tahoe and was tidying up a few loose ends. Seems to be some confusion over how much they drank in the restaurant, manager says one thing, the waiter another. Who'd you speak to? Suppose it wouldn't be a problem if we could have found some bodies, would it?' Andy made his lie sound as boring as possible, just another lawman cheesed off with all the paperwork the tragedy had generated.

'Fraid I can't help you, Captain,' the Stockton reporter replied. 'I haven't been up there myself, the story was wired through from a central news agency.'

'Which one?'

'Don't know without checking.'

'Don't bother, thanks. Bye.' Andy had confirmed his suspicion that somebody had written one statement which had then been circulated to all the papers in the area so that the same story had been printed. No anomalies, no nosey reporters and no questions asked.

It had all been nicely boxed up and somewhere, he knew, Hutton had been involved.

He went back to the ranch and browsed through the *Sacramento Times* out of general curiosity. The world was certainly not getting a better place to live in as Allsop had hoped, people were at each other's throats in most of its corners. Then the name 'Madden' leapt out from one page. The article was no more than a couple of inches.

> The badly burnt body recovered from a wrecked car has been identified from dental records as a Mr Derek Madden from Washington DC. Mr Madden, a businessman, was thought to have been on vacation in the area and it is understood that his car hit a deer on the notorious stretch of the Boreal Ridge Road and crashed into the sheer rock face.

The article was not credited to any reporter. Poor old Derek, his whole life didn't even warrant more than a couple of sentences on page twenty-nine of some local rag. Andy checked himself. What was he thinking about? Derek was lying at the bottom of the lake and this corpse was a stand-in, no doubt obtained from some mortuary by that bastard Hutton again. Everything all neat and tidy, just in case something had gone slightly wrong with the plan and bodies had begun to turn up. Hutton had wanted three bodies on the boat and had got three – even in death Derek had been used as a scapegoat.

Andy's temper rose and he was glad when Maureen got back early. He needed to talk, just talk to stop his mind racing.

'What's the latest news at the plant then?' he asked, bringing her some coffee.

'Panic, and more panic, as far as I can see. Clay had everyone assembled in shed B at shift changeover time and explained what had happened to Allsop, and then in as many words said the show must go on and irrespective of the tragedy production must come first – cynical little bitch, aren't I? The big bosses in Sacramento are going to appoint a new technical manager as soon as possible, and I understand they've already had several enquiries.'

'My God, so soon? The man's shoes aren't cold yet!' Andy replied, genuinely taken aback.

Maureen shrugged. 'This is California, Andy. It's dog eat dog with the unemployment situation as it is. Some people will have had their CVs posted as soon as they read the first editions. Believe you me, some guys read the obituary columns before the situations vacant ones!'

'Will you apply?'

'No, I'm not qualified – they're looking for a pucker mineralogist. No, I'm quite happy at the moment, although I wouldn't mind Clay's job when he retires in two years' time. Have we got any wine?'

There wasn't any, so Andy agreed he would drive into town while she cleaned herself up. He searched out the same label as they'd drunk before up on the ridge. He'd enjoyed the effect, and if it made him aggressive again then it was just too bad – he wanted Maureen tonight more than anything else at the moment. The transformation was incredible when he got back; she looked stunning. She had tied her hair back and wore a white stretch top and a blue loose flowing skirt. They sat, drank and talked.

'So you're quite happy staying here around Bullen then?' he asked.

'Yes, unless some great big strapping Australian fella wants to whisk me off to see his kangaroos!' She came across to him, lifted up her skirt and buried her crotch in his face – the pubic hair had gone. This was the start. Their lovemaking carried on for most of the night and Andy had no idea what time they eventually fell asleep. He did remember having one strange thought, though; he wondered if Derek was having as good a time in heaven as he was in this hell-hole in the desert. He hoped so.

They crawled out of bed just before midday and he came back into the world of reality with a jolt. He'd been so engrossed with Maureen, he'd forgotten to phone Simon. He cursed to himself and suggested they go into town to buy something for a picnic, some more wine and then spend the rest of the day on her favourite spot overlooking the plant. She agreed to do the shopping whilst he sought out the one and only public phone in town.

'Hello, Simon, have you got any news for me?' Andy stood there praying for the right answers. This call was now his last hope of finding out anything on Hutton. but all Simon did was add to his frustration by going into great detail on how he'd had to almost goad one of his former colleagues to find out the information. Andy cursed under his breath, for God's sake just get on with it please!

'My friend has not only gone through all the armed service personnel but has also checked out the name against all government employees, and there are twelve Huttons listed, of which two have a first name beginning with the initial "O".'

Andy's heart leapt, at last he was going to be able to track down that fat twisted bastard. His euphoria didn't last long.

'Unfortunately, one is an ordinary seaman and the other one is female and works as a secretary.'

'What about the others?' Andy almost snapped back.

'I'm afraid it's the same story. There is no Hutton either in the army or drawing a salary commensurate with such a rank. Would you like me to read out who they all are and what they do?'

Andy said hastily, 'No thanks, Simon, I believe you. So what's your conclusion then – that Hutton is an alias?'

'No it's probably his real name, but he could be using an alias for all his business and financial affairs.'

'I don't follow you.'

Simon explained, 'When my friend drew a blank with the government personnel disks he tried the major credit card company computer and again couldn't find any trace of this man, so we have come to the conclusion he's "hydeing".' Simon spelt out the word. 'A lot of prominent people – pop stars, politicians and the like – do it. They adopt another name for all their financial affairs. It's all perfectly legal and usually set up by their accountants. Their new signatures are genuine and are recognised by the credit houses and banks, and as long as the IRS is getting its tax then everybody's happy. I don't know how important Hutton is, but perhaps he's adopted this method.'

'So your friend could have his name on file but not recognise it?'

'Sure, but without a further link he'd never trace it.'

Andy knew it was over. From the start, Hutton had always known what was going on and had planned for things accordingly; whereas he was just floundering about in the dark. He tried not to let too much disappointment show. 'Thank you, Simon, for all your help. Next time we meet it will be to look at your plants, I promise. Bye.'

Maureen was waiting outside the phone booth and knew immediately from his look that something was worrying him. He told her he had a domestic crisis and would have to leave in the morning and head back down under. She didn't speak at all on the way out to their rock, but if this was to be their last day together then she was determined they would both remember it for many years to come.

Andy woke at six the following morning and felt across an empty bed. Maureen had already gone to work. He found the note propped up against a cup on the table.

> Dear Andy, I'm not the best person with words but I think you should get the drift of what I'm trying to say. You have been very kind and dear to me and I think I love you, no, I know I love you! I shall miss you so please, please, please keep in touch and please come back and see me. You will always be very welcome here and there will always be a job for you and a roof over your head. With all my love, and lots of it, Maureen.

One line had been struck through many times with the pen. Andy tried to decipher the words underneath and as far as he could make out they read, *'I will come to*

Australia if you want me to.' He had never received a note like this from any woman before. He folded it neatly, found the pen and pad and scribbled out a reply. Words like 'love' didn't come easily and were few and far between; however, he felt she would appreciate the message and sentiments. He'd said in his note he would come back one day; the big and only question was when.

He turfed the entire contents of his holdall out onto the bed and changed into his crumpled suit. The last time he'd worn it had been at Ben's funeral all those weeks ago. He stuffed his two passports, Maureen's note, Derek's diary, travel documents and credit cards into various pockets. The two bundles of money stared back at him. It would be a gamble taking it out of the country, but what the hell, it had been won on a gamble. If he was stopped he would tell the truth about winning it and then act with complete ignorance. He rammed the rest of his belongings back into the bag. Two items remained on the bed. The contents of the syringes were of no use now so he emptied them onto the desert floor, put them back in the padded envelope together with the gun and buried the evidence under the porch.

He was now ready for the long flight home and took one last look around the old ranch house. It had given him some very happy memories and perhaps even maintained some of his sanity. He had been in the States for almost three months now but it seemed more like years. A lot, too much, had happened from what had seemed at first a wild-goose chase.

He drove slowly down to Los Angeles and was late arriving at the terminal. He was given one of the last vacant seats in the middle of a centre aisle and sat with headphones on for the entire flight. He wanted to stay in his world, but certain horrible images would not go away. So he tried thinking about Maureen – each time she was replaced by Derek with a gaping bullet hole in his forehead and the fat little General laughing at him. He knew he'd reached the lowest of ebbs and felt totally isolated. He made up his mind, once back on his side of the water he would break with the stupid rules and would ask for, even demand, a meeting and some explanations from his people. After all, the Commander had seemed like a reasonable man – even Derek had been impressed. The thought began to cheer him up and he decided he would make the call his first priority once inside the terminal at Schiphol.

The answer both surprised and floored him. After the usual delay while they presumably figured out whose charge he was, the man's voice said they would be delighted to see him for a debriefing session. Eleven o'clock Monday morning was suggested and an address reeled off. He hadn't had to argue at all, in fact, from the tone of the conversation, they would have been in touch anyway.

With his morale boosted Andy took the train into Amsterdam and then hailed a taxi to Westermarilt Straat, got out at the wrong end and joined the dozens of other people on their way to work on this wet Saturday morning. The sign read *Van Hoeff Antiques*, and antiques were on display in the window and sold in the front part of the shop – but behind, in two small dingy rooms, anything went. Van Hoeff had no scruples and no principles; if you wanted something and were prepared to pay for it he would get it for you with no questions asked. Andy had been introduced to this dubious character during his more secretive army days and this would make his third visit. He showed the little ferret of a man the dollars and was invited into the back, where they were all inspected and counted. Hoeff suggested gold was the thing to be in these days as the price was rising steadily, thanks to Chinese interest, and worked out some figures on a well-used calculator. Exchange rates were thrown into the conversation frequently but eventually a deal was struck and Andy was given the equivalent of fifty-three thousand pounds sterling in small gold bars bearing a South African hallmark stamp.

His next stop was within walking distance and Andy was glad of the fresh air after the stale smell of cigar smoke which pervaded every corner of the antique shop. The offices belonged to a small private bank whose main business was hiring out safe-deposit boxes. Again this place had been recommended by a senior army man who had insisted such a box was very much part of the job. Andy extracted his key from his plastic credit card wallet, signed the book and was given a second key and a private cubicle. He emptied the entire contents of his box onto the scratched table; two handguns and eight clips of ammunition, some letters, a set of inherited skeleton keys from his old 'teacher' and a small box which contained about ten thousand pounds' worth of cut diamonds. He put them all carefully back in the box, then added the gold bars and dug about inside his holdall until he found the two tapes, which had become separated amongst his clothes. He studied the covers and thought how innocent they both looked with their country-and-western pictures – but he knew that the tunes they played were not easy listening. Finally he reread Maureen's letter and placed it gently on top of all his hidden treasures and closed the lid. He was now ready to return home to England.

15

The scientist woke up with a splitting headache and slowly looked around the large bedroom, the just off-white décor made him squint. All the furniture looked very solid and expensive but whether it was genuine antique or just reproduction stuff be neither knew nor cared. The bed he was in was more than king-size and would have slept three or four people comfortably; again, the carved mahogany headboard matched the rest of the bedroom suite. He looked under the sheets and found he was wearing blue silk pyjamas. They weren't his – he didn't own anything as outlandish as this. He tried to sit up but felt weak and dizzy as if he was getting over the effects of influenza, and every bone in his body ached. He inspected one particularly painful shoulder and found that it was covered in bruises. With great difficulty he swung his legs out onto the floor and after a minute or two found the energy to stand, but then immediately dropped back onto the bed in agony. His left leg hurt like hell so he slowly undid the pyjama cord and pulled the trousers down. A large sticking plaster had been placed across his thigh.

He remained seated and continued his inspection of the room from his higher vantage point. It was much bigger than he had at first realised, and the only conclusion he could reach was that he was in some five-star hotel suite. There was fruit and bottled water on a table by the window, and although it was only twenty or so feet away it took him ages to shuffle across. He slumped into one of the chairs and took three full glasses of the liquid; the relief on his throat was immediate. With curiosity rising he continued his inspection of the room. There were no clothes in the wall-to-wall closet. A door led off into a bathroom and he just stood in the doorway staring at the sunken bath; he had never seen one so big in all his life, it would hold the same numbers as the bed. Even with his fuzzy brain he thought of the cost of the hot water – he had never been one to fritter money away unnecessarily. He just about made it back to the chair and fell asleep again. When he woke from this nap he felt a bit better, the aches were still there but at least the construction work in his head had stopped. He peered through the net curtains on the window and realised it was a patio door, but it was locked.

A voice behind him made his heart jump. 'You'll need this.' Hutton stood there, dressed in white shirt, shorts and socks and looked like some throwback to British Colonial days. In his left hand he held a small black box. 'Everything is electronically controlled here, including the door you were trying. It's very nice to see you up and about, Charles. How are you feeling now? Would you like some medication?'

'Not too bright, but I'm anxious to know where I am and why have I got a plaster on my leg?'

'Just temporary, like the bruises. I do apologise, Charles, but we've taken the liberty of implanting a small radio transmitter in your leg so that we always know exactly where you are. The bruises were unfortunate and unnecessary – my man was a bit too rough with you when he manhandled you into the boat – but I can assure you he has been duly reprimanded.' Hutton looked across at his guest and smiled. Wilenius would never know that there were two devices in his leg. The second and bigger one was radio-controlled and at the touch of a button would detonate a very small explosive charge which in turn would break a metal vial and release a chemical into his bloodstream, triggering a massive heart attack in less than a minute. Obviously, he hoped that such a device would remain immobile for ever, but there was always an outside chance that one day Wilenius might try and escape so they had to be ready for such eventualities.

'You haven't answered my question, where am I?' Wilenius repeated.

'Your new home, my dear Charles, your new home.

Would you like something to eat first or would you like me to give you the guided tour?'

Although he didn't know it, it was now four days since he'd last eaten, but the very thought of food made his stomach churn and anyway he desperately needed to find out where he was, so he asked for the tour.

'In that case,' Hutton replied, 'please bring the control box with you and you'll soon get the hang of all its functions – for instance, press number three.'

Wilenius did as instructed and the net curtains slid back whilst the patio doors swung open. Hutton offered his arm, which Wilenius took gladly, and together they walked slowly out into the garden. The change in temperature from the air-conditioned room was dramatic and the sun beat down on both their balding heads. Wilenius stopped and took in his new surroundings.

The sky was a uniform blue and the bungalow, its roof covered in orange pantiles, reminded him of buildings he'd seen on holiday in Mexico. The gardens and the lawn he was standing on were kept in immaculate condition and all the flower-beds had recently been watered and a colourful range of dripping blooms offered their faces up to the sun. They ambled on round the corner and the bright greens changed to blue. The whole area was devoted to a huge oval swimming-pool and Jacuzzi, and at the far end terracotta pots stood by the dozen on a large semi-covered verandah which housed a barbecue in one corner. The garden ended here and large evergreen bushes ran around the entire perimeter, making it impossible to see any of the surrounding countryside.

Wilenius managed a question. 'What's on the other two sides, Oliver?'

'Oh, just another bungalow like this, they're link detached.' Hutton replied. This brief explanation was all Wilenius was going to get. The fact that three staff had taken up full-time occupation in the hidden part of the building was of no concern to his new guest. Hutton continued the walkabout, then, after the right button had been pressed, led on through more patio doors on the verandah into another large room. 'Living room,'

Hutton said briefly and walked on without allowing Wilenius the chance to absorb all its expensive trappings. They came out into a long corridor with at least six doors opening off it and at each one they shuffled past, Hutton reeled off their function, sometimes adding a question mark. 'Gym, steam room, kitchen, shower room, library?, study?' He missed several out. 'I'll explain these later, I think it's time you rested some more, my dear Charles.'

Wilenius noticed the security cameras – they weren't hard to miss – so Hutton told him. 'There isn't one in the master bedroom, we do allow you some privacy!'

Wilenius was pleased to climb back onto the bed. The tour round had exhausted him but he summoned up enough energy to ask, 'Where am I, Oliver, and what do you want from me?'

'As I've said, you're in your new home and we would like you to work for us. As you can see, your conditions and surroundings are excellent and you will have everything you require, every imaginable luxury – even your food and wines will be to your exact specifications. There is only one house rule though, you will not be allowed to leave us.'

'You keep mentioning "us". Who are you? Who will I be working for?'

'The American people,' Hutton answered. 'Charles, you are still tired. I suggest you get some rest and we can discuss this in more detail later on.'

Hutton left Wilenius and let himself out through one of the doors he had deliberately overlooked. He walked down the small corridor and gave instructions to the staff to be vigilant and to observe all rooms on their monitors. The first few days were always the most anxious, ensuring that a new guest didn't try to do anything foolish. Hutton didn't envisage Wilenius giving him any problems once the various anaesthetics and drugs had worn off and he was back to thinking rationally again. He laughed to himself. It always amazed him that the 'truth drug' – he preferred the words 'speech maker' – that Albert had put in all the bottles of wine he could find on Allsop's boat always gave his 'clients' severe headaches for days afterwards. It didn't seem to affect him, in fact he liked taking it – it gave him a buzz and a feeling of dominance, and he was not averse to having some on a regular basis.

When Wilenius awoke it was almost dark, so he fumbled about with the gadget until he managed to turn some lights on. A small table had been placed by the bed and on it stood a food tray and a blue folder. He took the lid off the plate – turkey salad, and it was done just the way he liked it. Whilst he ate he read all the newspaper clippings – his own obituaries.

Hutton was sitting in one of the armchairs drinking coffee when Wilenius stirred the following morning. He poured him a cup – it was obvious from the way Wilenius got out of bed that he was nearly back to his old self.

'Have you had a chance to read the contents of the folder?' Hutton asked.

'Yes.'

'Then I think you understand the position you are in?'

Wilenius nodded and then asked, 'So you are going to hold me as a prisoner here?'

'Charles, I prefer to think that you will be our guest. You are surely one of the greatest research people in the world; here you will be able to devote your entire mind to pure research. Just think of it, just think of the possibilities. You will have no more mundane worries, no more interruptions to break up your daily routine, no more unnecessary meetings, none of the thousand and one things that can eat away at the day. I have taken the liberty of ordering breakfast for both of us in the living room. First, I would like to show you something. Bring your little box with you, please.'

They walked down the corridor and stopped outside one of the unknown doors. 'Press L please, Charles.' The door slid back. It was not a room but a small elevator. 'Please,' Hutton beckoned for his guest to join him inside, pressed the one and only button and they moved slowly downwards. As soon as the room came into view Wilenius gasped, before him lay a large fully equipped laboratory.

'Just shout and anything else will be provided, excluding a telephone, of course!' Hutton laughed at his own humour.

They walked round and Wilenius could feel himself becoming excited again. This was his world, a place where nobody else could argue with him. At one end there was a fully furnished office and a smaller, as yet empty room.

'Perhaps a library or even a refreshment room, the choice is yours,' Hutton added.

Back at the far end a separate room had been created. Wilenius poked his head through the door. Larry Fletcher would also have recognised the way it was set up ready for animal experiments. Again Wilenius noticed the abundance of security cameras scattered around the laboratory; he was going to have to get used to working with them peering over his shoulder all the time, there didn't seem to be any alternative. A large double set of metal doors with no handles also caught his eye. Hutton pre-empted the question. 'To bring in supplies and equipment.'

They returned to the living room upstairs, where Wilenius ate his breakfast in abject silence. Hutton had expected as much. It was always the same with new boys until they got over the initial shock of what their future was to be. He had allowed for this and would give Charles up to one month to acclimatise to his new surroundings and accept the inevitable. Hutton looked across at the other man. They were of a similar age and had experienced the same period of history, which made things somewhat easier. They even believed in most of the same doctrines. Given the right pampered conditions his guest could provide them with at least, what, fifteen years of valuable research?

Hutton broke the silence. 'I regret that you don't have a wardrobe yet. I'll get the tailor to visit you later on this afternoon, and please remember, don't skimp on anything, whatever you want you will get. Would you like to retire for an hour or so?'

Wilenius shook his head.

'Good, then let me tell you something about your

new surroundings. As you can see from the weather we are in desert country and your bungalow is one of ten, all of similar design. At present four, now five are occupied. The nearest civilisation is about fifty miles away, so you can see we will be left undisturbed. Our little venture is on the outskirts of a much larger military base which has been in existence for nearly fifty years now, so I'm sure the other countries monitor us through their spy satellites, but so what? Incidentally, there is a thirty-mile no-fly zone around the whole complex. As I have said, you have complete freedom to move around your new premises, day or night, but I must warn you that beyond your garden boundary is a rather nasty electronic security barrier and it would not be wise to come into contact with it. At present we have a staff of twenty-seven, all hand-picked and vetted by myself and all totally dedicated to looking after all the needs of, now, five scientists.' Hutton waved his arm around the room. 'If you would like the décor or the furniture changed in any way then please shout, it will be carried out immediately. Oh, by the way, when you meet some of the staff don't discuss things like hostages or freedom – you will only be wasting your time and theirs.'

'Will I have any information provided about what is happening in the outside world?' Wilenius asked. 'It would be good to know scientific developments, for instance.'

'Good Lord, Charles, of course! You will have access to everything and anything you want. I believe there are at least three television screens scattered around the place already; all work off your little box of tricks and all receive world satellite programmes. The sets themselves are inaccessible – just a precaution, we don't want our guests building small transmitters from the parts, do we now? We will also automatically obtain copies of all scientific reports and new books published for you to examine. We will also get you all the latest videos of your choice. Our guest in bungalow three is a workaholic, he hardly uses his domestic quarter. However, once a day in the afternoon he likes to return to his bedroom to watch young ladies doing things to each other with an assortment of fruit. Incidentally, he's very happy here. Later on, there is no reason why you cannot take a holiday. We own a very nice property on one of the Californian Channel islands – you might even like to go sea fishing. One day you might like your wife to join you here, but of course the move would have to be one way and final. Still, all these things are in the future and needn't concern you yet. You need some time to familiarise yourself with all of this first.'

'What happens to me if I don't make the grade or when I become too old and senile to be of any further use to you?' Wilenius enquired.

Hutton protested, 'Charles, you will be our star! Your past record shows it. Don't worry about your future – we will always look after you.'

Hutton's last remark carried no basis of truth whatsoever. He hadn't a clue at this stage what would happen to old and useless scientists. He wasn't going to concern himself about possible future problems – it was all happening now.

'You said that, including me, there were five scientists here now. Do I take it that we are all chemists?' Wilenius asked.

'Yes, although all in different fields. It was felt that from an administration point of view it would be better to have similar research people all under the same roof so to speak so that equipment, livestock, chemicals and that sort of thing would be basically common to you all. Obviously, more stringent precautions have to be taken with boffins who are into electronic and laser research, for instance – God knows what they could be up to!'

'Does that mean there are other centres around for people like them?'

Hutton smiled. 'I certainly hope so! They are not my responsibility though – this is my project.' Hutton waved his arms around the room again and puffed out his already oversized chest proud of all his efforts.

'Aren't you worried that I or some of the other people here might make something to poison you all with?'

'No, we trust you all,' Hutton replied, still smiling back across the table at his captive audience. They had built into the design of the building as many safeguards as they could think of; a master switch could override the little black box and close down the whole bungalow, outside shutters could be slid across all the windows in a matter of seconds and the air-conditioning reversed to emit knock-out gas. And only he ate the same food and drank the same wine as the guests.

Wilenius asked what he was expected to work on.

'I would be grateful if you would do exactly what you have been doing so well over the past years – the uses amino acids and similar products can be put to – but really anything else you would like to get your teeth into. You have a new start, Charles. For the first time in your life you have the unique opportunity to carry out pure uninterrupted research with the objective of providing the United States with the best that can be invented.' Hutton paused. 'I think it might be apposite to tell you about some of your new colleagues – it will help you understand the type of things going on here. One of them is a mere youngster, Geoff Temby.' Hutton knew from the blank look he received that the name meant nothing. 'Geoff spent many years working for the Council for Tobacco Research and some of his work was rather outlandish, not to say unethically orientated, and would have caused a huge public outcry if it had leaked out. In the end his bosses fired him, having thoroughly discredited his reputation so that nobody else would employ him. But we knew that he was discussing offers from South Africa and Korea, so we invited him to come here.He's absolutely no trouble, in fact he told me he would have paid us, if he had the money, so he could continue his work.'

Wilenius said hesitantly, 'May I ask what's so delicate about his research?'

'Certainly, it's the conversion of certain chemical substances into mind-altering gases – the more you smoke the greater the effect, type of thing. I understand that the work officially started off to find a safer cigarette, one that wouldn't give you cancer yet at the same time still provided the fix that you get from nicotine, but he just got carried away with all his tests. His latest work is very exciting, I can tell you. Perhaps you would like to see his latest report?'

Wilenius nodded and said, 'I'd be delighted, thank you.'

'One day in the not too distant future I hope to be able to arrange group meetings where you can all exchange ideas – perhaps over informal dinners, that sort of thing. In time I envisage that our little centre will become one of the greatest think tanks this country has ever had – I cannot say "seen" for obvious reasons.' Again there was muted laughter from Hutton. 'I must say I think you will get on famously with our Doctor Michael Brantham, for instance.'

Wilenius was startled. 'Michael Brantham? But he's dead!'

'So are you, my dear Charles, so are you! Yes, the very same doctor. You obviously know the man already.'

'Yes, I used to enjoy listening to his research papers when he was on the circuit.'

'Then you will probably recall that the good doctor ran amok seven years ago now. A gas station clerk refused his particular credit card so he went back to his car, found his gun and shot the man at point-blank range through the forehead. The medical reports concluded that he had finally cracked up and gone over the top – too much stress. He was sentenced to prison for manslaughter and was eventually sent to a secure prison for the criminally insane or whatever fancy name they give such places nowadays. He officially died two years later.'

'Yes, I know, I followed the case closely at the time. Dr Brantham was brilliant, nobody came near his work on genes.'

'Well, you'll be delighted to know that Michael is not only alive and well but fully recovered from his earlier aberration, and getting on with more research into his sole purpose in life – genetic engineering.'

Wilenius asked, 'Does he know I'm here?'

'Not yet. Patience please, Charles!' Inside Hutton was glowing; not only was Wilenius going to be a great asset but he had just about settled in already. The next question brought him back down.

'What if I completely refuse to co-operate and do nothing at all?'

'Charles, I can't treat this as a serious question. You are a communist spy and already dead anyway. Besides, you would be refusing the chance of a lifetime.'

Wilenius exchanged long eye contact with the General; they understood each other perfectly.

Hutton rubbed his long beak of a nose and looked at his watch. He would have to leave Wilenius to his own devices very shortly as he had two meetings to attend. The first, in Washington, he would enjoy as it was with his young team of logicians. He liked the way they were so enthusiastic about the Purflo project. They had already come up with two interesting ideas – first to make sure that the final destination of product from both Bullen and Melford was rescheduled so that only one country received one type; and second, that the treated filteraid from Melford might offer the brighter future, as it could be in their best interests to keep certain, even large, parts of the world in submissive mode. He was looking forward to learning what else they had now discussed amongst themselves.

The second meeting when he got back was going to be more difficult. All was not as straightforward as he made out to his new arrival. One of the other guests was proving troublesome. He had been brought to the complex against his will – there was nothing new about that, but he resented the fact and steadfastly refused to settle in. The man spoke only limited English and refused to have an interpreter anywhere near him. In the month he'd been with them he'd smashed up most of his living quarters as well as destroying all the plants in the garden and now he was refusing to eat. They had tried drugs, but it was no good having some doped-up brain which couldn't think straight. Hutton had already made his mind up he would tell the man he had one last chance to mend his ways. If that failed he would tell his team to dispose of him. It would be a great pity, a brain that knew so much about virus technology was hard to find. Still, there would be other scientists, perhaps not as brilliant to start with, but it was amazing how a good brain turned into an even better one once the dross of everyday life was put to one side and total devotion given to the main thought process.

Hutton returned his thoughts to his new arrival. 'I shall have to leave you now, Charles, unless there are any more points you wish to raise. I will be away all of tomorrow, so take the opportunity to explore your new surroundings in more detail and perhaps even work out what laboratory equipment you require. Anything you need, just press the call button on your machine or in any of the rooms. You have three staff operating a twenty-four-hour system. I'll let them introduce themselves to you – they're all very charming ladies.'

'There is one question,' Wilenius said. 'What's happening to the filteraid products?'

'They're exactly as you left them. We have our own ideas, of course. In fact, I'm attending a meeting tomorrow on the very subject. Perhaps I can run through some of our suggestions with you, say, the day after tomorrow. How about I join you for dinner? I would also like your views on who in Decker, or elsewhere for that matter, is the best person to take over from you.'

Hutton said his goodbyes and left. He was a very happy man. He was also surprised. All week he had been rehearsing a whole variety of answers to the stream of questions he was sure would be raised, but Wilenius hadn't asked any, apart from the filteraid project. He hadn't asked about his two dead friends or, surprisingly, about his wife and family. Charles Wilenius would be a good asset, he had no doubts about it any more, his priorities were already in the right order to accept his new role in life, and so they should be. After all, he was a communist spy who had enjoyed the fruits America had to offer for a quarter of a century and he probably knew in his heart it was now time to contribute something back into the system.

Hutton swaggered to his car, flushed with pride and convinced that one day, maybe in a century's time when news of all this was made public, his name would be remembered as one of the great heroes whose foresight had helped protect the American nation if not the Western world. But it was easy for him to fantasise – he crossed the thin red line between madness and genius many times in a day.

Horse Guards Parade was empty. The pouring rain had made sure that any tourists pursued indoor activities. Andy pulled up the collar of his raincoat. No wonder people caught colds, he thought. Last week had he been sweltering in a desert and now here he was soaking wet and cold – and as good as lost. He had come up from Eastbourne by train and decided to walk across Westminster Bridge to the parade ground. The address of the building would be easy to find, he had reasoned. It wasn't, and he was getting wetter by the minute. He admitted defeat and asked the first official-looking gent he came across, who without saying a word pointed to one of the many archways leading into the labyrinth of God knows what government buildings.

He pressed the button and announced himself through the small microphone grille. The door began to open automatically so he followed its direction. Once he was beyond it, the piece of heavy oak with a mind of its own swung back and clicked itself shut. He was now trapped in a small corridor between two identical solid bits of wood. A security camera moved and adjusted its gaze on the intruder. Andy did his best to dry his hair and smarten the creases out of his suit, and every time he moved so did the electronic eye. Bolts could be heard being drawn back on the inner door and a middle-aged man appeared. Just one look put Andy's back up, he epitomised everything he hated about jumped-up authority. He wore a drab dark grey suit, an old club or school tie and looked as if he hadn't seen any sunshine for years; his skin was dry and flaky. He didn't possess any manners either. He demanded some form of identification and looked down his nose at Andy as if he was some sort of low life. Once satisfied that the passport photograph matched the face in front of him the 'civil' servant led the way along the corridor into a waiting-room. Like the rest of the building the room was centuries old and smelt musty, and the two small leaded windows were criss-crossed with sturdy iron bars. What was needed was some good old-fashioned London fresh air to blow the cobwebs away, Andy concluded as he sat down on one of the two well-worn leather arm-chairs. There was another camera attached above an old fireplace and its eye followed him around until he sat down and then just stared at him.

The wait lasted nearly half an hour before the insipid little man poked his head around the door and beckoned Andy to follow him. They climbed three flights of bare wooden stairs with cameras placed at strategic points on each landing, old oil-paintings of somebody's distant relatives festooned the walls. He was ushered into a very large office where once again the style, furniture and décor were from a bygone age. Two men were standing in the bay window at the far end, watching the rain lash down on the diamond leaded panes. They turned round together at the sound of Andy's footsteps on the varnished boards. One made the first move down the single step.

'Andy, my dear chap, welcome, it's nice to meet you at long last. Let me make some introductions, I'm Crawford Murdoch and this is Philip St John Travis.'

Both men took it in turn to shake Andy firmly by the hand.

'A drink, perhaps, to celebrate your excellent results?'

Andy accepted a glass of very good, and expensive, single-malt whisky and then said, 'I thought the Commander would be here.'

'Sends his apologies but he's had to fly off somewhere, I'm sure you understand' Murdoch replied. He was older than Travis, probably coming up to retirement age, Andy guessed. Murdoch moved across to the gas fire and warmed his backside.

'Please sit down , Andy. We want to hear all about your tremendous and successful operation.' The request came from Travis, whose accent was clipped and affected. Money, and a lot of it, had been spent on this one's education, Andy guessed. In fact, from the cut and look of his suit, he wasn't short of money at all. From first impressions he wasn't the sort of person Andy liked, he was one of the breed that got into places like the Foreign Office, not on merit, but because of old family connections. Andy sat and watched their faces and wasn't sure what to say.

Murdoch broke the silence. 'There are some very senior people who are delighted with the way things have worked out. Tell us, how did you know the two ingredients were coming via Sarius Chemicals?'

Andy related the sequence of events and every time he skimped on some detail they almost took it in turn to ask for elaboration, both listening intently to his every word. He paused once to explain that all this surveillance had cost money and that at one stage he'd even bought a camper. He was curious to see the reaction of these two senior government men who had no doubt not stopped congratulating each other on the success of the mission. The reply was exactly as he had expected; when it's the taxpayers money who cares?

Andy felt the time was appropriate so he reached inside his breast pocket and produced his handwritten accounts and receipts. He'd added on about another thousand pounds for incidentals and hadn't bothered to mention the money he'd got back on the camper. The bottom line came to just over eight thousand pounds. He handed it over to the Murdoch fellow, who never even glanced at it; it was dismissed as an aside, a nuisance, which had interrupted the flow of things.

'You'll have a cheque before you leave, Andy old boy. Now let's return to more important matters, shall we?' Murdoch insisted.

Andy continued his story right up until the boat exploded. As far as he was concerned, that was all he was supposed to know, but he had to ask his burning question sometime, so why not now? 'Are you both convinced that the death of these four people is the end of the operation?'

'What makes you think otherwise?' Travis asked. 'Please explain further.'

'Well, we never actually got involved with the Oregon plant and we never established whether there was a paymaster. The numbers involved may be significantly higher than those accounted for so far,' Andy lied.

The two senior people made subtle eye contact. Travis got up from his chair and went over to a bureau by the window and returned with the decanter in one hand and a red leather folder in the other. He handed the folder to Murdoch, who fiddled in his trouser pocket for a key and unlocked the small fastener. More large whiskies were poured out for everybody.

Murdoch put on a pair of reading-glasses before he spoke. 'You must understand, Andy, that Philip and myself, because of our more senior positions, are privy to some information which you unfortunately are not. We have here a transcript of General Hutton's taped conversation with Charles Wilenius whilst they were on the boat. You knew, of course, that the General was wearing a concealed tape recorder – or at least you must have realised he'd be wired, as I believe our American friends call it. In a nutshell, Wilenius ended up confessing to everything and admitted that it was his idea from the start and that nobody else, apart from Allsop and Warren, knew anything about it. If you ask me, Wilenius sounded like a bit of a madman, out to get revenge on the world just because the Soviet Union had fallen apart. So you see, Andy, both we and the Americans are perfectly happy that the whole affair is now a thing of the past. I hope that this puts your mind at rest as well?'

'Yes, as you said, I wasn't aware of the final conversations on the boat so I didn't know the whole story. Now I do, thank you.' Andy bit the inside of his bottom lip and tasted blood in his mouth.

'You were damn lucky to have escaped before that gas cylinder exploded,' Travis remarked.

'Yes, very lucky indeed,' Andy replied, inwardly cringing.

'It's a great pity about your partner. I understand you got to know each other quite well. According to reports from Hutton, you were becoming quite a well-oiled team.'

Andy didn't reply, it was now bullshit time.

'Doesn't it say somewhere in the text that the General remarked on more than one occasion that he thought he could smell gas?' Murdoch said, aiming the question at his colleague. 'Perhaps you'd be good enough to find one of the passages, please, Philip, and read it out to Andy.'

'Certainly, old boy. Ah yes, here's one reference to it. Wilenius has just explained about a new product he's making for Bullen, the General interrupts and says he thinks he can smell gas and asks if someone has left something on the stove in the galley. Wilenius tells him that the smell is coming from the boat's exhaust blowing back in because they're only moving slowly ahead on low engine revolutions. There's at least one more later on. Please give me a second and I'll find it.'

Andy held up his hand. 'No, please don't bother on my account, the General told me all about his suspicions when we were on the other boat.'

Murdoch stood up, walked round to the fire again and started to warm his hands, rubbing them together like a modern-day Scrooge. He didn't look directly at Andy when he spoke next. 'For the record, there were only three people on the boat when it went down. We all felt that it would be for the best if Mr Madden was excluded from the numbers. We don't want some very nosey reporter to find out that it was more than just some unfortunate fishing trip, do we? Now that it's all over it's best left that way, as I'm sure you understand.'

Andy nodded but did not reply. He understood all right. It had all been prearranged so that every eventuality was covered and no loose ends would be left dangling, and poor old Derek had always been a disposable item, a complete nonentity to these bastards.

Andy's lack of comment took Murdoch by surprise. He had expected an answer or at least a brief discussion about their decision. Their assessment of Lockwood was obviously wrong, he was more cold-hearted than his records showed, not asking about his dead friend's welfare. He felt he now had to say more. 'Of course, the

Americans won't just forget him. Oh no, they will report he was killed in action somewhere else, all in the line of duty, of course, and his next of kin will be well looked after with pensions and that sort of thing.'

'Are there any other pieces of information you need to complete the picture?' Travis asked.

'No none, thank you,' Andy replied, chewing harder on his lip. 'It's nice to know that the whole nasty business is over and I can start drinking wine and beer again – as well as Scotch!'

There were long guffaws of laughter from the two liars before Murdoch said, 'All over and all down to you, Andy. It'll obviously take some months before all the contaminated filteraid gets through the system, but all new material produced will now have only one purpose in life – to clarify – and in years to come nobody will ever know the plot even took place.'

Andy stood up ready to leave but Travis stopped him 'There are one or two minor irritations left on this side of the Atlantic which we would like you to deal with please, Andy.'

Murdoch took several minutes to outline these 'small difficulties', as he put it and then suggested methods by which they could be eliminated. 'But of course any other *modus operandi* you choose will be fine by us as long as the end results are the same, as I'm sure you understand. Then take some leave, old boy. Sorry it can't be a long one though, you're too experienced to leave lying around idle for long.' Again there was a pause for more false laughter. 'We need you back out in Hong Kong. There are some nasty little episodes going on, as I'm sure you're aware from all the news bulletins. Find out who's behind it, will you? You're to liaise with a Captain Lu Young, Special Branch, and you're expected there, let me see . . . ' Murdoch referred to his pocket diary. 'Ah yes, two weeks yesterday.' He looked at his watch and added, 'We musn't detain you any longer from your leave, must we? Thanks once again for all your efforts.'

Travis pressed a wall button, Handshakes were exchanged and a general feeling of false bonhomie – or was it relief? – pervaded the room, Andy was glad when the standard-issue civil servant knocked and entered the room. He was handed the expense sheet and given some short instructions then led Andy past dozens of anonymous doors and eventually told him to wait outside one of them. Half an hour passed before the grey man returned and in complete silence thrust a cheque and brown envelope into Andy's hand, indicating that he was to follow him again. Eventually he was let out of the building, this time by a different door.

It had stopped raining but he put on his raincoat, stuffed the paperwork into one of the pockets and set out across the parade-ground, trying to walk in a reasonably straight line now that the whisky was beginning to affect his legs as well as his head. He was convinced that at least two pairs of eyes were monitoring his progress. As soon as he turned the first corner he slowed down and shouted out a string of obscenities. Two old Japanese tourists took the full impact of the words full in the face and if they hadn't heard the words before they would certainly know them now.

Andy's mind was in turmoil. He'd been invited for the first time in this career to visit his bosses, and he'd hoped for some explanations, but their real reason was to assess whether he was still a risk. The anger boiled up inside him. They had even invented stories about the smell of gas being mentioned. Liars, the lot of them, including that 'nice man' the Commander – the man Derek had said he would like to work with was no better than Hutton. They were all lying bastards – all in the same plot together. What would they have done if they had not been convinced he was happy with their answers? Arranged some convenient accident for him? They still might. Andy was annoyed with himself, he had been well and truly used and was powerless to do anything about it. He also felt aggression creep into his body and he wanted to smash something – anything. It was exactly the same feeling he'd had in Larry's office all those weeks ago when they were playing human guinea-pigs, only this time he didn't need any ingredient X.

There was a souvenir seller in the distance, following tourists, pestering them to buy his exclusive rubbish. Andy found himself muttering out aloud, 'If he comes anywhere near me I'll ram those fluffy toys down his bloody throat.' He stopped walking and leant against a wall. What was he thinking about? That's all they needed to find out, that he'd been arrested for assault and then they'd definitely know something was still troubling him. He had to remain calm, act naturally and behave as if he hadn't a care in the world. It was going to be bloody difficult, he was the only outsider left who knew that two countries, at least, were up to no good. A feeling of total isolation crept over him. He turned up his collar and walked on again. The old pedlar saw the look of thunder on his face and gave him a wide berth.

Andy needed coffee, and lots of it. He found a small buffet in the station and sat and mulled over the last few hours. How he hated all their patronising ways and their glib expressions, and what did things like 'it's in everyone's best interests' mean? That it was in their best interests, more likely! And what about the few loose ends that 'needed tidying up'? If the whole sorry affair was over and done with, why should any loose ends matter? They had even laughed about it and agreed that it would be perfectly all right to drink normal beer and wine again soon. They. (Hutton, the Commander, Murdoch, Travis and God knows who else) were all lying through their teeth, why? Andy could only come up with one answer and that was that they were going to continue where Wilenius had left off. For all he knew, the man was not even dead so they could still use him to come up with bigger and better inventions, if that was their plan.

How far up the ladder did knowledge of it spread and who ultimately was responsible for deciding how far it all went, anyway? The Foreign Secretary? The Prime Minister? The whole bloody Government? Maybe none of them knew anything about it in the first place and it was a dark secret in the hands of the intelligence departments; after all, if they could lie to him why not to people up the pecking order? Behind the façade offered to

Parliament, covert methods still carried on as they had done for decades. Secret-service organisations did not have to go cap in hand every year to the Exchequer, whatever they asked for they got; after all, the nation's security was at stake. Nor were members elected, they were there for life, during which time they could grow very powerful, more so than the temporary politicians. The more Andy thought about it all, the more confused and depressed he became, and his embryo of a headache wasn't helping matters either.

He needed some fresh air. It had started to rain heavily but it felt good on his face. He wished it would penetrate into his brain and wash all his thoughts away. He walked for about an hour, trying to empty his mind, but doubts started to creep back. What if he'd got it all wrong and his imagination was getting the better of him and the filteraid saga was well and truly over with now? Perhaps they'd saved Wilenius in order to use his incredible brain-power for the benefit of mankind. He could understand them all wanting to avoid world publicity and the boat explosion had been a nice tidy answer, but why kill Derek as well? Andy shook the rain from his hair. There were too many flaws in the argument and too many loose ends and question marks.

When he'd been invited to change from an army career to this invisible service, he had been told that it was an honour. It would provide him with a greater opportunity to serve Queen and Country in a more challenging role. He would be there to help protect the people from dangers they weren't even aware of, and they would be able to continue sleeping soundly in their beds thanks to people like himself, the unsung heroes. The rhetoric had all sounded very patriotic and commendable at the time and he'd enjoyed the years, firmly believing that what he did was for the welfare of the ordinary people – people like his mother. But now he was having his doubts; if his bosses could lie and mislead him then what thoughts did the ordinary man in the street warrant? In dictatorships the secret police were there to nip anything in the bud before it got out of hand, to protect their pampered masters from their own downtrodden kind. But in Britain, people were free to do what they wanted, when they wanted – or was this just a sham as well? Were the activities of the populus confined within certain strict parameters? The powerful élite couldn't afford to let the masses do just what they liked, otherwise they would begin to lose control, and in time their large estates, wealth and power would crumble. Whatever happened, the peasants had to obey their rules and follow their orders in exactly the same way they had throughout all the past centuries, only the rules were far more subtle now. What better way to prevent the common people from having ideas above their station than through hard work. At the end of the day all people wanted to do was to relax, unwind and sleep. Television provided the most brain-soothing remedy and people watched endless hours of it; perhaps some of the programmes were even made to subconsciously influence the thought process along the right tracts. Then what? Unemployment rose sharply, people had time to think about their lives. They became restless, no longer happy with their lot and began to see through the veneer. They banged on the walls of their small existences and demanded more from their masters. Alarm bells started to ring in the lofty corridors of power. Then somebody suggested giving them ingredient Y to drink in their beer to calm them down again and restore the status quo; smiles spread across faces once more, and comments such as, 'It's for their own sake, you understand', were heard as they adjourned to their respective empires.

Andy shook his head. Water ran down his neck and he could feel the damp where the rain had penetrated through the shoulders of his raincoat. All his adult life he had obeyed orders without giving them so much as a second thought, and now here he was walking down Oxford Street querying everything. He'd never had such crazy notions in all his life, but if there was even the slightest bit of truth in any of it then he was one of the flunkeys who did the dirty work; signing the Official Secrets Act was proof of that.

He needed to eat something. He wasn't particularly

hungry but knew that food would help get rid of the knotted feeling in his stomach and the awful taste left in his mouth. He played with the sandwich and contemplated bringing over the two tapes and giving them to the most active and investigative journalist he could find, but he knew that as soon as even a sniff of it reached his bosses they would slap some official notice on the press banning publication and then dismiss any rumours as the ravings of some nutcase and the contents of any tapes as fictitious ramblings. Or they could argue that they had stopped it well before it could do any damage, and reassure the country that due to their vigilance it was all over and everything was back to normal now. Such a statement could only add kudos and ensure that they became even more dispensable. If they were asked why they hadn't come forward of their own accord, they would probably say that 'it was in everyone's best interest not to' in order to avoid any false panics, adding, 'you understand, of course. 'Whichever way they reacted they still held all the trump cards. And Andy would be dead – the Americans would demand his head on a plate for a start.

There was only one option left open to him. He had to remain exactly where he was and work from the one position of strength he had left. He had to knuckle down to their orders, pretend to have forgotten about the 'last job' and most of all remain alive. Once he had blended back in he might just have the chance to find out something more tangible and catch one of the bastards, hopefully Hutton, by the balls. Now it was time to get down to some action again; the sooner he got the loose ends out of the way the sooner he could try and relax a bit and spend some time with his mother.

He took the brown envelope out of his pocket and read the two pages relevant to Hong Kong; he didn't like the contents one little bit but this could wait. A separate sheet of paper contained two addresses and one telephone number. He put this page back in his pocket but shoved the larger note, together with the cheque, into the envelope, licked the gum, sealed it down and addressed it to Eastbourne. Two addresses to visit, one in Belgium, one in Ipswich. He decided he would visit the European one first and checked all his damp pockets for credit cards, driving-licence and passport. He had no spare clothes with him, they would have to be purchased along the way. He bought a stamp, posted the letter and telephoned his mother to tell her not to expect him for a couple of days. He felt a lot better now his mind was focused on having something to do; Derek would have sympathised with him.

The young woman in the travel company was very helpful, but try as she might she couldn't find a vacant seat on any evening flight to Amsterdam. He would have to visit the address in Ipswich instead. He booked a flight from Stansted for the following morning, and organised two hire cars, one for one day from Schiphol, the other for at least a week to be picked up from Stansted that evening and probably returned to Heathrow.

He was totally unprepared for the job in hand, so he ran through a mental checklist of things he might need and decided he could pick most of them up at a late-night do-it-yourself store.

On the outskirts of Ipswich he stopped, bought a street map and homed in on the address. He drove past the building several times whilst it was still light. The Victorian house was set back in its own large garden down a quiet tree-lined road. The front garden had been sacrificed to make way for a tarmacadam car park which he guessed would take nine or ten vehicles. A large sign by the entrance proclaimed that the offices belonged to Babcock, Neame and Partners – Solicitors, Notaries and Commissioners for Oaths; underneath and in brackets, were the words *founded in 1923*. All the large houses he drove past were now offices and most seemed to belong to the local social service departments. At least he wouldn't be bothered by nosey neighbours.

He 'lost' the car in a multiscreen cinema car park about half a mile away and changed into blue overalls and a black donkey jacket – it was all the store had had to offer – but at least he blended in and looked like a manual worker on his way home from his last shift. He timed his walk back so that it would be dark when he reached number 128 and was pleased to have some more fresh air to work on his still thick head. The front door was up three steps and incorporated into a fairly new porch. Entry was gained by means of a push-button coded lock. The sequence of numbers would have to be something easily remembered by at least ten employees, Andy thought. Established 1923! The door opened on his third attempt – 19238. Once inside he was safe from prying eyes, which was just as well – the second door, which would have been left open during working hours, was a pig to open with the bent bits of wire he had at his disposal. Once through this obstacle he sat on the floor in the hall and let his eyes acclimatise to the semidarkness. The house appeared to have changed very little since it was first built and a huge, imposing staircase led off to the former bedrooms. It seemed a reasonable assumption that any safe would not be up there, either being too heavy to carry up in the first place or because the floors would not be strong enough, so he would concentrate on the ground floor first. Names on doors began to appear out of the gloom. *Secretary to Mr V. Neame* – the door was unlocked and there it stood in the corner, a huge vintage Chubb safe which somebody had hand-painted and adorned with pot plants.

Andy sweated and cursed as he tried time and time again to get the lock to yield, and what would have taken him less than a minute with the right tools cost him thirty minutes. After all his efforts the only contents were a small petty-cash box and a set of keys – there wasn't a scrap of paper inside the voluminous cavern. Each key was labelled; someone had taken the time and trouble to meticulously print the function of each one on the small tags. With the aid of the dim red light from the cheap torch, Andy read through them all. He was most interested in the one for the records-room; now it was just a question of finding the place. Andy went round the whole ground floor, without finding the room, and was on the point of going upstairs when he noticed a door at the far end of the hallway. Bingo, the key turned in the lock. Originally the small room under the stairs would have been used as a larder; there were no windows and a vent had long been sealed off. He went inside, closed the fireproof door, switched on the light and quickly threw his jacket across the small gap at the bottom. Shelves ran floor to ceiling and were packed with box files, whilst different-coloured flat files, tied up with ribbon, were stacked tidily in a pile in one corner. Everything was neatly labelled, again in the same fair hand as on the keys. At first glance it all looked a bit disorganised but whoever was responsible deserved full marks, everything was in strict alphabetical order. He found the box file he wanted, *Mr and Mrs Fred I.Clarke*,and there was only one unopened envelope amongst the pile of paperwork. Carefully Andy opened it, read it and put it in his pocket. That should have been it, that was his sole reason for being in Ipswich, but other thoughts began to drift into his head so he sat on the floor and read the entire contents of the file. It was almost an hour later when he relocked the safe and retraced his steps, making sure everything was left as he'd found it.

He drove straight to Stansted Airport. The terminal was deserted at that time of the morning so he had the toilet to himself as he washed, shaved and changed back into his crumpled shirt and suit. He rammed the workmen's clothes back into their original plastic carrier bag and would lose them somewhere on the Continent. He was in Amsterdam by seven o'clock local time.

Andy phoned the number at the bottom of the sheet immediately he was inside the airport and obviously woke up the contact in Brussels, who was none too pleased by the sound of it. They agreed to meet outside a café overlooking the Grand Place at three o'clock that afternoon, so he had plenty of time to photocopy the letter, visit his deposit box and retrieve his skeleton keys and then drive across into Belgium.

The stranger wanted to see his passport as some form of

identification before letting go of the brown envelope and only uttered one word 'when', and this came out with a thick accent attached to it. Andy kept up the thriving conversation by replying 'tonight', and that was it; but he wasn't too concerned about this job, he'd visited the European headquarters of Union Mining and Minerals before and had got in easily, thanks to the cleaners.

He chose the same time and parked almost outside, but things never go as you expect them. Tonight there were no cleaners in the building, the place was in darkness and the pavement was for ever busy with people off to enjoy themselves for the evening. He looked up at the building; the first four floors were devoted to offices but the two above them looked like flats. A different approach was necessary, and the residents had to have some form of stairs or lift to their apartments. He locked up the car and walked round the back of the building into a large car park with lots of reserved spaces marked out. A set of double doors led into the building but they were well and truly locked. He was just about to reach into his pocket to get his special keys when he heard a noise and turned. An old couple were standing next to him. He must be losing his grip, he thought, he hadn't heard them approaching at all. The old man grunted out a greeting, pressed a button, spoke briefly into the microphone and then the door clicked open. The woman held it open for him. He was glad he'd decided to wear the workman's clothes again, perhaps they thought he'd come to repair something – it didn't matter, he was in. He watched and pressed a different button in the lift to ensure they got out first and once on his own laughed out loud. It was sod's law! All the trouble to get the right 'smart' keys and he hadn't had to use them yet!

He walked down the stairs surrounding the lift shaft to the office floors. Blank doors stared back at him, fire exit doors with no signs of any locking mechanism visible; if they were the 'break glass bolt' type he was sunk. He banged each corner of one with his fist – he was in luck, they were only fastened by a panic bar. He kicked the middle of his chosen door hard with his foot and heard the bar unlock. A few more gentle taps with his fist and it swung open a few inches enough for him to reach in and pull the bar fully upwards. He was quite convinced he would find a long corridor with more doors and locks to negotiate, but he didn't, he walked straight into the main central office, immediately recognised his surroundings and made his way to his intended victim's office.

Travis had said that this job was a small favour to the Americans, and although they did not suspect the European sales manager of being involved in the plot they had a niggling feeling about him and would feel better if he was removed from office. An incriminating package would see to that, they had said. Andy was not going to follow orders so blindly from now on so he ripped open the envelope. The contents sickened him. The lights from the street outside showed up the photographs quite clearly. There were dozens of pictures of men doing indescribable things to very young children, plus several magazines and a list of organisations which specialised in obtaining children for such activities. He found the desk and hid the envelope in the bottom drawer and imagined what would happen next. The police would receive an anonymous tip-off, raid the place just after the office opened, find the contents in the drawer and arrest the man. The adverse publicity, and there would be plenty of that arranged, would leave Union no alternative but to get rid of the man, guilty or not. But what was the real reason behind it? So that Hutton and his British buddies could put in their own tame man, so that they could control Europe as well and distribute whatever they liked to whatever chosen country they liked? Again unanswerable questions convinced Andy that the problems with filteraids were not over with. Everything was just being rearranged to suit, and it all stank. Damn it, the Purflo could just be the forerunner of worse things to come. Andy shivered. It was time to get away from this office and drive back to Holland.

He slipped up badly with his timing and returned to

England just in time to catch the morning rush hour on London's orbital motorway. Three lanes of slow-moving traffic crept along the concrete, occasionally drivers with long faces looked across at him, but nobody smiled, nobody looked happy, the same routine day in day out had taken its toll. They reminded him of Derek's termites; they could move from lane to lane so they had some variety, but they all had to go in the same direction. Technology had moved on though, now the workers were propelled along in metal boxes and the guards, who were no longer present, could watch their progress from afar through television cameras. Tonight the great phalanx would drive in the other direction heading for their homes, tired and miserable, where they would watch television which they had no control over, sleep and then be ready to do the same thing the following day, they had no choice, they had to conform to this routine in order to live.

The loose ends were now out of the way. Andy posted Clarke's Ipswich letter to his bosses and no doubt they would have already heard directly from their contact in Brussels about the other business. He had obeyed orders and there could be no element of suspicion in their minds that he was anything but a loyal operative. Now he had his own loose ends to see to.

He took his mother out on several occasions, slept a lot and began to lose some of the nightmares that filled his head. When she led her own life and saw her old circle of friends he stayed indoors and wrote. He wrote page after page until he had a dossier of his last mission. He mentioned everything – his suspicions, all the names and every action he had been involved in. He wished he'd kept more of Derek's faxes; in due course his two tapes would have to be his main prosecution weapon.

He visited his local bank. They were very efficient and took good care of any bills his mother brought in, as well as keeping his financial house in good order. He was not at all surprised to learn that in the various accounts they'd set up for him was a total of just under one hundred thousand pounds – after all, he'd hardly touched his salary over the years, everything he did for the service was on expenses. The hardest part of his first week's leave was trying to organise his next trip from London to Hong Kong via Amsterdam and Cyprus. Connecting flights were hopeless after Cyprus and he had no choice, he was going to have to stop over in Bahrain for a day. His starting date was Tuesday of the following week, so he still had four days to enjoy himself before God knows what in Hong Kong.

The girl in the travel agent's had trouble understanding exactly what he wanted on the receipt, so she called the manager over and he explained again. He wanted the full amount receipted but no mention made of the European flights.

As Andy left the shop, the manager turned to the girl and remarked, 'Another salesman fiddling his company's expense account by slipping in a short holiday when he should be working. It's all right for some, isn't it?'

16

Andy left his bag in a locker at the airport and caught the local bus into Paphos. The less paperwork, such as car-hire forms, the less chance they had of finding out he'd been to Cyprus. It was the end of a beautiful hot June day. He knocked on the front door and Gill Clarke answered it. She had a friendly smile which enhanced her tanned face.

'Good evening, Mrs Clark, is your husband at home? Sorry to bother you so late but I've just got here on holiday myself and thought I'd take the liberty of dropping some more details off on houses that have come up for sale recently in Suffolk.'

It worked, she invited the stranger in and called out for her husband. Andy let out a silent sigh of relief. The last thing he wanted was to be seen arguing at the front door. Fred appeared barefoot and dressed only in his shorts. He had lost weight and looked a lot fitter than at their previous meeting, Andy thought. The original smile on his face changed into a scowl as soon as he recognised who it was.

'You! What do you want this time – somebody sprayed the wrong stuff on the land again? I suppose your little friend is skulking about outside somewhere? Listen, I have nothing further to say, so please leave my house and leave us alone, Mr . . . I can't even remember your name. Gill, this is one of the men I told you about who said they were from the World Health Organisation and were investigating that pesticide that had got through into beers, remember?'

The look on Gill's face also changed. She was hardly likely to forget Fred's mood swings all those months ago, and now this tall stranger had reminded them both again. 'But you said you had some house details for my husband. What's going on?' she asked.

'I'm sorry to have lied to you, Mrs Clarke,' Andy replied. 'But I didn't want to be seen hanging around at the door. My name's Andy Lockwood, and I'm not from the World Health Organisation, never have been. I work for British Intelligence and I need to talk to you both. I need your help, please.'

The three of them stood staring at each other, then Gill took the initiative. 'Come into the lounge, Mr Lockwood. We can't stand in the hallway all night. Would you like a coffee?'

Fred sat down and stared at the stranger. He was still very suspicious of him and with good reason. Gill returned with the tray of drinks, sat down next to her husband, handed the cups out and they both sat watching their uninvited guest, waiting for him to speak.

Andy started his story and with each and every sentence broke every official secret act going. He explained about the original visit to their villa to glean information and then the trek to America and how they'd discovered that there was a plot to add two different types of ingredient to the world's beer and wine production and how they'd tracked down those responsible, and how – minus one – the guilty had been eliminated, along with his friend Derek. At this stage he asked them if they had any questions, both shook their heads in unison and sat transfixed, so Andy continued. He told them that in his opinion the plot had not been eliminated but had merely changed hands and that at least two governments were implicated, and one of them had the original inventor alive and well – and that he was convinced they would continue to use the products to control world events, as they saw fit, and even improve upon the original formulae. Andy finally concluded that he felt his own safety was in jeopardy and that was why he was asking them for their help. He looked at his watch. He had talked non-stop for well over an hour.

Fred stood up and stretched his legs. 'A very convincing story, Mr Lockwood, or whatever your name is. But how do we know you haven't made it all up? You lied to me before, why not again? We've no proof about any of this. Look, it's late, I think it's time you left.'

Gill stood up, but Andy remained seated and reached into his trouser pocket. A look of fear came over his hosts' faces and he realised what his action meant. 'No, please don't worry, I promise I'm not going to harm you. In fact, quite the reverse,. I desperately need your co-operation. Here, read this.' He handed across several sheets of paper.

Fred's face froze in horror. He and Gill sat down again. 'It's a copy of my original letter to the British Government! Where did you get it from, Mr. Lockwood?'

'I was asked to retrieve it from your solicitor's in Ipswich. The original is with my bosses in London. Mr Neame doesn't, and won't, realise it's gone.'

'Why?' Fred asked.

'Because they want to tidy up any loose ends so there's no proof left of what they're up to, is my guess.'

Gill was puzzled. 'How did they know there was a copy at our solicitor's?'

'My fault, I'm afraid. I found out from our first meeting and told them. Mind you, that was before I knew I was being used as well.' Andy looked across at the two older people opposite. Stress had returned to their faces and they began to look their age. Inside he felt rotten at having ruined their retirement, but it was too late to retract anything now. Like him, they would have to live with it.

Gill asked the most leading question so far. 'If what you say is all true, won't we become "loose ends" too?'

'I honestly don't think so,' Andy replied, 'otherwise this visit tonight wouldn't have been through the front door, I'd have been instructed to do something more sinister, probably when you were asleep. It's true your husband started the whole thing off with this letter, but as long as they think he's forgotten all about it then you're not in any danger. They don't know I've been here, so as far as they're concerned you don't know about anything really and are no threat to their plans. I also think you're even more secure on Cyprus, well away from their immediate thoughts, and I am one hundred per cent confident no harm will come to you provided you remain as you are. That's why I lied to you at the door. I didn't want anybody, including your neighbours, to see me arriving tonight, so there's no connection between us.'

Andy had laboured the point and the eye contact between Fred and Gill hadn't gone unnoticed. He knew why, but the remedy was his trump card and would have to wait.

Gill broke the momentary silence. 'What sort of help are you looking for, Mr Lockwood?' she asked.

'I have two tapes of the final conversation on the boat, including the murders, and I've also written out a complete report on the whole episode, together with my misgivings about my bosses. These are locked away in a safety deposit box in Amsterdam. What I am asking is that in the event of my death, you send the envelope off to the press – it's addressed already.' Andy took out a small brown envelope from the same trouser pocket. 'If you agree to my request you will need to sign this form. It makes you a joint key-holder to the box. The key, as you can see, is already labelled with all the details you'll need. I must stress that nowhere in the report is there any mention of yourselves.' Andy put the key and form down on the coffee table.

'Why us, why involve us? We've nothing to do with this, why not go straight to the newspapers yourself?' Fred asked the question with a certain amount of panic in his voice.

'Because I'd be dead within days and they'd use every trick in the book to stop the story being printed, probably say it was all fabrication anyway, dreamt up by some nutcase. Look, I've given all of this a great deal of thought over the last few days; in fact, I've thought about nothing else, Mr Clarke. After I leave you they're sending me off to Hong Kong on another mission and as far as I can see it's going to get pretty nasty out there. I don't know but maybe they hope to get rid of the last eyewitness. I hope I'm wrong, please God, but if I do get killed then I firmly believe the story will have that much more impact. The fact that I've left a note predicting they will try and eliminate me should arouse some curiosity, I hope.'

Andy handed across his instructions relating to his Far East visit, hoping this further weight of evidence would finally convince them.

'I must say that I have not the slightest intention of getting killed if I can help it,' he added, 'because the longer I live the more chance I have of getting hold of one of them by the scruff of the neck and wringing a confession out of him in front of witnesses. However, I need a back-up in case anything does go wrong. Can I count on you, please?'

Fred was still not convinced. 'Don't you think you're going over the top on all this?'

'Sometimes, yes, and then I remember how little they think of people who get in their way, like our mutual and very dear acquaintance Derek.'

Gill brought the conversation back from its present sombre note. 'Are you married, Mr Lockwood?'

'Andy, please. No, it's not the sort of job where you feel in a position to get hitched. You're on the move most of the time so it's very difficult to have a stable relationship and in the end you become a bit of a loner, I suppose.'

Gill offered more coffee or something stronger. Andy accepted a glass of the local wine. When he felt the moment was right, again he asked them if he could count on their support, but before he got an answer Fred grabbed his wife's arm and led her into the kitchen. He could hear lots of talking, sometimes quite loud, but he couldn't make out the gist of any of the conversation.

Fred returned first. 'All right, we will agree to your request, but I still can't see for the life of me why you had to pick on us, and anyway we'll be moving back to England again shortly.'

'I know, Mr Clarke,' Andy replied, and turned to face Gill. 'When I was retrieving Fred's letter from you solicitor's I took the liberty of going through your file so I know a lot about you both. I know you rent this place and would dearly love to buy it but can't afford it. Well, you could, just, by taking out a loan against your pension, but then you'd be strapped for cash. You also want to stay on this lovely peaceful island, and who can blame you? But all the properties you like are even more expensive than this one. So in the end you asked Mr Neame to request estate agents to send lists of two-bedroomed bungalows in Suffolk – hence my cover story tonight. I'm sorry it hasn't worked out as you planned.'

'And I suppose all your secret service pals know all my life's details as well.' Fred retorted angrily.

'Fred that's not fair!' Gill said, scolding her husband. 'I think you should apologise to Mr Lockwood. From what he's said tonight I don't think he'd dream of doing that.'

Fred held out his hand and apologised. Andy shook it firmly. It was hot and clammy.

'I have a proposition to make. I would like you to stay in Cyprus and carry out my request if necessary,' Andy said as he stood up, stretched his legs and looked down on two very perplexed faces. He then handed Fred a building society pass book.

'It's ours, Gill. Where did you . . . ?' Then the penny dropped. 'But it can't be ours, we don't, there shouldn't be . . . what's going on? It's got more money than we ever had, than we put in, I mean a lot more, what I mean is . . .' Fred stumbled over every word so Andy put him out of his misery.

'What your husband's trying to say, Mrs Clarke, is that there is exactly fifty thousand pounds more in your account now, enough in total to buy this place and leave your pension alone.'

Gill grabbed the book from her husband's hand and over the next minute it went back and forward as if it were a game of pass the parcel.

'The money is genuine and yours,' Andy stated. 'As far as anyone else is concerned it is now at the bottom of a lake in America.One of the men on the boat won it at a casino but it slipped from his pocket before he was blown to pieces, so you will not be depriving anyone of their life's savings or anything like that, I can assure you' The story was almost the truth. Andy had got his bank to transfer some of his money across to the Clarke's account, but with his own windfall now tucked away in gold bars he certainly wasn't out of pocket.

Fred Clarke was very confused. 'But why?'

'Call it blackmail, bribery, or what you will, but it's my gesture to you both for helping me out, okay? And from a selfish point of view it would be better for me if you remained on this island, far away from London. I'm sorry if it sounds crude but here you're out of the way and now your letter's vanished, completely forgotten about, just a retired couple spending their last years together in the sun. Back in England, who knows you might start drinking beer again, Fred, and be tempted to write more letters.'

The last sentence brought a smile to Gill's lips. You could almost bet on it, she thought.

Andy continued, 'Also, you create a much lower profile out here and it would be better for me to visit should the need arise.'

'Won't they track the money down to you eventually and then implicate us?' Fred asked.

'It's a chance we're going to have to take but I doubt it. As I've said, I don't think they're bothered about the likes of us any more. If, on the other hand, they are monitoring every single thing we do, then it's all too late for any of us anyway – they've won.'

'What about this pass book? Won't Mr Neame know it's been taken?'

Fred certainly liked to press a point. Andy's life was on the line and all Clarke was worried about was his book. He kept his cool and replied as calmly as he could. 'I doubt if he knows he's still got it so don't tell him! All you have to worry about now is getting the money out of your building society to buy this place before someone else does. If somebody asks where the new money came from, tell them you were left it by a distant cousin.'

Gill tried to broach the subject but couldn't find the right words. Andy put her out of her misery. 'I'll send you a postcard once a week from wherever I am, signed "Aunt Martha". If you don't get any for a month then please do the deed.'

It was late and Andy had stayed much longer than intended. Gill insisted he could stay the night in the spare room – she still hadn't grasped that he shouldn't be seen with them. He made to leave. Fred shook his hand and wished him good luck, but it was his wife who volunteered the message he'd wanted to hear and which had taken all this time to discuss.

'Andy, we hope it doesn't happen, of course, but we will honour our promise and do the deed if we don't hear from you.' She kissed his cheek and told him to be careful in Hong Kong. She sounded a bit like his mother; it was warm and considerate of her.

'And don't forget to burn that letter as soon as possible,' Andy reminded them, and with that was gone. Although it was way past their bedtime he doubted if the Clarke's would get much sleep that night.

It was too late to get a bus back, so he decided to lie low in one of the nightclubs until daylight. It was small beginnings but he was very slowly building up a small circle of people he could trust. He raised the first large whiskey and quietly toasted Derek. 'One day, my friend, one day you'll have the last laugh.'

Andy caught the first bus back to the airport, picked up his holdall from left luggage and left the island the way he had come in, using his Australian passport. The flight to Bahrain was nowhere near full so he decided to stretch out across the empty seats in his row and allow himself the luxury of some much needed sleep. He was just beginning to drift off when a small Arab boy in the row opposite started to make a scene. His mother gave in to his demands. She fumbled for something in the luggage compartment and almost threw it at her offspring. Good, Andy thought, peace once again. But he was wrong. The repetitive noise of synthetic music rang out in his ears. He tried to ignore it but it got to him and the harder he tried the more he could hear it. He sat up and stared across at the spoiled brat, who had some sort of electronic game in his hand. In the mood he was in, he would have loved to snatch it from him and smash the expensive toy underfoot and restore the previous tranquillity. The boy misinterpreted the scowl on Andy's face; he thought the big man opposite wanted to have a go. He came across and shoved the box into his hand.

'You play, you play,' he commanded.

The gadget was no bigger than a book, with a small four-inch screen in the middle, three buttons on one side and a small joystick on the other. Andy didn't have a clue and shook his head to indicate his ignorance of the thing. The boy, who was not more than six or seven years old, gave him a demonstration and his little fingers moved with lightning speed over the controls. The picture was very sharp and appeared to be three-dimensional. One large spaceship was firing laser beams at smaller craft, which rapidly came and went from view and in turn fired back. Each time somebody managed a hit, the machine made a booming sound and a score flashed onto the screen, whilst the incessant and tuneless music played on. Andy went through the motions but failed miserably; the rules and technique were completely beyond him. He handed the game back with a shake of his head and the boy returned to his seat and whispered to his mother. the pointed finger suggested he was telling her that he was stupid.

And then like a sudden kick up the backside it dawned on him. He and Derek had been specifically chosen for the last job because of their lack of up-to-date technology. they were both from the old school of espionage, good legmen, thorough methodical plodders who got results the hard way by old-fashioned detective methods. They were people who would physically watch and wait for days or weeks if necessary for something to happen and then rely on their own judgement and instincts as to the next step to take. But they were in the wrong age group; the world of men in raincoats standing in doorways was over and they had been left behind by it all, probably considered too old to retrain.

Murdoch had said Hutton was wired up with a tape recorder when he was on the boat, but that skin-tight outfit he had on would have shown up every bump. Was that big big black box in the camper and the device on the roof some form of sophisticated satellite system which relayed everything to his headquarters, and their little tape recorder just an aside, something to keep them happy? Andy shook his head. He hadn't a clue. But if he was right, then the whole idea was that they didn't know too much. Once they had broken into places and ferreted out Wilenius by traditional methods, their usefulness had come to an abrupt end and they had been discarded as obsolete models past their sell-by date.

Andy thought back. there was not one job he'd done over the years that had involved learning new methods. He was probably an embarrassment to them when they were surrounded by dozens of young graduates still in their twenties who could complete modern-day missions without even leaving their computer terminals. Both Ben and Simon were typical examples, and had found out information in a matter of minutes which would have taken him months if at all. The number of new jobs they could use him on might be very limited, and he could turn into a nuisance factor just like Derek. He also knew a lot of details about the filteraid scam; the old-fashioned methods meant you did, perhaps the new computer people didn't read or understand the significance of what they got, but just handed disjointed paperwork over, unaware of all its hidden meanings. They certainly didn't get a feel for how their 'enemy' lived or any backdrop to a plot and were probably safer as a result. Maybe this trip was designed to be his last and he pictured the headlines.

DIES IN CROSSFIRE

Mr Andy Lockwood, 40, a tourist, was shot dead when he was caught up in gunfire between two rival Triad gangs. Police believe Mr Lockwood unwittingly strayed into a part of Hong Kong which is definitely considered to be a no-go area for all visitors. His next of kin have been informed.

He wondered if his obituary would warrant as many column inches in the paper as Derek's and he could visualise the satisfied faces in London saying, 'It had to be done of course, obsolete model, no longer viable, in everyone's best interest, you understand.'

No, he suddenly resolved, he wouldn't let any of his fears happen. His bosses weren't inside his head, they didn't know how he felt. They probably thought his guard would be down after his 'holiday' in the States, might even think he was going to be a soft touch, but this could work to his advantage. From now on he would be on his guard and treat everything with suspicion; he would return to thinking like a professional soldier once again. He would re-equip himself with new skills and knowledge – what better place than Hong Kong to start doing it – and they would not know anything about it. He would survive and become as double-edged and devious and calculating as they were, until such a time as he could penetrate their inner world and drag them screaming to the people, begging for mercy. He hoped – how he hoped! – Hutton would be first. They were good but they were not invincible. They had made at least two mistakes already: he had the tapes and he was still alive. Those élite, powerful men would make other errors as well and they would be let down by their own protectors, people like himself, because they had one serious flaw, just like Derek's termite guards. He now knew that all termite guards were born blind. Either the workers didn't know about this shortcoming or were too frightened to overpower their formidable cousins; but the opportunity was there to creep up on them when they least expected it and he would use this to his advantage.

Andy felt more at ease with himself than he had done for weeks. He was now ready to face the challenge. There was also another reason for staying alive – Maureen. Not only was he beginning to miss her but he'd never got around to asking her why she'd gone and had that bloody great tattoo embroidered across her chest. One day he was determined to find out.